The Highmore Circle

The Highmore Circle

Cricket Reynolds

THE HIGHMORE CIRCLE

iUniverse books may be ordered through booksellers or by contacting:

iUniverse
1663 Liberty Drive
Bloomington, IN 47403
www.iuniverse.com
1-800-Authors (1-800-288-4677)

ISBN: 978-1-5320-0676-0 (sc)
ISBN: 978-1-5320-0677-7 (e)

Library of Congress Control Number: 2016918123

Print information available on the last page.

iUniverse rev. date: 12/30/2016

3201300371664

For my sister Faith and for all my other sisters
who make my circle complete.
For my boys, simply put, you rock my world.

So here it was I first found myself, not in some meaningful exploration you read about on one of those trendy blogs but in a small musty room at the local community center. I must admit I was nervous. My best friend, Chloe, had convinced me to enroll in this "support" group. Chloe thought it would be a great place to pick up guys. It turns out the support group was for women only, which she secretly knew but hid in a way only she could.

"Hey," she said one day while enjoying my last blueberry muffin, "I just read about this great support group at the center. You go and bitch about how screwed-up your life is because your mom died, and they all agree because they're in the same boat."

I wasn't really listening—I was watching the way her mouth curved in a funny shape when she said *c* words. It was one of those weird things in life that twenty minutes later you totally forget, but it seems mesmerizing as hell at the time.

"Gracie? Are you listening to me?"

"What?"

"Hello? It's a great place to pick up guys." Chloe had a way of turning any event into a possible dating-game adventure.

"Why would a support group be a great place to pick up guys?"

"Because they're there to lean on someone, and that someone could be you."

"Why would I want a guy who is looking for some emotional crutch? I have enough problems of my own. Plus, Les and I just broke up."

"You broke up six months ago. And it's still my belief that—"

"Yes, I know. That Les was a closet homosexual just looking for a mother figure to take care of him."

"He did dress *really* well." Chloe thought any man who didn't wear white socks and sandals dressed well. And any man who dressed well must be gay. She definitely had her own take on the world, which was one of the reasons I loved her so much.

"Why do I need a support group anyway? I get enough support with you hanging around," I said, watching her reaction. She loved it when I acknowledged that she was my own personal Freud.

"It's a group that deals with parental loss. And since your mom ..."

"My mom died twenty years ago. I'd be pretty pathetic if I needed support after all these years."

"We're all screwed-up in our own way. This just gives you an excuse to be cray-cray. I think it will help you as you approach being a mother yourself."

"I haven't had sex in six months. Unless I'm reinventing immaculate conception, being a mother is the farthest thing from my mind."

"Okay," she said, looking at me with a level of intensity I hadn't seen since our high school prom when we caught my date, Fred Johnson, enjoying some solo action in the parking lot. "This is how I see it. Since your last birthday, which I know I'm not allowed to acknowledge, I've noticed that you talk more and more about how many years you have left. Life isn't a waiting game, sweetie. We roll with it and make the most of it. But you're not even doing that. You need to talk to someone besides me, Gracie. Plus, since you're a town resident, it only costs ten bucks. You can't even pick up a *Cosmo* and a cappuccino for that. Go—it'll do you good."

"I'll think about it," I said, hoping the subject would change quickly.

"Better think fast. I already signed you up. Group sessions are every Tuesday and Friday from six to eight, starting this week." She smiled that slightly off-center smile, and I could see in her eyes she was proud of herself. Chloe had won again, like she always did.

"Why Friday nights? Don't they think I have a life?" I tried to sound offended, but we both knew my life was severely lacking. No dates. No pets. Not even any good chick flicks on my DVR. An exciting Friday night for me was *People* magazine hitting my mailbox a day early.

"Since I'm guessing," she said, tucking her auburn hair behind her ears, "that was a rhetorical question, I will be looking forward to a full report tomorrow night. I've gotta run. Rick will be home soon. It's Monday night. You know what that means." Chloe and her husband, Rick, had "private time" (as she called it) every Monday night, just like clockwork. They never missed a session. How romantic.

"Don't you ever get tired of the same old routine?" I tried to sound disgusted, but at least Chloe was getting some action on a regular basis.

"Every once in a while, we vary things."

"Like what?"

"Like who gets the beer afterward. Honestly, the routine does get a bit old, but we're not like we used to be. Remember those days with Les? Oh yeah, you probably don't because—"

"He was not gay!"

"How many times did you guys actually do it?"

"A lot in the beginning, until he realized *Dancing with the Stars* was on two nights a week."

"With a name like Lester, you're bound to be a geek, a serial killer, or into some serious deviant stuff."

"That's an awful thing to say. Blame it on his parents, not on him. Just because his name is Lester doesn't make him anything."

"Besides a loser for breaking up with you. What was his reason again?"

"He needed space to see life for himself."

"See life? He's an optometrist, for God's sake. If he were a proctologist, he still couldn't find his head up his ass."

"Maybe I still love him."

"You never loved him, Gracie. You were used to him. He's like an old pair of shoes. You've stepped in dog crap and everything else in them, but you still keep them around because they're comfortable. Just go tomorrow night to this group thing, and you'll be amazed at how much better things look, even in this rinky-dink town."

Chloe smiled at me, and I felt like crying—not because I knew she was right but because there was something *so* right in her words that the pain of the words lingered heavy on my heart.

"Okay," I said. "I'll call you tomorrow."

"Now give me a hug and knock 'em dead tomorrow night. Well, don't do that. That's what sent you there in the first place. Let me know about the guys. Bet there's a slew of them there."

So here I sat in a musty community center room, waiting patiently for the beginning of my new life. I was early, like always.

"Hello." The voice startled me. I had been watching the second hand tick on my watch when she walked in. I was even more surprised when I lifted my head to see her, although I'm not sure what I was even expecting to see.

"Hi, I'm Gracie." I hated the way I said my name. It sounded like I was blowing vowels out of my nose.

"I'm Gloria, but you can call me Ginger."

"Uh, okay. Which side of the imaginary couch are you on?" I smiled, and she stared blankly at me. No response. "Are you here as part of the group or as the ringleader?"

"Oh," she replied nervously. "I'm part of the group. I wasn't sure what you meant. My brain doesn't always move too fast."

"What do you do?" I asked, trying to enter a safer playing field.

4

"As a job or in general?"

"Either." I glanced down at my watch again. Not even close to six. God help me.

"I'm a dominatrix."

"You're shitting me." Had I really just said that out loud?

"Why would I be shitting you?"

Yep. I'd really said it. "I'm sorry. It's just that I've never met a dominatrix, and no offense, but you don't look like one, or at least what I thought one would look like." It was the truth. She was at least five foot ten and had long brown hair, which was knotted in a tight ponytail at the base of her neck. She wore catlike glasses and no makeup. Her turtleneck hung loosely past her waist. Looking at her closely, I could see nothing exceptional about her.

"I've heard that before. But it's what I do. I even have my own business card." She began digging in her purse, rummaging through things that made clanking noises. I couldn't help but wonder if handcuffs were somewhere in her goody bag. She handed me her card.

I read the slogan printed on the card aloud. "'Let me whip you up some fun. Guaranteed to hurt so good or your money back!' Well, that really says it all, doesn't it?" I was trying not to let my disgust show on my face. Somewhere in the world, I thought Gloria Steinem had probably just thrown up.

"Business really picked up after my cards went into circulation."

"I bet." I looked closer at her card. In the photo her hair hung loosely over her bare breasts. She wore black leather pants and stiletto heels and was biting down on a whip. She was stunning in the picture, wearing makeup and blue sapphire contacts in place of glasses. "Well, Gloria ..."

"It's Ginger. It was my mother's name, and since she went away, I decided to start using it."

"I thought this was a support group for people whose mothers had died?"

"Yeah, she died. I like 'went away' instead of 'died.' You know, 'died' sounds so permanent."

"I know what you mean." My eyes caught hers, and for a minute I completely understood. "How did she die, if you don't mind me asking?"

"Decapitated."

"Excuse me?"

Ginger slowly repeated the word. "Decapitated."

"Jesus. Sorry." What was there left to say? I had critiqued her career and gotten her to admit that her mother had died because of loss of her head. I was really making friends now. There was a moment of awkward silence, and then she spoke again.

"I had to identify her body. It was so hard—you know, with her not having it all, well, connected. But nobody else was going to do it, so it had to be me."

Just as I was about to say something even less comforting, another victim walked in the room. She was short and stocky. Her eyes were chestnut brown and her clothes tight. She was misty-eyed with a blotchy face—a bit too rosy for makeup or a natural glow. She had probably been sitting in her car crying. Her eyes met mine, and she smiled slightly.

"Hi," I said.

"Uh ..." She said nothing else.

"My name is Gracie, and this is ..." Wait, why was I introducing Ginger? What the hell? Any girl who could whip people for a living had to have the ability to introduce herself.

"I'm Ginger."

"My name is Sarah, and my mother is dead." She began to cry. Huge tears slowly made their way down her face like a stream etching out a mountain. Silence permeated the room.

Then another woman entered. She glided into the room like she owned it. She was confident and held her head high. I couldn't take my eyes off her. She was breathtaking. Blond hair cascaded down her back, accentuating her tan skin. She was lean and muscular, filling out her clothes like a model. And then it hit me. Even beautiful people have parents who die.

"Sorry. Am I late?" she asked.

I smiled and shook my head.

Two other women walked in and took their seats. I looked around the circle. Six strangers sat there with seemingly only one thing in common, a connection none of us wanted to have.

"Good evening. How's everyone?" I watched her walk into the room as she spoke. She commanded the space, her presence taking ownership of the circle. I noticed her long arms, out of proportion compared to the rest of her body, and wondered how many people she had wrapped them around in order to bring comfort. "My name is Dr. Gretchen Love. I hold a PhD in psychology with a specialization in bereavement counseling. It is my pleasure to serve you for the next six weeks and hopefully beyond that." She gave each of us a quick glance and then took a deep breath and continued. "We will start promptly at six, and I will provide coffee, water, and tissue."

Listening to her, I wanted desperately to escape to the comforts of anywhere but here. Maybe my mom had been gone too long for me to feel like the rest of these women. I did not belong here and resolved to wait out the two hours and then kiss room 26 good-bye. My wound was not fresh. It was old and beyond scarred. I had made my peace with God and everyone else for taking my mom. There was nothing left for anyone to do for me.

My attention drifted back to Dr. Gretchen, who was still talking. "For the next six weeks, I will be your guide ..."

Why do we need a guide? I thought. *It's not like an African safari. "And on your left, you will see the ghost of your dead mother approaching ever so softly right behind the wild boar."*

Suddenly and without warning, Sarah began to sob loudly. I grabbed the box of tissues and motioned it toward her. She nodded her head and from the depths of her bag pulled out her own box and buried her face in it.

Dr. Gretchen continued her monologue. "First of all, I want you to know that we are in this together. No one here is alone. I am available to you when you need me." She pulled business cards from her pocket like a good magician's trick and handed them out.

I took mine and carefully placed it on my lap. There was something about business cards with this group. I had already collected two, one from a dominatrix and the other from a shrink. *For a good time, call me, and to figure out why you needed that good time, call me.*

"Now, who'd like to start?"

The words that came out were a surprise even to me. "My name is Gracie, and my mom died from cancer when I was fourteen. Not the quick kind—the long, drawn-out, suffering kind that stole everything from her except her last breath. That she took on her own terms." My memories suddenly came rushing back. All the years of my self-recovery mysteriously evaporated, and I felt like a lonely and frightened girl again.

The beautiful blond spoke. "My name is Ellie Bradshaw, and my mother died in a car accident last year. And my dad"—she trailed off for a moment—"died two months later from a heart attack." Why was she really here in this musty community center? She had money or came from money or maybe both. She could have afforded any therapist in the world, and yet here she sat next to me.

"I think I'm gonna be sick." Sarah barely got the words out before a tidal wave of vomit erupted from her mouth.

I jumped up as the splash of vomit hit the floor and then my body. The circle quickly lost its shape. As I stood trying to assess the damage, the door flew open, and in someone ran. His foot hit the vomit, and he grabbed me for support. We both fell to the floor, him on top of me and me in the pool of vomit. I opened my eyes to see him staring back at me.

"Jack!" Ellie said. "What are you doing?"

He looked up. "Sorry, sis. I thought something was wrong."

"It's wrong you're on top of Gracie. How about *dismounting* her?"

He rolled off me, managing to miss the cesspool I was swimming in. I lay there with both my arms outstretched, not sure what to do next. He reached for my hand to help me up. The more he tried to pull me up, the more I slithered around in the vomit. Most of my body was now covered in it. I finally managed my way out of the puddle.

"Hey, look, a puke angel!" Ginger declared, pointing to the place my body had just occupied.

"Well, considering the circumstances, maybe we should call it a night and pick up where we left off on Friday?" Dr. Gretchen suggested. Relieved faces stared back at her, especially my own.

"Are you okay?" Jack asked me.

I nodded, not making eye contact with him.

"I need to clean up a bit," he said, wiping his hands on his shorts. I looked down at myself, knowing I had to do the same.

I made my way to the pool locker room. I removed my wet clothes, replacing them with a dry hoodie and sweats I found in the locker room lost and found. I rinsed my hair in the sink and blotted it with a pool towel. I never looked at myself in the mirror, afraid of what would be looking back at me.

As I exited the locker room, Ellie stood waiting for me, holding my jacket. "This one belongs to you, right? It was the only one left on the hook."

"Thanks."

Ellie slipped on her Stella McCartney jacket. It fit her perfectly, unlike mine. I always felt embarrassed by my body, always wanting to be taller or thinner or flatter, always wanting to be something I wasn't.

"Do you live far from here?" Ellie asked.

We had made our way down the hall. The smell of chlorine and sweat hung heavy in the air. The community center was nothing more than an old glorified gym.

"Just a few blocks. You?"

"Actually ..." She stopped and turned so she could look at me. "Jack and I need to decide what to do about my parents' home, so I'm staying here for now, but I live in New York."

"Where's your parents' house?"

"Hillside Estates. Are you familiar with it?"

Was I familiar with it? Could I spell m-o-n-e-y? Hell yes, I was familiar with it. Hillside Estates was one of those places we called the Gates. Our little place on the map was filled with the Gates— places you couldn't get into without permission or an invitation. The Gates were a not-so-invisible reminder of the division of classes, of rank, of importance. "That's in Westminster, right?" I said.

"Yes. It's a lovely home, very nice amenities." She sounded like a Realtor. We began walking again. Ellie suddenly called out to her brother. "Jack, you obviously met her earlier since you fell on top of her, but I'd like for you to officially meet Gracie."

"Nice to meet you, Gracie."

I had been so shocked when he landed on top of me that I had barely registered him as human. But now as I really looked at him, he was more than real to me. He was unbelievable. I had never seen anyone that good-looking in person before.

His blond hair was tucked under a baseball cap he wore backward. He was clean-shaven, with the hint of a five o'clock shadow around his chin. He towered above me, but that was never hard for anyone taller than five feet four. His white teeth glistened through his parted lips, and I felt my stomach flip. I noticed a small bead of sweat dancing above his lip and fought the urge to touch it. I had been a sucker for jocks in high school—well, one in particular, and that had ended about as well as my first group session. I knew I didn't stand a chance with this jock, but that didn't stop me from wanting to taste the sweat lingering on his lip.

"Sorry," said Ellie. "That's my cell ringing. Would you please excuse me?" In my heated frenzy, I hadn't even heard her cell phone ringing. She quietly stepped out the door, and alone we stood in the middle of the community center. And for me, the world stopped completely.

Jack's crystal-blue eyes looked me over slowly, and every hair on my body stood up. All he needed to do was breathe my name, and I would have stripped myself naked for him. "You look good wet," he said, leaning into me closer. He smiled at me, and I felt a surge rush between my legs. And I was pretty sure it was more than leftover vomit remnants causing that sensation.

"You think?"

His eyes flickered slightly. Just as he opened his mouth to speak, the banging of the outer door broke his train of thought. We both turned to see Ellie.

"That was Bruce. His flight is delayed, so he won't be getting into O'Hare until after midnight. Would you please?"

"Yes. I'll drive you there later. I know how you feel about fighting airport traffic. This is what I get for being an older brother."

"You're older?"

His piercing eyes caught mine again. "We're twins, but I'm one minute and thirty seconds older than El. That gives me seniority rights."

I laughed.

"Gracie, we'll walk you out," Ellie offered.

In another situation, I would have taken their politeness to be insincere and fake, but they seemed to be the real deal, straight out of a good Gates upbringing. At the entrance, Jack pushed open the old metal door for us.

The cool autumn wind tugged at me as my hair tossed carelessly in the night. I knew it wouldn't be long before winter settled in. I noticed that ours were the only cars left in the north parking lot.

"I'm guessing the Honda is yours?" Ellie stood by her car, waiting for Jack to get me safely to mine.

"Yes. Good night, Ellie. See you on Friday."

I watched her drive away. "What does Ellie do?" I asked, turning back to Jack, whose eyes were on me.

"She's a buyer—works a lot of the runways in New York." He was leaning against my car now, adjusting the zipper on his pullover fleece. I wanted to reach up, grab the zipper, and pull him to me, but instead I kept my hands to my side, trying not to be distracted by my thoughts.

"Aren't you cold?" I motioned to his shorts, which stopped just above his knees.

"Me? No. You?" He touched his fingertips to the tip of my nose, red from the chilly air. I rested my elbow on the car and my head in the palm of my hand, allowing the car to support my weight. It was also a way to keep my hands to myself as the urge to run them all over his body became overwhelming. I was freezing but wasn't about to admit it.

"Are you this concerned about everyone you meet?" I asked. I wasn't even sure what I was saying exactly; words were running from my mouth without my brain's permission.

"Just the ones I lie on top of."

My body temperature rose at least ten degrees, and just as I was about to offer up a response, Jack's phone chirped.

He reached into his pocket and studied the text message. His tone of voice quickly changed. "I've got to run. See you around?"

I fumbled for my keys, stunned at how fast our conversation was ending. "See ya."

He grabbed the door as I was opening it, allowing me room to get in. Our fingers touched, and I felt a shot of electricity run through my body. Nestled behind the steering wheel, I was closing the door when he spoke again.

"Oh, and Gracie?" He leaned in his head, just inches from my face. I could feel his breath on my cheek. "I'm sorry for your loss. Drive safe." The door shut, and away he walked.

Driving from the parking lot, I studied his car through my rearview mirror until I turned the corner and could no longer see him. "I'm sorry for your loss." I repeated his words over and over the rest of the night. It wasn't until much later that I realized I hadn't even said the same thing back to him, being so lost in him and his words that no words of my own would come.

And no matter how much I tried to convince myself that this boy would never go for a girl like me, I could still feel the warmth of his breath on my cheek, and suddenly, the possibility didn't seem so far beyond my reach after all.

2

Chloe has an unbelievable sixth sense. The night my mom died, she appeared on my doorstep, and the first words out of her mouth were "I know." After running the three blocks from her house to mine as fast as her legs could carry her, she stood on my doorstep and cried with me.

Chloe was the closest thing to a sister I'd ever had. Although my parents never officially told me, I overheard Grandma Blake tell someone my mom had had a partial hysterectomy right after I was born. She probably had her first brush with cancer then, but she never mentioned a word of it to me.

Chloe had seen me through more of life's challenges than I ever thought I could face. I spent half my life wanting to be her and the rest just thankful to be with her. It was no surprise to hear my phone ringing as I struggled to release the house key from the lock. Chloe's sixth sense was hard at work again.

"I have to call you back," I said, knowing it was her.

"What are you doing home so early? And most importantly, what's his name?"

I rolled my eyes, shook my head, and smiled. "Someone in session threw up on me, so that pretty much killed the night."

"What's his name?" She was pressing hard for the scoop.

"You mean, what's her name? It's a support group for women. There are no men in there—not one single guy looking to be saved."

"So how did you meet him?"

"Meet who?" I tried to sound confused, but she somehow already knew.

"I know you met someone. What's his name?"

"Jack."

"Good name. Does this Jack have a last name? Or is it just Jack?"

"Jack Bradshaw. But I only know that because his sister was in the session with me."

"Twins?"

How does she do it? I wondered. "Yep. At first I thought she must be a supermodel, but she works behind the scenes."

"Okay, but who cares about her? Tell me about *him.*" I could hear the radio playing classic rock in the background. Chloe said all the good music had happened in the seventies, and I reminded her that unless you were tripping out on LSD, nothing about seventies music made much sense.

"He's hot. What else can I say? He probably has some gorgeous girlfriend who knocks his socks off every night."

"So he's not married?"

"Oh, I don't know. He could be, I guess. He doesn't wear a wedding ring, but how many married men do these days?"

"Only the good ones. What does he do?"

"I don't know. His family has money—Hillside Estates."

"Oh, a Gates boy."

I had grown up and still lived in Highmore, but my grandparents were Gates people. I often felt out of place inside their gates. Once you crossed over the border from Highmore into Westminster, gates were everywhere. Every subdivision had a gate, some of them with a guard.

"He seemed really nice," I continued. "He walked me to my car, and before I left, you know what he said?"

"What?" I could hear her hanging on my words.

"He said, 'I'm sorry for your loss.'"

"Shut the front door! He did not!"

"We hadn't even been talking about Mom when he said it. He was so close I could have licked his face."

"Well, that would have been fun. You know what this means, don't you?"

"What?"

"It means you have to stalk him. A nice boy with manners who has money falling out of his ass? Either get knocked up by him or stalk him. Either way, it's a win-win situation."

"I'm hanging up now."

"Hey?"

"What? I have papers to grade."

"Liar. Listen, how was it really? Are you going back on Friday?"

"It was better than I thought it was going to be. I'll go one more time, and if it's lame …"

"You'll still go back because how will you get knocked up if you're not there to seduce him?"

"Night, Chloe."

"Good night, toots." After my mom died, Chloe and I had made a pact to never say good-bye to each other. Chloe decided "good-bye" was boring anyway, so we started saying "good day" or "top of the morning" or "good night." It made us sound worldly, and when you live in the Midwest, you have to dream big.

As a professor at a local college, I did have papers to grade, but actually, I just wanted to soak in a hot bath and think about Jack. At one point in my early college years, I was going to be a journalist, traveling across the world covering breaking stories. But somewhere between English lit and Newswriting for the New Century, I felt a calling to become a professor, which meant a PhD, which meant a dissertation and lots more money sucked up in classes. Although we were always more disconnected than connected, if it weren't for my dad, I never would have made it. He helped me out when my money was running low. My grandma wanted to help as well, but there was always a catch with her, so I just smiled and told her I was fine, even when a box of macaroni and cheese was the lone soldier in my kitchen cabinet. I had finished my education with a PhD and that box of macaroni and cheese by the time I turned twenty-seven.

I caught a glimpse of myself in the mirror. What did Jack see when he looked at me? Light-colored freckles dotted my nose and cheeks in little clumps. My eyes were pale green and my lashes long, but I never really wore makeup. My hair was bottle-blond. It used to be naturally blond when I was a little girl, but age had darkened it. I still kept the "sun-kissed" blond facade going, but I drew the line at having *all* my hair bleached. That service was offered, but for me, my carpet and drapes didn't need to match. That area was an invitation-only destination, not open to public viewing anyway.

How would I survive until Friday? Would Jack be there again? I'd definitely give him an invitation into *that* territory. Hell, I'd draw him a map and mark it with an X just in case he got lost along the way. My mind took me to all kinds of places but always brought me back to Jack.

I managed to struggle through three days of classes and two nights of bad TV before Friday finally arrived. Chloe took me shopping for an appropriate "Let's discuss our dead mothers" and "Please hump me" outfit to ensure all bases would be covered. After our successful selection of a semi-tight-fitting sweater and jeans, it was time for a late lunch.

"Are you nervous?" Chloe's eye peered over the restaurant menu.

"About what?"

"About what you will say to your future husband?"

We both laughed, but she continued to stare at me.

"He probably won't even be there."

"I'll bet you dinner he will be." Chloe had won every single bet we'd ever made, every single one.

"How can you be so sure?"

"Because"—she paused—"he wants to be there as moral support for his sister, and he wants your jelly, girlfriend."

"At this stage in the game, I'm just hoping he remembers my name."

"Go a little early, which is no stretch for you anyway. He'll be there. I just know it."

And as always, Chloe was right. I pulled into the parking lot and instantly saw his car. Well, maybe I had been scouring the parking lot for it, but nonetheless, there it was. What would I say to him? Why had I gotten engrossed watching YouTube videos instead of planning out a witty conversation? The YouTube videos with all those kittens doing crazy things made me laugh every time. I could talk to him about that, or I could slit my wrists with a dull butter knife and call it a day. Tough call.

I pulled the heavy community center doors open, looked around the empty hallway, and contemplated my next move. In the last three days, I had envisioned at least a dozen different scenarios for this exact moment. None of my fantasies, however, started off with me standing in a musty hallway with my new lace undies riding up my backside. They barely covered either of my cheeks anyway, so it seemed pretty pointless to have worn them in the first place. I walked slowly down the hall. I could barely think straight because my panties had almost been swallowed whole by my butt. I was so caught up in what to do about them that I didn't hear him come up behind me.

"There you are." His voice startled me.

"Hi, Jack."

He smiled at me but said nothing more. I felt the need to break the silence, and what I said next was nothing short of a history-making moment. "Hey, did you see the video with that amazing pussy?" As soon as I said it, I realized what I had done. Kitty, not pussy. Kitty, not pussy.

He laughed out loud. "I'm not sure. Which amazing pussy might that be?" He inched closer to me, and I felt my face go flush. I needed to change the subject quickly in order to save the smallest shred of dignity I somehow still had.

"You surprised me. I didn't expect to see you here."

"Really? Why not?" Tonight there were no sweat droplets above his lip, and he was dressed in jeans and a button-down shirt. His hair was slightly gelled, and his eyes were bluer than I remembered.

I was so lost in admiring the piece of artwork standing before me that I forgot he was talking. "What did you say?"

"Why are you surprised I'm here?"

"I don't know. It's Friday night, and I would think a guy like you would have better things to do than hang around a community center."

"A guy like me, huh?" I couldn't tell if he was amused or offended by the words I was throwing out there without regard.

"You know what I mean. Don't you have, like, a wife or girlfriend or something like that?"

Jack took a very long look at me before responding. "Something like that." His eyes never deviated from me. "Can I ask you a question?"

I honestly couldn't believe he was interested in me enough to ask me anything. I wanted to tell him the answer was yes to anything he might ask me, but I caught myself before the filter in my brain permanently malfunctioned.

"Sure."

"What's your full name?"

"Gracelynn Faith Anderson."

"Was your mother religious?"

"Probably not in the way most people think. My mom loved feeling the sun in her face, hiking at daybreak, walking along the beach, watching the stars come to life at night. That's when she said she felt closest to God." I hadn't talked about her in so long that I was surprised it came so naturally with someone I barely knew. Les and I had spoken about her only once, and it was simply because a picture of her had fallen from a box I was putting away. He picked it up, looked at it, and asked me if it was her, and when I told him it was, he handed the picture back to me. I put it away, along with all the memories of her. Up until now, she had been packed away in a quiet, untouched place. Now she was with me again.

"And how about you? Are you the same?" he asked, seeming sincerely interested in my answer.

"I'm not that good. I need God's hands to push me, not guide me. Every once in a while, he also kicks me in the ass just to remind me who's boss."

He laughed, and then silence again fell.

"It's beautiful."

"What is?" I looked at him, confused.

"Your name—it fits you."

I wasn't sure what to say next. All the words, all the witty lines, everything I had practiced saying the last three days escaped me. I was at a loss for words and completely wrapped up in him. His cell phone shattered the silence, and he glanced down momentarily.

"I should probably take this."

"Sure."

He looked at his phone again. "They'll call back." He hit the ignore button, and I felt my heart begin to beat again. His blond eyelashes touched the edges of his eyebrows.

"I'm so sorry about your mom and dad. That must have been incredibly hard for you."

"Thanks. I know you understand what others don't." His face blushed slightly. I could tell that he was wounded by it all. Still trying to make sense of something, he would never find the answers. "Do you look like your mom?" He tilted his head slightly, as if to survey my looks.

"I've been told I do. She had blond hair and green eyes."

"How about freckles?"

"Oh, those." I reached up and touched my nose, feeling embarrassed about them.

"I like them. My mom had freckles. Hers were brown, though." He was quiet for a moment. "Did she have your lips?"

I brushed my finger over my lower lip. Did she? I felt a pang of uncertainty and a moment of awkwardness because I couldn't remember. "I don't remember. It was a long time ago." There, the confession.

He nodded.

"Do you look like your mom?" I asked.

"Kinda." A partial smile crept on his face as he thought of her.

"She must have been very special." The words fell flat between us.

"How about you?" His eyes met mine. "You have someone waiting for you at home? Boyfriend? Husband or something?" His fingers traced the lines in the wall next to where we stood. He clearly did not want to talk about his mom.

"Or something."

His phone pulsed again.

"Man, someone is trying to reach you."

"Not really."

"How about a question for you?"

"I'm not sure how I feel about fielding a question from a girl who gets a regular ass whooping from God."

I laughed. "What do you do for a living? I mean, besides hanging around community centers on a Friday night? Are you a reformed convict or something?"

"It's worse. I'm a lawyer—corporate law, no less. And I bet you thought we never left the bottom of the lake."

I laughed again, and he smiled.

"You seem pretty dressed-up for the community center, Jack.

You hiding your shorts under those?" I reached out, pretending to touch his leg, and he leaned forward. My hand met his jeans. I felt my heart surge.

"You smell amazing, Gracie."

My cheeks instantly flushed. Chloe had convinced me to spray perfume on my body in places that should never smell like country wildflowers. I looked up at him but could say nothing. My hand still rested on his leg. He leaned in closer. He smelled like a sample out of a magazine. For the first time in a very long time, I almost felt real again. Almost.

Words finally found their way out of my mouth. "Do you like what you do?"

"Every day except those that end in a y."

"Then why do you do it? Why not try something else?"

"I'm not sure. Maybe because I'm really good at it. And you don't walk away from something you're good at. That wouldn't make much sense, would it?"

"It would if you're not happy."

His eyes clouded. "That's what my mom used to say." Silence filled the space between us once more. "Listen, I have to run. It was great seeing you again."

His mother was reaching beyond the grave, channeling career advice through me, and Jack was having no part of it. How unsurprising that I had killed another moment like this.

"It was great seeing you too," I said. I had turned to walk past him when he grabbed my arm.

"I wanted to see you, Gracie. That's why I came."

He moved past me and out the doors. I wanted to stop him. I wanted to say something that would make him turn around and come back to me, but the only words I could find, out of all the words in my extensive vocabulary, could not bring the moment or Jack back to me. "Thank you," I said. And then he was gone.

Everything was a blur. I was confused and dazed and not sure what my next move should be. I couldn't remember the last time I had wanted something so badly and felt so utterly clueless about how to get it. I walked through the heavy steel doors into the parking lot. The wind howled like a dog begging to come in from the cold. My heart sank when I saw the empty space where his car had been parked. I took a step back before catching a glimpse of his car next to mine.

The wind whipped at my hair as I walked toward the cars. My eyes began to water as each gust hit my face. I glanced into his car but saw only stacks of files and a gym bag in the backseat. Then his silhouette appeared beside my car.

"Hello, Jack."

He jumped. I had startled him. "Gracie, what are you doing here?" His lip quivered as he spoke.

"Maybe I should ask you that. Are you in the market for a Honda? You know, grand theft auto is a pretty serious crime."

No response. He held a piece of paper in his hand. It was folded in half.

"Whatcha got there?" I motioned toward the paper.

"Nothing." He looked at me. "You look cold. Your nose is red."

"One of the many perks of being Irish, I suppose. I always get rosy cheeks and a red nose when the temp drops below fifty."

Jack looked over at the center, where Ellie was walking through the doors. "You'd better go. I think your session is about to start." He seemed anxious.

"Is that note for me?" I pointed at it.

Jack was silent.

"C'mon, just give me my note."

"Your note? This isn't for you."

"I know it's mine, so you can either give it to me or get in your car and take my note with you." I wasn't exactly sure it was my note, but I was taking the chance.

He walked past me to his car. "Night, Gracie." He got in, started the car, and drove away.

I stood there motionless. I was not cut out for love or lust or anything like it. I was not that kind of girl—the girl who finds her soul mate and has everything fall into place so easily. I was the girl who handed her heart to someone completely and got it handed back in a million little pieces.

3

His name was Sam Patterson. We met in second grade, and I instantly fell in love with him, as did all the other girls. He had black hair, big brown eyes, and dimples that creased his cheeks like half-moons. I was not a shy kid. I was giggly and outgoing and never let anyone or anything rattle me—that is, anyone or anything except for Sam. I was shy around Sam for no other reason than I liked him.

For years, Sam barely acknowledged my existence. During the summer between seventh and eighth grade, Sam finally took notice of me. While Chloe was spending the summer with her grandparents in Rhode Island, my Midwest summer was long and boring.

One uneventful night as I sat on my porch watching the stars, Sam's dog, Mascot, came bounding into my yard. Sam's voice trailed slightly behind the dog's fast-moving feet. "Mascot! This is the last time, dog, I'm going to go chasing after you." As he was securing the leash to his dog's collar, Sam finally looked up and saw me sitting there.

"Hey, G."

"Hey, Sam. Mascot got you on the run tonight, huh?"

He stood up with Mascot by his side. "Yeah." It was quiet for a minute. "How's your summer been?"

"Okay, I guess. Yours?"

He walked my way and stood near my porch. "Okay. Chloe's gone this summer, right?"

I nodded. Mascot was pulling at Sam, looking to go on another adventure, whether Sam wanted to join him or not. Lightning bugs lit up the night with their brief flicks of light.

"Well, better get going."

"See ya, Sam."

He started to turn but stopped. "I may go bowling tomorrow night. You can come if you want. I mean, if you want to come, that's okay. I mean, that would be cool."

"Sure." I was happy to have someone to hang out with, even if it was just for one night and it was bowling.

Like he was at every sport he touched, Sam was exceptional at bowling. The day after bowling, we went to my grandma's to swim. She had this amazing in-ground pool. For those of us on the outside, the pool was something really special. For a house inside the Gates, it was like having a water sprinkler. We swam all day, and Grandma ordered takeout food from the country club. We sat with my grandparents, eating and watching a horror movie. Slasher movies were my grandma's guilty pleasure. For a woman who had been bred to be prim and proper, this enjoyment of horror movies was surprising. She especially loved it when the beauty queen took one to the throat. She herself had been Miss Lake County, so the irony was not lost on me.

Every day for a month, Sam and I were inseparable. One night, I was sitting on my porch watching the stars when I caught a glimpse of Sam walking up my steps.

"Hey. What's going on?" I asked.

In the shadows of nightfall, his frame danced on the sidewalk. He came up and sat next to me on the porch swing. He didn't say anything. Instead, he reached over and took my hand. My fingers got lost in his. My head started to swim. I wasn't really sure what was happening.

"G?"

"Yeah?" My heart was in my throat. I could barely speak.

"Can I stay here tonight?" Something was wrong; I could tell.

"Are you okay?"

He pulled me to him. He held onto me like someone broken, and I held him while he fell apart. It seemed like a real and grown-up moment.

"Sam? What is it?" I never wanted to let him go.

"Don't ask me." He lifted his head, looked at me, and kissed my lips softly and quickly. His cheeks were wet with tears. I could feel his heart beating like a drum, and I felt mine doing the same. I took my fingers and wiped away a tear running down his face. I kissed his cheek, finding the trail the tear had made. One of the half-moons creased where my lips had just been. He looked at me again, his chestnut eyes clouded with water.

"I have to ask my mom. Stay here, okay?"

He nodded but said nothing. He was still crying.

Cassandra Marie Desiree Smith had been a beautiful baby with big green eyes and chubby cheeks. She had blossomed into a beautiful woman, with long blond hair and a petite frame. Cassie, as everyone except my grandma called her, had a magnetic personality. In high school she had been head cheerleader, honor roll student, and volunteer at the local soup kitchen. I think my grandma had expected my mom to become the next trophy wife in a long line of nameless, faceless women lost in the shadows of their husbands. My mother definitely had other plans.

A year before this night, my mom's health had begun to deteriorate. Her once-long hair was gone, replaced by a Bears cap she wore daily. Her eyebrows, long lashes, and trendy bangs were absent. At the height of her beauty, she had worn clothes like she was walking a Milan runway show. Her skin now hung on her frame like an overcoat over a skeleton. She weighed less than ninety pounds. She slept most of the day away, exhausted from fighting the endless night sweats.

I found her in bed watching an old movie. Stacks of classic movies sat piled by the TV—*Made for Each Other, Bringing Up Baby, It's a Wonderful Life, Adam's Rib, To Kill a Mockingbird, Casablanca.* She loved old movies and watched them nonstop. Tonight it was *It Happened One Night.* Her favorite was *It's a Wonderful Life,* and we had watched it together for as long as I could remember.

Bottles of pills and wadded-up, bloodstained tissues spilled over the nightstand and onto the floor by her bed. She glanced over when I walked in the room.

"Hey, Mama." Claudette Colbert and Cary Grant kept the conversation light in the background.

"Hey, sugar."

"Can Sam spend the night?"

"Sam? Well, that's a surprise. Why?" She paused to cough and motioned for the box of tissues on her nightstand. I reached over and handed it to her. She wiped a few droplets of blood from her lips with a tissue and motioned toward a glass of water. She grimaced as she took a long sip. Her eyes closed and opened slowly. Tiny droplets of dried blood were splattered across her shirt collar like an original piece of artwork.

"Can he?" I was growing impatient, thinking about Sam waiting for me on the porch.

"Is it okay with his parents?" Her eyes were sullen, and dark circles encased them like defining rings. She was on the verge of death. It would come for her soon after, but at that moment, my mother was not ready to let go of life. Not ready to let go of me. Not ready to let go of my dad. I'm not sure she ever really became ready, but her body wanted to shed her like an old skin, and she fought it every step of the way. My grandma and grandpa had taken my mom to every specialist, every premier hospital. They refused to accept that nothing could be done for her. They assumed that money would keep my mother alive, that it could buy her a miracle. The day my mom stopped treatment, she looked at my grandma and said, "Enough." She would say nothing else, and for the first time in a very long time, my grandma was left speechless. My mother had taken her own path her entire life in everything she had done, and she did the same when it came to walking toward death.

"I think so," I answered.

"Think or know so?" My mother never missed a beat, just like her mother.

"I'll make sure he calls them. Okay?" I looked at her as her head slid back on the pillow. "Thanks, Mama. Love you."

"Love you more." Claudette and Cary filled the room again.

I ran back to the porch, worried that Sam might have changed his mind and left. I found him in the exact spot I'd left him. He hadn't moved at all.

"My mom said it was okay as long as your parents are okay with it." Silence. "They are, right?"

He looked at me and then looked up at the sky. "Is your mom real sick?" He was avoiding answering my question.

"Yeah." I pretended to be looking up at the sky as well, but I was looking at him out of the corner of my eye.

"Cancer, right?"

"Yeah."

"Is she going to die?"

My heart stopped. I struggled for words and felt only a rush of tears. I knew she was getting worse, but not until that moment did I realize the answer. And it hit me like a lightning bolt to my heart.

"What's happening, guys?" My dad's voice startled me.

"Nothing. Sam is spending the night." I wiped my falling tears.

"Gracelynn, inside for a moment, please."

I followed him into the house. I knew that my dad, home late again from work, was in no mood for diversionary tactics or lies. Straight up, no chasers—my father demanded the truth. And I gave it to him. "Stay here." He ordered me stationary in the living room as he made his way to the front-porch swing and to Sam. It seemed like forever before Sam and my dad came inside. "I'm taking Sam home. Say good night to your friend, Gracie."

"Night, Sam." I looked at him, hoping to read his mind. I could tell by his eyes that he had been crying again, but he actually looked relieved. "Call me tomorrow?"

"Sure. See ya, G." He glanced at me and then headed out the door.

I sat on the couch, waiting for my dad to come home. Almost an hour passed before I heard the key in the lock.

"What are you still doing up?" My dad plopped down next to me on the couch and laid his head back.

"Is Sam okay?"

"He will be. He's just going through a rough patch. Understandable with his parents' divorce and all …" He trailed off, fighting sleep.

"Divorce?"

I heard my dad's breathing slow. No response.

"Dad, go to bed. It's late."

"It is, isn't it?" He looked at me, rose slowly, and shuffled up the stairs. I sat there thinking about Sam as I watched the stars blink on and off in the sky until I could fight sleep no more.

Sam did not call. He wasn't at the town summer festival, and every call I made to his house went unanswered. He simply vanished from my life.

Over the next couple of years, we would see each other only in passing at school and at parties and, of course, at my mom's funeral. Then, one boring night, on the eve of my sixteenth birthday, Sam called me.

"G?"

"Yes?"

"It's Sam. How are you?"

Sam had become an outstanding athlete, a mediocre student, homecoming king, and a ghost to me. But I'd never stopped missing him, even after he'd forgotten who I was and what I thought we'd meant to each other. I hadn't kept close track, but the last I'd heard, Sam was dating a girl from Westminster named Millie, spelled with an "ie" with little hearts over the *i*'s, I guessed.

"Good, Sam. How about you?"

"Whatcha doin'?"

"Nothing much."

"Your birthday's on Sunday, right?"

How did he remember that? "It is, but you know I don't do birthdays." It was common knowledge that I had no interest in birthday celebrations. No one was allowed to decorate my locker, give me cards or presents, or bake me a cake. It offended some people, but if they knew the real reason I was antibirthday, they might have felt the same way.

"I'd like to change that. Can I come over?"

I did really want him to come over, no matter why.

"Give me a few minutes." I hung up and bolted to my room. My dad was traveling on business again. Since my mom's death, my dad spent most of his time on the road. He hated being home, hated being reminded of what he no longer had, and I was part of that reminder. For the most part, I was raising myself, left alone for long periods at a time, but I didn't mind it. My grandma checked on me regularly, bringing groceries as needed. I brushed my hair, changed my clothes, and put on some mascara. I rarely wore makeup, but I suddenly felt the need to look more grown-up. I was in the middle of flossing my teeth when the doorbell rang.

"Hey," he said as I answered the door. There he was, six foot four, with those half-moon dimples, standing in front of me. He walked past me and turned around with a bag in hand. "To celebrate."

"What did I tell you about my birthday? Not going to happen."

The half-moons pulled back into a smile. "How about a one-time exception for an old friend?"

I shrugged my shoulders and opened the bag. Inside were two cupcakes topped with pink icing, along with party hats, noisemakers, and a birthday candle.

"Allow me." He put the candle in a cupcake, put one party hat on me and then one on himself, lit the candle, and asked me to make a wish.

I closed my eyes, blew out the candle, and felt his lips on mine. Startled, I pulled back. "What are you doing, Sam?"

"Something I want to do every time I see you. I think about you all the time. Do you think about me?" He was inching closer to me. "Yes."

He pulled me to him, and we kissed. At first, it was just our lips that touched, but as the kisses became longer, our tongues tangled and crashed. I felt Sam's hand reach into my shirt and up my back. I was confused, caught off guard. He was kissing my neck, sucking on the skin around my collarbone. He pulled me to the couch, and I could feel how much he wanted me.

I looked at him, pulling the string of his party hat to me. "Do you know what I wished for?"

"No."

I kissed him and pulled the party hat off. It dropped to the floor. I took his hand and guided him to my bedroom. As I laid him down and climbed on top of him, I whispered softly in his ear, "I wished for this."

There were so many things in my life I could not control—things that no matter how much I wanted to take back as my own were no longer mine. I often felt like a prisoner in my own world. I had never been able to break free of the emotional handcuffs and shackles that had weighed me down nearly my whole life. And in this moment, I was going to take no prisoners, nor would I be a prisoner myself. I had complete control over this situation, control over Sam. I knew this would go as far as I wanted it to go. I wanted to leave the wounded girl I had become behind me. I wanted to run, not walk, away from her as fast as I could. This was my chance.

I straddled him, my legs on either side of him. Strands of blond hair fell into my face as I leaned down and kissed him softly. My tongue traced the edges of his lips. His hand moved to pull my hair away. He was looking at me. I moved my lips down to his neck. I reached my hands under his shirt and tugged at it. He arched up, and I pulled it over his head. His hands reached up the back of my shirt, and I felt a rush of excitement surge through my body. My hands rested on his chest. I could feel his heart racing through my skin. He pulled me to him, and our mouths pressed more intensely against each other. His hands were shaking as he tried to unfasten my bra. I stopped him.

His breathing was hard and his eyes closed. He opened them and looked at me. "Is this okay? We don't have to ..."

I reached behind my back, and with one quick release, I was exposed to him. My heart was racing so hard, I felt like it was going to stop, but I knew what I wanted. I took his hands and placed them on me. Heat pulsated through them, and when they touched my cool skin, I shivered slightly. Moonlight lit up half the room, creating flashes of light across my face.

He grabbed by legs and quickly flipped me over. He was on top of me now, and the weight of his body made me want him even more. I unbuttoned his jeans, and he wiggled out of them. They dropped on the floor. He gently pulled at my waistband, and I helped him until nothing was between us. He was kissing my chest now and had slid partially off me. Droplets of sweat fell from his forehead and landed on my bare chest. I heard soft moans coming from inside my throat. I wanted him inside of me, and I pulled him on top of me again. It felt so good, so right, at that moment that I didn't want it to stop. He leaned over the bed and pulled something from his jeans. He struggled for a few moments. I wanted to help him, but I had no idea what to do, so I just lay there with my head turned away.

He moved back on top of me, and I could feel him trying to find his way inside of me. A rush of pain replaced the previous sensation of pleasure. I winced at the immense pressure. Finally, he was inside me. I tried to find the rhythm of his moving body. His head was next to mine as my hands raced up and down his back. Just as I was beginning to keep in time with his rhythm, he pulled me to him with one final push. Then there was nothing more than his heaving chest. He kissed my neck and rolled off me. His arms found their way around me. My head rested on his chest.

Our legs were intertwined, and our fingers interlaced. I felt the tendrils of sleep pulling at me. Sam said something and then fell silent. I woke first. Sam lay next to me still. His chest rose and fell slowly. I delicately traced the lines of his stomach with my fingertips. He began to stir. He placed his hand over mine and guided it down below his waist. I moved my hand at the pace he wanted me to keep. As I continued, the rate of his breathing increased. His back arched slightly as he moaned. I had never done anything like this before, but I could tell I was doing it right.

The moonlight bounced off the half-moons. His eyes remained closed, and he interlaced his fingers back with mine again when it was over. It wasn't long before he was asleep again, but I lay awake, looking out the window. There she was, the brightest star, shining at me through the dark night. We'd never had a chance to talk about what to expect the first time I was with a boy like this. I was too young, she was too sick, and then she was gone. Being with Sam wasn't so much about the physical part, which truthfully hurt as much as it felt good. For me, it was more about having this boy want me in a way I had never thought he would. I closed my eyes, holding onto him as tight as I could, never wanting this moment or Sam to leave me.

As the morning sunlight beckoned me to greet the day, I reached over for Sam, and he was gone. I sat up in bed, trying to wipe the sleep out of my eyes. He had disappeared sometime while I slept. I looked around. He had left no loving note, nothing telling me how much last night had meant to him. The house was silent. He was not in the bathroom or in the kitchen making me breakfast like people did in romantic movies. He had taken what he wanted from me and snuck out like a thief in the middle of the night. I sat there naked in my bed, and the shackles I thought I had broken free of again tightened themselves around my hands and feet; I was a prisoner once more.

Saturday rose and fell, and as I lay in my bed looking at the dark sky, I became overwhelmed with the pain of my mom's absence. I knew that in this moment she would have known what to say or do to make the hurt all go away. Tonight, nothing could comfort me, and the brightest star only added to the realization that I was, in fact, alone.

★ ★ ★

The next morning, I awoke to clanking sounds in the kitchen. "Grandma?" With each cabinet door that opened and closed, an invisible sledgehammer hit my head. I stumbled to the kitchen, trying to shield my eyes from the glare of the morning light.

"Gracelynn, you look a mess. Are you not feeling well?"

I found my way to the kitchen table and shrugged my shoulders. I sat and rested my head on the table.

"Off the table," she said, tapping my head slightly.

I glanced at her. My grandma looked perfect as usual. Designer clothes, trendy haircut, perfect makeup.

"Rough night?" She put a glass of orange juice in front of me.

I shrugged my shoulders.

"Your shoulders cannot speak, Gracelynn. Kindly use words."

Tears welled up in my eyes. I said nothing.

She sat next to me, wrapping her manicured nails around a cup of coffee. "I will assume by the tears that this is about a boy."

Tears left my eyes and dropped to the table.

"Samuel?"

I looked up in disbelief. "How did you know?"

"I pay attention. You have liked that boy your entire life, and he has liked you."

I shook my head.

"Did I ever tell you about Teddy and me?"

I shrugged my shoulders again. Teddy was my grandma's friend or boyfriend or whatever you call an old person who dates another old person. My grandma and Teddy had known each other forever.

"Yeah, he's your friend," I said as I wiped my nose. I liked Teddy. He was funny and nice, and he made my grandma laugh. If you knew Grandma Blake, you knew that wasn't an ordinary feat. Teddy wore novelty T-shirts all the time. They were really funny, sometimes on the verge of being offensive.

"Well, actually, he has always been a bit more."

I was confused. "What?"

Grandma stood up, poured another cup of coffee, sat back down, and proceeded to tell me the story. As she unfolded her life in words, it became clear to me that my grandma had many layers. She was complex in ways I had never imagined.

Blake Desiree Honoree had been born of money, not new money but old money. My grandma was a snob, but she came by it honestly. Her family lived in a sprawling gated home on top of a hill, with servants and maids. It was pretty clear the path my grandma was expected to take in life. She was to be educated in order to properly engage in social situations. She was to marry someone who also came from money and be a dutiful wife, as her mother had been before her. Under no circumstance was she to divert from this prearranged path.

My grandma met my grandpa Will and Teddy, who were best

friends, when they were all teenagers. My grandma liked both of these boys, and as time moved along, she found herself faced with a decision. The year she was named Miss Lake County, she also turned eighteen. She was now considered an adult, and as such, the expectation was that she would marry.

"Yeah, I know. You chose Grandpa Will. End of story." I was slightly bored, picking at the blueberry muffin my grandma had placed in front of me.

"Not exactly."

My interest was suddenly piqued. "What do you mean, not exactly?"

She parted her perfectly painted pink lips and continued her story. My grandpa confided in Teddy that he was planning on asking my grandma to marry him. Teddy knew his window of opportunity was closing, so he had to do something quick. The night before my grandpa was to propose to my grandma, Teddy asked her to meet him in Central Park by the old oak tree.

"I know that tree," I interrupted. "It's the tallest one, right in the middle of the park."

"Gracelynn, it is not polite to interrupt," Grandma said before continuing. My grandma knew that if she met Teddy in front of that tree, he would likely propose marriage, and she would have a decision to make. Her parents had discounted Teddy long ago. My grandma had been told that she would marry Will. His family was more respectable in the social hierarchy, so there was no need for discussion. She also knew that if she went to the park, her life would be forever altered.

"So you didn't go." I leaned back in my chair, confident in my assumption.

"I went."

My mouth literally dropped. "I don't understand. Did Teddy propose?" I was leaning over the table now, waiting impatiently for her next words.

"He did."

"And?"

"I said yes." My grandma loved both boys, but when she thought about the two, she decided to pick the one she felt she could not live without, and that was Teddy.

I couldn't believe it. "But you married Grandpa Will."

"I did." She reached into her sweater and pulled out a necklace. A simple gold band filled with a small row of tiny diamonds hung on it. "This is the ring Teddy gave me that night."

My grandma met Teddy under that big oak tree. He proposed, and she said yes. Knowing her parents would not approve, they decided to run away and elope. The plan was to move to Madison, Wisconsin, where Teddy would work for his uncle, who was in the garbage business. They would raise their family there, and only after the right amount of time had passed would they return to Lake County and to her parents. That night under the sprawling oak tree, they made their relationship official, both physically and emotionally. They agreed to meet by the same tree the next day and leave for Madison.

"Then what?" I asked.

Halfway to Madison, Teddy's car broke down, and he was forced to call his father. Instead of going to Madison, they were driven back to her parents' home. My grandma's parents were furious with her. She was not to marry Teddy but was to marry Will, and it would happen right away. In a time when running away was considered an act of social treason, my grandma knew she had lost her one chance to be with Teddy. She placed the ring he had given her on a chain around her neck, hidden out of sight. She wore the chain as a reminder of what she had and what she had lost.

The following Saturday, my grandma married my grandpa, and Teddy left for Madison alone. He would take over his uncle's business and expand it to Illinois, Michigan, and Indiana. He would never marry. I had known Teddy all my life. He was at all our parties, holidays, and birthdays. He was seemingly always around, never missing an opportunity to see my grandma. He was there the night my mom died. It was the first time Teddy found nothing funny, sitting by our front porch swing, tears falling.

My mom was born less than a year after my grandparents married. Grandpa Will never said much about Teddy, even when my grandma would disappear and he would find her at the park, sitting under that old oak tree. I wondered how my grandpa must have felt, finding her time and time again under that tree.

Grandpa Will died not too long after my mom. On his way to work, he collapsed on the sidewalk in front of First National Bank and Reserve, one of the three banks he owned. He was dead before his head hit the pavement. Teddy sat next to my grandma at my grandpa's funeral and never left her side again.

We sat quietly for a moment before Grandma spoke again. "My point with this story, Gracelynn, is that you never know where your life or your heart is going to take you. We do not own destiny, and we certainly do not own love. It is handed to us in strange and unique ways."

I leaned into her. She felt warm and genuine then, two things I had never known my grandma to be.

"Now ... tell me what happened with Samuel."

"I thought he liked me, but I guess he doesn't." Tears found their way to my eyes again.

"And what makes you think he does not like you?"

"He wanted to celebrate my birthday with me, and we did, but he hasn't called or come around since."

"Your birthday is today. In addition, you refuse to celebrate your birthday. Has that changed?"

"I made an exception for an old friend."

"Well, what did you do for this birthday celebration?"

My stomach jolted. Telling my grandma about it felt weird. She looked at me, waiting for an answer.

"Uh, we just hung out." I hoped that answer would be enough for her.

"Doing what?" My grandma was relentless. She always had a way of pulling information out of people. Lying to my grandma was useless. She would have made an exceptional interrogator.

"Not much." The silence at that moment felt like two walls closing in on me. She was going to squeeze the truth out of me. "He brought me a birthday cupcake."

"That is nice." The walls continued to close in. "Did you not have a good time? I mean, did something happen that upset you?" She raised her eyebrows and made me look her in the eyes. "Anything at all?"

"No, Grandma. We had fun." I looked away.

"Then what exactly is the problem?"

"Well, we had fun, and then he left, and well, that's about it."

"He will be back again. I guarantee it."

"I doubt it."

I stumbled to the living room and was lying on the couch, a pillow over my face, when I heard my grandma's voice again. "Gracelynn?"

"Yeah?" I said in a muffled voice from under the pillow.

"If you ever want to talk about things, I am here." She lifted the pillow off my face and looked at me. "I know you miss her so much more at times like this, especially today." She dropped the pillow back down on my face. I heard the door close.

Especially today. I slept most of the morning away. About noon, I finally got up to take a bath. Passing by my parents' room, I caught a glimpse of her old movies sitting on a shelf and paused. Those movies were the source of the only major fight my dad and I had ever had. Right after my mom died, we were packing up her stuff to donate when I noticed the movies were gone. She had dozens and dozens of them. Dust framed the shelf like a police chalk outline.

My grandma had thought it would be good to pack some things away "so we could move on." Packing up her room meant putting closure to her life. Our nerves were edgy, our hearts weighed down with bricks.

"Where are the movies?" I stepped away from her nightstand and stood up.

"What?" My dad was in her closet, removing shirts from their hangers.

"Her movies? Where are her movies?" I felt my anger rising up.

"Oh, I already packed those." He went back to her closet.

"Packed them? How could you pack those?" I felt a hot burst of tears come to my eyes.

"Gracie, what are we going to do with all those movies?"

Grandma had wanted to hire someone to pack my mom's things away, but my dad had politely refused. Now deep into a project neither of us wanted, we were ready to come to blows over old movies.

"How about *watch them*?" We stood face-to-face now, a silk lavender blouse in his hand, her glasses in mine. "She loved those movies. We are not getting rid of them." I took a step forward. Tears slid down my face like acid.

"Why keep them? We'll never watch them."

"Just because you don't want them doesn't mean I don't. How dare you take them away without talking to me first?"

He was sitting on the bed now, clutching the lavender blouse. "They aren't going to bring her back to us." He was staring at the blouse, gently rubbing it between his fingers.

"Do whatever you want to do with them then." I stormed out of the room. I stayed in my room the rest of the night, watching the stars in the sky. I wanted to grab the brightest one, reach up, and pull it down—bring it back to me, bring her home. He was right. The movies wouldn't bring her back to us. She was gone, and no black-and-white movie was going to change that.

The next morning, as I walked past their room, I noticed all the boxes were gone. The room stood empty and silent—empty except for the stacks of movies placed neatly back on the shelf.

4

He knew he never stood a chance with her. From across the football field, he watched her, blond ponytail bouncing up and down as she kept in time with the other cheerleaders. He knew she came from money; all the girls from Westminster did, and none of them ever gave guys like him the time of day.

"Anderson! Get your head and your ass in the game!" His coach's raspy yell dissolved his thoughts of her.

Out on the field, he was the game hero again, leading Highmore to a victory over Westminster. He wasn't picky about where he would go to college, as long as it was miles and miles away from the small house next to the railroad tracks where he had grown up. For him, football was his chance to really begin life instead of watching it pass by on a fast-moving freight train. College recruiters were calling, and he knew freedom was within reach.

Running to the locker room after the game, he saw her again. She was running as well, until she bumped into another cheerleader and dropped one of her pom-poms. He ran over to her and picked it up. They made eye contact, and he felt his heart pound out of his chest like the nightly freight train that barreled past his bedroom window.

"You dropped this." He smiled at her, black smudge running down his face from sweat.

Big green eyes stared back at him. "Thanks. Nice play out there."

He towered over her petite frame. *She is out of your league. No way is Westminster mixing with Highmore,* he kept telling himself as he got lost in those big green eyes. He knew she would never go for a guy like him. "Gotta go." He turned and started for the gym.

"Hey!" she called out to him.

"Yeah?" He stopped and turned back.

She was standing there with her pom-poms on each hip. "You got a name?"

"Anderson."

"Is that your first name or your last name or both?"

He shook his head. "It's Jeff. Jeff Anderson."

"Hi, Jeff Anderson. I'm Cassie."

"Hi, Cassie." They stood there looking at each other. He waved and headed to the locker room.

As the hot water beat against his face in the shower, he told himself, *Never gonna happen, Anderson. Forget about her.* He quickly got dressed and sidestepped wet towels and dirty cleats scattered across the floor on his way out. As the old gym door clanked behind him, there she stood, blond ponytail whipping around in the wind, a big block *W* on her jacket, with the name Smith scrolled across the back of it. He hesitated for a second, wondering if she was waiting for him or someone else.

"So I was thinking," she said, walking toward him, cheerleading skirt popping up and down with each gust of wind.

"Yeah?" She was so pretty that he wasn't sure if he could even say anything else right then.

"I'm going to the movies tomorrow night, and I could use someone to block and tackle for a good seat. You up for the job?"

"I'm sure I could manage." He shoved his hands in his letterman's jacket pockets, trying to hide the fact they were shaking.

"Here's my number. Call me tomorrow." She handed him a

small folded piece of paper, and he took it and slipped it into his back pocket. They went their separate ways.

That night, as the freight train traveled along the creaky tracks next to his bedroom window, he focused on the small unfolded piece of paper on his desk: "Cassie Smith 799-3455." He wanted to call her right then. He had wanted to call her the minute she walked away from him. The freight train took him to a new place that night. It took him to Cassie and to the beginning of the life he didn't have to go miles and miles away for. He only had to cross the tracks.

It was easy to be with her. She was funny and outgoing and always had an opinion about something, but she always said it in the politest of ways. They became fast friends but nothing more. He wanted to kiss her so many times—felt the urge to grab her and pull her to him. But something always stopped him. He wasn't sure what it was, but every time his instincts told him to take her hand, his mind told him to stop. Every night, he would listen to the freight train and think of her. Football season turned into basketball season. They were never without each other.

One winter night, she snapped a picture of them together. She later gave it to him in a card signed "Always, C." He kept the picture by his bed. It was the last thing he looked at each night before the lull of the freight train carried him off to sleep. He knew if he didn't tell her soon how he felt, it would be too late. He was closed off when it came to his feelings and hadn't really been with many girls, and none of them had come close to how he felt about Cassie.

Her problem was much different. She had been hiding their friendship from her parents, mostly from her mother. One night after sneaking back home well after curfew, she found her mother waiting for her in the dark of her room. She confessed everything, including the bombshell that she was in love with this boy from Highmore. And even more, he lived by the tracks on the poorest side of town. The horror on her mother's face said what the cold and direct orders out of her mouth would next confirm. She was never to see this boy again. She was to break it off immediately. Money was not to be diluted and definitely not with a boy from the other side of the tracks. Her mother reminded her that there was a bridge between the two towns for a reason. "Physical separation, Cassandra, is society's way of reminding us that there is a ranking order."

No matter how many angles Cassie tried, her mother could only see her fragile social foundation cracking. There would be no discussion. Let him find a suitable girl of his own kind. A respectable Gates boy would be selected for her. Her mother's departing words sent daggers to her heart. "Boys like that are only looking for a ticket out of their circumstance, Cassandra. I certainly did not raise you to go to the slums for anything more than entertainment."

She sat in the dark thinking. There would never be anyone else for her. She had known it the night he handed her pom-pom back to her. She would follow him across the world if that's where his life was taking him. She waited an hour and then quietly snuck out the back door, with a plan. As she drove over the bridge into Highmore, she finally felt free.

He let her in, and she immediately put her arms around him and kissed him. After months and months of their wanting something more, it was finally happening, and neither wanted to stop. That night, the fast-moving freight train took them both to a new place, and her mother could never take that away from her. Her grand plan was to date in secret. Once they were away at school, her parents would never know they were together.

"And then what, Cass?" He was holding her hand as they sat in the far corner of Central Park, out of sight. "Hide forever? Not an option. No more secrets. No more hiding." He kissed the top of her head. "We are going to do this the right way."

He graduated at the top of his class at Butler. He went on to finish grad school at Northwestern. Cassie made a point never to be far from him, even selecting Northwestern for her graduate studies so they could be together. It wasn't until he was recruited by a pharmaceutical company for a junior executive role that her mother began to acknowledge his presence. It was seven years before he could walk into the Smith home through the front door, seven years before her mother would refer to him by name, seven years before a more suitable Gates boy was not part of the discussion.

Seven years and one month after he and Cassie had become a couple, Jeff Anderson walked into the Smith home, sat down with Cassie's parents, and told them he finally felt good enough for their daughter.

There was a long silence. Finally, Will Smith quietly said, "We appreciate all you've done, but the truth is, you were always good enough for our daughter." He looked over at his wife, who smiled, vodka tonic in her hand.

Jeff Anderson had done the impossible. He had beaten Blake Desiree Honoree Smith at her own game.

I had heard the story of how my parents met and how my dad won over my grandma in varying forms from varying people over the course of my life. It wasn't until my mom's funeral, though, that I realized how hard it had been for my dad. He spent years trying to prove he was good enough for my mom, never letting what seemed to be the impossible keep them apart. In the end, he was the last one with her. The funeral concluded, and the infinite line of mourners paraded in front of us, saying their last good-byes to her. Grandma Blake, Grandpa Will, Teddy, and I stood in front of the casket. I felt myself floating outside my body, not sure if she was really, truly gone from us.

Grandma squeezed my hand. "Your father needs a few minutes."

He sat motionless on the couch in the front row. Tissues spilled out of his hands. He looked at us, tears falling into the creases of his lips. My grandma ushered me out of the room, closing the doors nearly all the way behind us.

In the opening between the doors, I watched him. He sat on the couch, looking at my mom. Finally, he stood up, walked over to her, and eased down so their foreheads could touch. Tears dropped from his face onto hers. He kissed the Bears cap she wore, leaned in, and whispered something. From inside his suit coat, he pulled out the old picture of them and tucked it next to her. He kissed her lips softly, his hand cradling the side of her face. He stood and slowly walked away from her. He stopped and looked back one final time. Over the earlier years, my dad must have felt victorious, thinking he had removed every last thing keeping him from my mom. Then the realization came that he had failed. There was one last obstacle he could never overcome—death.

After my mom's death, my dad seemed to just be going through the motions of life, picking up scattered pieces of our new existence that he really didn't know what to do with. He was expected to build a new life for us. He had always been good at solving problems, but when it came to our relationship, he remained puzzled. Without my mother, we were fractured and fragmented. He was an exceptional defenseman, but his offensive game was severely lacking. His best move was avoidance. We quickly became very good at playing that game.

Thankfully, my family didn't expect too much from me on Sunday. I lay in bed, looking out the window. Clouds covered the stars; I couldn't see her staring back at me. I closed my eyes and tried to remember the good times until I realized those were too few and far between now.

Monday slithered into my life. As I navigated around teenagers talking about each other in the school hall, I glanced up and saw him. He stood with a group of jocks and cheerleaders, his head slightly down. He lifted his head as I walked by. Our eyes met, and then he looked away. I heard them all laughing as I walked past. I turned the corner, and Chloe stood at my locker. She grabbed me and half-pushed me in the bathroom.

"What is it? What's wrong?" she asked as tears instantly fell from my eyes.

"I'm hor …" I tried to talk, but only a string of saliva came flowing from my mouth.

"You're what?" She was rubbing my hair, trying to soothe the words out of me.

"I'm hor …"

"You're horny? Oh, it's okay, sweetie. This is high school. Everyone is horny."

I shook my head. "No. I'm horrified." Finally, it was out. And horrified was how I had spent my weekend. The bell rang. We were late for class.

"Meet me in my car. I'll go get us out of class," she said, handing me her keys.

I just stared at her.

"I've got this. Now go."

The cold wind bit at my already-red nose as I walked to the parking lot. I fumbled with the car keys. How would I tell her what had happened?

A few minutes later, a tapping on the car window roused me from my thoughts. "Open up. It's freakin' cold out here."

I opened the door, and Chloe jumped in. She waved her fingers across the car vent.

"How did you get us out of class?"

"This time of year, Gracie? I just told Mrs. Periwinkle you were having a hard time because of your mom. She asked if you wanted to go talk to Mr. Prankiss, and I said your best friend could help you more than our half-assed guidance counselor."

"What did Mrs. Periwinkle say?"

"She knows Mr. Prankiss, for God's sake. She agreed."

I smiled. Even with misery saddled on my back, Chloe made me feel like a small weight was lifted.

"We just have to stop by later for the homework assignment. No biggie." We sat in silence for a minute. "You just missing your mom, or did something happen with your dad?"

I shook my head. "I saw Sam."

Chloe rolled her eyes and made a face. "I hate that guy. What did he say to you? He's always got some stupid thing to say."

Tears dropped from my chin onto the steering wheel.

"What did he say, Gracie?" She reached over and grabbed my hand.

"It's not what he said." I paused. "It's what we did."

I felt her hand loosen slightly. "Why? What did you do?"

I looked out the window, watching the flag whip against the flagpole. I knew I had to tell her. I knew it would make me feel better—help remove the burden from my back.

"Gracie? You can tell me anything."

I took a very deep breath and began talking, starting with the phone call and ending with the hallway sighting. "I can't believe I even thought I was good enough for him ..."

Chloe broke her silence to interrupt me. "Good enough for him? It's him who's not good enough for you. I'm going to go find that tool and give him the swiftest kick to his nuts he's ever had. Maybe if he spends all winter trying to remove his frank and beans from his throat, he'll think twice about what he's done."

"No. Don't. I guess he got what he wanted from me, and now he's done." I leaned my head back on the headrest. "I feel so stupid. How am I ever going to face him again?"

"There are only two things you aren't going to do when it comes to him. You aren't going to let him see how this has made you feel, and you are not, under any circumstances, going to talk to him again. Understood?" She reached over and pulled at my sleeve.

I looked at her. I knew I could clean up my face and make a good show of it to the rest of the world. But asking me not to acknowledge him was like asking my emotions to hide away, and they were presently on a rogue mission.

Chloe looked at me. "Promise, okay?"

I finally nodded. "Promise."

For the next three days, I managed to avoid him. Normally, I would see Sam in the hallway between classes, but I started taking a different route. There was only one time when our paths naturally intersected, so every day I ducked into the bathroom and hid until I was sure I would miss him. Friday came without a Sam sighting, and I was finally back to my old self. As I opened my gray, discolored locker door, a note fell from the top where it had been shoved. The small folded square of paper hit the ground at my feet. I picked it up, puzzled, shoved it into my book, and headed off to English Lit. It was a movie day, and *Romeo and Juliet* illuminated the dark room. When Romeo was at Juliet's window, I decided to open the note. My hands began to tremble when the unfolded paper brought the message to life:

G,
We need to talk.
Don't hate me, I can explain.
Sam

I folded the note back up and shoved it in my book. I tried to concentrate on the movie but couldn't. I had promised Chloe I would not see him again, but what would it hurt to just see what he had to say? Truth be told, I desperately wanted to see him, soak in his face, take his hand in mine, and tell him I forgave him for how horribly things had ended. As Romeo and Juliet kissed, I realized what I needed to do. I had made a promise to Chloe, and I was going to keep that promise, no matter how much I wanted to break it. My prison was once again built, the shackles securely fastened, chains around my feet. I dragged them out of class, down the hall, and out the door.

The walk home was cold and long. I was avoiding the bus, knowing Sam might be on it. He had a beat-up truck but used the bus most days. Autumn was quickly turning to winter. Thanksgiving was on the horizon, and the uneasiness of another depressing holiday was in front of me. The leaves crunched under my feet. I started a game of stepping on the ones that made the loudest noise to hear them echo in the near darkness. A small leaf I thought would crunch fell silent under my feet, but a loud crackle from a leaf under someone else's foot came from across the street. That's when I saw him. He was keeping time with me, remaining a few steps behind me. I quickened my pace, forgetting my leaf game. His pace grew faster. I turned the corner; my house was only a few feet away.

"Did you get it?" His voice caused my feet to stop.

"Yes." My back was to him.

"We need to talk. Can I cross the street?"

"It's a free street. You can go wherever you want to go on it." I turned to look at him, and he already stood in front of me. He must have sprinted over.

"You can only hide out in the bathroom for so long avoiding me."

I felt my face flush. "I have to go, Sam. Say what you have to say so I can get home." I tried not to look at him, knowing it would weaken my resistance.

He was quiet, saying nothing. I could feel his eyes on me. I wasn't sure what to do next, but I knew I didn't want to have my heart broken again out in the open. "I'm leaving now. Bye." I turned away from him.

He grabbed my arm. "Don't be like that, G. That's not who you are."

I looked at him. I could feel the coldness of his fingers as they gripped my forearm. "What else could you possibly want from me, Sam? You already took what I had to give, so just leave me alone." I pulled my arm away and walked the last few feet to the safety of my front steps. Only when I was inside did I peek from my front window, trying to catch a glimpse of him. He was gone. Again.

I had kept my word to Chloe but not without effort. I dropped my coat and backpack. The note sat in my English lit book, safely tucked away. It was proof he was not done with me yet, as my grandma had said.

My dad was gone again. The house was silent. I braided my hair, took a long bath, and put on a Bears shirt, one of the few things I'd kept of my mom's. The phone rang as I was surveying the refrigerator for dinner options.

"Hey, Chloe." I'd known it was her as soon as the phone rang.

"Hey, toots. Want to hang out tonight? I could come over and watch a movie." Chloe was trying to take care of a girl like me when she was still just a girl herself.

"I think I want to just lie low tonight."

"Are you okay?"

I was quiet.

"Is it still the Sam thing?"

"Nah. I just have a little headache. That's all."

"Well, if you hear a knock at your door tonight, it will be your bestie making sure you are not sitting at home wallowing in self-pity."

"Understood. See ya."

"Later, gator."

I was just finishing dinner when I heard the knock. Chloe obviously had figured me out. As I opened the door, I said, "Listen, why do you feel the need to check on me? Really?" I looked up and took a quick step back.

"Hey, G." The half-moons stood in front of me. "Can I come in?" He walked past me, not waiting for me to welcome him in.

My heart began to pump ferociously. I shut the door and took a deep breath.

He looked at me. "Hope you weren't busy."

I shrugged my shoulders. It felt awkward for a minute. What if Chloe decided to come over? Seeing Sam here was definitely not something she would be happy about since I had made a promise I was breaking from every angle.

"What's up?" I said. We stood in the living room. My eyes found their way to his face. Those big brown eyes looking back at me caused the hairs on the back of my neck to dance around.

"It's about the note."

"Did you mean to put it in someone else's locker?"

He shook his head and walked to the couch. Sitting down, he pulled off his jacket. A royal blue shirt outlined his chest like a perfectly drawn shape. "Nah, it was for you."

I stood there, not sure what to do.

"I want to talk about what happened." He was staring at his shoes, turning each foot on its side over and over again.

I felt a craving for him rise up inside of me; my skin was beginning to heat up to the point of burning. "Well, since you're here bothering me, you at least want something to drink?"

He looked up from his shoes, smiling as his eyes met mine. "That would be cool."

I walked into the kitchen, feeling my knees begin to wobble. "What would you like?" I yelled, only to turn and find him right behind me.

"I'll take whatever you got."

"Root beer okay?"

"Sure, minus the root."

"Sorry, I can only give you what I've got." I had to stand on my tiptoes to reach the glasses. I was holding onto the counter with one hand for support when I felt his hands grab my waist. I paused and closed my eyes, trying to remember what I was doing.

"You look like you could use some help." He was still holding onto my waist.

I turned around, glasses in hand, and he immediately leaned in and kissed me. At first I tried to pull back, but as his mouth pressed harder against mine, I knew it was useless to resist. I pushed my tongue through his parted lips. He grabbed the glasses from my hands, putting them quickly down. He hoisted me up on the counter, spreading my legs. I wrapped them around his waist. He was pushing up against me as I began kissing his neck. My hands found their way up the back of his shirt. My fingernails ran up and down his hot skin. He pulled his shirt off, and I did the same with mine. He grabbed me by my hair and tilted my head. His lips began sucking on my neck. I pulled at his sweats, trying to find my way inside them. I was having a hard time hearing anything inside or outside my head. My desire for him was frenzied. It was Sam's voice that finally brought me back to consciousness.

"Someone's here." He pulled back from me slightly. My Bears shirt lay on the floor; Sam's sweats were below his hips, exposing a green and black checkered pair of boxer shorts.

"What?" I was leaning into him, my lips still pressing into his collarbone.

"Stop. Someone's here."

I stopped. The knock at the door came again. This time there was no mistaking it. "It's Chloe," I said. I pushed him off me and jumped down from the counter, grabbing my shirt.

"Great. She hates me."

I looked at him. There was no way she could know he was with me. I wanted him to stay, but I was panicked thinking about Chloe.

"She can't see you here." The knocking grew louder.

"You want me to leave?" He raised his eyebrows, waiting for my answer.

"No. I don't know. What do you want to do?"

He pulled me to him and kissed me. The knocking escalated to pounding.

"Don't say a word. You hear me? Not one word." I shoved him by the back door and ran to the front door. My hands were shaking as I tried to open the door.

"Jesus, Gracie. I was worried." Chloe pushed past me and plopped on the couch. "What were you doing?"

"I was lying down. I told you I have a headache." I was trying to adjust my clothes and put everything back in place when I felt the tag of my shirt. In my rush, I had put it on inside out.

"You look horrible. What's up with your face? And your neck? It's all splotchy."

I covered the spot where Sam's mouth had been just a few minutes before. "I told you. I'm not feeling good. I was sleeping."

"Is your shirt on inside out?" Her face scrunched up in mild disbelief.

I shrugged my shoulders, trying to make it seem like no big deal. "Is it? I just grabbed it out of my closet. Didn't pay attention." I noticed Sam's coat on the opposite side of the couch. The evidence was within inches of her. If she saw it, life as I knew it would be over. I needed to get her out of the house and fast.

"I'm really not feeling well. I think I need to go back to bed," I said, hoping she would get the hint.

"Something else is up with you. What's going on?" Chloe's sixth sense was in overdrive.

From the corner of my eye, I saw Sam's shadow move across the kitchen. I felt a rush of panic. He was standing in the shadows, close enough to hear. "You know, the week's been hard." I tried to stop myself, but my eyes kept darting between Sam's jacket, Chloe, and his slightly moving shadow in the kitchen. I felt like I was standing tiptoe on the edge of a building, teetering on the verge of plummeting down headfirst.

"You know, sweetie, I really didn't come over to check on you. I came over to let you know the reason Sam is bad for you."

I looked over at his moving shadow. It stopped when she said his name. "I really don't want to talk about Sam." I knew that whatever she said was not going to be good.

"Tough. Come sit next to me." She patted the couch, nearly touching the sleeve of his jacket.

I went over and in the process of sitting down shoved his jacket under a nearby pillow.

She took my hand. "I really want you to be happy. But it's never going to be with Sam."

"Why would you say that?" My panic was turning to anger. I wanted to tell her that Sam was in the kitchen and was here because he wanted to make things right. Instead of letting me get the words out, she kept talking.

"Why do you think Sam flies in and out of your life and leaves you when he does? Because he's a coward, that's why. He wants you only when it's easy, not when it could get hard. He's just like his dad."

"What do you mean about his dad?" I had no idea what she was talking about, but she obviously had the inside scoop on the Pattersons.

"His dad left his mom. Met some woman in Michigan and took off—left Sam and his mom to fend for themselves. That's why she works at Valu-Mart. I'm sure it's not because she wants the employee discount. No one ever aspires for that."

"How do you know this?" I was getting mad at her and was embarrassed for Sam that people knew his personal business.

"My mom and Mrs. Patterson sit next to each other in church."

"Just because Sam's dad took off doesn't mean Sam would do the same to me." I felt the need to defend him for both of our sakes.

"Gracie, he's done it to you time and time again. Why would tomorrow be any different than yesterday with him?"

A moment of uncertainty hit me. "Maybe it will be."

"He couldn't have a relationship with someone if he tried. He just loves the hit-and-run of it all—gets off on it. You know, once a coward, always a coward." Chloe stopped and looked at me. "What's that on your neck?" She was pointing to the spot where I had once felt pleasure and now felt pain.

"Uh, I touched myself with a hot curling iron yesterday. Maybe that's the spot."

"Huh. I didn't even think you owned a curling iron." She

shrugged her shoulders and stood up. "You look even worse than when I got here. Go get some sleep." She headed to the door but paused before walking out. "Gracie, you sure it's just the headache and nothing else?"

I pointed at my head. "Nah, just this."

The door closed behind her. I stood there waiting until I was sure she was gone. Finally, I turned, expecting to see Sam behind me, but he wasn't there. "Sam?" Nothing. I walked into the darkness of the kitchen. "Where are you?" I felt a chill at my feet, and then a gust of cold air hit me as I noticed the back door. It was ajar. Maybe he was standing outside. I opened the door and stuck my head out. "Sam?" My breath blew his name into the wind. "Sam?"

A stray cat hissed back at me. I closed the door. Sinking to the floor, I knew. Same ending to the same story.

I got up, pulled his note out of my book, ripped it up into small pieces, went outside, and let the wind take it away from me. I was done. I needed to be done. After midnight, I left my house on foot with his jacket. The smell of his jacket brought the memories of him back to me. I missed him already. I walked past the eight houses I used to count in my head, the only things keeping me from him. I quietly set the jacket just inside his screen door. I didn't knock. I just left it like he'd left me.

I ran as fast as I could back to my front porch and sat outside on the swing, watching the stars. She was bright tonight, shining down on me, promising me that one day things would get easier. I wanted to undo what had been done, rewind my life and make it different, but I knew that would never be possible.

A weekend of old movies brought me perspective. I no longer ducked into the bathroom every day at school. Instead, I walked by him and looked in the other direction. I faked my way through enjoying the daily grind of school, desperately trying to create a new existence. Two weeks of loosened chains around my feet didn't help me feel any better. It was the Monday before Thanksgiving when my life made a U-turn and sent me back in the same old direction.

American history was one of my favorite classes. Shortly after my teacher, Mrs. Tandra, began her lecture, I learned an important lesson about history repeating itself. The large wooden classroom door creaked open, and in he walked. He handed her a note, and she told him to take an open seat. There were three open seats in the room. One chair was near Alex Pictor, a boy blessed with brains but cursed with acne; another was by Rose Greenblatz, a cheerleader who kept her BMW keys displayed on her desk for all to see, even though no one really cared about her expensive wheels except her. Then there was the seat behind me. As he walked past Alex, I thought he would make his way to Rose. He smiled at her with his half-moon creases as he took the seat behind me. I could feel myself sink into my chair.

"Hey, dude," Johnny Baker whispered to him. "How'd you end up in this class?"

"Issues with my schedule. Needed to make a change," Sam whispered back.

Mrs. Tandra continued talking, and I tried unsuccessfully to pretend he wasn't behind me. When the in-class assignment was handed out, I took my copy and held the others over my left shoulder without looking back. His fingers grazed mine as he took the sheets. I pulled my hand away.

"Thanks, G."

I nodded my head. When the bell rang, I left class as fast as I could. I hurried down the hall and into the bathroom, the chains dragging behind me, the shackle around my neck squeezing the air out of my throat.

During yearbook class, I wanted to tell Chloe about Sam, but I decided against it. She was in a good mood, heading off to see her grandparents for Thanksgiving. I found myself preoccupied with thoughts about Sam. Chloe quickly picked up on it.

"Hey, girl. You okay?" She was busy editing Ms. Andrews's butt to make it fit in the student council picture.

"What?" I was writing an article about life in our generation. I'd gotten as far as the word "Life" when my mind wandered off.

"You seem off today."

"Just thinking about how bad my holiday is going to suck."

"I invited you to come with me. But you're sticking it out here for what? Thanksgiving at the club? Blah."

Every year, I was forced to endure Thanksgiving dinner at my grandma's country club. It wasn't even at dinnertime for normal people. It was at eleven o'clock, and by one, all the silver-hairs would be drunk off cognac and vodka. We never missed a country club Thanksgiving. It was a miserable way to spend a day you were supposed to be thankful for. The only bright spot in the whole day was Teddy. He made me laugh, and I knew he would try to make the misery somehow less painful.

"But who will run to the bar for my grandma if I'm not there to keep the vodka tonics flowing?"

We both laughed.

"How's it going with Ms. Andrews?"

"Well, if her butt weren't so big that you could land a twin-engine plane on it, I would already be done."

"You'll figure it out." I leaned in and rested my head on her shoulder.

"Don't I always?"

I bit the inside of my cheek. "Yes, dearie, you certainly do."

By Wednesday, I was ready for the week to be over but was dreading having to spend quality time with my fractured family. The day was winding down as Mrs. Tandra tried to keep the class on track. "Class, I know you are anxious to start your holiday weekend, but one last thing before you leave me: the decade assignment."

The class groaned in unison.

Mrs. Tandra ignored the protests and continued. "Each of you will work with a fellow classmate for this one. You will be responsible for a written paper and an oral report, both worth one hundred points each. You are expected to work together because you will turn in one paper and give one oral report." My mind raced to calculate what less than two hundred points would mean to my grade. I was pulling A's in all my classes, and I was determined to keep it that way. "I will give you the decade, but you and your partner are responsible for picking one topic from that decade. By Monday, I need to approve your topic. To make things easier," Mrs. Tandra said, clearing her throat, "I have picked the partners."

What? A crappy partner would mean a bad grade, and I wasn't going to sacrifice my GPA because of a slacker. I surveyed the room. Johnny Baker? He could land a three-pointer from midcourt, but he thought the Boston Tea Party had happened in Chicago. Mariam Coultier? She was our French foreign exchange student who was still struggling with the fact that we couldn't drink wine with lunch. Prentiss Franklin? Yeah. I could totally work with him. He once had gotten so upset about missing an extra-credit question on a test that he had to go to the nurse for an antacid. Yep, Prentiss was the way to go.

While I was surveying the possibilities, Mrs. Tandra had been announcing the partners and their decades. I tuned in just in time to hear my fate. "For the sixties, Patterson and Anderson." In my rush to find the perfect partner, I'd forgotten about Sam. I felt his eyes burning a hole in my back as the details of the assignment were handed out. I was stunned. The bell rang, and I sat there in disbelief.

"Guess we're partners, huh?" he said from behind me. He was still sitting in his seat too, even as the classroom was emptying out. "G?"

"Yeah, I guess so." I darted out of the room and straight to the bathroom. I locked myself in a stall, trying to wrap my head around this development. I kept telling myself I could make it through the assignment. If Mrs. Tandra gave us class time to work on it, I would barely need to see him, I reasoned.

When I exited the bathroom, he stood waiting for me. "So we should probably get together over break, right? Our topic is due Monday."

I initially nodded in agreement but quickly came to my senses. "Why don't I call you on Sunday and we can decide on a topic then?" I walked past him without making eye contact.

"G, I'd rather get together on it."

"Call you on Sunday." I walked out, and the wind slapped me back to reality. Who was I kidding? I would never survive this.

Thankfully, Chloe offered to give me a ride home. She was especially talkative, excited to be heading out of town. She didn't take a breath until we were in front of my house. "You have an awesome holiday with the entire club gang. Don't let any of the old pervs put the moves on you. Those gray-hairs can get pretty frisky."

I had stopped listening the block before when I saw Sam on Frances Street, making his way home.

"Earth to Gracie, come in." She snapped her fingers by my face.

"Oh, right. Yeah, I'll beat them off with a stick if I have to."

Any other time, Chloe would have stopped and made me tell her everything, but today, she was anxious to get home, so the conversation ended without incident. After a quick hug, I stepped out of the car, and she was quickly down the street and out of sight.

I expected a quiet house but instead was met with Grandma opening and closing cabinets. As I walked into the kitchen, I saw a half-empty bottle of vodka and my mom's recipes strewn across the table.

"Grandma? What are you doing?"

My grandma turned around with a confused look on her face. Flour, sugar, eggs, and every dish we owned filled the counter space. A broken egg lay on the floor at Grandma's feet.

"Gracelynn, I am so glad you are home. I have been baking."

She grabbed her vodka tonic, took a swig, swirled it around in her mouth, and swallowed hard, closing her eyes in euphoria.

"You've been what?" My eyebrows raised in disbelief.

"Baking. Yes, baking." A piece of eggshell rested in her highlighted hair. It was official: my grandma had gone completely and utterly mad.

"Baking? Why would you be baking?"

"Why, for Thanksgiving, of course." She smiled, taking another gulp from her tumbler.

"Baking for what?" I still wasn't getting it.

"To eat, of course. Now go put your coat away and help me. I am having a few ... what should I call them? Challenges. Yes, challenges."

"Grandma, the club always has like a thousand desserts." I dropped my coat by the door.

"We are not going to the club this year."

"Why? Is it closed or something?"

She sat down at the kitchen table, struggling to read one of the recipe cards. "Oh, I suppose they are open. We will just not be there." She said it so casually that I thought she was joking. "Now ... where did I put those reading glasses?"

I walked over and took the red rhinestone glasses from the top of her head and handed them to her.

"Thank you. Kindly wash your hands and help me."

"I still don't get it. Why aren't we going to the club? We never miss a year." It was true. Even when my mom was sick and couldn't go, my mom insisted we go to the club without her. It was a miserable meal, eaten in record time so we could return home to her.

"I thought it would be nice this year to have Thanksgiving at home." My grandma shifted her glasses up and down to make sense of the small print on the recipe card. "Your mother had horrible penmanship. I never could get her to write any better than a third grader. What is this word, anyway?" She held the card up to me.

Seeing my mom's handwriting sent a small shot of grief to my heart. "Baking powder, Grandma."

"Oh, I thought it said barfing power. That explains some things."

"We have never eaten anywhere but the club on Thanksgiving. Is everything okay?"

"Certainly. I just want to start a new tradition this year. I think it is time." She smiled at me, perfect capped teeth exposed.

I half-smiled, raising my eyebrows. I started toward my room, half-yelling, "Why would a recipe say barfing power? Really?"

"Baking powder? Yes, of course." She was still talking to herself when I reentered the room a minute later.

"Grandma, what are you trying to make?"

She held three recipe cards in her hand, eyeing each one like she was trying to decipher a code. "Pie. At least, I think."

I heard the front door open and the heavy sound of my dad's feet making their way to the kitchen.

"Jeffrey? Is that you?" A sense of relief came across my grandma's face.

"Indeed it is, Dee Dee." A large brown bag entered the kitchen with my dad behind it. My dad was the only one ever allowed to call my grandma anything besides Blake or Mrs. Smith.

"Were you able to pick it all up?" She stood to help him but then pointed at me. "Gracelynn, be respectful and offer your father some assistance."

"Of course, Grandma." I reached over and pulled the smaller, handled bag from my dad's arm.

He shifted his weight and set the larger bag down on the table. A puff of flour exploded in the air. "Whoa. What do we have here?" My dad looked around the kitchen, not sure of the exact cause but able to see that a small explosion had occurred.

"Grandma was baking." I tried not to laugh as Grandma wiped a faint layer of flour from her face.

"Well," my dad said, "Santori's threw in a couple of crème pies, and I think Teddy was going to pick something up as well, so I think we have desserts covered." My dad reached into the bag and pulled out a large bottle of vodka. "My compliments to the chef." He handed her the bottle.

She took it like he was giving her a priceless diamond. Her face lit up. "Oh, son, you always know just the right thing." She reached her hand up and touched his cheek.

He smiled. Day or night, my dad was there to help my grandparents. It was my dad who had helped my grandma with everything after my grandpa died. My dad had become my grandma's constant in a way, and he never complained about it once. I never would have gone to the same lengths to please her, especially after everything she had done to refute him early on, but they had formed this bond that, although the outside world didn't understand, made perfect sense to them.

"What's the deal with Santori's?" My family had obviously forgotten to let me in on the grand plan.

"It's for Thanksgiving dinner." My dad pulled out a ham, a turkey, mashed potatoes, green beans, salad, rolls, and two trays of varying meats and cheeses. It seemed like the bag was never-ending. With the lack of available counter space, I ended up holding most of it. "Just heat and serve tomorrow. Mr. Santori left detailed directions for each dish."

"Delightful!" Grandma could hardly control her excitement, an emotion I rarely saw in her. She motioned to the refrigerator. After all the containers were placed safely away, my dad and I looked around the kitchen.

"Now, what do we do with all this?" Grandma put her head down, accepting defeat.

My dad placed his arm around her shoulder. "Dee Dee, you can't expect to be good at absolutely everything. You're pretty close to it, though."

She nodded her head in agreement.

I heard the front door open and Teddy's voice from the other room. "I come bearing gifts!" Teddy's entrance into the kitchen ignited the room. "Uh-oh, it looks like my baby doll was attempting the impossible."

I laughed. My grandma peered at me just above her glasses.

"Stopped at Rosenwinkle's to pick up the pie and apple slices."

I ran to Teddy and hugged him.

"Well, if that's all it takes to get a hug from a pretty lady, I'll place a standing order with them." Teddy's shirt featuring a turkey holding a sign that said "Eat more fish" made me smile.

Teddy moved into the kitchen and began cleaning. "I ran into Mr. Lee today. He sends his best. Says he misses seeing you two." Teddy pointed a wooden spoon at my dad and me as he spoke. Grandma stood by him, watching him in awe as he cleared the counter seemingly without effort.

"How is Mr. Lee?" asked my dad. Mr. Lee and his wife owned Wok-n-Run, a Chinese restaurant we had ordered takeout from once a week when my mom was alive. We always had the same order, and Mrs. Lee always asked the same thing, every time: "Throw in some egg rolls for your girl?" Egg rolls always came along with the order, even when we politely refused.

"Business is going well. Said Mrs. Lee has been sick." Teddy loaded the last of the dirty bowls in the dishwasher.

"Sorry to hear that. Hope nothing serious?" My dad was sitting at the table, picking up one recipe card after another.

Teddy paused for a minute before starting the dishwasher. "Cancer."

We all stopped what we were doing, loathing even the sound of the word. Cancer never truly leaves you, even when you try to forget it. Unapologetic, cruel, and brutal, it steals the best parts away. It is a thief, a rogue, a criminal.

"What is the prognosis?" Grandma asked, filling her tumbler with vodka again.

"He says they think they got it all. She is doing better. Touch and go for a bit, though."

My dad nodded and went back to the recipes. "Glad she's doing better."

"Man, I miss their sweet and sour chicken," I said, sliding down in a chair as I remembered the double order my mom and I used to share every Monday for dinner.

My dad smiled. "Hey, we should get some for tomorrow—you know, in honor of your mom."

I nodded quickly. For the first time in a long time, I felt like I was on the same planet with my dad. We were still a million miles apart, but at least the worlds between us had moved out of the way.

My grandma objected. "Not a traditional Thanksgiving meal. I would prefer we save it for another day." She did not look happy.

"C'mon, Dee Dee. New traditions, remember?" My dad took my grandma's hand and squeezed it. "Cass would have loved it."

Grandma looked at my dad with no facial expression.

"I'll go call Mr. Lee now." My dad returned quickly, sitting back down at the table in front of the recipes. "Mr. Lee said sure about the sweet and sour chicken. Mrs. Lee said she will throw in some egg rolls just for you, Gracie."

I laughed. I never could tell Mrs. Lee, but I couldn't eat her egg rolls. They gave me heartburn.

The doorbell rang. My dad placed a recipe card back in its box before standing. "I'll get it. I think it's the shipment I've been waiting for."

Teddy wiped the last crumb off the counter and sat next to my grandma. "Well, what should we do tonight now that things are under control?"

We all looked at one another, not really sure what normal families did the night before a holiday. It had been so long since we'd had a normal existence that I'd forgotten what one felt or looked like.

"Gracie, you have a visitor," my dad called from the living room.

Teddy looked at me, eyebrows raised.

"I thought Chloe was traveling to the East Coast," my Grandma said.

"Yeah. Not sure who could be here for me." I stood up slowly.

Teddy jumped to his feet. "Maybe it's a boy." He stepped in front of me, heading to the living room.

"Doubtful." I rolled my eyes. But as my feet hit the threshold of the living room, I heard Sam's voice. I stopped, not wanting to take a step farther.

"Well, who do we have here?" said Teddy.

Sam, who was sitting across from my dad, talking, rose to his feet when Teddy walked in.

"Teddy, this is Sam," my dad said.

"You Gracie's guy?"

I felt a flash of embarrassment.

"Uh, well ..." Sam was struggling to find the right words.

"No, Teddy. He is not my guy." I moved from behind Teddy and into the forefront.

"Hey, G. Hope I'm not interrupting anything."

"Well, actually, we were ..."

"Never an interruption." My grandma had joined the awkward party, much to my dismay.

"So, Sam, how are things?" My dad motioned for Sam to sit back down. My grandma practically shoved me to the open spot next to Sam.

"Pretty good." He smiled, the half-moons melting my icy exterior.

"Rough season, eh?" My dad leaned into the space between him and Sam.

Teddy look puzzled.

"Teddy, Sam is Highmore's QB," my dad explained.

"Our Jeffrey played football not only in high school but in college as well. He was one of the best." Grandma always felt the need to one-up someone. It was in her DNA.

"My mom told me," Sam said. "Lineman, right?"

My dad nodded. "How is your mom?"

"She's good." The room fell quiet again.

"Samuel, may we offer you something to drink?" Grandma shook the ice in her vodka tonic as a call-out for beverage requests.

"Grandma, I'm not sure Sam can stay ..."

"A drink would be great. Thanks." The half-moons appeared again.

My grandma nodded at me. "Gracelynn, kindly get your friend something to drink."

I stood up and was mumbling about how I wouldn't exactly call us friends when my grandma shut me down.

"And please do not talk to yourself. It is off-putting."

I walked into the kitchen and stood there, trying to block out the last time I'd gotten a drink for Sam. I shook my head to erase the memory. I grabbed a bottle of root beer out of the refrigerator. Returning to the living room, I handed the bottle to Sam without looking at him.

"What are your holiday plans, Samuel?" Grandma motioned me to sit back down by Sam, which I reluctantly did.

"Oh, not much." Sam took a long drink from his root beer.

"Are you not dining with your mother?" Grandma looked surprised.

"Nah, she has to work."

"That's too bad. She at Valu-Mart still?" My dad seemed to know a lot about Sam's mom. He barely knew anything about me but managed to know her whereabouts.

"Yes, sir. She's the night manager."

My dad nodded like he'd somehow already known.

"Valu-Mart? Where might that be located?" asked my grandma.

I rolled my eyes. My snobbish grandma couldn't find a discount store if it walked past her gates and knocked on her door.

Teddy put his arm around my grandma's shoulder. "Doll baby, it's right off the highway."

"Oh, the large gray dirty-looking building?"

I shrank down farther in the couch.

"That's the one."

"They need to do a better job cleaning the parking lot." Grandma pinched up her nose like she was smelling parking lot trash. "Samuel, you must join us for Thanksgiving tomorrow. I insist." My grandma occasionally felt the need to do charity work, and in this case, the charity was sitting right in front of her.

"Grandma, I'm sure Sam has better things to—"

"That would be cool. I was just going to hang out at home tomorrow. My mom has to work a double."

"It's settled then, Gracie's guy."

"Teddy, he is not my guy. I told—"

"What brings you our way tonight?" My dad was back in the conversation. I was glad he could get a full sentence out. I certainly couldn't. Why was I even in the room if I couldn't get a word in edgewise with these people?

"G and I have to work on a project together. I thought I would come over to talk about it."

"She failed to mention that." Grandma's eyebrows arched as she looked at me disapprovingly.

"Well, Grandma, I didn't have a chance. I was busy helping you with barfing power, remember?"

My grandma frowned at me.

"What power?" Sam looked confused.

I shrugged my shoulders. "Sam and I are partners on an American history project."

"And?" Grandma gestured with her hands, motioning for more details.

"It's a decade assignment. Our teacher gives us a decade, and we have to pick a topic from that decade to research and present a report on."

My dad, Grandma, and Teddy all nodded at the same time. I sank farther into the couch, wanting to be past the conversation.

"What's the decade?" My dad seemed interested. I was not.

"The sixties." I rolled my eyes, only to widen them at the sound of my grandma's shriek of excitement.

"I loved the sixties—so much excitement!"

"What?" I looked at her.

"Have you come up with a topic yet?"

Sam and I shook our heads. "Not yet," I said. "I was thinking about—"

"You have to do the sexual revolution."

My mouth dropped open. My grandma not only had just said the word "sex" but was actually encouraging us to talk about it in a room full of sex-crazed teenagers.

"Uh, no, Grandma. Bad idea." I crossed my arms over my chest.

"Why not? I kinda like the idea," Sam said.

"Nothing like the Swinging Sixties to put everyone in the mood." Teddy hit my dad's back as he spoke. They all laughed except me.

"Gracelynn, the counterculture, especially as related to sexual awakening, really set the tone for future decades to come." Grandma sounded like a documentary.

"I was thinking more like the assassination of JFK." I liked my idea better.

"No one did the sexual revolution like JFK," Teddy said. "Good to be a Kennedy boy for a while." Teddy slapped my dad's back again. By the looks of them, I guessed all men were created equal, at least when it came to sex.

"I'll have to think about it." I stood up and excused myself to the bathroom. I felt like I was in an alternate universe, having a normal teenage existence. I knew it was all a lie. I sat next to the sink on the floor, thinking about my mom. A knock on the bathroom door startled me.

"Yes?" My voice was failing me.

"Gracie, you okay?" It was Teddy.

"Uh, sure. Be out in a minute." I stood up and reluctantly opened the door. Teddy stood there and folded his big arms around me in a bear hug.

Teddy somehow always knew when I needed a hug. He gave me the one thing my dad never could with those hugs—comfort. Teddy and I didn't have the kind of relationship that needed to be defined. It was one of the few easy things in my life, and I was grateful for it. "Okay, your grandma has reluctantly agreed to pizza for dinner. You game?"

I smiled and finally let go of him.

"Gracie?"

"Yeah?"

"You are so special. Never let anyone make you feel anything less, you hear me?"

I nodded. We walked back into the living room, where the same suspects were still seated.

"Gracelynn, I just asked Samuel to stay for dinner. Are you okay with that?" Grandma's words were in the form of a question, but I knew this was more of a statement.

"Sure, Grandma." I looked at Sam, and the half-moons responded.

We ate greasy pizza from Rico's and watched *What You Don't See Will Hurt You*, the latest horror movie out on video. Of course, the movie had been my grandma's choice, and she'd gone with a guts-and-gore flick. My dad dozed in the chair while my grandma and Teddy sat next to each other on the love seat. When the movie began,

THE HIGHMORE CIRCLE

Sam and I were on opposite ends of the couch, but as sorority girls started disappearing into the woods one by one, he began inching over, until our legs were nearly touching. I pretended not to notice. When sorority girl Britney took a hook to the throat from out of nowhere, I jumped, and Sam grabbed my hand. He never took his eyes off the TV, but as I settled back on the couch, he squeezed my hand harder. When the movie ended and the murderer turned out to be outcast Tracy, his hand still firmly held onto mine.

"Well, Sam, it's getting late, and you best be getting home." Teddy's voice woke my dad out of a sound sleep and caused my grandma to nearly spill the melting ice out of her empty glass.

"My, it is late, is it not? Do you need a ride home, Samuel?" My grandma's feigned level of concern was funny to me, but Sam took it as sincere.

"It's okay. I only live a block away."

"See you tomorrow then. One o'clock. Please be on time." Grandma polished off her melted ice and nodded to Sam.

Sam stood, our hands still locked. My grandma looked at our hands. I pulled loose and took a few steps away.

"Thanks for the pizza. And movie."

As the door closed behind Sam, I figured that would be the last time I saw him before Monday. He was a runner, and he would continue to run away from me and from the thought of us as long as I let him do it.

She was bright in the sky as I watched her, waiting for sleep to take me away. It was not long before she joined me in my dream. She was sitting on the porch swing, holding my hand. In my dream, she was healthy, vibrant, and fully alive. Her blond hair moved slightly with the wind. She said nothing, but she didn't have to speak. I was just happy to have her next to me again. A noise pulled me away from her. I woke, and reality instantly hit me. My heart sank. I looked out the window. The swing creaked in the cold wind, empty.

75

"Gracelynn? Are you finally awake?" My grandma stood near me.

"What?" I looked at her, surprised to have someone else in the room with me.

"It is nearly ten. There is still a significant amount to do." Grandma looked perfect, as always—not a hair out of place, makeup perfect. She rarely looked anything but perfect. The night my mom died, I saw the real her. And in that moment, I realized perfection was nothing more than a facade. It's a carnival mirror.

"Ten?" I was surprised.

"I bought you a new top. Please take a bath and get dressed. And Gracelynn?"

I looked over at her. I knew it was coming.

"Kindly make an effort with yourself today."

"Yes, Grandma." The dream still haunted me as I looked at the new top. My grandma frequently forgot that I was not comfortable in my own skin, so her repeated attempts at putting me in slenderizing outfits rarely worked. But I knew the day was important to her, so although I loathed the thought of it, I made the effort and put on the top. It was a tight red tank with a sheer top over it. The long sleeves flared out just before the wrist, and it stopped just below my waist. The neckline was curved lace that zigzagged by my collarbone. The more I looked at myself in the mirror, the less I hated it.

I reached into my top dresser drawer and pulled out the velvet box. Inside sat a gold chain with a small diamond star. It was the last birthday present I'd received from my mom. I had looked at it a thousand times before but had never worn it. I gently took it out of the box and placed it around my neck, where it would remain daily after that. I touched the star gently. I smiled and walked out of the room.

"Okay, Grandma, what do you need help with?"

My grandma was busy pulling containers out of the refrigerator. She stopped when she saw me. "Gracelynn ..." her voice trailed off.

"What do you need help with?" I started to take the containers out of her hand, but she pulled away.

She set the containers down and pulled me to her. She hugged me tighter than she ever had in my entire life, including the night my mom died. I wasn't sure what to do in response. This was new territory for Grandma and me.

My dad walked in and was surprised to see my grandma hugging me. "What happened? Dee Dee? Gracie?"

I pulled away from my grandma and turned to look at him. My dad's eyes widened.

"I know," Grandma said as she reached over and took his hand. "She looks just like—"

"Cassie." He looked at me like he was seeing a ghost. "Why haven't I ever seen it before?"

I stood there wanting to tell him the truth. He had been blind to me all these years. Even before she died, it had never really been about me. My dad had taken such good care of my mom before and after she was sick. I always knew where I stood with him. He had never seen it before because he had never really seen me.

"I guess that answers the question once and for all of whether I look more like my mom or my dad." Instead of speaking the truth, I made light of the moment.

"Well, I'll be. Look at my girl!" Teddy stood by the back door, bringing in firewood.

"Nice shirt, Teddy." His "You Are What You Eat" shirt with turkey feathers around the words was perfect for the day.

"Do not forget, the knife goes on the right side of the plate." Grandma hovered over me with a vodka tonic in one hand and a meat thermometer in the other as I set the table.

"Grandma, I thought the turkey was already cooked. What's the deal with the thermometer?"

"Appearances, dear Gracelynn, are everything." Even among family who knew dinner came out of a bag, my grandma felt the need to keep up the charade of a home-cooked meal. We stood looking at the table, surveying our work which had somehow taken nearly three hours to bring to life. I glanced at the clock. It was ten minutes before one. Up to that very minute, I was sure Sam would be a no-show.

The doorbell caused my grandma to almost spill her drink. "That would have been a huge misfortune," she said, tracing her finger up the side of her glass, returning the escaped vodka back into the tumbler.

Teddy patted Sam on the back as he entered. "Ah, Gracie's guy."

I shook my head. The half-moons met me.

"Wow, G. You look ..." Sam stood there looking at me.

I felt myself blush. "Thanks, Sam," I mumbled. He was still standing there in a weird zombielike daze, holding a large casserole dish. "What's that?"

"Oh, from my mom. She thanks you for having me over." He handed it to my grandma, who looked like he had just given her a scientific experiment. "It's pierogies. She makes them herself. They're so good." He smiled.

"I am sure they are lovely, Samuel. Do tell her we said thank you." She placed the dish on the table, holding it slightly away from her nose. "With Polish and Chinese as part of our traditional meal, we might as well invite a German to bring something." She was mumbling now, and the more she said, the more I laughed.

"Strange dinner companions, huh, Grandma? I bet that's what people thought when they heard about the Pilgrims and the Indians."

She raised one eyebrow and looked at me. "Yes, definitely just like your mother."

I shrugged my shoulders, but on the inside, I was happy to be compared to her.

Grandma made sure the meal was a formal affair, with our best china, cloth napkins, fancy glassware, and even place cards. Thankfully, Teddy kept the mood lively. My grandma seemed especially happy in the moment. My dad even acted like he wanted to be there, which was new for him.

When the meal was over, my grandma turned to me. "Gracelynn, would you mind clearing the table?" Again, a question from my grandma was not really a question; it was a statement.

"Absolutely, Grandma." I stood up, and Sam stood up with me. "I'll help," he said.

I was standing at the kitchen sink, rinsing out the glasses, when he walked up next to me.

"This is great. Thanks for having me over."

I smiled, continuing to rinse out glasses.

"I had a hard time saying anything when I saw you. You look so pretty." He moved closer and kissed my neck lightly. I leaned in, and his lips stayed on my neck for a moment.

"In the living room, please." My grandma's voice took Sam's lips off my neck. Silently, we went to the living room.

My grandma began speaking as soon as we were seated. "Since we are here together, I thought it would be nice for each of us to write down what we are most thankful for this year. We will write it on the paper and place it in a dish. I will then read each one."

We all nodded. As Teddy passed out the paper and pens, I noticed how quickly everyone else wrote something down. I sat there for a few moments, and then it came to me. I wrote mine down and folded my paper.

"Delightful." Grandma stopped to take a drink of her vodka tonic. "I will read each one."

We all sat back and waited.

Opening the first paper, she said, "An old oak tree." When my grandma looked up, Teddy winked at her.

Grandma unfolded the next slip of paper. "Family." I wondered whether that was my dad's or my grandma's. She paused to take a drink. "Now here is the next one—a bright star on the darkest of nights."

She selected the next piece of paper with her long, manicured fingernails."New traditions." She smiled at Teddy as she spoke.

Grandma took the last piece of paper out of the dish. She struggled for a minute to open it, but it finally relented. "Gracie."

5

"That's my favorite one. Wish I could take credit for it," Teddy said, breaking the silence. I sat there embarrassed.

"Samuel and Gracelynn, have you decided on your topic?" My grandma was back at it again.

"No, ma'am. Not yet." Sam smiled at her, and my grandma smiled back. No one was immune to the half-moons.

"I'm fine with the sexual revolution," I said. I had decided that, like most everything else in my life, there was no use fighting this. I dreaded telling Chloe everything, but I would deal with her when the time came.

"Teddy and I will gladly share our thoughts and provide insight if you are interested. Factual sources are critical." Grandma never missed a chance to put herself out there.

"Well, can't say I remember all the sixties," Teddy said. "A couple of years are hazy, but I can for sure fill you in on the rest."

My dad chuckled.

After dessert, my dad, Grandma, and Teddy excused themselves to the basement to watch my grandma's least favorite thing, sports. Teddy was a sports fanatic, so she tolerated it like he tolerated everything else about her.

Sam and I sat on the living room couch, legs touching. "Thanks for agreeing to the topic."

I nodded.

"I'm glad Mrs. Tandra paired us together."

I kept my head down, looking at my fingernails. I felt just the opposite but wasn't going to tell him that. I looked up at him. "Did you really have a schedule conflict?"

His response was immediate. "No."

"Oh." I looked at my fingernails again.

"I wanted a way to see you." He reached over and took my hand.

"Like the hallway isn't enough?"

He laughed. "More like the girls' bathroom." It was the truth. I spent as much time hiding from him as I did facing him.

"How did you get into the class?" I asked. I could barely get them to give me a hall pass to go to the bathroom.

"I have a few connections in the office."

I nodded. Connections and favors were probably very easy for a star athlete like him. He was rubbing my hand now, tracing each of my fingers with one of his own.

I needed to do something before I gave in to my urge to kiss him. "Do you feel like watching TV?"

"Uh, sure, if that's what you want to do."

I started flipping channels. Nothing seemed as interesting as him, so I kept pushing on the remote. "Stop me when you see something you like."

"You mean besides you?" About five channels later, he stopped me, and my heart sank. "Hey! My mom and I watched this one before. You ever see it?" He seemed happy to have found something. Little did he know it felt like a knife piercing through my heart.

"George Bailey lassoes the moon," I whispered. The scene was unmistakable. *It's a Wonderful Life* played in black-and-white in front of my eyes. I could find no more words, only the cloudiness of tears.

"Hey? You okay?" Sam leaned over to look at me.

I turned my head away. "Just something in one of my eyes."

I pretended to be struggling with my eye, but every word out of Jimmy Stewart's mouth fractured my heart a bit more. "I'm not really feeling TV." I turned the TV off.

He sat there looking at me. "Now what?"

The clouds cleared from my eyes. "You like cards?"

The half-moons reappeared. "Sure."

"Poker?" I stood to get the cards.

He grabbed my hand and pulled me down to him. His lips met mine, quickly but with purpose.

"What was that for?"

He smiled, not answering.

As I sat across from him at the coffee table dealing cards, I could hardly believe the moment was real. We were using peanuts for chips, and as my winnings kept growing, Sam's competitive spirit amped up.

"Card shark, eh?"

"Not really. Just used to play with my grandpa," I said, collecting another pot from a three-of-a-kind win.

"You must have played a lot."

I shrugged my shoulders.

"Okay, I guess this may be our last hand since you pretty much own my nuts."

"As it should be."

"So ... let's make the hand worth something."

"Like what?"

He smiled, saying nothing right away. "Give me that paper over there." He pointed to blank sheets of paper left behind by my grandma. "You write down what you want if you win, and I'll do the same. Whoever wins gets what has been put up as the prize."

"Ha, easy win." I grabbed the paper and wrote down my prize. He scribbled something and folded his paper up. He dropped his in the middle of the table. I did the same. I dealt the cards.

As the hand continued and I drew to a full house, I knew I

had him beat. My hand was too good. When we went all in, my confidence was at an all-time high. "Okay, pretty boy, get ready to go down." I slowly laid down each one of my cards, three fives and two tens. "And that, my friend, means the house is full."

He raised an eyebrow and, one by one, placed each of his cards neatly on the table: one queen, two queens, three queens, and finally a fourth queen next to the other three. "And that, my friend, is what happens when the queens take over your house."

I sat there in disbelief.

"As soon as you pick your mouth up off the table, I'll collect my prize." He flicked the piece of paper across the table. It landed perfectly in front of me. He placed his chin on his hand. "Go ahead, open it."

I picked up the paper and opened it: Go to winter formal with me. I sat looking at the words.

"Read it out loud," he said.

I shook my head.

"Then just say yes." He leaned over and took my hand. "C'mon, G. Say yes."

"Isn't the girl supposed to ask the guy to winter formal?"

"Why do you think I had to bet you for it?"

What would I tell Chloe? No way would she believe I had lost a bet on it. Friendship massacre? Who was I kidding—she would kill me before she killed our friendship.

"Let's do this: I'll give you your prize, you give me mine, and we'll call it a fair trade." He picked up my piece of paper and opened it. "Really, G?"

I shrugged my shoulders.

"Brownie bites?"

"They are really good."

He pulled me to my feet.

"What are you doing?"

"We are going to get your brownie bites so you will go to

winter formal with me." He leaned in to kiss me, but I pushed him back.

"Where are we going to get brownie bites at this time?"

"I know a place." He grabbed me and kissed me. "C'mon, it'll be a quick trip."

For some reason, my dad had no problem with me leaving my house in the middle of the night with a boy for brownie bites. He actually told me to "have fun."

Sam's truck was dirty and cold. Climbing into the front seat, I stepped on empty fast-food bags and pop cans.

"Sorry," he said, pushing them away. As we drove into the darkness of the night, we said very little. The loud humming of Sam's truck made it difficult to hear, and I was glad for it. We turned the corner, and the Valu-Mart sign glowed in front of us.

He took my hand as we entered the store. People were everywhere. I wasn't sure why so many people felt the need to be at Valu-Mart after midnight.

"Hey, Mom!" Sam's mom stood near the shaving cream, restocking shavers. He leaned in and kissed her cheek.

"Gracie? How are you?" She walked over and hugged me.

I was taken aback by her embrace. "I'm good, Mrs. Patterson."

"You look just like your mom," she said, surveying my appearance. "Pretty, Sam, huh?"

He smiled and nodded. I felt uncomfortable.

"What brings you kids here tonight?" She went back to restocking.

"Gracie needed some brownie bites."

She laughed. "Those can be addictive."

I smiled. "I know, right?"

"I gotta grab something," Sam said. "Be right back." He darted down the opposite aisle.

"So, Gracie, I hear you and Sam have a project together."

"American history. We have to talk about the sixties."

"Oh boy, so much unrest and social change then. Lots of possible topics, though."

I glanced away awkwardly. There was no way I was telling her about our topic. As she continued stocking the shelves, I asked, "Can I help at all?"

She stopped and smiled at me. "That is so incredibly sweet, but I got it. Hey, how's your dad?"

"He's fine. He asked about you too."

"He did?" She seemed to perk up when I said my dad had asked about her, almost like she was excited about it.

"Yep. He remembered you work here."

"Well, I just saw him here a few weeks ago, so it's not been that long."

My grandma did all our shopping. Why would my dad be at Valu-Mart? I took a long look at Mrs. Patterson. She had a firm build, not thin but not heavy. She had passed down her dimples to Sam; hers were the original half-moons. She wore no makeup, and her hair was pulled back in a messy ponytail. I suddenly felt a pang of sadness for her, knowing the job she had to do in order to provide for her and Sam.

"Thanks for keeping Sam entertained. I feel bad there's nothing to keep him busy."

I laughed.

"Something I said?"

"I think Sam stays pretty busy."

"Well, sports keep him busy, but he's really missed out on a normal family life."

I laughed again. "I'm not sure he gets that with me."

She held a packet of razors in her hand. "You underestimate yourself, Gracie. He talks about you all the time."

"He does?"

"He does what?" Sam was back with a grocery bag.

"Nothing," Mrs. Patterson and I said at the same time.

"Got your brownie bites. Ready?"

I nodded, and Sam reached over and hugged his mom.

"I'll be home around six unless we get a call off," she said. "Then who knows."

"Nice to see you, Mrs. Patterson."

She reached over and hugged me again. "Tell your dad I said don't be a stranger."

I nodded, thinking it was a weird message to deliver. I took Sam's hand in mine, and we turned to leave.

"Patty!" a voice from behind us called out.

Sam kept walking.

"Patty!"

Sam dropped my hand and turned around. Julie Wilks and Fred Johnson were walking toward us.

Fred looked at Sam and then me. "Hey, man. What's going on?"

"Just hanging out. You?"

"Jules and I were hoping to score some brews. No luck. You got any?"

"Me? No." Sam seemed anxious.

Julie looked at me with disgust. "How about you?"

"Me? No, not my thing."

"Damn, Anderson, is that you?" Fred looked at me with surprise.

"Yep, it's me."

"You look hot. You get one of those mall makeovers or something?"

Sam frowned at Fred.

"What's going on here?" Julie pointed her bloodred fingernail at us.

"Nothing," Sam immediately responded.

I looked at him and felt my heart sinking.

"Gracie's family let me hang out with them. My mom's working, so I was an orphan today. Did you see her?"

"I must have missed her," Julie said, smiling at Sam. I knew she wanted to sink her teeth into him. It was disgusting, made worse by the jealousy and insecurity I felt. "Sam, come hang out with us?" Julie smiled, fangs drawn.

"Nah. Thanks, though. Maybe another night?"

She motioned with her hand for him to call her. Sam pushed me toward the door.

We walked to the truck in silence. It was clear he didn't want them to know we were together. How were we supposed to go to a school dance together if he couldn't even acknowledge me in front of two people at Valu-Mart? Sam opened my door, pressing his hand against my back.

"Thanks. I got it." I pulled myself in and shut the door.

In front of my house, the truck came to a stop. I wanted out of the truck and out of his life.

"G, I know you're mad." He pulled me back from reaching for the door handle.

"Really? And why would that be?" I was straddling two different emotions: anger and pain.

"What just happened? It's just that—"

"It's just what? You're embarrassed of me, right?"

"Why would I be embarrassed of you?" He reached for my hand, and I pulled it away.

"Because I'm not good enough for your friends—I'm not good enough for you, I guess."

"Why would you say that? And those aren't really my friends."

I laughed at the stupidity of his comment. "You know they're your friends, Sam. And you made it perfectly clear you weren't going to tell them about us. I mean, you, me, whatever this is."

He pulled my arm to slide me closer to him. "You don't get it, do you?"

I looked down at a crushed straw wrapper on the floorboard, saying nothing.

"I don't want anyone to mess with what we have. And with those two, it would be all over school by Monday if they knew. You're too important to me to have them trash this."

"Yeah, I bet." I was still focusing on the straw wrapper.

"You have any idea how long I've liked you?"

I said nothing.

"G, look at me."

I bit my lip and turned my head to him.

"Forever, that's how long."

"Then why do you do it?" I wanted answers from him once and for all.

"Chloe's right about me. I get freaked when I think it will get tough. I'm a runner. I get scared, and I run." As always, Chloe had been right. I could almost hear the "I told you so" at that very minute.

"Then why bother?" I said.

"Because no matter where I run, I always want to run back to you."

"Have you really liked me forever?"

The half-moons appeared. "Longer." He leaned in and touched his forehead to mine. I moved my lips to his, and we began kissing.

"I should get going," he said. He was sweating.

"Or you could come in for a while." I placed my hand on his inner thigh.

"That would be great."

We quietly slipped in the front door. The house was still. "Where's your dad?" Sam asked, his arms around my waist.

I pointed to my dad's bedroom and took Sam's hand and led him to the basement. It was dark and cool as I laid him on the couch. I felt confident then, wanting and willing to do anything with him. The more he told me how great I felt, the more I wanted to do. I moved down to let my tongue swirl around his belly button; this was the most I'd done with any boy. I felt the excitement and energy pulsate through me. I had never imagined it would feel this good to be with someone.

He reached into the Valu-Mart bag and pulled out a box. As he struggled to open the little package, I smiled.

"Expecting to get lucky tonight?"

"Nah, just hoping."

This time I didn't look away but helped him. The minutes turned into hours. We lay there entwined with each other. His head rested on my chest.

"You have to get going?" I never wanted him to leave, but I knew daylight would eventually take him away from me again.

"I just need to get home before my mom. She works until six. So I've got a little more time."

I smiled and closed my eyes.

"G?"

"Hmm?" I was fighting sleep.

"I'm glad it was you."

I opened my eyes and looked at him.

"It wouldn't have meant anything with someone else." He kissed my chest softly. I felt my senses coming alive again. I ran my fingers through his hair. I pulled at his hair until our lips were connected again. He pulled back from me quickly. "What are you going to tell Chloe about us? She hates me."

I felt a sense of dread rush over me. "I wouldn't say she hates you."

He laughed. "Totally hates me."

"I guess she does." We lay there for a minute. "I'm not sure. What should I tell her about us?"

He interlaced his fingers with mine. "Tell her tomorrow will be different than yesterday."

He slipped out the back door just before six. I watched him slide into his truck, and as the old engine grumbled to wake up, I felt exhausted yet fully free. The chains were no longer weighing me down. I took a long bath and fell asleep. This time, sleep offered me a safe retreat.

My dad was gone by the time I woke up. The house was silent. Wiping the sleep out of my eyes, I tried to focus on myself in the mirror. Three large marks were inked on my neck. They were bluish, almost purple. A curling iron mishap in three different spots wouldn't pass Chloe's sniff test. Fortunately, by the time she returned from her trip, they would be faded. I ran my fingers over the marks and smiled to myself. They were proof that everything was real and Sam was part of my life in the way I had always wanted.

My grandma called at four to make sure I was still alive. "Gracelynn, did you survive the night okay?"

"Yes, Grandma."

"And Samuel?"

I sat there silent for a second.

"Did Samuel have a nice time?"

"Definitely."

"What time did he leave?"

I hesitated. "I don't know. It was pretty late. We went to see his mom at work."

"That's nice. Teddy and I are going to the club for dinner. Would you like to join us?"

"That's okay, Grandma. I think I'm just going to stay at home." I was hoping to see Sam, but we'd left each other with nothing but a kiss, so I wasn't sure when I'd see him again.

"Do you have anything to eat?"

"Yes, I'll be fine. Grandma, I'm gonna get back to studying."

"Gracelynn, if I thought you were actually studying, I would not have called you. No need to lie to either one of us." Of course, she knew I wasn't studying. She was masterful. "You should go out and have some fun," she continued.

"Chloe is gone. Who am I supposed to go have fun with?"

"We both know the answer to that."

After a hot bath and soup, I curled up on the couch with a documentary on the sixties. Not long after it started, the phone rang.

"Hello?"

"Hi." Sam's voice made my heart jump. "Whatcha doing?"

"Watching a documentary that's super interesting."

"Wanna know what's more interesting?"

"What?"

"My mom's working tonight. What about your dad?"

"Gone until Tuesday."

"See? Definitely interesting."

I could almost see the half-moons through the phone. "Wanna come over and watch the documentary with me?"

"I thought you'd never ask. Be there in a minute."

I put on a shirt from my grandma. It was a sapphire-blue one that fit so snugly that not much was left to the imagination. I looked in the mirror as the knock on the door came.

When I opened the door, he stood there looking at me. "Unbelievable."

"What?"

"You look totally amazing."

I grabbed him by the coat and pulled him to me. He closed the door behind us, and we tore at each other like ravenous dogs. It wasn't long before my skin melted into his. His sweat ran down my chest, and the more his body pushed against mine, the more I wanted it to go on forever. I suddenly felt a surge rise up in me and had a hard time catching my breath. Sam must have felt the same as our bodies convulsed into one. Afterward, we sat next to each other on the floor. It was starting to snow outside, and as we silently watched white flakes fall outside the window, it was Sam who spoke first.

"My dad wants me to stay with him during break."

"Okay." Those words meant little to me at the time. I would soon learn that what seems inconsequential, a radar blip in time, can turn out to be life-altering.

"I promise to be back before winter formal."

I nodded, still lost in our perfect moment of time.

"I was also thinking ..." He reached over and slid my hand into his. "Maybe we should just keep us to us, at least for now."

He finally had my attention. I looked closely at him. "Why?"

"I just think it would be better that way."

I nodded and grabbed my pants. Struggling to put them on, I could feel my raw emotions tearing at me. I stood up and moved to the couch. "Maybe we should skip winter formal." The words cut my mouth like barbed wire.

"Why?" He pulled himself up to the couch, next to me.

"I just think it would be better that way."

"You're totally missing the point, G."

"And what point is that, Sam? The here-we-go-again one?"

He shook his head. "You don't get it. It's not that I don't want to be with you. It's just that I don't want the whole world knowing. They'll rip it to shreds."

I wasn't buying it. "What's the big deal, Sam? Who cares who knows? It's not going to change how we feel about each other. Sorry I'm not in your super-cool clique of fake friends."

"That's not fair," he said, sounding frustrated. "You're not being fair."

"Are you really kidding me right now?"

"Oh, and you think Chloe will be okay with this, with us? You think she's going to high-five you for being with me?"

"Who cares?" I acted like her opinion didn't matter, but I knew it mattered more than anything to me.

He paused before speaking again. "I know you don't understand because you aren't allowed in our world."

"My apologies for not being mean enough to make the asshole

invite list to your world." We sat there for a minute, silence eating away at me like a parasite.

"When I get back from Michigan, we are going to tell everyone you are my girlfriend. Until then, I want to just enjoy it being you and me—our thing that no one else can touch, not Fred, not Julie, not Chloe."

With that, the moment spun around and headed in a completely different direction. "Did you say girlfriend?"

He pulled me to him and kissed the top of my head. "That's okay, right?"

I nodded. I had my first real boyfriend, and it was Sam. The moment became perfect again, its frayed edges repaired.

For the next three weeks, Sam and I spent our school days barely acknowledging each other and our nights so consumed with each other that little else mattered. I told Chloe about being partners with Sam, which gave me an excuse to see him. She hated even the thought of it but accepted it as long as I promised to keep my interactions with him to a minimum. I agreed, knowing it was one of the few lies I would ever tell her. I hadn't told her about winter formal; I hadn't really told anyone except my grandma, who had proceeded to go out and buy me a very expensive red dress.

The night before he left for Michigan, we sat on my front porch swing, watching the stars. She was almost glowing in the sky, and I finally found the courage to tell Sam how I felt.

"Sam?"

Only his head was visible from under the big blanket we sat under. "Yeah?"

"I want to tell you something." I swallowed hard.

He was looking up at the sky, seemingly unaware. "I love you too," he said, keeping his eyes on the sky. He pointed to the bright star. "You think she's okay with that?"

"I'm sure she thinks you'll do."

He rested his head on my shoulder. I closed my eyes, feeling warm and real and finally alive.

That perfect moment never left my mind. It was one of the few things that kept me going, even after Sam vanished from my life again. There were lots of rumors about what really happened with him in Michigan. It would be years later before I knew the truth. I tried my best to forget about Sam, but he was never far from my thoughts or my fractured heart. And I hated him for it. I hated myself for it as well.

I didn't see or hear from him for over a year; he seemed to have disappeared off the face of the earth. It took me months to recover from what had happened. The chains I thought I'd left behind shackled me down so much that I could barely move my feet at times. They wrapped around my neck, sucking the air out of my throat time and time again.

I was silent about it with Chloe, embarrassed to tell her how things had gone so sideways with him. I went through the motions of my last year of high school, spending endless nights sitting on my front porch swing watching her, asking her for strength, asking her why things never worked out for me. I shed a thousand tears, and just when I thought I could cry no more, I shed a thousand more.

One unexceptional day, as I walked down the hall wondering why I had agreed to go to prom with Fred Johnson, there he stood, transplanted back into my world, on a Wednesday in early May. Time stood still. I felt my knees begin to give way. His hair was slightly longer, and a thin black beard masked his jawline, but he was otherwise unchanged. I walked by him as quickly as I could, not wanting to make eye contact, hoping he wouldn't notice me.

Three days later, I found myself at prom with Fred Johnson, wearing the backless red dress pulled from my closet, hidden away since the winter formal that had never happened. Fred had started asking me out right after Sam left town. I had turned him down so many times that I was surprised when he came back for more with prom. I wanted to say no, but my grandma reminded me it was senior prom, an event I should not miss. "Even if you have a miserable time, Gracelynn, at least you can say you went." Fred probably wet himself when I said yes, if the screams of delight were any indication of his happiness.

We were waiting in line for pictures when Sam appeared. "Hey, guys." He wore a black tux with a white tie. His hair was gelled slightly, and the beard remained, though freshly trimmed. Looking at him, I felt my heart begin to beat quickly, pulsating beyond the scotch tape holding it together.

Chloe looked at him with her usual lack of admiration.

"Wow, G. Amazing. You look so unbelievably …"

"Thanks, Sam." I wanted to wrap my arms around him and beg for another chance with him. Instead, I stood there with Fred's sweaty, soft hand in mine. It was cold and clammy like what I imagined holding a dead fish would feel like. As soon as I got the chance to take my hand back from him, I did.

As the music played on, my eyes searched for him. Mrs. Tandra took the stage as the DJ faded the music into the background. "Welcome, everyone. It gives me great pleasure to announce Highmore's king and queen, who have been chosen by your votes cast earlier tonight. Your queen is …" Mrs. Tandra was handed a piece of paper. "Julie Wilks!"

Half the crowd cheered, and the other half stood silent. Obviously, it was a majority and not unanimous vote. Julie took the stage in her strapless pink gown, dangling diamond earrings, and matching studded necklace. The tiara was placed on her head, and she exposed her fang-like teeth.

Mrs. Tandra smiled as she continued, "Your king is Sam Patterson!" The crowd erupted into resounding cheers. "It's the king and queen's dance, so they get to pick who they want to dance with for this next song."

I wondered who Sam would pick, and as he walked by each overpriced, over-the-top dress, my pulse quickened. He stood in front of me, hand extended. The spotlight and all eyes were on me. "Dance with me?"

I heard collective gasps.

"Please," he said.

My shaking hand found its way to his. He guided me to the center of the dance floor. "Make You Feel My Love" began to play. At first, the gawking and whispers distracted me, but as our bodies began to move as one, everything and everyone faded away until it was just Sam and me. I felt his breath on my neck as we inched closer. The warmth of his hand on my lower back sent a rush through me. His fingers pressed against my skin, exposed by the openness of the dress.

As the song ended, I knew I needed to leave Sam behind me. My eyes opened when he pressed his lips to my ear. His voice was soft yet clear. "It's a long life. We're not done yet." He began to pull away and then leaned in again. "There will never be anyone else for me but you." His lips slid across my neck. He lifted his head, kissed my forehead, and walked away. He was out the door before I could move.

Chloe grabbed my hand and dragged me into the bathroom, demanding an explanation. At first, I wasn't sure what to say because I was still recovering from the moment. She wanted to know what he'd said, and I replied, "Nothing."

"Liar."

I stood there, still feeling his lips on my ear, his words inked on my heart like a tattoo.

"What did he say? I saw him whisper something to you."

"He just told me it was a long life."

"Yeah, Einstein, it's a long life. What the hell does that mean? What did he say after that when he leaned back into you?" Chloe's pale blue dress swished and swayed with her words.

"I'm not sure. Couldn't hear him." I remembered clearly but would never tell Chloe.

"Well, we better go find your date. Poor Fred has no idea he never stood a chance with you."

Our uncomfortable heels and weighted-down dresses made it nearly impossible to even walk. The parking lot was filled with cars. I looked for Sam's truck but didn't see it.

"Look, there's Fred's car," said Chloe. "Let's go see if he's in there crying like a baby."

As we walked up to the car, close enough to see inside, we quickly realized that Fred was calming himself in a completely different way.

"Jesus!" Chloe cupped her hands over her mouth. My eyes widened. We both turned and walked away as quickly as possible.

Later, Fred thought he could make it better by telling me he had been thinking about me during those moments. That actually just made me throw up a little in my mouth. I wondered whether that was why his hands were clammy all the time but quickly dismissed the idea because I couldn't stand the thought of it.

That night was the last I saw of Sam. I searched for him everywhere for years, leaving shattered pieces of my heart like petals behind me for him to find. I finally learned to wear the chains and shackles nestled around me like jewelry, bringing me comfort even as they nearly squeezed the life out of me.

6

I was still standing in the parking lot, lost in my thoughts, when I heard a familiar voice behind me.

"Are you coming in?" It was Ginger. She was struggling to throw things back in her car, and the clanking of metal broke me free from my memories. She stumbled a bit, trying to grab something falling out of the backseat. Obviously, her business traveled with her.

"Absolutely." I half-smiled at her. "How are you?"

"Running late. I have to work after this, so I needed to pack my stuff. I forgot a couple of things." I wasn't sure how she was going to have enough time to pull herself together since she looked exactly the same as she had three days ago, only this time the cat glasses were slightly crooked, compliments of the nosedive she had taken while trying to keep a pair of handcuffs from falling onto the pavement.

"Where do you have to go?" I wasn't sure why I asked her. I didn't really want to know the answer.

"Downtown on Michigan." Having finished with her car, she was now walking next to me. From the corner of my eye, I could see her nose running. After a quick snort, she asked, "You live close?"

"Not too far from here." We were nearing the door.

"You by chance have some duct tape and a Coke bottle?"

Her question was serious, so I stopped for a minute to think. "The duct tape I have for sure. Don't think I have the Coke bottle. I have root beer. Will that work?"

"That's okay. I'll stop at Valu-Mart, but thanks."

"Sure." As we continued to walk, the reason for the Coke bottle finally occurred to me. I shook my head to get the image out of my brain.

"My client tonight is pretty famous, you know. I love that famous people can be normal like the rest of us."

I smiled. I really wanted to tell her that normal people didn't use duct tape and Coke bottles for fun, but instead I said nothing.

Inside the meeting room, we took our seats next to each other. Sarah suddenly flew into the room, her cheeks flush and her eyes racing back and forth. She clutched her purse and tripped over two chairs before grabbing the empty seat by us.

"Are you okay?"

"My mother is in the other room."

"Sarah, sweetie," I said, lowering my voice, "I'm not sure how to tell you this, but your mother is dead." She didn't appear incoherent or high, but at this point, anything was possible.

And then Sarah did what she did best: she began to cry. Her face disappeared in her purse. The three of us were right back where we'd started.

"Good evening. How are we?" Dr. Gretchen was struggling with bags in her hand as she entered. "Oh my, what's this?" She dropped the bags and reached out to Sarah. "What's going on, Sarah?"

From deep within her purse, a mumbled sound came. Sobs took over for her words. Dr. Gretchen looked at me, and I shrugged my shoulders. "She thinks she just saw her mother in the other room."

"Ah, completely understandable." Holding on to Sarah, Dr. Gretchen said, "Once you begin exploring feelings about your loss, memories surface. For some, they are so vivid they become real."

As time progressed, I would find myself in Sarah's shoes, but at that moment, I thought it was impossible.

"Sarah?" Dr. Gretchen was trying in vain to coax Sarah out of her purse. "Let's go to the room where you saw your mother, okay?"

No words. Just sobs. Finally, like a wounded animal, Sarah lifted her head from her purse and nodded in silence. And with that, Dr. Gretchen took Sarah to the next room to show her that her mother was not in the arts and crafts room, scrapbooking her trip to the great beyond.

With the two of them out of the room, it was back to Ginger and me. She began talking again. "You know, I have a large client base, an even larger following. The hits on my web page are huge—thousands of likes on my Facebook page. People live for my blog."

"Really?"

"Oh yeah," she said, correcting her cat glasses, "but I always keep my professional and personal lives separate. In my business, it's a cardinal rule." I wasn't exactly sure how a cardinal rule could be written when it came to whipping someone, but I didn't know *all* the cardinal rules, so maybe a spanking clause was in there somewhere. "I've never been in love, though, so it's never been a problem. How about you?"

"Been in love?" I really hadn't loved Les. I knew I'd loved Sam, but that was so long ago that I wasn't sure it counted. It was too early with Jack to tell anything. I shrugged my shoulders.

"I once had a client tell me he loved me right after I performed the thirsty camel in the desert on him."

I had no response for that one, so I just smiled, and she smiled back. There was a moment of silence before she spoke again.

"People think I'm weird."

Looking at her, it struck me. She was different from me and Ellie and Sarah, but that wasn't a bad thing. It made her unique and memorable. She left a lasting impression on everyone she met. I barely made a ripple.

"Not weird, Ginger. One of a kind. That's a good thing."

"It is?" She was clinging to my every word now.

"It is." Without even thinking, I put my arm around her shoulder and squeezed it gently.

"Do you want to know what happened to my mom?" she asked. She leaned into me, shifting her weight to evaporate the personal space between us.

"If you feel like telling me."

"It was the garage."

"It happened in the garage?"

"No. I mean the garage door. She was trying to fix the garage door and had rigged it to see what was wrong with it. The pulley broke when she was under it, and the door came down on her neck. She was the only one who believed in me, the only one. You probably have lots of people who believe in you, but without her, I don't know … I guess I just feel out of place. You know? No control." Ginger began to cry, and tears flooded my eyes as well. No control. I knew exactly how she felt.

"Maybe that's why I do what I do, to have control. Because really"—she paused to wipe her nose with her hand—"it's the only time I have complete control, the only time." She sank into me, and we both sat there quietly for a minute. "Anyway," she finally said, "this is me now."

I knew what she was doing—trying to wipe away the pain with masked words. I knew it because I was a master at it. "I think you're really brave, Ginger."

She pulled herself up. "You know, I could show you some of my work—teach you how to use some things to take your game to the next level."

I had been to those private home parties where they sell things to spice it up. The only time I had tried to use one of those things, I had spent a night in the ER having it removed. I wasn't sure whether Ginger was really serious, but the memory of the night Chloe had to accompany me to the hospital made me shift uncomfortably in my seat.

"That's really nice of you. I'm not sure that's my thing." I was wondering what to say next when Ellie's entrance saved me.

"Hello," she said. Hints of her perfume danced through the open air. Her pants were neatly pressed, and her sweater fit her perfectly.

"How are you, Ellie?"

"I'm well, thank you. I just arrived from New York—big runway season coming up. I came straight from the airport. I've been in the washroom trying to make myself presentable. I was worried the session already started. Is Dr. Gretchen here?"

"She is. She's in the next room with Sarah."

"I see." Ellie paused like she was going to say something else. The other two circle members walked in just before Dr. Gretchen and Sarah.

"Well then, I think we're all here," Dr. Gretchen announced. "Let's get started, shall we? I don't believe we heard from Mindy or Mandie last session. Ladies, we will definitely hear from you this evening." Both of them nodded, although neither look thrilled about being the first sacrificial lamb.

I already felt emotionally spent, and the session hadn't even started. Sarah's eyes were puffy, and she kept glancing over at the door, waiting for the ghost of her mother to take an open seat. Ginger's glasses once again sat precariously on the tip on her nose. And then there was me. I had no idea what to expect from this group, yet my hopes hung on Dr. Gretchen. I wanted her to save our motley crew, cleanse our lost souls, bring us back to a sense of normal. I wanted her to heal us, fill in our voids, and strip our pain away. It struck me then that what I wanted more than anything, I was never going to get. I wanted my mother.

"Thank you for joining us again." Dr. Gretchen stood behind Sarah, gently rubbing her shoulders. "Remember, in this room, we make no apologies for our emotions. We respect each other, even if we do not understand or agree with what is being said. It is my responsibility to make sure you feel safe enough to explore your loss and that which ultimately brings you here today." I hung on her every word, engulfed in the rhythm of her voice and the comfort it brought me.

"Gracie? Would you like to start?"

"Start?"

"Can you share with us your most vivid memory of your mother?" Dr. Gretchen's eyes were imploring me to speak.

"Well, let me think." Blood rushed to my cheeks. What did I remember most about her? Her hair? Her smell? Her laughter? I couldn't remember any of those things. I couldn't. And the more I tried, the further away the memories of her ran from me. And then it hit me. "She loved to decorate, every holiday, every room, inside and out. The day after one holiday ended, another round of decorations came out for the next holiday. Even our toilet paper was themed. I used to hate going to the bathroom around Presidents' Day. It was totally creepy with Lincoln and Washington joining you for number two."

Everyone laughed.

"My mom never missed a holiday—well, until she got too sick. Then holidays became, well, ordinary."

"Anything else?"

"She used to make this Christmas candy. It was this hard marshmallow stuff. She always blew up, like, two hand mixers making it. Every Christmas, she always got two new hand mixers from my dad. He would have bought her twenty mixers if it would have made her happy. And he didn't even like the stuff, but he ate it because she loved making it."

"When's the last time you had it?" Sarah asked meekly.

"Not since her last Christmas with us."

"You don't have the recipe?" Ginger leaned in with interest.

"Oh, I think I have the recipe."

"Then why haven't you had it?" Sarah placed her purse under her chair.

"Because she's not here to make it."

Five heads nodded back at me.

"What is your mother's name?" Dr. Gretchen had not looked away from me the entire time.

I was still lost in the memory of the red- and green-wrapped candy pieces sitting in a crystal bowl. "Cassandra. Everyone called her Cassie." My voice quivered. Her name sounded foreign coming off my tongue. Occasionally, my grandma would talk about her, but as the years crept by, everyone had talked about my mom less and less. My dad and I never talked about her. We talked about the weather, local news, and sports but nothing more. She was the love of his life and the woman who had given me vibrant green eyes and blond hair and a sense of humor in times of desperation. Why had she faded away? She had been a fighter for her life, our lives, until the very end. Why had I let them get away with not talking about her? It would not happen again, I promised myself. Never again.

"Ellie?" Dr. Gretchen had moved on. I felt a sense of relief.

Ellie flashed a nervous grin. "Her name was Elizabeth." She reached for the hair cascading across her forehead with a manicured hand. A single hair slipped out of place, and she smoothed it back.

"That's a pretty name. What's your most vivid memory of her?"

"She would dress for an after-five event with my father, but as soon as they could sneak out, she'd be right back in sweats. She was wonderful. She was almost too good for this world. Maybe that's why she's not in it anymore; perhaps because she was needed more somewhere else."

"Where else would she be needed?" Ginger looked puzzled.

"She was needed in heaven, Ginger." Ellie smiled at her without any hint of frustration or agitation.

"How do you know?"

"I just have a feeling. She was an angel here on earth, but she was called by a greater power."

"Called on the phone?" Ginger was completely serious.

"No, Ginger, not on the phone. She was called spiritually."

"By …?"

"By God. She was called by God."

"I see. She was called by God. That's why she's dead. Do you think the same thing happened with my mom? She was called by God?" Ginger was putting it all together. She managed to also push her glasses up, which had slid down to the tip of her nose again.

"I hope so." Ellie smiled at Ginger, who smiled back.

"Do you think they're in heaven talking about us right now?" Ginger asked.

Ellie looked confused. "Who?"

"Our mothers. Maybe they have their own group there. Maybe they're Daughterless Mothers. Do you think they miss us as much as we miss them?" Ginger's question sank deep into my heart.

"I hope so," Sarah said, her voice sounding stronger. "My mother's name was Mary. My mother is dead."

I saw it coming. I reached over, picked up her purse, and handed it to her. She took it from my hands and buried her face in it.

"Now, Sarah," Dr. Gretchen said. "What did we talk about in the other room? Remember what I told you?" She was trying to coax Sarah out of her bag, which seemed to be her safe place.

"Mother. Dead. Okay." Sarah cried harder with each mumbled word.

Ginger quietly sat on the floor next to Sarah's feet. "It's okay to talk about your mom with us. We're in it together." Reaching up, she began to stroke Sarah's hair and whispered something in her ear. Sarah nodded. A moment passed, and Sarah pulled her head out of her bag and handed it to Ginger. Ginger took the purse, walked to the closet, opened it, and casually tossed the purse inside of it. She turned around and said, "Now, Sarah, tell us about your mom."

"Mary. Her name was Mary. She raised me. All those years, it was just us, and she promised she would never leave me. We were supposed to always be together. It's been three years since she broke that promise." Sarah began to cry again. "I'm not sure how to … what to do." Sarah was starting to crumble again. She cupped her hands over her eyes and started rocking back and forth. Ginger reached up and pulled her hands away from her face. She placed one hand on the side of Sarah's face and the other over Sarah's heart. "Your mom's right here."

Ginger looked down, suddenly introspective. "My mom's name was Ginger."

"Our Mama's name was Dorothy," Mindy offered. Mandie nodded.

Dr. Gretchen looked at them and then spoke. "My mother's name was Bethany. Now let's talk about your mothers. Tell me their stories."

For the next hour, we talked about our mothers. Ellie talked about the day her mom was killed. She talked about her father and how he had never recovered from the loss. She talked about Jack and his ability to make everything seem better, even when they became orphans in the blink of an eye.

Ginger talked about her mother and recounted the garage door tragedy. She talked about how the loss of her one true confidant had left her corner of supporters empty. Her glasses fell as many times as she pushed them up, the tears coming fast and furious. She never knew her father. Her mother had worked three jobs to make it, sacrificing everything for Ginger. The reality of that, knowing her mother had given more than she got from beginning to end, made the pain worse for Ginger.

Sarah's mother's story was masked by Sarah's periods of uncontrollable crying. What I think I understood was that Mary Bland had been a secretary by day and a closet gourmet by night. She had written and published a couple of cookbooks. She died of anaphylactic shock from a reaction to shellfish. The irony is that she had no known allergies, but something in her system changed, and Mary Bland died quickly and unexpectedly because of it.

Mindy and Mandie spoke of their mother next and how she had fostered them since they were toddlers before finally being able to adopt them when they were teenagers. Then it was my turn. I talked about how the night sky brought me comfort time and time again. The more I talked, the more memories of her started sneaking out of the recesses of my mind. I remembered her hands vividly all of a sudden. They were delicate, fragile. Her wedding rings would spin around her finger every time her hand moved. She made my grandma put tape around them so they wouldn't fall off. Not even death could remove them. I didn't speak about the day she died; I just couldn't. Talking about her was both refreshing and heart-wrenching.

We spent a few more minutes talking, and then Dr. Gretchen concluded. "It's been a powerful night. We are starting to break down some walls just by talking about your mothers. Next Tuesday, I'd like to talk about how your world revolves without your mother in it. Thank you for being supportive of each other and for giving me the chance to get to know your mothers."

I almost felt a hint of sadness that the session was over. I felt close to these women, these emotional drifters. For a little while, thoughts about Jack and Sam had left me, and my feelings belonged only to these women. For the first time in a very long time, I felt connected. In this circle my loss was not bigger than I was. I was becoming part of them, and they part of me. For all the words I could not bear to speak to others, I spoke freely to these women. And the chains and shackles that still dragged behind me everywhere I went, I easily left at this door.

As the group members collected their things, Dr. Gretchen approached me. "Gracie?" We met halfway, and she spoke softly. "I'd like to thank you for your participation. There's something about you, Gracie. I can tell. I hope I didn't put you on the spot too much."

"Honestly, I'm not sure what I have to offer. It's been so long since my mom died." I tried to sound distant from my loss, but she knew better.

"But don't you see, Gracie? You have the most to gain. You've survived the years that make the wound less apparent but the scars so deep."

"Maybe." I wondered if she was right.

"Your mother would be proud. Have a great weekend, Gracie."

Thoughts of Jack had slipped out of my mind during the session but sat front and center now. The wind lashed at my face. Leaves flew back and forth, creating their own rhythmic dance against the night sky. As I approached my car, I saw it: a note tucked under my windshield wiper. It flittered and fluttered, holding on for dear life. My heart began to pound as I reached for it. It slipped out, free from its restraint, and the wind quickly took it away. It flew from me and managed to stay one grab away halfway across the parking lot. It finally became trapped at the base of the light pole. I grabbed it quickly. The simple note was written in clear, precise penmanship:

Gracie:
I'm in desperate need of career advice. Call me.
(312) 210-0803
Jack

I stood in the middle of the parking lot, trying to figure out what to do next. Too caught up in the moment, I didn't notice the car pull up beside me. The note tried to break free again in a gust of wind. I was tightening my grip on it when a voice broke through the brisk air.

"I'm waiting."

I looked up, and sapphire-blue eyes stared back at me through the open car window.

"Well?"

"Well what?" I walked over and leaned into his car window, trying to fight off the night air tugging at me.

"Career advice?"

"Oh, I see. Well, it will cost you." His car smelled amazing, just like him.

"Hold on." He turned his car off. He stepped out and walked over to me. "This is better." He was standing in front of me now, his dark gray wool coat protecting me from the blistery wind.

"When would you like this career advice?" I was cold and could feel my nose turning a deep red.

"How about now? Or do you have plans?"

"Plans?"

"It is a Friday night, and you look great, so I thought you might have plans."

"Lucky for you, my calendar just opened. Five minutes later, and you would have missed your chance."

"Definitely lucky then."

I looked down, smiling through the cold.

"Hey, follow me." He grabbed something out of his car, turned and headed back toward the community center.

"Jack, I heard them lock the doors. I think it's closed for the night." He either didn't hear me or was pretending not to since he just kept walking. I followed him along the side of the building, toward the back entrance. I wasn't sure where he was going, but I followed him intently, excited to be in the moment with him. He stopped at the back of the building. The exterior lights that lit the front of the building were missing where we stood. It was dark, and the wind blew colder. I heard the sound of keys and then a turn of a lock.

"C'mon."

I hesitated as he slipped through the open door. "Jack? I can't see you."

He grabbed my hand and pulled me into the building. His hand was warm and enveloped mine completely. We were inside the janitor's room now. I could smell the chlorine in the air. Jack's hand still firmly held mine.

"I think there's a light in here somewhere." Fumbling around for the switch, he stumbled over a mop and bucket, nearly toppling us both to the ground. I pulled my hand away to regain my balance. I caught the switch with my hand and flipped it on. The glaring light made us both squint.

"If your next career goal is serial killer, you're right on pace, dragging me into a dark building with no one around."

He laughed. "Not sure there's a big demand for serial killers. I didn't drag you, by the way. You came willingly."

"True." Neither of us said anything for a long moment. "So did you forget something in here?"

"No." He stared at me, saying nothing.

"Okay, now I'm thinking serial killer might already be on your résumé."

He laughed again. "Follow the leader."

Again, I followed him, this time not taking his hand. We walked past all the rooms I knew until we were by the pool doors. He grinned, raised his eyebrows, and walked inside. I let the doors close behind me. The smell of chlorine was overwhelming at first.

"I love the water," he said as he sat at the edge of the pool.

I took a seat next to him. "Do you swim here?"

"Since I started coming here, I do. I have my own pool at home, but I like this one." He glided his hand through the water, letting it fall between his fingers.

"This one's nice, though, because it's inside so you can swim all year round."

As he looked up at me, it seemed like the blue from the water was mixing with the blue in his eyes. "My pool's indoor at my place too, but this one … I don't know … seems better for some reason."

"Of course your pool is indoors—because really, why wouldn't it be?"

He flicked a few droplets of water at me in response. I reached in and cupped a handful of water and threw it at him. He shifted, grabbed my hand, and pulled me toward him. His hand wrapped around my wrist as our lips nearly touched. I could hear the pounding of my heart through my ears.

"Hi." The breath of his word got lost inside my mouth.

"Hi back."

"Wanna play a game?" He leaned back and stood up.

"Oh, okay." I stood up, slightly dizzy from the moment.

"Let's play truth or dare."

"Really, Jack? How old are you?" I smirked, but I could feel the energy pulsating between us.

"Well, not really truth or dare, but close enough." He smiled, and blond strands of hair fell onto his forehead.

"What are the rules?"

He stepped to the other side of the pool, directly across the water from me. "I'll ask you a question, and if you want to answer it, then answer it."

"And if I don't?"

He raised an eyebrow. "Then you remove a piece of clothing."

My heart jumped, and my pulse raced. I bit my lip. Maybe the questions would be easy. I definitely wasn't stripping in front of him. No way was I showing him any of my body.

"You ask me anything too. If I don't want to answer, I'll take something off."

"I think I need alcohol for this game."

He nodded, walked back around the pool, and handed me a thermos pulled from inside his coat.

"Classy. What's in the thermos, a roofie?"

"Ha! No, just one of my specialty drinks. You like vodka, right?"

I nodded, and he handed me the thermos. I took a swig. It instantly took the edge off.

"Let the games begin," I said, watching him walk back to the other side of the pool. I wanted to take off my coat because the heat from the pool and my nerves were causing my underarms to sweat. But I also wanted to keep as many layers on as possible in case I needed them.

"Ladies first. Let's lose our coats, though. I'm dying in here."

I took my coat off and tossed it to the side, taking another swig from the thermos.

He walked over, dropped his coat on top of mine, and took a long drink from the thermos. He wiped his mouth and smiled. "Good stuff." He filled the thermos's cup and returned with it to his place alongside the pool. "Don't go easy on me. I'm a big boy. I can handle it."

"Tell you what? Since it's your game, I'll let you go first." I wanted to follow his lead.

"Okay, ready?"

I took another drink from the thermos. I was starting to feel the buzz of the vodka. "Sure, pretty boy, ask away."

"Have you ever been married?"

"Nope. You?"

"Nope." He drank from the thermos cup. "Kids?"

"Nope." *This is going to be easy*, I thought. "You?"

"Not that I know of."

I laughed, my voice echoing off the pool walls.

"You ever been with a girl?"

I nearly choked. "Not that I know of."

He laughed.

"You?"

"Of course." He looked at me for a moment. "You ever think of me?"

I hesitated, not sure whether I should admit it or not. I decided to take off a shoe instead.

"I get to ask another question since you failed to answer that one."

"No way! It was either answer the question or take something off. I chose to take something off."

"Okay, but let the record show I object to not being able to ask you back-to-back questions."

"My turn." I hesitated. "You ever think about me?"

"Yes." His eyes met mine. "Have you thought about me since we met?"

"That's the same question, Jack."

He nodded. "I have the right to do that."

"Then I'll answer it. Yes, I've thought about you."

He smiled. I was suddenly nervous again.

"What's your full name?" I asked.

He smiled and took off a shoe. I took another swig from the thermos.

"Have you thought about kissing me?" he asked.

I took off my other shoe. "Have you thought about kissing me?"

"Yes."

I shook my head in disbelief.

"Do you wonder what I would feel like?"

I looked at him. Now I was sorry I had wasted a shoe on an easy question. I either had to tell him I did or had to take off my sweater. I could get away with no sweater since I had a tank top on underneath it. I pulled my sweater over my head, letting it drop to my feet. I could feel his eyes on me, and I was both embarrassed and aroused.

"Do you ever feel unhappy?" I asked.

He opened his eyes wide, surprised by my question. He took off his other shoe. "What do you like best about me? I mean, when it comes to this?" He motioned his hand up and down his body.

"Your eyes."

"Not my six-pack?"

I smiled and shook my head. "Haven't seen it, so have to go with what I know."

"You have a beautiful smile."

I blushed. "I didn't ask you that question."

He shrugged. "Well, if that is what you're going to ask, that's my answer."

"Nope. What do you miss most about your mom?"

He paused, seemingly trying to find an answer, and then slowly unbuttoned the top of his shirt and pulled it over his head. His body was perfect, his abs concrete. I couldn't take my eyes off them.

"Hey, eyes up here!" he exclaimed.

We both laughed.

"What's your best friend's name?" he asked.

"Chloe. Yours?"

"Ellie." Not an obvious answer, but a sweet one. "What's your most embarrassing moment?"

"You mean, other than now? Too many to just pick one, kinda like boyfriends."

"I bet."

"Have you ever been in love?" I asked.

He stopped middrink, lowered the cup, and tilted his head slightly, as if to think. "Real love? I thought so, but now I'm not sure. You?"

"A long time ago."

"What happened?"

I shook my head. "Not your turn to ask the question. Favorite kind of movie?"

"Porn."

I nearly spit a gulp of drink from my mouth. "Really?"

He started laughing and took off a sock. "Nah."

Socks! Of course, why hadn't I thought about my socks?

"Boxers or briefs?"

I laughed again. "Boxer briefs," I answered.

He nodded. "That's good."

"Favorite kind of date, out or in?" I asked.

"In. Perfect night is takeout and a movie."

"Agree."

"Favorite spot to be kissed besides the lips?"

I looked at him, thinking about his lips on me. "Neck."

"Good to know."

I stared at him. "Favorite spot to be kissed?"

"Stomach. Most kinky fantasy?"

I instantly took my sock off, and he laughed.

"Dog or cat?" I asked.

"Are we talking about my kinky fantasy?"

I laughed and shook my head.

"Kidding. Dog, definitely."

I nodded. "Me too."

"Worst thing that's ever happened to you?"

I thought about Sam and my mom. Neither seemed like the right thing to talk about then, so instead I took my other sock off. "Worst thing for you?"

"Identifying my mom's body at the morgue."

I felt my heart sink for him. He looked at the water for a brief minute and then back at me. "Do you want me to kiss you right now?"

My heart began to beat uncontrollably. Flickers from the water bounced off his face. He was amazing. I wanted to answer yes, but instead, I reached for my sock.

He smiled. "You're out of socks."

I looked down at my bare feet. I had to answer or take off my jeans. Then I remembered the star necklace I never took off. I reached up, unhooked the clasp, and gently placed it on top of my sweater.

He shook his head. "I don't think jewelry counts."

I shrugged my shoulders.

We looked at each other, the heat from the pool adding to the electricity in the air. "I want to kiss you right now," he said. "Really want to kiss you."

I couldn't believe he had just said those words to me. "With tongue or without?" I felt powerful in the moment.

He walked over to me, with one sock and one bare foot. He stopped in front of me and put his hands on either side of my face. "With."

He leaned slowly into me, his eyes locked on mine. When his mouth finally reached mine, a surge of excitement raced through me. His lips were soft and full. With each soft kiss, I felt my heart pump. I placed my hands on his stomach and felt the hard muscles underneath my touch. His hands ran through my hair as his kisses became longer. I searched for his tongue and found it. Our mouths pushed harder against each other, the kisses deeper. He pulled me so close I could feel him through his jeans. He pulled away from my mouth, and his tongue wrapped around my earlobe and then slid down my neck. He pulled down the strap of my tank top and began kissing my shoulder. I was in a state of euphoria.

"Next question is mine," he whispered as his lips worked their way to my collarbone.

"What?" I could barely talk.

"Do you want me?"

I could find no words.

"Answer the question or take off your jeans," he whispered.

I struggled to find the button on my jeans.

"I'll help." As he pulled back from me to reach for my jeans, we lost our footing on the wet floor. Into the water we fell, holding on to each other. The water sent a rush to my head, and his weight caused me to sink toward the bottom. I felt him pulling at me, struggling to get us back above the water. I swallowed a gulp of water, and the chlorine stung my throat, causing me to choke. I tried to cough but instead took in another gulp of water.

He pushed me up out of the pool and onto the concrete floor. I was choking. The more I wanted air, the more I struggled to find it. The taste of chlorine in my mouth made my stomach churn. Jack was talking, saying something I couldn't understand. I panicked more with each gasp of air I could not find. I felt his hand hitting my back, the blows hard and fast. Finally, the water relented, and I vomited it out my mouth. I lay there heaving, exhausted in my pursuit of air.

"You okay?" Jack was rubbing my back.

I couldn't talk; the rapid heaving of my chest continued. The pressure of the water had pushed my already-unsecure tank top down my stomach, leaving my breast exposed.

"I'm sorry, Gracie. You okay?"

I nodded, tears rolling down my face. He leaned me against him. I was shivering, and the warmth of his body brought me no relief.

"Let's get you out of here." Jack grabbed my clothes, and I saw it being launched into the pool. My panic began again. I tried to find the words as he helped me to my feet, oblivious to what was now lying at the bottom of the pool. I tried to speak but could only cough.

"Gracie, don't try to talk now." He was trying to help me to the door, half-carrying me. I was pushing back, trying to turn around to retrieve it. "Gracie, it's this way." He was moving me in one direction when I needed to move in the other.

I finally found enough energy to stop him, pointing to the pool. "Ne … eck … lace." It was painful to say, but not saying it would have been unimaginable.

"What?" He leaned into me.

"Neck … lace. Po … ol." I started coughing again, feeling my throat burn.

"Your necklace is in the pool?"

I nodded in relief.

"Got it." He set me down gently and dove back into the pool. He returned to the surface with it quickly. When he stood before me with the necklace in his hand, the smell of the chlorine falling off his body made me vomit again. He leaned down and secured the necklace around my neck. I grabbed his arm and smiled. He looked at me, pulling my tank top back up over my breast and putting my strap back in place before wiping away a line of mascara running down by cheek. "You have a little something on your face." He used his shirt sleeve to wipe the side of my mouth. It was watery vomit.

"Thank you." My voice was raspy, but the slow burn was fading. I watched him clean the concrete floor with pool towels, placing them in the dirty towel bin. I shivered as we made our way to the door.

"Here." He placed his coat around me, the bottom so long on me that it dragged on the ground. "It's cold outside."

We walked to our cars in silence, the night air shredding my face. "Will you be okay?"

I nodded, knowing this would be the last time he would ever want to see me.

"I'd feel better if you let me drive you home."

"I'm fine."

"I know you only live a few blocks away, so it's no problem."

I stopped and looked at him. "How do you know that?"

He smiled, saying nothing.

"Definitely a serial killer," I softly said.

"Give me your phone."

Puzzled, I searched for it and handed it to him.

Quickly, he typed something and then handed it back to me. "I really am sorry, Gracie. You sure you're okay?"

I nodded.

He opened the door for me, and I caught my reflection in the rearview mirror. Dried clumps of spit sat at the corners of my mouth, mascara lines drew maps down my cheeks, and my hair perched in a clotted mess on top of my head. I looked over at Jack. He looked like he had just taken a casual lap in the pool. His hair was slicked back, and his appearance, even half dressed, was perfect.

"Here's your jacket," I said.

"Keep it. I'll get it another time. I've got plenty."

"Okay." I avoided looking at him.

"Sorry again."

"Thanks for ..." I wasn't sure what to thank him for—the strip game, the thermos booze, the make-out session, the near drowning, the peep show I'd given him with my exposed nipple, the vomit he'd wiped from my mouth. All possibilities, but instead I said nothing.

"Yeah, it was fun."

I raised my eyebrows. He smiled and closed my car door.

At home, I lay in the bathtub until my fingers were nothing more than wrinkles. I ignored Chloe's repeated calls. I knew she would try to make me feel better, and all I felt was humiliated.

I was drifting off to sleep when my cell phone chirped. I lay there assuming the text was from Chloe. Finally, something made me reach over and grab it anyway.

(312) 210-0803

Check your calendar for tomorrow. Reply Y that you can make it. Jack

I pulled up my phone calendar, and there it was: "6pm Dinner with Jack on dry land." Maybe things would be different for me this time. Maybe for the first time in forever, happiness would find me. Maybe ... another chirp.

(312) 210-0803

Truth—I had the best time I've had in a really long time, minus your near drowning. Reply Y

I smiled as my fingers searched for the right keys.

Me

Truth—me too, minus my near drowning. Y

(312) 210-0803

I'll pick you up at six. What are you doing?

Me

K. Nothing much. You?

(312) 210-0803

Thinking about you when I should be working. Thinking about me?

Me

Yes

(312) 210-0803

Are you wondering if I'm wearing boxers or briefs?

Me

Lol. Wondering why you have a key to the community center.

(312) 210-0803

I paid for the renovation of the pool so they gave me a key in case I wanted to swim after hours. Boxer briefs, BTW.

I suddenly remembered about the anonymous donor who had paid for the entire pool renovation. It was a massive undertaking, made possible by Jack.

(312) 210-0803
Truth—my favorite kind of movie are the classics. Nothing beats the old black-and-whites.

Me
And I was hoping you would stick with porn.

(312) 210-0803
I can definitely go back to that answer.

Me
JK. I love old movies too. They remind me of my mom.

(312) 210-0803
So not porn? I'll cancel our private showing of Deep Throat for tomorrow.

Me
What are you working on?

(312) 210-0803
A merger—nothing fun.

Me
What do you wish you were working on?

(312) 210-0803
My golf game. Lol. Nonprofit. I wish I was doing something to help others. Mergers only help the rich get richer.

Me
No offense, but aren't you one of the rich?

(312) 210-0803
Yes. Doesn't mean I like it, though.

I couldn't imagine not liking being rich. Didn't everyone enjoy having enough money to burn?

Me
I'm sorry about tonight.

(312) 210-0803
Sorry about what?

Me
I was a mess. I ruined the night.

(312) 210-0803
You made it memorable. How was your session?

Me
Good. Ellie was gone before I could say good-bye to her.

(312) 210-0803
Runway season coming up. Did she talk about our mom?

We had made a pact to be a safe circle. I couldn't break it, not even with Jack.

Me
We all did. That's the point.

(312) 210-0803
True. I hear there's a dominatrix in the group. You get any pointers?

Me
Not really.

(312) 210-0803
Bummer. What kind of food do you like?

Me
I'm pretty simple. Pizza or burgers work for me. Wish I was more exciting.

(312) 210-0803
I think you're pretty exciting. Do me a favor. Add me to your contacts. I want to be more than just a number.

Me
Will do. Add me to yours.

(312) 210-0803
Already have. You're under my contacts as Career Counselor. Add me now. I'll wait.

Me
Done.

Jack B
Is it tomorrow yet?

That night, I dreamed of my mom. She sat next to me at first, saying nothing. Then she bent down and slowly removed the shackles from my feet. She took the chains and tossed them aside. When the last lock was released, she looked up at me and said one word: "Freedom."

7

I spent every Saturday morning the exact same way: at the club with my grandma and Teddy, for a 9:00 a.m. breakfast. Occasionally, Chloe would join us, which gave me a break from the guilt trips my grandma would give me. I filled Chloe in on my night with Jack and, of course, our upcoming date. I swore her to secrecy, which lasted almost one hour.

"So did Gracie tell you she has a date tonight with a Gates boy?" Chloe looked at my grandma while putting way too much pepper on her scrambled eggs.

"No, she failed to mention it. Which Gates?" Grandma looked at me like I had been keeping a life-altering secret from her.

Chloe responded, "Hillside."

"Oh, that's a pretty ritzy one," Teddy said, wiping hot sauce gone awry off his "I'm somebody's Boo" T-shirt.

"I would not say nicer than ours, but it does have its merits." My grandma hated to think of anyone living in a snobbier neighborhood than hers. "What is his name?"

"Jack." I smiled, looking down at my omelet.

"Gracelynn, what is his family name?" Grandma stopped cutting her grapefruit, waiting for an answer.

"Oh, Bradshaw. His sister is in session ... I mean, I know his sister too." I hadn't told my grandma I was in the support group.

To her, I might as well cut out my tongue as talk to strangers about our family issues.

"Bradshaw? Elizabeth Bradshaw's children?" Grandma pulled her rhinestone glasses down her nose slightly, watching me for a response.

"Uh, yeah, that's their mom ... or was."

"You have a date with the Bradshaw boy?" My grandma half-chuckled. "Impossible."

"Why is that impossible?" I was starting to feel the slow burn in my throat again, caused not by chlorine but by my grandma.

"If he is Elizabeth Bradshaw's son, he is engaged to some model." My grandma went back to cutting her grapefruit.

"You sure?" Chloe asked, looking over at me. She wanted my grandma to be wrong.

"I have it on good word that her son is engaged to some famous model. Margaret Rodden-Simmons told me about them during our women's guild meeting a few months ago. Elizabeth Bradshaw died in a car accident, correct?"

"Yes." I suddenly felt very sick to my stomach.

"And the husband died a short time late, correct?" My grandma was merciless when it came to making a point.

"Yes." My responses were growing fainter with each question asked.

"The daughter works in New York—does something with the fashion industry—and the son, Jack, is an attorney, and a very successful one, I understand. Is that them?"

I nodded, feeling like a fool.

"Too bad. He would have been a good catch, Gracelynn. Now pass the jam, please."

I silently handed her the dish.

"Well," interjected Teddy, "anyone who meets our Gracie for longer than two minutes would be a fool not to snatch her up. I bet she isn't half the girl our Gracie is."

I smiled at Teddy, trying to fight off the swelling disappointment inside me.

"Her name is Angela or Angelina or something. She is on the cover of magazines or some nonsense like that." Grandma was spreading jam on her English muffin, oblivious to the anguish her words were causing me. "I am not sure why these young girls feel the need to show everything God gave them. It is embarrassing and completely disrespectful."

"Wait. Angelique Depardieu?" Chloe looked stunned.

"Yes. That is her," Grandma stated nonchalantly.

"She's, like, on the cover of every magazine out there. She was on the cover of the swimsuit edition, for God's sake." Chloe looked impressed until she saw my face. "I bet she's a total skank."

I said nothing.

My grandma looked over at Chloe. "Chloe, darling, we do not use the word *skank*. Perhaps *whore* is a better choice?"

Chloe smiled. "Of course."

"You sure he's still with her?" Teddy asked as he saw my demeanor crumbling.

"I assume he is, but you never know with those Hillsiders. They tend to be so ... what is the word ... flighty." Grandma took a sip of hot tea. "It has been a couple of months since I saw Margaret, and we all know how much can change in a short period of time. You may have a chance after all, Gracelynn." She smiled at me with her perfect white capped teeth.

I tried to swallow a bite of omelet that was in jeopardy of coming back up. "What has Dad been up to?"

My grandma stopped drinking her tea. "Did he not tell you?" Grandma looked over at Teddy, who shrugged his shoulders.

"Tell me what?" I looked at Teddy first, who promptly looked at my grandma.

"Well, it is best he tell you himself."

"Tell me what, Grandma?"

"Not my story to tell, Gracelynn. He will tell you when the time is right."

"She's not even that pretty," Teddy said, looking at a picture on his smartphone.

"Who?" I grabbed for the phone.

"Don't do it, Gracie. Not a good idea," Chloe implored.

I took Teddy's phone and stared silently at the picture. In a bikini the size of a Band-Aid, there was Angelique. Her long brown hair fell below her waist as she stretched out across a white sandy beach. Her skin was tan, and her mouth was open in an expression of ecstasy. Chloe was right: I had seen her before, on every magazine at the grocery store and anywhere else I looked for that matter. Of course this was Jack's girlfriend. It made sense. I wasn't sure what he was doing with me—likely slumming while she was on some exotic location shoot.

"Gracie, you know none of that's real, right? I'm not the smartest guy, but I do know trash when I see it. And that picture is trash. If she was with us right now having breakfast, she'd look just like the rest of us." Teddy was trying to make me feel better like he always did.

"Yeah, like the rest of us if we were all six-foot-tall supermodels." I slumped in my chair.

"Oh, Gracelynn, quit being so dramatic. He asked you out, correct? He obviously sees something in you that he cannot get from that inappropriately dressed girl." And with that, my grandma made it real for me.

"I hope you plan on wearing something other than"—she used her butter knife to motion down my body—"whatever that is you are wearing. How many times have I told you that you have to put something eye-catching in the storefront window for men to want to take a closer look?"

"Yes, Grandma, you've told me, more than a few times."

"As a matter of fact, Gracelynn, I am heading over to the boutique after breakfast for a few things. You will come with me.

I am sure we can find something suitable for you to wear." She smiled. "Chloe, join us if you are available."

"Thank you, but Rick and I have plans."

My grandma smiled. "See, Gracelynn, this is what you could be enjoying if you just did something with yourself to attract a man who is worth your time."

Chloe rolled her eyes at me.

"Doll, leave our girl alone," said Teddy. "When the right fella comes along that is good enough for her, she'll know it. Until then, let her be picky. She deserves to be." Teddy put his arm around me.

"Thanks, Grandma, but I'm sure I have something in my closet that will work."

Grandma peered at me above her rhinestone glasses. "I'm sure you do if he is taking you to a track meet."

I lowered my head.

"Hiking in the woods?"

I shook my head.

"Wild game hunting? Bingo at the senior center?"

"Grandma, I get it. I'll go with you."

By early afternoon, I had added four new shirts, skin-tight jeans, a wrap dress, heeled black boots, and a skirt to my closet. I lay in the bathtub thinking about Jack and, of course, Angelique. I had promised Chloe I wouldn't Google her. I was grabbing my phone to do it anyway when the sound of a text went off.

Jack B
Hey. How about a pre-date drink at five?

Me
Pre-date?

Jack B
So by the time the real date starts we won't be nervous.

Me

Are you nervous? Shouldn't I be the one nervous since you
are clearly a serial killer?

Jack B

Clearly. Five work for you?

Me

I can probably squeeze you in then.

Jack B

Truth—I'm looking forward to tonight.

Me

Truth—Me too.

Chloe came over to help me pick out an outfit. It turned out to
be a burnt-orange silk top with a keyhole opening at my chest and a
pair of tight jeans with black boots. We took a wave iron to my hair
and mascara to my eyelashes. When I was ready, I felt like I could
be decent competition for Angelique—well, not competition at all
with her but pretty good competition against another Midwest girl.

Chloe smiled at me. "You look amazing." She touched the
star peeking out from the keyhole opening. "Your mom would be
knocked out by how you look. And your grandma ... well, I'm sure
in her own way, she would be pleased."

We looked at each other and laughed.

"Hey, what do you think is up with my dad?" I asked as we sat
on the couch, drinking a glass of wine.

"I'm getting this weird vibe about him. Is he seeing someone?"

"I guess he could have something on the side."

"He wasn't that old when your mom died. I can't imagine being
so young and alone."

"I never really thought about it." I had always assumed my dad was content with his life, happy to have his job and my grandma and Teddy and, I guess, me to fill the void. Maybe like everyone else, he needed more.

"I mean, I know he spends a lot of time with your grandma and Teddy, but unless he's looking for a Mrs. Robinson, there's nothing much happening for him at the club."

I nodded. "I couldn't handle him being with someone younger than us."

"Now that would be gross." Chloe took a swig of wine and stood to leave. "Call me later, or hopefully, you can't call me later because you'll be doing some nasty business with Jack." Just as she was stepping out the door, she stopped. "Oh, I Googled him, and he is freaking hot." She kissed me and closed the door behind her.

I cleaned my kitchen sink, and emptied my dishwasher while waiting for the time to pass. I was caught up organizing a closet when the doorbell rang.

He stood at the door, flowers in hand. "Here, for you."

I took the flowers from him and was trying to remember the last time someone besides Teddy had given me flowers when it struck me that no one ever had. "Thank you."

He reached over and gave me a hug. It seemed awkward. Was he nervous? He had dated a supermodel, so I wasn't sure how he could be nervous around me.

"So ... where to for dinner?" I asked, handing him a glass of wine.

"I was thinking maybe Sonny's downtown first and then a movie back at my place?"

"Sounds good."

"I'm not sure why, but I'm nervous," he said, laughing a little.

"Me too!" I leaned in and squeezed his arm. His bicep was rock-solid.

"It's like I've never been on a date before."

As we sat drinking our wine, conversation between the two of us started to flow easily. It wasn't long before we were talking freely and laughing. It was completely dark outside. I looked at the clock. It was nearly seven.

"Hey, I don't want to be the one to tell you this, but we're late for our date."

He looked at his watch. "Crap. We have to go. Our reservations are now." We grabbed our coats and headed to his car. He picked up stacks of files from the passenger seat and tossed them into his backseat. "Sorry about that. I use the passenger seat as a filing cabinet."

"That's okay." Maybe Grandma was wrong about him and Angelique. She had been known to be wrong before. Well, actually she was never wrong, but maybe this would be a first for her.

At the restaurant we were led to a private room. "This was one of Al Capone's places," Jack said. "I thought you might like having dinner in an old speakeasy."

A waiter in an all-white jacket handed Jack a menu. "Thank you, Mr. Bradshaw, for dining with us this evening. May I start you off with something from the bar?"

I nodded at Jack.

"We'll take your specialty cocktail. Is the chef ready? I apologize for being late."

"No apology needed. I can understand why." He looked over at me and smiled.

Jack grabbed my hand. "Yes, it's all her fault."

I laughed as food began appearing at our table out of nowhere. By the time I grabbed my second piece of gourmet pizza, washed down with another cocktail, my waistband was begging for mercy.

"Anything else, Ms. Anderson?" The waiter motioned to me.

"No, thank you. It was amazing." My stomach hurt from the combination of alcohol and food. I needed to stand and move around.

"With that, Mr. Bradshaw, we will leave you two to enjoy the rest of the evening."

Jack handed the waiter what looked like multiple hundred-dollar bills.

The waiter nodded. "We look forward to serving you again soon."

As the waiter left the room, Jack started to close his wallet and then stopped. "Can I show you something?"

"Sure."

He took something out of his wallet and handed it to me. It took me a minute to focus in on the card. My contacts were dry, and my vision was slightly blurry from the alcohol.

"Elizabeth Bradshaw. Your mom's driver's license?"

Jack nodded. "I carry it with me. Silly, huh?"

I looked up at him and instinctively leaned over and kissed him. "Not at all." I looked again at her license. Then I noticed it. "Her birthday?"

"Yeah, it's coming up."

"It's the same day as mine." I handed it back to him.

"Really? Cause for celebration." He placed the license back in his wallet.

"I'm not really into birthdays. I mean, other people's are fine, just not mine." I looked down at the table, my stomach beginning to cramp.

"Why not?"

I didn't want to talk about it. I really just wanted to get up and walk around. I shrugged my shoulders. "Hey, ready to head out? I can't wait to see what's next on the agenda—before you kill me, of course."

"Oh, the serial killer part comes later, so we have time."

I laughed.

We headed down Lake Shore Drive and pulled into a building a few blocks away. It seemed like the elevator was taking us to the sky, but it stopped just short. The doors opened, and we walked into Jack's place. The walls were windows overlooking Lake Michigan. It was expansive.

"It's a shame, Jack, that you live in such deplorable conditions."

He chuckled, kissing my neck slightly. I felt a rush go through my veins.

"Well, the first floor is the main living room, kitchen, master bedroom, couple of bathrooms, and formal dining room. The second floor—"

"Wait, how many floors do you have?"

"Counting the pool and patio area?"

"Sure."

"I guess technically four, but I don't count the pool area as indoor. The ceiling retracts during the summer for outdoor use."

He walked me through each room leading up to the top-floor which was breathtaking. The entire area was encased in glass, so from one view there was the lake, and from another, you could see all the stars you could imagine, including my mom.

"It's amazing, Jack," I said, looking up at the stars.

"Maybe we should move away from the pool. I'd hate two near drownings in one week."

I hesitated. "You know how you keep your mom with you in your wallet? I keep my mom here." I touched my star necklace, and then I pointed to the sky. "And there."

"Why a star?" We were sitting on the patio furniture, staring at the sky.

"When she was dying, she told me she would always watch over me. She would be the brightest star on the darkest of nights. She gave me this necklace as a reminder."

"That's why it was so important that I got it from the pool?"

I nodded. "It wouldn't have been an issue if I had just been wearing a double layer of socks."

He laughed and slowly leaned in to kiss me. Our lips touched as he placed his hand on the side of my face. I placed my hand over his. We sat there kissing until the loud beating of rain on the ceiling broke us apart.

"Want to go watch a movie?" He stood, pulling me up with him. He wrapped his arms around my waist and started kissing me again.

"I'd rather go pretend to watch a movie with you."

We moved to the theater room, and for the next couple of hours, Jack and I lay on the couch, kissing and exploring each other. I was excited and exhausted at the same time. The alcohol that had sent my pulse racing earlier was now causing me to feel groggy. I lay next to Jack with my head on his chest.

He kissed the top of my head. "I should probably get you home. It's nearly one."

"Really?" I couldn't believe how fast the time had gone.

"Do you want to just stay? I can drive you home in the morning."

"It's closer to tomorrow morning than to last night."

"I guess you're right."

"I should probably get home."

I started to sit up, and he pulled me to him. As his tongue grazed the inside of my mouth, his hand slipped up my shirt.

"Time to go," I said, pushing him off me a little.

He stopped and dropped his head onto the couch. "Gracie, you have no idea what you do to me."

Laughing, I stood up. "Feeling is mutual, Jack."

We were almost out the door when I saw it—a picture sitting among a number of other family photos. Her face was instantly recognizable. It was Angelique. In the picture, her arms were around Jack's neck, her head tilted slightly to the side so her hair cascaded like a waterfall down his shoulder. They looked happy.

I stopped short of the door, wondering whether I should say something. Jack was talking and didn't notice I had stopped until he ran into me.

"She's pretty." I pointed to the picture and walked out the door. "Yeah, I guess."

We got in the car, saying nothing else. I felt sleep and disappointment overtaking my body. Jazz music filled the car as Jack weaved in and out of traffic. I sat looking out the window, saying nothing.

In front of my house, he finally spoke, but not about the picture or her. "It was an awesome night, Gracie." He leaned in to kiss me.

I gave him a quick kiss and opened the door. "I had fun. Thanks, Jack." I closed the car door behind me and walked up to my door without looking back. The picture burned in my mind. My grandma had been right, yet again. I was definitely not going to be the warm-up act when the main show was not available. I would rather be alone.

I expected to lie awake for hours, but sleep came easily. It was well after ten when I heard the knocking. I stumbled to the front door.

"Gracelynn, my word, are you going to sleep all day?" Grandma brushed past me and placed two cups of coffee and a box of croissants on my coffee table. I walked over and sat next to her on the couch, wincing from the brightness of the day. "So I stand corrected."

"About what?" I was trying to rub the sleep out of my eyes.

"Well, Jack, of course." She leaned in and removed a fleck of mascara from my face.

"The thing is, Grandma, I don't think so." I started to take a sip of the coffee, only to recoil as a hot drop of it touched my lips.

"I was definitely wrong. I talked to Margaret last night at bunco, and she told me the full story."

My second attempt at coffee was abruptly stopped by her words. "Wait? What?"

"Last night, Margaret told me that—"

"No. I mean you were playing bunco? The dice game?"

Grandma shook her head casually like it was no big deal.

"Since when do you play bunco?"

"A few of the club ladies and I play. It is one of the benefits of outliving your husband. You actually get a seat at the table again."

I raised my eyebrows. My grandma was actually a little independent. Who knew?

"Gracelynn, I did not come over to talk about bunco. I came to tell you what Margaret told me."

"Grandma, you could have called."

"I called, but apparently you like to sleep half the day away and do not bother answering your phone."

I thought for a minute. "I must have left it in my coat. Sorry about that."

She nodded and took a sip of coffee, without the same second-degree burns I suffered. "Your Jack is definitely not with that Angie person any longer."

"Well, first of all, he isn't *my* Jack, and second, her name is Angelique."

"Whatever her birth name is, she goes by Angie, and he might as well be yours because he certainly is not hers any longer."

I smiled. My independent grandma was also a gossiper. The earth was tilting off its axis right then. "Okay, I'm listening. Tell me." I sat back, intently listening to my grandma's story.

"According to Margaret, they were due to marry this winter. Jack was going to move to California where she lives. He flew out there as a surprise and found her indisposed with another gentleman, some action-movie star. His name is something like Brad Blohard. Why anyone would watch those horrible things is beyond me."

"Bryce Blohunk? Grandma, he's like the biggest action-movie star there is. And you watch those awful horror movies—not sure there's much difference."

Grandma waved her hand in my face like I was speaking nonsense.

I thought for a minute about the possibility of Bryce and Angie. "That guy is so old, like sixty or something."

She frowned at me. "Need I remind you, Gracelynn, age is but a number?"

I nodded, since we both knew my grandma had stopped aging at forty-five. Or at least that's the age we had been celebrating with her every birthday for the last twenty-plus years.

"That's true, but the dude is like twice her age."

Grandma continued, "What I understand from Margaret is Jack broke it off immediately, but Angie kept begging for another chance, so he gave her one."

"And?"

"The same thing happened again, so he called off the wedding and has been focusing on getting his parents' home ready to put on the market. Still mending a broken heart, I imagine."

"Wow."

Grandma looked at me and smiled. "Yes, wow indeed. So ... how was your evening with Jack?"

"It was great, but ..."

"But what?"

"I saw a picture of the two of them when we were at his house, so I just assumed they were still together."

"Gracelynn, follow me." She pulled at the sleeve of my baseball shirt. We walked into my kitchen and stood in front of my refrigerator. "What is that?" She pointed to an empty magnetic frame.

"An empty frame?"

"And up until a month ago, what was in it?"

I dropped my head slightly. "A picture of Les and me."

"Yes, and why did you still have it on your refrigerator months after you were no longer together?"

I shrugged my shoulders.

"I am sorry—what did your shoulders just say?"

"Because, Grandma."

"Because a picture is a lasting memory, and as long as you have that, you still have something."

I nodded yes. "I'm not even sure if he will ask me out again. I mean, I'm no Angelique." I glanced at my feet: half of my toenails were partially painted, and the other half were naked.

"You are so much more than your storefront window, Gracelynn."

I looked at her, and she grabbed my chin.

"But you need to brush your teeth. Your breath is atrocious. No man likes a woman with unattended halitosis." She pulled me to her and hugged me, the smell of her perfume wrapping around me. "Teddy and I would like to take you and your father out for dinner this week. How about Tuesday?"

I started to say yes but remembered what I now did on Tuesday nights. "I think I have something on Tuesday. How about Wednesday?"

"I'll confirm and let you know. I need to get going. Teddy and I are attending an Oktoberfest party."

"On a Sunday? You live a wild and crazy life."

"Well, one of us should. And Gracelynn, it should be you and not your forty-five-year-old grandmother."

I nodded.

After my grandma left, I dug my phone out of my coat. Sure enough, there were four missed calls from my grandma. There were also six text messages.

Chloe
Hey, toots. How was the night? I got called into a surgery.
Will talk to you later.

Jack B
Hey

Dad
Be home Tuesday. Want to get dinner?

Chloe
Surgery delayed. Bored waiting for the doctor to show up. Damn surgeons. Remind me why I became a nurse and not an architect?

Jack B
Heading to my parents' place today around noon. Thought maybe we could hang out if you don't have anything going.

Jack B
Truth—I hope you don't have anything going.

I texted Jack first. It was almost noon, and I was worried I had missed my opportunity with him.

Me
Hey there. Sorry, just saw your message. I have rearranged my calendar to hang out with my favorite serial killer at noon if you're still free.

Ten agonizing minutes passed with no message back. I kept checking my phone to make sure I didn't miss it. I was washing my hair when I heard the chirp.

Jack B
Great. How many serial killers do you know that you have a favorite??

Me
You'd be surprised. Want me to meet you at your parents?

Jack B
That would be great. I'm already here.

Me
What's the address?

Jack B
1123 Hillside Drive. Just give the guard my name.

Me
Cool. I'll pick up lunch.

As I pulled into Hillside Estates, I felt out of place. My Honda seemed like a beater car in this very upscale subdivision. I stopped at the gate.

"Delivery?" The security officer stepped outside his gatehouse and looked at me.

"Sorry?" I said, confused.

He pointed to the large white bags of food on my passenger seat. "Are you here on a delivery?"

I felt my face go flush. He thought I was bringing someone takeout food. "No, I'm here for Jack Bradshaw."

"Ms. Anderson?"

I nodded.

"My apologies. I'm Joe. Pleased to meet you. Mr. Bradshaw is expecting you. Straight down this road. It's the house at the end of the street."

As I reached the end of the street, my mouth dropped. In front of me, double wrought-iron gates protected a massive house. I was used to large homes in my grandma's neighborhood, but beyond these gates was something I'd never seen. In the middle of the gates was a large B.

The gates slowly opened, and I drove past them and into the circle driveway. The double red doors opened, and out Jack walked.

"Joe thought I was the delivery guy."

"You're way too pretty to be the delivery guy." Jack leaned in and kissed me.

We entered a massive foyer with a large winding staircase. "Jeez, Jack. I thought your place downtown was big, but this is crazy."

"It's been in my family for a long time." He led me to the back of the house and into the kitchen, which was nearly the size of my entire house. We sat at the counter eating and talking. "I made a specialty drink in honor of the occasion. Want to try it?"

"What's the occasion?"

"I convinced you to go out with me twice."

"And you haven't killed me once."

He laughed, putting a blue concoction in front of me.

"And what are we drinking today?"

"It's called blue passion. Try it and tell me what you think."

I took a sip and instantly felt the rush of alcohol. "Whew. It's strong."

"You don't have to drink it if you don't like it."

I shook my head. "It's really good, but I better go slow—too early in the day to be falling-down drunk."

He took two big chugs of his drink and smiled at me. "You want a tour?"

As he walked me through the house, I stopped in the hallway to look at the family pictures hanging on the pewter-colored walls. Jack stood behind me. I could feel the warmth of his body on my back, and I was starting to feel surges of excitement pulse through me.

"Those are my grandparents." He pointed to a young couple with serious faces. "My great-grandparents are in this one."

I glanced at the photos and finally found a familiar face. "This is your mom and dad, right?"

He leaned in with his cheek nearly touching mine. "Yes. That's them." His dad stood in military uniform, tall, blond hair, brown eyes. His mom wore a satin wedding dress, and her brown hair enveloped her face in waves. Her blue eyes were bright, and her red lip stain outlined a beaming smile.

"Your mom is beautiful." He was still standing behind me, with our cheeks nearly touching. He slipped his hand into mine, interlacing our fingers. I was just about ready to turn and kiss him when I saw another familiar face. "I know this one too."

Jack pulled away from me. "Yeah, that's me and my ex. C'mon. I'll show you the rest of the house."

"We're not done yet?"

He pulled me away from the wall of photos. "Nah, we're just getting started."

My tour ended in the classic car garage, and as we sat in a vintage Stingray, Jack finally talked about the picture. "I thought after you saw the picture of Angie and me last night, you wouldn't want to see me again."

"Well ..." I wasn't sure what to say but decided to be honest. "I wondered if you guys were still together. It felt weird thinking I was invading someone else's territory."

"We were together for a long time. We broke up this summer." He was rubbing his hands around the steering wheel.

"What happened?" I didn't want to tell him I already knew because what I'd heard might not even be the real story.

Jack looked at me. "Tell me this, Gracie. You ever cheat?"

I bit the corner of my lip. "Once."

"Really?" Disappointment moved across his face.

"At cards against my grandpa. I probably could have beaten him fair and square, but I couldn't resist the temptation."

He laughed.

"It felt dirty to win that way."

"But you've never cheated in a relationship?"

"No."

"I didn't think so. You don't seem like the type."

"So I'm guessing, by the line of questioning, she cheated on you?"

"Yes, more than once."

"You don't deserve that. No one deserves that."

"That's really nice of you to say."

We were silent for a minute. "You still love her?"

"I'm not really sure."

I felt my heart sink a little. "How long were you together?"

"Forever."

"Kind of like me and my ex."

He looked over at me, eyebrows raised. "Do tell."

"Nothing really to tell. I thought we were happy, but I guess we weren't." Talking about it, I felt a sting in my heart.

"Did you break up with him, or did he break up with you?"

"I guess it was mutual. I asked him one night if he ever thought about getting married, and he said yes, just not to me."

"Damn. Really?"

"In hindsight, I dodged a bullet, but then it felt like a knife to my heart. I don't think I loved him anyway."

"I thought you said you had been in love before?"

"Yes, just not with Les."

"If he didn't want to be with you, he must not be into girls."

I laughed. "You sound like Chloe."

He smiled.

"How about you? I asked you if you had ever been in love, and you said no."

"I don't think what I had with Angie qualifies as real love."

"I see."

"The first time I caught Angie cheating on me, my dad told me to overlook it, like a personality flaw."

"That's a pretty big flaw."

"Like everyone, my dad was caught up with what she looks like on the outside instead of who she really is on the inside."

"Looks great in the window, but doesn't match what you find inside the store."

"What?" Jack gave me a puzzled look.

"Just something my grandma says. People are like store windows. You have to look good on the outside for someone to want to get to know you on the inside. Sometimes people can look great on the outside, but on the inside, their racks are empty."

"I wish I could completely forget about her, but it's not that easy. She's Ellie's best friend."

I nearly choked on my tongue. "Really?"

"Yeah. That's how I met her. She does modeling."

I nodded, tugging at the bottom of my emerald blouse.

"You could model."

"Hardly." I laughed, expecting Jack to laugh with me.

But he continued looking at me straight-faced. He was serious.

"Jack, no way in hell."

"Why not? You have the most beautiful eyes I've ever seen. And your smile? It's amazing. Trust me, I definitely stopped at your store window."

"I'm too short."

"You're gorgeous, Gracie."

"That's what all serial killers say to their victims."

"I'm pretty sure they don't."

I grabbed the collar of his shirt, pulled him to me, and kissed him. He pulled me on top of him, and my right butt cheek pressed against the steering wheel, causing the car horn to blow. I tried to adjust my position and found myself wedged between the steering wheel and Jack. I was uncomfortable, and even though I should have been enjoying what he was attempting to do to me, I was feeling just the opposite.

I tried to pull away from him slightly. "Jack?"

He said nothing, continuing to run his hands up my back.

As I shifted again, his hand got caught inside my shirt, his fingers pinching my skin. "Ouch!"

"What?" He stopped and looked at me.

"I'm squished."

"Oh, sorry." He attempted to push me off him, but the more he pushed, the less I was able to move.

I felt a buzzing against my thigh. It started soft and then gradually grew stronger.

"That's my phone," he said. With one final push, I was free from the steering wheel. Jack pulled his phone out. I tried not to look, but as I moved, I saw the name on the screen: Angie.

"You need to get that?"

He looked at it and put it back in his pocket. "Nah." He took my hand and helped me out of the car. "I hate to do this, but I have a ton of work to do before tomorrow. Do you mind if we continue this another time?"

I felt my heart begin to splinter. "Sure. No problem."

"Sorry about that. I'll need to pull an all-nighter to get this brief done." Holding my hand, he led me to the door. We were standing at the door when his phone began to buzz again.

"I can see myself out," I said. He leaned in and kissed me lightly on the lips.

I got in my car, knowing he was giving me the brush-off. I was never going to be able to compete with an ex-fiancée, especially one still tied to him. As I slowed up by the entrance gate on my way out, Joe waved at me. I waved back, wondering how many women he had waved good-bye to for Jack over the years.

I called Chloe on my way home and relayed the story to her.

"Well, I think you have a problem."

"What's that?"

"You like him way too much."

I was silent for a moment, knowing she was right. "What do you think about him?"

"He's not a lost cause, but he's definitely damaged goods. I don't think it will be as easy as it seems to be with him. You just have to decide."

"Decide what?"

"Decide how much of yourself you're willing to give him."

I thought for a moment. "How much should I give?"

"Oh, sweetie, you've already given too much."

"I should forget about him then?"

"I'm not saying he's not right for you. He very well could be. But before you try to fix someone else, you need to fix yourself."

"You think I'm broken?" I felt hurt by her words.

"No, not broken—more like a work in progress."

I hung up with Chloe, not feeling any better. She was always my sounding board, my voice of reason, but her words had just gotten tangled up in my already-complicated feelings.

A hot bath and an old movie didn't make me feel any better. I was heading to bed when my phone chirped.

Jack B
Hey. Sorry about earlier.

Me
No worries.

I really wanted to say it caused me big worries.

Jack B
Truth—I got a little freaked out when Angie called. Felt like I was cheating on her.

Me
Ironic, huh?

Jack B
Yeah. I like you. I'm just not sure what to do.

Me
Would you rather just be friends?

Just typing the words made my heart sink. I didn't want to just be his friend, but I knew I had to make the offer and chalk it up to another ill-fated romance if he said yes.

Jack B
No. U?

Me
No.

Jack B
I'm not great at this, but I'll do my best to get it right. How about dinner on Wed?

Me
I have dinner with my family on Wed. Maybe Thursday?

Jack B
How about we do dinner with your fam on Wed and Thurs just you and me?

Me
Two more dates with a serial killer? How can I say no?

Jack B
Serial killers can be so irresistible.

I wrapped myself up in a blanket and sat on my front porch swing. I wasn't sure when I dozed off, but the feeling of someone caressing my hair woke me. It was soothing, like the endless times I had spent nestled beside my mom.

"Gracie, it's time. It's time." The voice kept repeating this, over and over again.

"Time for what?" I tried to open my eyes.

"Time to wake up."

"Wake up for work?"

"Wake up for life."

I opened my eyes and felt the cold rush of night air hit my face. I looked around, rubbing my eyes and trying to focus. Leaves rustled in the night air, taking flight, not caring how far they traveled, just happy to be on a journey.

I sat there on my swing, alone. It was then I caught a glimpse of her standing in the shadows, watching me.

"Mom?" Leaves blew back and forth. The shadow did not move. "Is that you?"

The shadow moved farther back into the darkness of the night. *It's time to wake up for life, Gracie. Time to wake up.*

8

Monday came without much fanfare. I was still bothered by the experience of seeing my mom. I was unsure if it was really her or just a figment of my imagination. Maybe Dr. Gretchen was right about memories manifesting themselves into actual visions. I made it through my classes, watching my students feverishly working on their assignments.

As I sat reading a journal on the impact of parental loss on children, it struck me: I had never melted down after my mom died. I had never sought comfort in drugs or deviant behavior. I had never lashed out at someone. I had never set fire to our house or dyed my hair blue. One day I was at her funeral, and the next, I was working on school assignments. My scars ran so deep that I wasn't even sure where one stopped and another one started.

Why didn't we talk about my mom anymore? I didn't expect my dad to talk about her since he barely could talk to me at all. Teddy always wanted to protect me, so talking with him would be tough. But Grandma, she never pulled any punches. She never sugarcoated anything to save me from pain. She certainly never shied away from tough conversations; I think she thrived on them. Why didn't she talk about her? It began to eat away at me, so much so that it was all I could think about. I knew I needed answers, and I needed them immediately. I tried her house phone first only to be met with her very polite, but not overly friendly voice mail. I quickly dialed her cell phone.

"Hello, Blake Desiree Honoree Smith speaking." She always answered the phone that way, even though she had caller ID and knew it was me.

"Hey, Grandma. It's me."

"Yes, Gracelynn?"

"Where are you? I called the house, but no one answered." It was after three, and by this time, Grandma was usually back from running errands. For normal people, errands meant the grocery store, bank, post office, dry cleaner, car wash. For my grandma, errands meant hair salon, spa, lunch at the club, boutique shopping, and the occasional charity board meeting.

"I have one stop, and then I will be home."

"Okay, where are you going? I'll meet you there. I need to talk to you about something."

"What something do you need to talk about?" Her voice sounded different.

"I don't want to talk over the phone. Where are you? I'll meet you."

There was silence on the other end of the call.

"Grandma? Are you still there?" My grandma was never silent during conversations. She considered it rude not to respond promptly to people, especially over the phone.

"Very well. Meet me in the park by the old oak tree."

"Really?"

Silence again.

"Okay, I'll be there in a few."

As I pulled into the parking lot next to her Audi, my curiosity shifted gears. What was my grandma doing at the park? I remembered her telling me about going to the oak tree when she was younger, when she missed Teddy and the life she did not have, but why was she here now?

Daylight was waning as the leaves danced across the path. Teenagers playing soccer were trying to squeeze in the last remnants of the day. Two dogs pounced around as I walked past them, oblivious to my presence. A couple held hands, walking slowly, without purpose. As the walking path curved, I could see it: the massive old tree in the very middle of the park. Its branches reached up farther than my eyes could see. It was then I saw her, sitting on a bench by the tree. She sat looking at the tree, the wind blowing the leaves around her feet. She was motionless, her manicured hands resting on the bench.

"Grandma?"

She turned slowly and looked at me, saying nothing.

"Grandma, what's wrong?"

"Nothing, Gracelynn." She motioned for me to sit next to her, which I did.

"I don't remember this being here before." It was a beautiful oak bench. It looked fairly new, and ornate carved swirls served as arm rests.

"It has been here for two years." She looked back at the tree.

"Maybe it has been that long since I've been in this park." We sat in silence for a minute. The wind blew my hair back and forth. It tried to tousle Grandma's hair, but since she was a force all her own, not a hair moved out of place.

"Gracelynn, considering you could not wait to talk to me, what is on your mind?"

I hesitated for a minute, not sure how to start the conversation. It had been so long since we'd talked about her that the subject seemed taboo. "I was wondering why we don't talk about her."

"Talk about whom? You are an English professor. You should be more specific with your questions. I am sure you expect your students to provide clarity with theirs."

"Mom. Why don't we talk about Mom?" There, I'd said it. Taboo no more.

"Because you never bring her up."

I looked away, knowing she was right. "What are you doing in the park, Grandma?"

"I like it here. I find it comforting."

I looked at her. "Did something upset you?"

"Life upset me, Gracelynn." She remained still.

It was then I saw it—just behind my grandma's wool jacket, an engraved plate. "What's that behind your back?"

"It is a memory marker."

"What does it say?"

Her posture remained unchanged.

"Did you put this bench here?"

"Yes, I did."

"And that's your memory marker?"

"It is."

"Can I read it?"

She slowly turned her head to look at me and then moved slightly, exposing the gold plate.

In loving memory of our Cassandra
Even the angels carrying your wings
needed to rise up to meet you

"This is a bench for Mom?"

She nodded, saying nothing.

I thought for a minute. "Why here? She never really came to this park."

"It just made sense."

I was puzzled. Then a memory came rushing back. After my mother's cremation, we had gone to the funeral home to collect her ashes. I remained in the car, not wanting to be there, on an errand no one should be running. They stood in the parking lot talking, my dad nodding at my grandma. She hugged him, dotted her eyes with a tissue, and accepted the urn from my dad.

"Did you bring her ashes here?"

She nodded again.

"I don't get it. Why here?" I asked again.

"This is where her life began, so it made sense to bring her back here again at the end."

"That makes no sense. How could Mom's life begin at this tree?" As the words left my mouth, I realized I knew the answer.

She sat caressing the park bench. "It just made sense."

"Did Grandpa know about you and Teddy and ... Mom?" It was an unreal moment, made very real by my grandma.

"Yes. I was devastated about losing Teddy. I was angry at my parents for forcing me to marry your grandfather, and so I took it out on him. I withheld intimacy from him for as long as I could. Two months passed, and by then, I already knew I was with child."

"I don't get it. Why didn't you just leave Grandpa and marry Teddy if you were having his baby?"

My grandma looked at me and frowned. "Even if I thought about leaving your grandfather, I would have been ostracized by my parents. It would have been complete betrayal. I could stay with your grandfather and pray he would love the baby as his own or see if Teddy would take me back."

"You told Grandpa, right?"

"Yes, and he begged me to stay with him. He promised he would love your mother like his own. And he did. I knew it was the right thing to do."

I was somewhat stunned. "What about Teddy?"

"You mean, does he know?"

I nodded, feeling horrible for Teddy.

"Not until your mother was around four. He came back to town for his father's funeral, and that is when I told him."

"How did he take it?"

She pulled her jacket zipper up slightly. "He agreed to not tell your mother as long as he was able to have full access to her whenever he wanted. And we agreed."

"*We*, as in you and Grandpa?"

"Yes. Your grandfather agreed as well."

My emotional pendulum swung back to my grandpa. How horrible it must have been for him to know that not only did his wife truly belong to someone else, but so did his daughter.

"Did you ever tell Mom?"

She was quiet for a moment. "I did."

"What did she say?"

"Let me just say we both made our peace with it in our own way."

We sat quietly for a few minutes.

"How often do you come here?"

"Daily."

"Does Teddy know?"

"He is the one who had the bench made."

"And you come here every day? Grandma, the weather gets pretty bad for you to be trudging through the rain and snow."

"Teddy made arrangements to have the path plowed when it snows. I carry an umbrella in my car for when it rains and for the sun when it is too warm."

"I see." Thinking out loud, I said, "You had bronchitis last year. You were down for the count for like three days."

"Teddy came for both of us those days."

"Wait. Teddy comes too?"

"Yes. We do not come together, though. I like it to be just her and me—our time."

"So this is where she rests?"

"Her final resting place? No. She is not just here with this tree.

She is that bright star you seek out in the sky; she is that leaf moving in the air; she is the song in the wind. She is everywhere."

"Does anyone else know about this place? Know about Teddy?"

"No."

"Then why tell me?"

"Because I am too old to keep secrets, and you are old enough to know the truth."

"Thank you, Grandma, for telling me."

"Gracelynn, your mother is as alive as you want her to be. You can hide her away in your memories and pretend she never existed, or you can acknowledge that all that is real and good inside of you came from her."

We sat on the bench until the sun fell behind the horizon and the moon took over the fading sky. We walked back to our cars in silence. As we stood in the near darkness, I was the first to speak.

"I won't come again, Grandma, but I appreciate you letting me spend time with you here today."

"If you believe this will make you feel close to your mother again, I believe you should come here."

I nodded but said nothing.

"I am here later today than normal. Teddy will be worried." I could hear her cell phone ringing as she opened her car door. "That is probably Teddy."

As I was opening my door, she rolled down her window.

"I do not tell you because you should already know, but I am proud of you, Gracelynn. And I know she would be as well."

My heart sank slightly. My mom would have been my biggest cheerleader, the one standing next to me every step of the way. How sad for both of us that it was not meant to be.

As I walked in my front door, my phone chirped.

Jack B
You busy?

Me

Nah. Was just hanging with my grandma.

Jack B

I heard about her. Her reputation precedes her.

Me

Lol. She is a force of nature.

Jack B

I believe the word used was ballbuster.

Me

Sounds about right. Fair warning, she is one to reckon with.

Jack B

I'll take my chances.

Jack B

You know you're like no one I've ever met before.

Me

Is that a good thing?

Jack B

Better than a good thing.

I tossed and turned most of the night, until I knew sleep would not be mine. I wondered how my mom felt when my grandma finally told her the truth. Had she ever wondered about Teddy, considering that he was always around? I had assumed that Teddy remained close to us all those years because of my grandma, but in actuality, he was there for so much more. He was there for his family, woven together by secrets and lies.

All day long, it haunted me, this secret of mine, which really wasn't mine at all. As I pulled into the community center parking lot, it was all I could think of. I was on the verge of obsession.

"Welcome back," Dr. Gretchen began. "I trust you all had a thought-provoking few days. Tonight, I'd like for us to—"

"Who I thought was my grandfather all these years isn't. And who I thought was just a family friend turns out to be my grandfather." The words were out of my mouth before I knew they were coming.

"Gracie, it seems like you have something on your mind you'd like to share?"

All eyes were on me. My face blistered red. I had just handed my family secret, the one that was not mine to share, to six other people like it was the classified section of a newspaper.

"Uh, well ..."

Mindy smiled at me. "It's okay. You can tell us."

My grandma would not be accepting of this group or what I had just told them.

"Gracie, we're all sisters here." Ginger, sporting her sapphire-blue contacts, blinked her fake eyelashes at me.

Sisters? As I looked at each one of them and they looked back at me, I felt a sense of belonging rush over me. It was a strange feeling, one I had never felt before. I was safe in their arms.

"My grandma told me my real grandfather is a friend of ours. My mom actually has a different father than she was brought up to believe."

"And how does that make you feel?" Dr. Gretchen leaned into the circle toward me.

"Sad." It was an immediate response.

"Why sad?" Mandie asked.

"Not sad for me. Sad for her."

"Sad for whom?" Ellie raised a perfectly arched eyebrow.

"Sad for her mom," Ginger said.

I nodded.

"Why?" Sarah asked, her voice strong.

"Because it's not fair."

"What would you say to your mom if she were here right now?" Dr. Gretchen inquired.

"I would tell her I loved her."

"Of course you would. But what would you say to her about this secret you now know?"

I looked out the window for a minute. "I would say she deserved better than the fake circumstances of her life."

"Anyone else like to share thoughts?" Dr. Gretchen opened her question to the circle.

"I would tell my mom to hire someone to fix the garage door. It would have been money well spent." Ginger shrugged her shoulders as she spoke.

"I would tell my mom to leave my dad," Ellie said.

I looked over at her, surprised. I wanted to ask her why but didn't.

"I would tell my mom …" Sarah's voice trailed off.

I could see the waterworks beginning to form. Ginger used her stiletto boot to slide Sarah's purse beyond her reach.

"I would tell her I'm sorry for doing what I did. I just didn't see any life without her."

I noticed Ellie's already-perfect posture straighten even more as the words slipped from Sarah's mouth.

"What did you do?" Ginger's voice was filled with concern.

"I took some pills." Sarah's head dropped in shame.

"Sleeping pills?" Ellie asked.

"Diet pills." The room was silent. "All I got was diarrhea."

"Why did you take diet pills?" Mindy asked.

"It was either diet pills or gas pills. I thought maybe the diet pills would work better."

"I'm not really sure any pills would be the right choice, Sarah, ya know?" Ginger used a long red fingernail to adjust one of her eyelashes.

"Tell us about your life now, Sarah," said Dr. Gretchen, trying to break through to Sarah.

"What life?" Sarah sounded defeated.

I looked down, sad for her, wondering when her life had become nothing to her.

"Well, what did you do yesterday?"

"I worked, went home, ate, had sex, and went to sleep. Same thing I do almost every day."

"Say again?" I must have misunderstood her. I thought she'd said she had sex, but she must have said "played the sax."

"I worked, ate, had sex, and went to sleep." Yep, that's what she'd said. Sarah Bland was having sex, which was more than I was having.

"Does physical intimacy lessen your pain?" Dr. Gretchen asked Sarah.

She shook her head.

"Thinking sex takes away the pain is wishful thinking," said Ellie. "It's only an emotional mask. It never fixes the problem. It always comes back tenfold."

I looked over at Ellie. Twice tonight she had surprised me with her comments.

"Sarah, when was the last time you felt good about something?"

Sarah looked sideways at Dr. Gretchen. "Last Friday, when I left session. It made me feel good to be here."

"Well, that's a start."

Sarah smiled.

"I agree," Ginger said, readjusting her push-up bra.

"What do all of you think your best quality is that you got from your mom?" Dr. Gretchen nodded at Ginger to start.

"Strength," Ginger said.

Ellie was next. "Forgiveness."

"Humor," I declared.

It was Sarah's turn. She was quiet for a moment. "Intelligence."

I shook my head, and Dr. Gretchen frowned at me.

"No," I said. "I would say brave. And not just Sarah—it's all of you. You are brave in times when you feel paralyzed by your emotions. No one forced you to be here, and yet you sit here with me." My words came so quickly that I almost forgot I really didn't know these women and had no right to tell them how I felt about them.

Ellie slid her hands over her bangs. "Other than Jack, I've never really had anyone to talk to about losing my mother. No one really understood, until now. I'm not sure why I feel like I've known you all forever."

"Because in a way, you have," Ginger said. "Inside, we're the same person. We have holes so big inside us that only someone else with the same hole gets what that feels like."

I looked at Ginger for a long moment. She was someone else on the outside tonight, but the real her was still on the inside.

"How do you fill the hole?" Sarah asked with a glimmer of hope in her voice.

"You don't." Ellie's response was clear and present. "You don't."

For the next hour, we talked about our lives in the present tense. We were not allowed to talk about what we could not fix; we could talk only about what we could control. If we could choose our own path in life, with or without our mothers, Dr. Gretchen wanted to know, where would that path take us? And then the bigger question: what was stopping us from taking it? The answer was the same six times over: our own selves.

As the session drew to a close, Dr. Gretchen wrote each of our names on a piece of paper and placed them in a brown paper bag. The task was simple: draw a name, look at that person, and say one positive thing about her. In turn, the person was not allowed to self-deprecate or dismiss what was said. The only allowable response was "Thank you." I was the first to pick.

I looked at Ginger. "You're one of a kind. And that's a good thing. In a world filled with gray, you paint with bold colors."

"Thank you," Ginger said. She drew Mandie's name and turned to her. "You really care about people and you got a big heart." Mandie mouthed thank you and pulled Mindy's name.

"You pull no punches and call it like it is and that's awesome." Mindy laughed in agreement before pulling Ellie's name.

"You are beautiful on the inside and out."

Ellie said thank you and drew the next name. "Sarah, you have strength inside of you that will help you get through anything. You just have to find it."

Sarah picked the next name and was silent for a moment. She turned and looked at me. "You inspire me to want to live."

I instinctively started to disagree with her but stopped. "Thank you."

As the session ended, Dr. Gretchen gave us a homework assignment. We were to write a letter to our mothers and bring it to the next session.

"But you know we can't send them, right, because they're dead?" Ginger's question was serious.

"Yes, I am aware. Sometimes, though, it's helpful to write down your thoughts—what you're thinking and how you are feeling," Dr. Gretchen explained.

"Oh, I see."

At the session's end, all the women did something that caught me by surprise: they all hugged one another. Everyone trickled out of the room until only Sarah and I remained, gathering our things.

"Hey, Sarah."

"Hey, Gracie," she replied, rubbing the handle of her purse, something I could tell she did often because the leather on it was faded, worn, and cracked. "I want to get where you are now. I mean ... I want to get past the pain and find peace with it. You know?"

I hugged her tight. "So ... you work at the library?" I said, pulling away and shifting the conversation.

She nodded yes.

"Which library?"

"Loyola. I've been there for ten years."

"Wow. Impressive."

She half-smiled, soaking in the compliment. "That's where I met my fiancé."

I looked down at her left hand and finally noticed it, a sapphire and ruby ring surrounded by tiny diamonds. "Your ring is really pretty."

"Thanks. We're getting married in May."

"It sounds like you have some great things happening in your life. Why don't you think any of it is good?"

She was quiet for a moment. "I used to be different, you know. I wasn't like this. I'm surprised Jerry asked me out. I had some days I couldn't even brush my hair after she died. The simple things seemed so hard all of a sudden."

I nodded. "Are they getting easier now?"

"Not really. But I'm trying. I promised Jerry I would."

"Are you excited about getting married?"

"I guess."

"Are you having second thoughts?"

"About Jerry? No. About life? Yes."

"In your letter to your mom, tell her all the good things in your life now."

She thought for a minute. "I can tell her about you guys too."

"Yes. Make me prettier and smarter, though, okay?" I laughed, expecting Sarah to laugh with me.

But her face was emotionless. "Why don't you see yourself like others see you?" Sarah Bland practically knocked me off my feet with her words.

"I'm not sure."

"Then maybe you should ask your mom in your letter."

Later, I kept thinking about what Sarah had said to me. Maybe she was right. Jack liked me, so that had to mean something. I was almost hoping he would back out of dinner since my grandma could be ruthless. She found a thousand faults in me, but she found a thousand and one faults in anyone I dated. No one could measure up to her standards. She had been merciless with Les, often to his face.

"So, Lester, you are an optometrist? That is a fake doctor, correct?"

For years every conversation with her had started, "Gracelynn, how is your subpar boyfriend?"

So I was disappointed when Jack texted me to tell me he couldn't wait to have dinner with my family.

Jack B
Any words of advice when it comes to your grandma?

Me
Wear a shield of armor.

Jack B
It's laid out with my favorite tie.

Jack B
Was Ellie in session? She was having a fight with Bruce. I was worried about her.

Me
Yes. Everything ok with them?

Jack B
Bruce has a wandering eye. Ellie said it's harmless but that's what I thought about Angie.

Me
Why would he want to cheat on her?

Jack B
Directors have God complexes sometimes.

Me
He's a movie director?

Jack B
Ever see The Never Ending Night? That's one of his.

Me
Are you kidding me? My grandma loves those movies. There's been like seven of them. All of which she has forced me to watch on movie night.

Jack B
You have movie night?

Me
Sadly yes.

Jack B
Don't you ever get to pick the movie?

Me
I get one movie a month. She's in charge of the rest. Like everything.

Jack B
Good to know.

Me
What's your favorite movie?

Jack B
The Grand Illusion.

Me
Never heard of it.

Jack B
Old war movie, more about characters and their complexities than actual war.

Me
Sounds like dinner with my grandma.

Jack B
Yours?

Me
It's a Wonderful Life. Haven't watched it in forever though.

Jack B
We should have our own movie night and watch our faves.

A pang of sorrow rushed over me. I hadn't watched it since my mom died, and the thought of it still haunted me. My response was just the opposite of how I was feeling. "Sounds great," I typed.

★ ★ ★

By three o'clock, I was craving a nap to build up strength before dinner. I had a feeling I would need it. While I was taking a hot bath, a new emotion took over—panic. I barely knew Jack myself, and I was putting him in front of my grandma. What was I thinking? As I was stepping out of the bathtub, I heard my doorbell ring.

I opened the door to find a package containing two movies, *The Grand Illusion* and *It's a Wonderful Life*, along with movie candy and microwave popcorn. I opened the attached card: "I can't wait for movie night," the card read.

I knew the other shoe was bound to fall. I just didn't know when. Chloe said he was damaged goods. What if Angie came back for another chance? Old habits could die very hard. I knew that myself.

I put on a sheer black blouse with bold red and yellow flowers on it. The blouse was from my grandma, and I knew that if I didn't wear it, I would never hear the end of it. I paired the top with form-fitting black pants, and I had to admit I looked pretty good.

By the time Jack picked me up and we pulled into the club parking lot, we were officially six minutes late. It was a horrible way to start off the evening with my grandma.

Jack's hand found its way to mine as we walked into the club. He leaned in. "Don't worry, Gracie. I got this."

I smiled, feeling a sudden onset of spastic colon. As we approached the table, I saw Grandma and Teddy and five empty seats. This was strange because my grandma never allowed the table settings to be any more or less than the exact number of attendees.

"Hey, Grandma. Sorry we're late."

My grandma stood, looking not at me but at her watch. Teddy gave me a long hug.

"Teddy, Grandma, this is Jack Bradshaw."

My grandma lowered her glasses to give Jack a long once-over.

"Pleased to meet you both." Jack shook Teddy's hand. "I've heard a lot about you."

"And what have you heard?" my grandma curtly asked.

"Uh, well, all good things, of course." Jack was starting to fumble.

"Then you must not have talked to many people, Mr. Bradshaw."

Jack smiled. "Please call me Jack."

"Oh, Mr. Bradshaw, we are not even close to calling each other by our first names."

"Doll baby, give the boy a break. They just got here," Teddy said as she motioned for us to sit in strategically placed seats.

I shot a look at Teddy. Grandma was obviously on her A game tonight.

"So, Jack, I hear you're a lawyer. What kind of law?"

I smiled at Teddy. He was my knight in shining armor, yet again.

"Mergers and acquisitions, mostly."

Teddy nodded, wiping the butter off his "Boo-yah!" T-shirt. "Sounds fun."

"Gracie tells me you own your own business—garbage, right?"

Teddy nodded. "Supply and demand keeps me in business. There will always be trash, you know?"

Jack nodded and smiled. "True."

It was awkwardly silent for a minute. I could see the wheels turning in my grandma's mind.

"Grandma, what's with the extra seats? It's just Dad, right?"

"Finally," Grandma said, looking past me. My grandma stood and walked toward three people standing at the door.

I shifted in my seat and accidentally knocked over my water. Fumbling to capture the liquid and ice as it cascaded down the side of the table, I missed their approach. I stood, hitting my head on the edge of the table. "Ouch." As I was rubbing my head, I heard the introductions.

"This is Gracie's friend, Jack …"

"Bradshaw. Nice to meet you." I squinted, trying to shake off the pain, as Jack shook hands.

"Nice to meet you as well."

My eyes opened and focused when I heard the voice. It was a voice I could never forget. I turned to meet him, feeling the rush like I first had as a young girl.

"Hi, Sam."

9

There were fleeting times in my life when I felt like I had complete control, like nothing and no one could shake my rock-solid foundation. This was not one of those times.

"How long has it been?" Sam said.

I just stood there looking at him, not sure when my tongue had left my mouth, preventing me from speaking.

"You guys know each other?" Jack stared at both of us with a quizzical look on his face.

"We go way back. Right, G?"

I nodded, still not able to string words into a sentence.

"Well," said my grandma, "now that everyone is here, why don't we sit down for dinner?"

My dad took a seat next to Mrs. Patterson. I half-stumbled to my seat. Jack sat on one side of me, and Sam took the seat on the other side of me. I wanted to slide under the table and crawl out the door.

"So, Sam, what have you been up to with your life?" Teddy asked, trying to break the titanic block of ice.

"Well, I'm a high school teacher and football coach."

I tried not to look directly at him, but I couldn't help myself. Even hidden behind black scruff, the half-moons were still very much present. His hair was short, his body muscular. He looked exactly as I had thought he would look light-years from when we were kids. My heart began beating out of time. Jack reached over and grabbed my hand. I was literally stuck between an old love and a new love, a rock and a hard place.

"Good for you—turning your love of football into a career." Teddy turned his focus to the menu.

"At least I managed to do something good with one thing I love." Sam looked at me, but I pretended to be reading the menu.

"Lovely. Are you married?" my grandma asked, much to my dismay.

"No, ma'am."

"And why is that?"

"Grandma, that's none of our business." I felt embarrassed by her need to know everything like it was her right.

"That's okay, G. I don't mind answering. I let the right one get away."

Sam looked at Jack for longer than I thought was necessary. "You look familiar. Did you play high school ball?"

"Yes, for Westminster."

Sam tapped his hand on the table. "That's where I know you! I remember playing you. Tight end, right?"

"Yes. Wait, were you Highmore's QB?"

I could feel my stomach starting to churn. "Yeah, small world."

I smiled at Jack. He held my hand under the table, rubbing the top of my hand with his thumb. If Sam hadn't been sitting on the other side of me and my grandma directly across, I might have enjoyed this quiet display of affection.

"Jeffrey, shall you share your news with everyone?"

I looked at my dad. He shot my grandma a look.

"What news?" Sam asked, drinking from what was left of the water glass I'd spilled.

"Yeah, what news?" I looked at my dad.

"We're getting married!" Mrs. Patterson threw her hand up in the air to show off her engagement ring.

"You're what?" Sam and I said at the same time.

"Lovely! Just lovely!" Grandma exposed her perfect white teeth, and at that moment, I wanted to wipe that perfect smile right off her face.

"Are you kidding me right now?" I felt a hot burst of energy scorching inside me.

"Gracelynn, kindly refrain from acting out and share your congratulations with your father and Lacey." My grandma was treating me like a child, which was a mistake, considering it only fueled my anger even more.

"And how long have you known about this, Grandmother?"

My grandma pushed her glasses on top of her head, a sign she was ready for a fight, verbal or otherwise. "Long enough to be happy for them. You should do the same."

I looked at Sam, who sat dumbfounded. "How about you? Did you know?"

Sam shook his head. "Mom, you just told me you had a friend, not a fiancé."

Mrs. Patterson sat back in her chair. "Well, you haven't exactly been around for me to tell you."

Sam looked down. I could see the guilt of being an absentee son wash over him.

"What's your excuse?" I stood, scowling at my dad. "I talk to you all the time, and you have not once mentioned this relationship to me. Not once."

"Gracelynn, you need to calm down." My grandma pointed for me to take my seat.

"You need to stay out of this, Grandma. With all due respect, I'm done with family secrets."

"And how long have you guys been together?" I looked at Mrs. Patterson.

"A couple of years."

"C'mon!" My anger was at its brink.

My dad rose to his feet, slowly. "Gracie, a moment, please?"

"Really? A couple of years?"

"Gracie? A moment, please." This time it was not a question but an order. I had no interest in moving from where I stood, partially because my legs were shaking so much that I wasn't sure they would carry me anywhere else right then.

"You have something to say to me, you say it right here, Dad."

"Gracie, you are just like your mother." He put his hands in his pockets and shook his head.

"Hasn't that always been the problem? I'm too much like my mother?"

"What?"

I had clearly hit a nerve, for his eyes were glued on me now. "That's why you can barely be in the same room with me, right? You can't forget about her because that's all you see when you see me. You see her, and you hate it."

"Is that what you think?" My dad's eyebrows rose.

"No, that's what I know." I felt the angry tears welling in my eyes.

"Gracelynn, I do not know where you get such ideas," my grandma interjected. But she had no right to in this moment.

"Grandma, this has nothing to do with you, so I suggest you back off." I felt a hand grab my shaking hand for support. My eyes were still on my dad.

"Not true, Gracie," my dad responded.

"You know, Dad, I think you wish it was me and not Mom who died. I have always been second best with you anyway." Words that had been locked away for years, waiting for the chance to be free, were flying out of my mouth.

"Gracie, I'm not sure where you're coming from with all this. Maybe it's that support group you've been going to …"

"What support group?" Grandma sounded shocked.

I rolled my eyes. "Yes, Grandma, I am going to a support

group—you know, therapy, which is nothing more than telling complete strangers our personal business."

My grandma looked mortified. "What will people say?" I thought she was going to vomit.

"Gracie, what do you want me to say? You look and act just like your mother." My dad was still standing, faced off against me.

"That's not my problem. That's yours."

His lips curved downward. "Are you saying you aren't happy for us?"

"No, that's not what I'm saying, but how about giving me more than two seconds to process?"

"I didn't know I had to ask you for permission to live my life."

My mind was on fire. "You know, you have never bothered to include me on anything about your life. You talk to me about a thousand meaningless things, but when it comes to something big—huge—like this, you fail to mention it. For two years, Dad. Two years." I felt the tears rolling down my face. The hand connected to mine squeezed harder.

"I couldn't." My dad finally looked away from me.

"Why, Dad? Is it that painful to be around me?"

He rubbed his eyes, saying nothing at first. "Yes."

I stood there frozen. The truth, though I had waited for years to hear it, felt like a blow to my heart. "Well then, I think it's time for me to leave."

"Now, let's just take a minute and catch our breaths," Teddy said. He was trying as only Teddy could to fill in the cracks of our fractured family foundation.

"I don't think so, Teddy." I pulled at the hand still holding mine. "Jack, let's go."

Jack stood up to leave. As my eyes followed my arm down to our clasped hands, I finally realized it: Jack's hands remained by his side; it was Sam's hand holding onto mine.

The car ride home was silent. Jack drove as I kept replaying the scenario I had just lived through over and over in my head.

"Is Sam someone I should be worried about?"

"What?" I was lost in my own thoughts, oblivious to Jack's.

"Sam. Is he someone to you?"

"God, no."

We sat in front of my house. Jack looked at me like he wasn't sure he believed me. "I like you, Gracie, a lot. I just can't end up being the odd man out again."

"I have known Sam all my life, that's all."

"Those are the ones you have to worry about. They never seem to go away."

"Did you say you like me ... a lot?"

The disbelief on his face evaporated. "Maybe." He smiled and leaned into me, kissing me softly on the lips. "Tell you what, why don't we just hang out at your place tonight?"

"Sounds like a most excellent plan."

I ordered a pizza, and we sat down on my couch. He pulled me on top of him, and starting at my ear lobe, he worked his way down to my chest, kissing me. His lips felt soft and warm. The farther down he traveled, the farther I wanted him to go. I pulled at his shirt, untucking it from his jeans. I unbuttoned his shirt, kissing the naked skin exposed with each opened button. I made my way to his belly button, smiling at the thought of what I was doing.

The doorbell rang. I ignored it at first, until the third ring.

"Ready for pizza?" I said.

"Ready for something, but it's definitely not pizza."

I laughed and started to stand up.

He pulled me back down on top of him. "Maybe they'll just go away." He began kissing the side of my neck.

The knocking at the door finally broke me away from him. When I opened the door, I expected to see the pizza delivery boy.

Sam stood in front of me instead. "Hey, G."

I looked over at Jack, who was lying on the couch, shirt unbuttoned, oblivious to our unannounced guest.

I slipped out the door and shut it quietly behind me. "What's up, Sam?"

"Were you busy?" He looked at my tousled hair and uneven shirt.

I pulled at my shirt to straighten it. "Kinda. What's up?"

"I just wanted to make sure you were okay."

I took a long look at him as the moon sent a shadowy glow over his face. I felt a pang of love lost. "I'm good. Sorry about earlier."

"You shouldn't be sorry. Not cool what they did. Total ambush."

I nodded. "Thanks for checking on me. I'm surprised you knew where to find me."

"Teddy."

"Got it." I caught a glimpse of the delivery boy walking up with the pizza.

"I was just going to ask you if you'd eaten yet. Looks like you're just about to."

The door opened, and Jack stepped out in his bare feet, shirt half-unbuttoned. "Gracie, you okay?" Jack looked at Sam.

"Hey, Jack." Sam gave a quick smile. "Well, it looks like you guys are about to eat. I should get going. Just thought I'd check on G to make sure she was okay."

"You hungry?" I asked, expecting him to say no.

"Actually, I am. I took off not too long after you guys did. Never got a chance to eat. I was just going to hit a drive-through."

"By all means, join us," Jack said.

I shot Jack a look, and he shrugged his shoulders.

"Cool. Thanks." Sam stepped past Jack and me.

A large sausage and pepperoni pizza and a twelve-pack of beer later, the three of us sat on my living room floor, laughing and talking. It was almost eleven.

"Gracie, you forgot to tell me it was a party."

I laughed as Jack brought in a bottle of vodka and a lemon from the kitchen. There was no way I was going to match Jack and Sam shot for shot, so for every two they did, I did one, until the bottle was nearly empty.

Sam took a shot and flipped his glass upside down on the table. "Hey, I think I saw you in a rag magazine in my dentist's office. Weren't you with some model?"

"Yeah." Jack smiled at him with a lemon wedge in his mouth.

I laughed.

"She was smokin' hot," Sam said.

"I guess." Jack poured the last of the vodka into his glass and gulped it down.

"You definitely upgraded with this one," Sam said, pointing at me.

Jack nodded. "Definitely."

I lowered my head onto Jack's shoulder, feeling the weight of the alcohol.

"G, what else is in that liquor cabinet of yours?" Sam stood and walked toward the kitchen.

I felt myself drifting off; Jack's shoulder was better than my pillow.

★ ★ ★

The morning sun felt blinding. My head was pounding like a drum. I felt the heaviness of an arm across my stomach. I tried to open my eyes and raised my hand to wipe the sleep out of them. My mouth tasted like I had been chewing on a dirty sock all night. For the first time in years, I was feeling the ill effects of too much alcohol. I suddenly remembered why I never got drunk; I loathed hangovers.

Light snoring filled my ears. I turned my head. Jack slept next to me, his body curled up next to mine under a blanket on top of my bed.

I tried to look at the clock, but my contacts, dry and brittle, created shadows across the numbers. I focused on Jack. His blond hair fell onto his forehead; two freckles stood above his right eyebrow. His lashes, long and blond, curled at the end. His lips were full, though slightly open, letting air escape. He was shirtless, his bare chest moving up and down in a peaceful rhythm. I looked down at myself, worried something had happened during the night. I was fully clothed, much to my relief.

I lightly rubbed the blond hair on his arm. He moved slightly. He inched himself closer to me, nestling his head into my neck. I could feel the warmth of his breath on my skin. I felt blood pound into my heart, just slightly stronger than the pounding in my head. He slid his hand under my shirt and rested it on my stomach. I moved closer to him. His lips kissed my neck ever so softly.

"Great way to wake up," he whispered.

The heat of his body began to set mine on fire.

"If I didn't have to work, I wouldn't let you out of this bed today."

"Hmm ..." I turned on my side to face him, letting my hand travel to his lower back. I pressed my lips against his.

He kissed me back, mouth closed. "I have morning breath."

"I don't mind." I pushed my tongue inside his mouth.

He grabbed me by the back of my head and positioned his body on top of mine. Our tongues found refuge in each other's mouths. He pulled my shirt off, kissing my chest.

"Sick day?" I mumbled, the excitement of the moment taking over all my senses.

"I wish." Jack leaned up and glanced at the clock. "It's almost eight. I have a deposition at ten." His head fell on my chest.

I tousled his hair. "I can call in sick for you. I'll say you have typhoid fever ... or something."

He laughed. "Not sure that one will work."

"Well ..."

He was running his hand up and down my leg, inching a little higher up my thigh each time.

"German measles?"

"Try again." His fingers made circles around my hip bone. My head was swimming.

"Yeast infection?"

"Good, except that's not really in my wheelhouse, so to speak." He walked two fingers slowly up my stomach.

"You're tied to the bed with naughty things being done to you?"

"Perfect."

We both laughed. He shifted and gave me a long kiss, followed by a peck on the tip of my nose. He sat up in bed. I began kissing his vertebrae, one at a time up his back.

"You're making this tough."

"It's my job."

He nodded and kissed me on the forehead. "Big date tonight. Don't forget. I'll pick you up at six." After a pause, he said, "I expect to continue this without any interruptions later."

I followed Jack to his car, leaving him with a long kiss. The morning air was brisk, the oncoming winter sending preamble notes in the wind. My first class was at eleven, enough time to get the house and myself back together.

I was brushing my teeth and searching for aspirin in the medicine cabinet when I saw him in the mirror. I dropped my toothbrush and screamed. His reflection in the mirror looked back at me.

"Jesus, Sam! You scared the crap out of me."

"Sorry, G. I crashed here last night—too drunk to drive back to my mom's."

I thought about my morning with Jack and wondered whether Sam had heard any of it. "Did you just wake up?"

"Yeah, I heard you in the bathroom. Man, I feel horrible."

I handed him two aspirins. "I'll make coffee."

"Thanks. You don't have an extra toothbrush by chance, do you?"

I handed him one from the cabinet.

A few minutes later, we sat at the kitchen table, drinking our coffee in silence. His hair was sticking up in a million different directions, his beard scruffy.

"It's been a long time since I drank that much." He rested his head on his arm across the table.

"I know what you mean."

"It was fun, though. Jack's pretty cool. You guys been together long?" he asked without lifting his head.

"Not really."

He closed his eyes. "Never thought you'd go for a Gates boy."

"Is that so? Who'd you think I'd go for?"

He looked at me for a moment. "A Highmore boy, maybe?"

"Any chance of that ended with your last vanishing act."

He hesitated before speaking. "Yeah, I was pretty messed up. Watching my parents' relationship fall apart did a number on me. I convinced myself we would end up like them, so it was always easier to run, in order to keep you safe."

I felt my heart disintegrating, melting into a pool of forgiveness and what-ifs. "Keep me safe from what?"

"Safe from me."

"You should have told me how you were feeling. It would have saved me years of feeling like I'd done something wrong."

"Sorry about that. Probably better anyway, though."

"Why would you say that?"

"Because I'm not good enough for you."

All my life those words had belonged to me; now they were Sam's as well.

"You should have let me be the judge of that."

Silence sat between us.

"Since we're going to be like brother and sister, anything

romantic between us would be pretty much illegal in most states anyway."

"What the hell? You sure you had no idea they were together?"

"My mom never said a word about your dad. Every once in a while, she would say she was going out with a friend. I never thought too much about it."

"My dad never talks to me about anything that matters, so I'm not sure why I'm surprised by it."

"Yeah, I kinda got that from last night."

"Between my scene at the table and going to therapy, my grandma will be lecturing me forever."

"You like therapy?"

"It's a group thing, but yeah, I like going."

"Yeah, me too."

"You go to therapy?"

Sam's half-moons played peekaboo with me. "G, you were the only thing that mattered to me, the only thing, and I let my head get in the way of us—and everything else for that matter—so hell yeah, I go to therapy."

"Has it worked for you?"

"You mean, do I still run?"

I nodded.

"I do, just not as fast or as far."

"What are we going to do about our parents?"

"I guess we're going to be adults and be happy for them. We should start off small, like saying we're sorry for acting like kids."

"You're right."

"It's really nice to see you, G. You look just like I thought you would."

"You too, Sam."

"And you're a doctor—been published too. That's awesome."

"How do you know?"

He made a face. "I confess, Internet stalking is a little hobby of mine."

I glanced at him, the half-moons causing me to pause for a moment. "I better get ready for work. I have a class soon."

"Who would have thought that you would end up a college professor and I would be a high school teacher? Funny how life takes you to places you never thought it would."

He reached out to give me a hug. I stood, feeling the sense of home I had buried in him so many years ago.

"Teddy gave me your number. Okay if I call you sometime?"

"Sure."

He handed me a piece of paper with his number on it. "Here's mine in case you ever want to reach out."

I folded it up. Another note from Sam—I had thought those were forever gone with the wind.

At work it was hard to focus, between Sam and Jack and the massive hangover I was still nursing. My Thursday classes were juniors and seniors who actually wanted to be there, so the day flew by quickly.

Sam was right. I needed to apologize to my dad for being a child. I detoured by his house on my way home.

"Dad?" As I walked in the door, a rush of memories washed over me. I rarely went to my old house. I had lived too many lifetimes there and had no interest in revisiting any of them. I found him at the kitchen table, reading a sports magazine. "Hey."

He looked up and closed the magazine. "Hey."

"How was your day?"

"It was okay. Yours?"

"I had a massive hangover all day. Sam, Jack, and I had a drinking party of sorts last night."

"Really?" He raised his eyebrows. "Quite the mix of drinking buddies."

"I guess." We sat there in awkward silence, like we did whenever we were around each other.

"Jack seems nice."

"He is."

"Gates boy. Interesting choice."

"Why would you say that?"

"Just never pictured you with someone from the Gates."

"You ended up with someone from the Gates, at least your first go-around."

He looked at me, saying nothing right away. "Well, your mother aside, I never really thought too much of Gates people. I assumed it was the one thing you and I had in common."

"Grandma is from the Gates."

He shifted in his chair. "Your grandma could have grown up behind a dumpster and would still be the same person she is today."

I chuckled. "True."

He flipped the pages of his magazine, trying to fill in the blank spaces of silence.

"How mad is she at me?"

"She's not happy about the therapy thing at all."

"Chloe signed me up for it. It wasn't my doing."

"You're still going though, right?"

"Yes. That's my doing. I like it."

"Is that where you met Jack? Dee Dee told me about his parents. Sad."

"Yeah."

"I'm glad you have someone to talk to about ... well, you know." His voice trailed off. I realized he had yet to make real eye contact with me. Had he always been unable to look at me? I guessed I had always wanted to be somewhere else too much to pay attention to it.

"I'm sorry for acting like I did. I am happy for you and Mrs. Patterson."

He looked up at me briefly and then looked back down at the magazine. "She's really nice, Gracie, once you get to know her."

"I'm sure." Silence again.

"It was good to see Sam. He's made good on his life. Lacey was worried about him for a long time. He seems to have gotten it back together."

"There was a time he didn't have it together?"

My dad looked up again, seemingly trying to decide whether he should say something. "Your junior year, he tried to kill himself."

"What? I was with him our junior year." I leaned back in my chair, trying to piece my memories together.

"He tried to kill himself when he was visiting his dad over winter break. He was in treatment for a long time. His dad paid for someone to homeschool him so he could graduate on time."

"Why would he do that? He had everything going for him."

"Some people hide pain very well."

I nodded, knowing exactly what he meant. "True."

"Don't say anything to him unless he brings it up."

"I won't." I thought about how I'd been mad at him for deserting me when he was actually just hanging onto his life by a thread. "He's okay now, right?"

My dad nodded. "He just won a teacher-of-the-year award or something. He mentors at-risk kids, and his football team is nationally ranked. He seems to be doing better than okay."

"That's good." I felt a sense of relief.

He glanced up at me and then looked down again. "I still have a hard time without her." Silence again.

"Then why are you marrying Mrs. Patterson? Do you love her?"

"Of course, I love her. It's just a different kind of love. The love I had for your mom was all-consuming."

I nodded.

"It's the best and the worst feeling in the world—a constant struggle between whether you should be happy to have had that kind of love or miserable because you can't have it anymore. She was like a drug to me. The more I had, the more I wanted."

I knew we would never be able to really talk about her, so I let his words fade away. "Have you guys set a wedding date?"

"We were thinking around Thanksgiving. Want to make sure it works out for Sam—and you, of course."

I nodded. "Well, just keep me posted. I'm sure I can make it work." I stood to leave.

"Thanks for coming over to apologize, Gracie. That's nice of you."

I started to leave but stopped. "Dad, it's okay how we are."

He shrugged his shoulders. "I wish it was different sometimes."

"Me too." I left the house knowing we would never be more or less to each other.

Dinner with Jack turned out to be dinner with Ellie and her fiancé Bruce as well. As soon as I saw Bruce, I recognized him from the pages of my *People* magazine.

A bottle of wine and a bowl of pesto pasta later, the four of us sat inside the massive screened-in back porch at the Bradshaw house. Jack took his hand from mine and stood, announcing that he was going to the wine cellar in search of another bottle of wine, and Bruce offered to go with him. Jack paused to give me a lingering kiss before leaving. Ellie watched us.

When it was just the two of us, Ellie spoke. "Jack really likes you."

"I like him too."

She gave me an uneasy smile. "Just be careful, okay?"

"What should I be careful about?"

She leaned in. "He's on the rebound, and you don't seem like the rebound kind of girl." She smoothed a single strand of hair back in place. "I'm worried he's not over Angie yet, that's all. I wouldn't want anyone to get hurt."

"Has he said something?"

"He can't stop talking about you. But a month ago, he was talking about Angie. He's not a lightbulb; he doesn't turn on and off that easy—not usually, that is."

"Okay." She knew him better than anyone, and she was putting the warning signs up.

"Gracie, it's not you. You are amazing. It's just that Angie wreaked havoc on him in all kinds of ways."

"I thought you were friends with her."

"Oh, I am. That doesn't mean I like what she does sometimes. I accept her for who she is and not who I want her to be."

Bruce and Jack were laughing as they reentered the room. The subject changed as quickly as the cold night air.

Back at my house, I was intent on proving Ellie wrong. I couldn't get Jack's clothes off fast enough. I inched down his body until I found the place I knew he wanted me to go. Afterward, we lay there, sleep and consciousness pulling and pushing each other for control.

"Hey, you," he whispered in my ear. "I have to go. It's almost five."

I rolled into him, smiling, eyes still shut.

He kissed me softly on the tip of my nose. "Go back to sleep."

I rolled back over, not feeling the light of day until well after seven. My first thoughts were of Jack. The smell of his skin saturated mine.

Finally, it was Friday. I was exhausted by the week, both mentally and physically. My phone chirped. I grabbed it, thinking it was Jack.

(317) 456-0330
Hey, G. Great to see u. Think the wedding is in November??

I struggled to focus on my phone. It was Sam. I added him to my contacts.

Me

Yeah. That's what my dad said. Great to see you too.

Sam

My mom said something about dinner with us. Told her I'd look at my schedule and figure something out.

Me

Dinner for what?

Sam

No idea. Maybe to be their wedding planners?

Me

Lol

Sam

I'm color-blind and my idea of a good cake is a Twinkie, so sign me up.

I paused, thinking about Sam trying to take his life all those years ago. I knew I might regret what I was about to text, but I did it anyway.

Me

Didn't realize it until I saw you, but I've missed you.

Sam

...

I lay there, waiting for the three dots to disappear and his message to appear. I knew it was a mistake to tell him I'd missed him. I'd just spent the night with Jack, and Sam and I were never going to happen. Why even tell him how I was feeling in some sentimental moment? I placed my phone back on my nightstand and rolled over. I closed my eyes and was drifting in and out when I heard the chirp. I grabbed my phone to look at the message.

Jack B
Need to repeat last night

Me
Agree.

Immediately, there was another chirp.

Sam
I've missed you too.

And there they were, the two men in my world, bookending my life. As I drove to work, it hit me: I still had a letter to write. I sat at my desk during my office hours, struggling for words to say to her. The workday was nearly done when the right words finally came to me.

We were all seated quietly in the room, waiting for Dr. Gretchen to arrive and begin the session. I looked around nervously, feeling like one of my students. As Dr. Gretchen entered the room, I could feel everyone's anxiousness heighten.

"Hello. I trust we all had a good couple of days."

"I'd like to go first," Ellie announced.

Dr. Gretchen looked at her, surprised. "Very well." She smiled and motioned for Ellie to speak.

Ellie opened the letter, handwritten on pink paper. There was hesitation in her voice as she began reading. "Dear Mom, there are so many things I wish I would have said to you when you were alive. For so many reasons, I kept them inside of me. I am proud of you and all you did for Jack and me. You were a talented artist, so bright, and you gave it up to be a wife and mother. When I look back on your life, I think you cheated yourself. You could have been a famous painter. You lived a life in black-and-white when your world could have been full of colors." Ellie looked up, signaling that she was done.

"Thank you, Ellie. How did it make you feel to write the letter?" Dr. Gretchen probed.

Ellie placed her hands in her lap. "Sad in a way, but it was liberating as well."

"Do you think she ever regretted not pursuing her love of painting?"

"I'm not sure. She never really said. Well, I never really asked either."

"What do you think held her back from painting?"

"My dad."

I looked at Ellie, eyebrows raised.

"Why?"

"He felt like her place was being a wife and mother."

"How did that make her feel?"

"She always wanted to please him, so whatever he said was the way it was going to be."

Dr. Gretchen nodded. "Anyone want to be next?"

"I'll go," Sarah said as she pulled her letter out, written on a large recipe card. "Mommy, three years is a long time to be without you. It's been super tough, but a new friend of mine"—she glanced over at me—"said I should write about the good things in my life. Jerry and I are getting married in May. You'd like him. He knows some days are hard for me, but he says things will get better. And you know what? For the first time, I believe it. I also have some new friends. There are six of us, and we talk about what it's like not having mothers anymore. I'm sorry you'll never get to meet them.

Love you forever, Sarah. PS. I tried your carrot cake recipe. You're right. It's better with a pinch of nutmeg."

I smiled sadly. The "oh, by the way" moments, not the earth-shattering ones, were somehow the ones in which we missed them most.

"Sarah, that was simply lovely. One question, though."

Sarah's demeanor began to alter. I glanced for her purse. It hung on the back of her chair.

"Did you bring any of that carrot cake for us to enjoy?"

We all laughed.

"No, but I can for next session." Sarah smiled brightly.

In that simple moment, I was so proud of her. I stood up, walked over, and gave her a hug.

"You rocked it, my friend," I whispered in her ear.

She covered her eyes and began to cry. "It's okay. These tears are the good ones."

"I'm glad." I took my seat next to Ginger.

Ginger raised her hand to be next. "Okay, it's not as good as the ones Sarah and Ellie wrote."

"I'm sure whatever you have to say to your mom will be just the right thing," Dr. Gretchen reassured her.

"Here goes ... Howdy, Mom. What have you been up to? Have you run into Uncle Phil yet? How's Grandma Frances doing? Did she find someone to bet on the horses with? I had your garage door fixed. It was a broken cable, just like you thought. That neighbor of yours with the bulldog keeps letting him poop in your yard. Yesterday, he did it again, so last night I put it back in his yard and started it on fire. I don't think he'll poop in your yard again. Work is the same. Cubs are pretty good this season. Miss you. I love you." She folded up the college ruled piece of paper and looked out the window. I was envious of Ginger then. Honest, no-punches-pulled Ginger.

"Did your mom like sports?" Mandie inquired.

"Oh yeah, we went to games all the time, baseball and hockey mostly. She hung out with a lot of the Cubs players back in the eighties." Tonight, Ginger was back to her natural self—no makeup, sapphire contacts missing, loose sweatshirt covering her frame.

"Who would like to go next?"

Mindy and Mandie each went, and Dr. Gretchen asked them varying questions about their parents. Finally, I was the only one who hadn't gone.

"Gracie, yours seems to be the last letter. Ready?"

I felt a rush of panic. Pulling the paper out of my purse, I slowly unfolded it. "Yesterday Daddy held Mommy's hand as she faintly smiled. Yesterday Daddy kissed Mommy good-bye. Yesterday I watched a part of Daddy die. Today Daddy wiped her tears away. Today Daddy held her in his arms. Today Daddy promised peaceful days ahead. Tonight Daddy spoke quietly in the dark. Tonight Daddy spoke to heaven. Tonight God took Mommy home. Tonight Daddy cried alone."

"I don't get it," Ginger said. "It's not a letter."

"No, it's a poem," Ellie said, looking at me.

"She knows we were supposed to write a letter, right?" Ginger whispered, seemingly forgetting that I was seated right by her.

"You wrote that yourself, right?" Mindy asked.

I nodded again.

"What most surprised you about writing the letters to your mothers?" Dr. Gretchen asked, looking around at the entire group.

"I thought it would be hard, but then I just pictured her sitting across from me and wrote it like we were talking," Ginger said.

"It made me feel good at first, but then the same pain came back." Sarah's voice cracked a bit. She reached for her purse but then pulled back.

"Sometimes there just aren't enough words," I sadly said.

"I'm mad at myself for not taking the time or making the effort to tell her those things when she was alive," Ellie declared.

"Do you think it would have made a difference?"

"Maybe not, but at least it would have been said."

"Do you have any of her paintings?" I asked.

"Most of them are in her art studio at their house, but Jack and I have a few."

I thought back to my tour of the house, trying to remember her art studio.

For the rest of the session, we talked about our mothers and the regrets we had about our relationships with them. We all agreed we should have treated our mothers better and, given the chance, been more respectful.

"Hindsight is a miserable thing," Dr. Gretchen said. "It lets you see all the mistakes you made but never lets you go back and correct them."

"I wish I would have known my mom in a different way than I did. Cancer lived in every aspect of our existence. It was horrible," I said matter-of-factly.

Dr. Gretchen pushed her top lip inside her bottom lip, feeling the sting of my adolescence with me.

"So maybe as we wind down tonight's session, let's talk about one thing that happened to you this week that made you feel happy."

"I picked out my wedding dress," Sarah said.

"Nice, Sarah. Good things, see?" Dr. Gretchen was trying to reinforce the positive for Sarah.

"I learned a new technique this week," Ginger proudly announced.

I smiled at her, even as my mind raced to define "technique."

"The charity benefit in my mom's honor is coming along nicely—just a couple of weeks away," Ellie said. She pulled at her blouse, which was perfectly in place. Jack hadn't mentioned anything about a charity benefit. Maybe it was just a small thing.

Mandie smiled at Ellie. "A charity benefit? That sounds nice."

"Every year, we host a gala in honor of her birthday, with all proceeds going to the charity started in her name. This year, the count is over five hundred."

I looked at her, surprised.

"If you are interested in going, let me know. It's at the Drake on the twenty-seventh."

"Gracie? Did you go yet?" asked Dr. Gretchen.

"Well, my dad is getting remarried."

Dr. Gretchen raised her eyebrows. "Really? How does that make you feel?"

"I guess it's okay."

"Someone you know?" Ginger asked interestedly.

"Actually, yeah. My high school boyfriend's mother."

"Oh, girl, that spells drama!" Mindy leaned back in her chair, shaking her finger.

"Why?"

"Is the ex-boyfriend still around?" Mandie asked.

"I saw him earlier this week for the first time in years. It wasn't a big deal."

"Is he married?" Sarah asked.

"Married? No. Not sure why that matters, though."

Mindy leaned into the circle. "You've known this boy for a long time?"

"Since we were kids."

"This is like one of those Lifetime movies," Ginger said, adjusting her cat glasses.

"Not really, and I'm kinda dating someone else right now anyway, and it's going really well." I glanced at Ellie.

"Sure it is," Ginger replied. "That is, until the old boyfriend sneaks back into the picture."

Dr. Gretchen took back control of the conversation. "Next time, I want each of you to bring in something of your mother's. It can be something you have that was hers or that reminds you of her."

"Dr. Gretchen?" Sarah meekly asked.

"Yes, Sarah?"

"I will bring in the carrot cake next week if that's okay with the group."

"Sure."

"I can bring in something," Ginger said.

"I'm in," I responded.

"Me too," Ellie stated.

Mindy and Mandie offered as well. I looked at everyone in the circle. Although I felt emotionally tied to all these women, for some reason, I felt most connected to Ginger and Sarah. It was a revelation surprising even to me.

"Okay, well, it seems like we officially have a potluck of sorts," Dr. Gretchen laughed. And just like we had the previous session, we hugged one another good-bye.

Dr. Gretchen and I walked out together, talking. I looked toward my car, and there he stood.

Dr. Gretchen looked over at Jack. "Good things for you too, Gracie." She leaned slightly into me. "Good things are nice."

As I approached him, I thought about the benefit, trying to decide whether I should say something to him.

He kissed me. "How was session?"

"Good."

"Hungry? I stopped and picked up some takeout."

We ate back at my house, drinking wine by the fire in the living room. As Jack talked endlessly about his legal case, my mind kept returning to the benefit. I finally decided to say something.

"Ellie mentioned the benefit."

"Oh, yeah." Silence.

"I think that's awesome—keeping her memory alive while raising money for charity."

"The proceeds help fund the arts program in elementary schools. You want another glass of wine?"

"No, thanks."

He poured himself another glass.

"She said tickets are still available."

"Really?" He seemed distant.

"Aren't you involved with it?"

He glanced down at his wine. "Usually, but this year, work is keeping me really busy. I haven't been much help."

"It's at the Drake. Pretty fancy."

He took another drink of wine. "Not sure how much of it I'll be able to enjoy, if any."

I looked at him. "You're not going then?"

"Probably not. Haven't told Ellie yet. She'll be mad, but Bruce will be there, so I don't feel as guilty as she'd like for me to feel about it."

"Well, if you go, let me know. I'll buy a ticket."

"Definitely." He leaned in and kissed me.

By the light of the fire, we found our way to each other. Our clothes fell away until our skin met, and our bodies seemed to morph into one.

"I want you, Gracie," he whispered throatily in my ear.

I opened my eyes to look at him. Flickers of light from the fire bounced off his body. He was amazing, perfect in so many ways. I couldn't believe I was with him. I needed him—needed the reinforcement of being wanted. I felt like I was being tricked somehow. Someone had to be playing a joke on me, giving me Jack like this. But I didn't care. *Good things for you, Gracie*, I heard Dr. Gretchen say in my head.

"Gracie? You okay with this?"

I knew I should say no. I knew it was too fast, too furious to be where we were. I couldn't give myself to him so freely. I wasn't a rebound. I wasn't that kind of girl.

"Yes."

10

In my dream, I was lying across a tire swing, my arms and legs moving freely as the tire took me in all different directions. It was a rush, a sense of freedom, a sense of letting myself go. The more directions the swing took me, the more I felt an inward sense of calm. I heard a distant ringing. Then the ringing became deafening, causing me to lose my balance on the swing. I flipped over, and as my face met the ground, my body jolted awake. I opened my eyes.

As I stumbled to answer my ringing phone, I looked behind me. Jack lay asleep and naked on the floor, curled up with a couch pillow covering his stomach. I grabbed for the phone.

"Hello?"

Grandma's voice greeted me. "Gracelynn?"

"Yes?"

"What are you doing?"

I sank to the kitchen floor, fearful that my grandma knew what I had been doing all night with Jack. "Nothing. Why?" I reached for a kitchen towel, trying to cover myself up.

"Do you know what time it is?"

"No." I squinted to see the clock.

"Eight fifty-seven."

"Okay."

"Gracelynn, do you know what day it is?"

"Uh ..." I tried to piece together the days, scanning my memory. I'd had session on Friday. "Saturday?"

"Gracelynn, are you high?"

"What?"

"Are you under the influence of a controlled substance? Have you been ... what do they call it ... huffing?"

"Good lord, Grandma. No."

"Do you have the intestinal flu?"

"No."

"Are your car tires flat?"

"No."

"Your feet bound together, preventing you from walking?"

"No."

"Then why are you not here? We are waiting."

I leaned my head back against the wall: Saturday, breakfast at nine. "Sorry, Grandma, I'm not sure I can make breakfast to—"

"We will wait for you. See you in twenty minutes." A click on the line told me she was done with the conversation but just getting started with me.

I sat there with the phone in my hand for a moment. Standing up, I quietly walked back into the living room. Jack was gone from the floor. I heard a flush from the bathroom, and out he walked. He wore nothing but a smile as he approached me.

"Good morning. How's the most beautiful girl in the world today?"

I felt self-conscious, standing in front of him with a kitchen towel adorned with pink cupcakes barely covering me. He grabbed the towel and tossed it to the floor. He pulled me to him. I could feel him starting to come alive.

"Jack, I have breakfast with my grandma."

"Perfect. I'm starving."

I bit the corner of my lip. "You sure? It's my grandma. When it comes to creating uncomfortable situations, she's the expert."

"Sure I'm sure." He kissed me again. "Do I have time for a quick shower?"

"Can you take it in five minutes or less?"

"Not sure. I'm a dirty boy. You know, I really need to be lathered up." He kissed my shoulder.

"Okay, any other time, I would love to do the sexual innuendo thing, but we have exactly eighteen minutes to be sitting in front of my grandma. Get moving."

★ ★ ★

As we walked into the club, my grandma greeted me with her perfected death stare, and I instantly regretted bringing Jack.

"Glad you could join us, Gracelynn. I see you brought along someone without mentioning it to me, by the way."

Jack pulled out a chair for me to sit.

"Jack was hungry, so he came along too."

"Interesting that you had enough time to get yourself ready and coordinate picking up Mr. Bradshaw in a little less than twenty minutes," my grandma retorted.

I rolled my eyes at Teddy, who smiled as he looked down at the menu.

"Sorry we're late, Grandma. We lost track of time."

She pulled her glasses down, giving us both the once-over. "I can only imagine."

We ordered, and for a few minutes, I almost felt like we were going to get through breakfast unscathed. Jack and Teddy talked sports, and Grandma and I talked club gossip. Then my grandma turned her attention to Jack. I could almost feel the change in the air.

"So, Mr. Bradshaw, I understand you were once engaged."

I choked on my coffee, nearly coughing it up.

"Yes."

"A model, correct?"

"That's right."

"How long has it been since you ended your engagement?"

Jack did not flinch. "A few months."

"I see. And before that, you dated someone from Covington Estates, right?"

"Uh-huh."

"I am sorry, is that slang for yes?"

"Yes."

"She was a beauty queen, correct?"

"Well, I guess she won a few pageants."

"You seem to have a specific type."

"Not sure what you mean by that." He glanced at me.

"You date primarily based on appearance—that is, until now."

"I wouldn't say that."

"And this fiancée you had, would you consider her bright? To clarify, would you trust her to manage your finances?"

"My finances?" He laughed. "Definitely not."

"But I bet she looked lovely on your arm, did she not?"

"Grandma, what's the point? Jack dated pretty girls. No big deal."

"I am just wondering, why the sudden change in type?"

"Change in type?"

"Up until recently, your dating life seemed to involve a string of one pretty, shallow girl after the next. And now here you sit with our Gracelynn."

Jack leaned over and squeezed my hand. "Yep."

"And would you consider her bright?"

"Very." He winked at me.

"Trust her to manage your finances?"

"I guess. Sure."

"How about showing her off on your arm?"

"What?"

"Gracelynn is not the type of girl to be strung along, Mr. Bradshaw."

"Well, I ..."

"That is what I thought."

Breakfast came just as my grandma went in for the kill. I had never been so happy to see poached eggs and bacon in my life. I tried to eat as fast as I could, until I noticed Grandma staring at me.

"Gracelynn? What is the rush? Going home to tend to unfinished business?"

"No hurry, Grandma." I glanced over at Jack, who seemed to be in a staring contest with his waffle.

"Good. Now, time to talk about Lacey's shower."

"Shower?"

"Yes, shower."

"For what? She's in her fifties and has her own house. Why does she need a bridal shower?"

"Personal shower, Gracelynn. You know, where you give the bride-to-be intimates?"

I dropped my fork on my plate, sending a clanking noise throughout the room. "I don't think so, Grandma. First of all, ick, and second of all, ick."

"Let me see if I understand this, Gracelynn. It is perfectly fine for you and Mr. Bradshaw to engage in intimate relations when you barely know each other, but it is not okay for your father and Lacey, who are soon to be man and wife, to engage in them?"

I looked at her. "Okay, when do you want to have it?"

"I told Lacey we would work out the details Tuesday night over dinner."

"Tuesday? That night's not good for me."

My grandma held her mimosa in midair. "And why is that?"

"I have a meeting that night."

"What meeting?"

I stared at her, trying to decide whether I was prepared to drink from the fire hose. "Group meeting, Grandma."

She took a long sip from her mimosa, carefully placed the glass back down on the table, and then wiped the corners of her mouth. "You will stop going there immediately."

"Excuse me?"

"I certainly never felt the need to tell our family matters to others, so I'm not sure why you feel the need to."

"And how'd that work out for you?"

"I do not think you need to be discussing"—she lowered her voice—"our personal business with strangers."

"It's not even about that. It's about connecting with others."

"I see. And that is where you two met? By your tardiness today, I can tell you two have already connected, likely more than once."

"We did meet at the community center." Jack kissed the top of my hand.

"The community center?" My grandma looked aghast.

I braced myself for her next words.

"Gracelynn, you might as well have met at the city dump. What will people think if they see you there?"

"Grandma, I live in Highmore. It's my community center."

"Lower your voice. Try to be a little discreet about it."

"It's been very helpful."

"Just do not mention it to me again. It causes me angst, which is frightful for my complexion."

"Baby doll, I'm sure you and Lacey can find another day that works for Gracie." Teddy gently squeezed my grandma's shoulder.

"Well, maybe next Saturday after the family dinner."

"Sounds ... Wait. What family dinner?"

"I believe dinner is at six, if I am not mistaken." My grandma looked at Teddy, who was wiping the syrup off his "I'm Bringing Scary Back" Frankenstein T-shirt.

"That sounds right." Teddy looked up at me and smiled.

"Was someone going to bother to tell me?"

Grandma motioned for the server to refill her empty mimosa glass. "I just did."

"Maybe I'm busy."

She stopped and looked at me. "Really? And what do you think you will be doing a week from today?"

"Maybe Jack and I have plans." I glanced at him. He was nodding off, trying to force his hand to support the weight of his head.

"I see he can hardly wait."

I bit my lip and looked away.

"I expect you to be there. There are wedding plans to finalize."

Jack was asleep before we were out of the parking lot. I silently fumed all the way home. Another uncomfortable family dinner, only this time the family was expanding.

When we arrived at my house, I turned to Jack. "Jack, wake up." I shook his arm slightly. "Why don't you go home and get some sleep? Just text me later if you want to do something." I put him in his car with a kiss, barely able to wait to grab my phone as he pulled away.

Me
Hey.

Sam
What's up?

Me
You know anything about a family dinner next Saturday?

Sam

My mom asked what I was doing next weekend. That's about it. What dinner?

Me

Wedding planning kind of dinner.

Sam

No way.

Me

You coming?

Sam

How could I miss it?

Me

Just found out about it.

Sam

Let me guess. Your grandma told you?

Me

How did you know?

Sam

Figured it wasn't your dad.

Me

It will never be my dad.

Sam

He asked me to be his best man.

Me
He did?

Sam
Be prepared. My mom is going to ask you.

Me
To be her best man?

Sam
Worse. Maid of honor.

Me
That's not what dinner's about, is it?

Sam
If I were a betting man, I would bet on it.

Me
I learned my lesson already, never bet against you.

Sam
I remember.

I felt a resurgence of memories circle around me like a wind tunnel. Reconnecting with Sam was something I had never thought would happen and something I wasn't sure I should tell Chloe about. It had been years, so maybe she wouldn't even remember half of what had happened between us.

We met for lunch that day, and as we ordered soup, salad, and a plate of fries to share, I knew I needed to come clean with her.

"Are you freakin' kidding me? Sam Patterson?" Chloe placed her glass of diet pop down on the table.

"Yep." I bit the inside of my lip. "He's going to be my stepbrother."

She laughed. "Now that sounds like a Lifetime movie."

I frowned. "Turns out he had a pretty rough go of things."

"Really? How's that?"

I looked at her, trying to decide whether telling her the truth about him would matter. "He tried to kill himself in high school."

She stared at me blankly. "Is that so? When would he have had time to do that? He was always lurking around you."

"When he vanished for a long time, that's when."

She looked at the ice melting in her drink. She started to speak and then stopped. Finally, words broke the silence. "Well, I'm sorry he felt like he had to resort to something so extreme."

"I know."

"Did he tell you?" I shook my head. "Who told you?"

"My dad."

"Your dad actually talked to you about something important? That's a first."

"He said it took Sam a while to get his life back together."

"You know, I do feel really bad for him, but that doesn't excuse all those other years of poor behavior."

I felt an inkling of defensiveness creeping in; I wanted to protect Sam from Chloe. It was clear to me now, though, seeing my life in the rearview mirror, that she was right. "I think he was just immature."

"Who cares now anyway? I'd rather talk about a real man. How's Jack?"

I smiled, feeling a flash of happiness hit me. I told her about our night of no sleep, followed by our suffering through breakfast with my grandma. I ended with Ellie's warning to me about Jack and how I was going to prove her wrong.

"Hmm."

"What?"

"I'm not so sure she's wrong."

"What do you mean?" A sense of trepidation washed over me.

"Think about it—how long has it taken you to move past Les? And you weren't even close to marrying him."

"Well ..." I was at a loss for anything to say in return.

"You might be a rebound. But is that such a bad thing?"

"I'm not even sure how to be a rebound."

"You just need to make sure you're okay with getting hurt if push comes to shove."

"You think I'll get hurt?"

"We both know there are only two ways this is going to end: in marriage or heartbreak. There are no other possibilities."

"Can't there be other possibilities?"

"Not at this point."

"What should I do?"

"Enjoy the ride, but keep your eyes open. I wish I could tell you it will work out, but it's just not that easy."

"Why can't it ever be easy?"

Her expression changed slightly. "Because life can be really hard, and you know that better than anyone."

I felt a pang of sadness. "Well, enough about me. What's going on with you?"

She looked at me, took a breath, and then spoke. "We've decided to try for a baby."

I was shocked. Since her only previous pregnancy had ended in miscarriage years ago, kids had been off the table. "Really?"

"I don't want it to be just Rick and me years from now with nothing to do but wonder if I could kill him by poisoning and get away with it."

I laughed.

"Really, we just want someone to carry on after us."

"When are you going to start trying?"

"We actually started a couple of months ago."

"You never said anything."

She placed her credit card on top of the bill and slid it to the edge of the table. "I felt bad telling you."

"Why?"

She looked at me. "My life is moving along, and it seems like yours is … stuck."

"I wouldn't say stuck."

"Why do you think I signed you up for therapy?"

"To meet guys?"

"I don't want you to be stuck, Gracie. Being stuck doesn't get you to a better place."

"I didn't think the place I was at was so bad."

"Not bad, more like void."

"Translated, that means boring and sad."

"You said it. I didn't."

"Well, it's definitely not boring anymore."

Chloe smiled. "Gotta run. Grocery shopping is still on my list of things to do, which is what Rick thinks I've been doing for the last two hours."

"Can I ask you a question?"

"Shoot."

"Do you think it's weird that Jack didn't tell me about the charity event?"

She looked up at the ceiling, seemingly trying to pull her thoughts together. "Possibly. It's either because he's not going and didn't want to make a big deal out of it or because he is going but doesn't want to ask you to go with him. Which one do you think it is?"

"I really want to believe he's not going, but part of me has doubts."

"Then, my sweet girl, ask him."

Back home, as I listened to my dryer toss and tumble clothes, I thought about what Chloe had said.

Me
Hey there.

Jack B
Hey. I want to see you tonight.

Me
I think I can fit you in my schedule. My place?

Jack B
Is this a pajama party? Should I bring my toothbrush?

Me
Bring the toothbrush, forget the pajamas.

Jack B
I already forgot them.

My fingers paused.

Me
So are you going to the charity event?

Jack B
...

I waited for his response, wondering what he was thinking on the other end of the three dots.

Jack B
No.

A red flag popped up in my mind. It had taken way too long for him to reply with just one word.

Me
It's no big deal if you want to go solo.

Bald-faced lie.

Jack B
Not going.

Me
Ok.

Jack B
Think I'll be in Indy for a deposition anyway.

I felt a twinge of disappointment as I thought about him being gone that weekend.

Jack B
See you soon.

Three hours later, we lay sweaty and naked across my bed. He had barely made it through the door before he started pulling at me. I gave myself willingly to him, thinking the more I gave myself to him, the more he would need me.

I lay on my stomach as he ran his fingers up and down my spine, and I felt flickers of euphoria as he repeated the motion. I felt his lips on my sweaty skin, his hand sliding under my stomach. He gently rolled me over, and as his tongue pressed against my inner thigh, I felt myself tense up. I was far from perfect and was worried that the more he explored my body, the more he would see how flawed it was. I couldn't compare to the other women he had been with, and I knew he could see my imperfections glaring back at him. He found my hands and placed them on top of his head. I closed my eyes and let myself give into it.

The brightness of the morning light brought me back to consciousness. I glanced over at the clock. It was nearly ten. I wasn't sure when we'd fallen asleep, but exhaustion had finally won out sometime in the middle of the night. I slid quietly away from him, grabbing my shirt to cover my exposed body.

As I sat at my kitchen table drinking coffee, I wondered why I had been second-guessing Jack and the charity benefit. It was ridiculous to question him, and I vowed to put it out of my mind.

"Morning." He kissed me.

"You want coffee?"

"Yes, need coffee now."

I watched him walk across the kitchen, still not really believing we were together.

"Sleep well?"

He smiled at me. "Sorry I fell asleep on you. I wanted to pull an all-nighter."

I laughed. "I fell asleep too. You wore me out." That was true. My whole body was sore, some parts more than others.

"And I was just going to suggest we spend the day in bed." He leaned in and kissed me, pulling me to him. As he kissed my earlobe, he whispered, "Ever use the kitchen table for anything besides eating?"

He grabbed me and lifted me on top of the table, toppling our coffee cups to the floor. He stopped and looked at them. I grabbed him, caring little about the mess—I could clean it up later.

An hour later, we lay in the bathtub, bubbles surrounding us like a fluffy blanket. Jack's arms were wrapped around me, my body floating on top of his. His hand glided over my stomach and took a trip along the hilly trail of my body.

"I'm sorry my body isn't better," I said quietly.

"What are you talking about?" His hands rested on my hip bones.

"I'm not perfect."

"You're perfect to me."

I felt a sense of completeness with his words.

By five, we were cuddled up on my couch, eating grilled cheese sandwiches and watching *The Philadelphia Story*. I never wanted the day to end, but I knew that like everything, it would eventually.

As the credits rolled, Jack looked at me. "I should get going."

"Or you could spend the night." I lay my head on his stomach. I could feel the ripples of his abs pressing into my cheek.

"I have work to do."

"Anything I can do to convince you to stay?" I looked at him, raising my eyebrow.

"Well, maybe one thing."

I smiled and lifted his shirt, exposing his skin. It was warm to the touch of my lips.

He leaned back on the couch. "Wonder if I'm going home tonight."

As I worked my way down from his belly button, my tongue tracing the faint line of hair, we both knew the answer.

Monday morning came too soon, and Jack left just before daybreak. I thought about how I had spent my weekend, feeling the sense of rapture that comes only in the early stages of a relationship.

In the bathroom mirror, the reality of how I had spent my weekend looked back at me. My pale facial complexion was painted with blotches of red from the scruffiness of Jack's five-o'clock shadow. Small purplish spots left by Jack's lips dotted varying parts of my chest. My legs ached, and every time I went to the bathroom, I experienced a quick jolt of pain. It felt like I was recovering from a wild college weekend, except I was a thirty-something facing a normal workday.

On my way home from work that evening, I detoured by the park for some reason. I wasn't sure why since the day was quickly falling behind the horizon. In the parking lot, I saw Teddy's truck. I pulled up next to it and slowly got out. The wind grabbed at my jacket. I shivered slightly. Teddy sat next to the big tree trunk, brushing leaves away from its mammoth base.

"Teddy?"

"Oh hey, doll." He shifted his weight to face me. He wore a long-sleeved "I'm Just Here for Boos" T-shirt. "Everythin' okay?"

I sat down on the bench across from him and nodded. "Not even really sure how I ended up here. I just kinda drove in this direction."

Teddy nodded.

"Grandma says you come here every day too, right?"

"Our girl is here." He patted the tree. "I'm glad you came by, Gracie. I've wanted to talk to you about your grandma for a while now."

"Eh. Not really sure I'm up for that conversation today … or any day for that matter."

"I know she can sometimes be … well, difficult."

"To say the least."

"It's hard, I know, but you gotta try and understand where she's coming from."

"Which is?"

"She only wants what's best for you."

"She has a funny way of showing it."

"Do you know anything about how she was raised?"

"She grew up in a family with a ton of money, who prided themselves on being social snobs."

Teddy laughed. "Her daddy was a real interesting character. He refused to shake my hand—thought my hands smelled from handling trash all day. Funny thing is, my trash made me more money than he ever saw in his lifetime."

"Sounds like a real treat of a guy."

"Point is, your grandma was brought up by people who thought they were better than everyone else. She worked for years to break out of that mold. But some things can't be broken."

"Nothing I ever do is good enough for her."

Teddy shrugged his shoulders. "She tells me over and over how much like Cass you are, and to her, that's a scary thing."

"Why is that scary?"

"She's worried she will lose you like she did her. And as much as she loves me, if she ever lost you, she wouldn't be able to go on."

"Then why is she so hard on me?"

"It's just her way of dealing with things."

I thought about those words. "Why do you stay with her, Teddy?"

He looked at me as if I'd asked him something unfathomable. "Our hearts are connected. I knew it from the first minute I saw her. My whole life has been about her. She's given me more than I ever dreamed I could have."

"But she didn't tell you about Mom right away."

His hand glided over the side of the tree trunk. "No, she didn't. But I'm not sure I could have either if I were her."

"Weren't you mad at her for not telling you?"

Teddy's eyes rose to meet mine. "Nah, I felt blessed she told me."

"Why blessed?"

"Did you know my mama died just a couple months before Cass was born?"

"No, I didn't. Sorry."

"You know what my mama's name was?"

I shook my head.

"Cassandra Marie."

"My mom was named after your mom?"

"I'm pretty sure your grandma took a lot of heat for that. She

216

never admitted it, but I knew how ruthless her folks could be when they were backed against a wall."

"Were they really that bad?"

"Have you ever seen the scar on your grandma's lower back?"

I shook my head, fearful of the answer.

"Whip strap, a reminder from her daddy about knowing her place. Not the first or the last time he reminded her of her place. Your grandpa and me had to get her to a doctor outside of town one time when her daddy hit her so hard it knocked her out."

"Why didn't you guys do something to help her?"

"We couldn't. She made us promise. It would've ruined her family's reputation if word got out. There was a doctor in Crestin who treated Westminster socialites. He was discreet, so they liked using him."

"I can't believe she was abused like that."

"It happened all the time—men making themselves feel big by making their women feel small. My daddy wasn't like that. He taught me how to treat a lady. Your grandma was the only one for me, so my life started and will end with her."

I felt a need to run to my grandma. I knew she would be mad at Teddy for telling me, but I clearly needed to find a better way to navigate my grandma's frustrating moments, for both our sakes.

"How do you handle it when she's difficult?"

Teddy laughed. "I know when she's like that, it's really about something else. Take you and the Bradshaw boy. She's worried he'll hurt you. Gates boys tend to do that kind of stuff. She thinks he's going too quick, too soon after his breakup." Teddy flicked a fallen leaf off his shoe. "Truth is, she doesn't think anyone out there is good enough for you. She thinks you're that special. And she's right."

I stood from my bench and walked over and sat next to Teddy, placing my head on his shoulder. He put his arm around me.

"I love you, Teddy."

"Do me a favor. Don't tell your grandma I told you. She'd kill me. I said I loved her, not that I wasn't scared of her."

That night I lay in bed watching the stars, barely visible in the night sky. It was nearly eleven, and I hadn't heard from Jack. I was starting to worry.

Me
Hey there.

No response. I watched the clock until just after midnight, when sleep took over. Just before two, my phone chirped. I rolled over and pulled it close to my face in order to read it.

Jack B
Sorry it's so late. Just got home from work. Talk to you tomorrow. Sweet dreams.

I rolled back over, relieved he was safe and at home. I drifted off to sleep, phone still in hand.

As Tuesday morning turned into Tuesday afternoon, I remembered that I still needed to bring something to the potluck and something of my mom's. I wrapped up class early and threw together fresh salsa. Then I sat at my kitchen table trying to figure out what to take of hers to session.

Instantly, the thought hit me. I grabbed it and placed it in a bag with the salsa and some chips. I was sitting on the edge of my couch thinking about her when my doorbell rang. A delivery man handed me a huge bouquet of fall flowers. They were almost as big as me. I opened the card: "Wednesday can't come fast enough. —Jack."

Me
Hey, you. Just got the most beautiful flowers.

Jack B
From who? Should I be jealous? Because he sounds perfect.

Me
I wouldn't say perfect.

Jack B
Really? Then I still have a chance. That is, unless you're officially off the market?

I wasn't sure what to type. If I said I was, that meant we were exclusive, and if I said I wasn't, that meant it was okay to see other people—something I had no interest in doing.

Me
Off, I think???

Jack B
I feel the same way.

I thought about being a rebound and how things were moving fast between us.

Me
Too quick?

Jack B
Only if you're not sure.

Jack B
I'm sure. Are you?

Chloe was right. It was too late to turn back. I was in too deep. There would be no other options for me now.

Me
I'm sure.

★ ★ ★

Sarah went all out for the potluck—balloons, tablecloth covering a large banquet table, even place settings. She looked happy putting it all together. It seemed to give her a purpose.

"Well, ladies, I see Sarah has our places set already, so maybe tonight we can break bread, so to speak, as we talk." Dr. Gretchen motioned for each of us to sit in our assigned seats. Our names were written in calligraphy on our place cards, decorated delicately with tiny roses.

"Sarah, it's so beautiful." I touched her shoulder as I took my place next to Ellie.

"Thank you." She smiled, and for the first time, her posture seemed more erect, her energy more positive.

As I took my seat, I looked at all the food placed on the table along with Sarah's carrot cake. It looked amazing.

We filled our plates, talking about trivial things. Something dawned on me as I listened to the chatter. I tried to remember when the change had happened—when we had become comfortable enough to sit around an intimate table, eating and talking like a group of friends out for dinner. It felt real and honest and was an experience I knew I wanted to repeat. I wondered, if I had met these women under different circumstances, would I still feel the same for them? Probably not.

"Who would like to go first tonight?" Dr. Gretchen asked.

"I will!" Sarah beamed. "This"—she pulled out a recipe box—"was my mother's. From it, she created some of the most amazing dishes." She pointed to the carrot cake. "That cake is from here."

"How did you feel making the cake?" Ginger asked, placing a chip with salsa falling off it in her mouth.

"When I first held the recipe, I was scared. But then I felt powerful somehow."

"How so?" Mindy asked.

"Like I could create something from nothing. It felt, well, good."

"It looks delicious. And I'm not usually a sweets person, but I'm going to have a piece." Ellie touched Sarah's hand.

"This," Ginger said, reaching into her bag of tricks, "was my mom's." She held up a baseball with blue signatures all over it. "Baseball signed by the 2003 Cubs. Awesome year—well, almost." Ginger tossed the baseball up in the air over and over, catching it each time. She was a contradiction, a dominatrix with talents reaching way beyond whips and chains.

"What is it about that baseball in particular?" Dr. Gretchen inquired.

"We never missed a home game that year. My mom knew lots of the players, so it was cool to be part of the season." Ginger rolled the ball back and forth in the palm of her hand. "It sits by my bed next to her picture."

Mindy pulled out a picture of her mother and began talking about her mother's passion for creating safe places for kids to play. Mandie chimed in, passing around the picture of their mother pushing them on a park swing—a park she had single-handedly renovated. They had been trying in vain to raise enough money to build a park in their mother's memory since her death.

"How much money do you need?" Ellie asked.

"We have five thousand saved, but no one will touch it for less than ten," Mandie replied.

"My mother's charity might be able to help. Safe places for kids are part of our community improvement initiative. My brother Jack serves as chair, so as long as all the required papers are submitted, I'm sure we can help."

The Brown sisters both hugged Ellie.

"Now who would like to go next?" Dr. Gretchen asked, moving the conversation along.

Ellie raised her hand. "I'll go next. This is one of my mother's paintings," she said, removing a canvas from a black leather portfolio bag. It was a portrait of a woman, her bare back at the forefront, her head turned slightly to the right. A large strand of pearls draped down her back, the lowest pearl positioned at the curve of her spine. Her eyes were closed, long dark lashes resting on her upper cheeks. Her face seemed melancholy, her presence haunting.

"It's amazing," I said, breaking the silence.

"It's my mother, a self-portrait." Ellie rubbed the tip of her finger over her mother's painted face.

"She looks sad," Sarah observed.

"Yes, she was at times."

"Do you think she painted herself the way she felt on the inside?" Ginger was staring intently at the picture.

"Perhaps," Ellie said softly.

"Did she ever sell any of her paintings?" Ginger questioned.

"No. My father wanted her to focus on other things, so she only painted for enjoyment."

"How many did she paint?" Mindy asked.

"Enough to completely fill her art studio."

"You should sell some of them at her charity benefit—you know, to support the cause," I suggested.

"That's a brilliant idea," Dr. Gretchen declared.

"Would you be okay selling some of them?" Sarah asked, sensitive to Ellie's feelings.

"I guess so. I've never thought of it before." Ellie was still staring at the picture.

"I bet you could get a ton of money for them, and that means more money for our park," Mandie said, smiling.

We laughed.

"Okay. Maybe I will." Ellie gently put the portrait back in the bag.

"Well, I guess that leaves me," I said. "No matter how good or bad the days were for my mom, she enjoyed one thing." I reached down in my bag and pulled it out. I sat there holding it, feeling my chest tighten. It had been so long, and so many painful memories had been hidden away with it. I wasn't sure why I had decided to resurrect it.

"What is it?" Sarah leaned over to see it better.

"An old movie." I paused. "She spent hours watching them. They always took her to a different place, where she wasn't sick, wasn't slowly dying, a place where she could escape."

"Can we watch it?" Ginger asked.

"Well, I'm not sure we have time …"

"Can everyone stay?" Mandie asked.

Everyone nodded.

"Maybe dessert and a movie?" Sarah pointed at her cake.

"I thought we would never get to the cake!" Ginger squealed.

As the lights dimmed and the movie started, I sank down slightly in my chair. I closed my eyes, regretting the decision to bring it in an earlier, braver moment.

"Oh, I've seen this one before," Ginger said, licking the icing off her fork. "What's the name of it? I can never remember."

"*It's a Wonderful Life.*" I opened my eyes to face my fears.

11

The memories crashed so hard in my head during parts of the movie that I snuck out to throw up. I knew I had to face it sooner or later. I was grateful to see the credits roll, and as we cleaned up, Dr. Gretchen approached me.

"You okay?"

"Sure." I avoided eye contact with her.

"You seemed troubled during the movie. Was it okay that we watched it?"

"It's just ... well, memories, you know."

"Not all memories come wrapped in a ribbon and bow, right?"

"More like a hammer and ax," I said without hesitation.

"Do you want to talk about it?"

"No, thanks, but I appreciate the offer."

She placed her hand over mine, stopping me from wiping down the table. "Gracie, memories can be tricky; they take us to all kinds of places, some of them very scary."

"I know." It was the only thing I could think of to say.

As we were leaving, Dr. Gretchen left us with one final thought. "Ladies, next week, I would like for you to bring a guest to session with you, someone you feel would benefit from sharing this time with you."

Later, I lay in bed, on the verge of tears. The movie's effect on me had been instantaneous and emotionally detrimental. I glanced at the clock. It was after ten.

Me
Hey.

I lay there for a minute waiting for his response.

Me
Really need to hear your voice right now.

Me
Rough night.

Thirty minutes passed, and there was still no response. My insecurities reached a frenzied state.

Me
Forget it.

I saw it then—the red flag waving in front of me. Was he with Angie or someone else, someone prettier, someone not me? I tried to find her in the night sky. Even she was lost to me tonight.

Sometime after midnight, I heard knocking at my door. I had finally fallen asleep, giving into my emotional exhaustion.

"Gracie, open the door."

When I opened the door, Jack stood in front of me, tie loosened, sleeves rolled up, dress pants wrinkled.

He grabbed me and hugged me. "Are you okay? I just got your text messages."

I pulled away from him. I was trying to focus, and my eyes

burned from crying. "Where were you?" I rubbed my eyes in order to see him more clearly.

"Working. Sorry, babe. My phone was on silent. Forgot to switch it back after court." He put his arm around me.

I tried to push the red flag out of my mind. "I got worried."

He kissed the top of my head. "Didn't mean to worry you. What's going on?"

I leaned into him, feeling a sense of comfort rush over me. "Can we talk about it tomorrow?" I took his hand and led him to my room.

He lay next to me, the warmth of his body relaxing me, and I fell asleep. I awoke sometime later to a kiss on my cheek.

"I have to go. I still have a mound of work to do before court."

I looked at the clock. It was dark still, just before four.

"Thanks for coming over." I reached up and kissed him.

He wrapped his arms around me, pressing his lips against mine. We lay there kissing for a few minutes. I reached for his shirt, but he recoiled from me.

"Hey, I need to go."

"Okay." I rolled back over, feeling rejected.

"Don't be mad, okay? I promise I'm all yours tonight. You won't be able to kick me out, even if you try." He kissed my head lightly. "Get some sleep."

I lay there until six watching the clock. I felt uneasy, not sure whether it was the movie still or Jack's vanishing act causing my mood. I was edgy all day, on the verge of either crying or screaming. Jack was my addiction, and just as the highs were heavenly, the lows caused by my own insecurities were hell.

On my drive home from work, my grandma called.

"Hi, Grandma."

"Gracelynn, what are you doing tonight?"

"Not sure yet. What's up?"

"I need a favor."

"Okay, what is it?"

"Sam's vehicle broke down, and your father is away on business. Lacey cannot leave work. Would you mind picking him up?"

"Grandma, he lives like an hour away from here. Doesn't he have friends who can get him?" I was irritated by the thought of helping anyone at the moment.

"I am not sure. He called your father, who called Teddy, but Teddy is in Springfield until tomorrow night."

"I don't know, Grandma ..."

"I can do it, but you know how driving at night bothers me."

I rolled my eyes. "Yeah, sure, Grandma. I'll go get him. Where's he at?"

"Off the expressway, near Deloitte, I believe."

"Okay. I'll head that way now."

"Thank you, Gracelynn." She hesitated for a moment. "What is wrong? I hear something in your voice." My grandma knew every hiccup and hesitation in my voice.

"I watched *It's a Wonderful Life* last night."

"On purpose?" She sounded surprised.

"Yeah."

"No one tied you up and forced you to watch it?"

"No."

"Did you at least keep your eyes closed?"

"For some of it."

"I know what even thinking about that movie does to you. What would possess you to voluntarily watch it?"

"A momentary lapse in judgment."

"With lasting effects, I presume."

"Yes."

She sighed. "Was this part of your *group therapy*?" She said "group therapy" like it was a parasite she was spitting out of her mouth.

"Yes, but it was my decision to bring it."

"Why did you need to bring anything?"

"We were asked to bring something that reminded us of our mothers. I chose the movie."

"But you could have chosen any of her movies. Why that one?"

"I thought I was ready for it."

"I see." She paused. *"Adam's Rib* would have been a better choice."

"Yeah, I realize that now."

"This therapy thing … are you finding benefit from it?"

"I am, Grandma."

I could hear her breathing on the other end of the phone.

"It's about knowing I'm not alone in how I feel, more than anything else."

"I never realized you felt alone." She sounded disappointed.

"It's hard to describe the way being with these other women has made me, somehow, less closed off to things."

"I do not approve of therapy. Hogwash is what I think most of it is."

"I know."

"That being said, if you are finding benefit in it, I make no promises, but I will try to be supportive. Under no circumstances, however, are you to share my personal business with them."

I hesitated. "Thank you, Grandma. I love you."

"Yes, yes, Gracelynn." After a moment, she added, "As I do you."

Me
Sorry, might have to rain check tonight.

Jack B
Why?

Me
My grandma has me running an errand of sorts.

Jack B
Disposing of the bodies for her?

Me
Nothing that exciting.

Jack B
I won't accept the fact we aren't seeing each other tonight.
How long will you be?

Me
Maybe a couple of hours.

Jack B
I'll wait.

I decided to give him an out to see if he would take it.

Me
Really, you don't have to if you have other things going.

Jack B
Nothing more important than you. Let me know when
you're done. I'll be around.

★ ★ ★

As I made the turn off the expressway using the directions Sam
texted me, the gas station he was at illuminated the night. He stood
waiting, two coffees in hand.

Once inside the car, he handed me a cup. "I feel like I owe you
at least a coffee."

I laughed, taking the cup from him. "Not a big deal."

He took a sip of coffee. "Hope I didn't take you away from anything special tonight."

"Not really." I glanced over at him. "Where to?"

"Good question. I live in Brighton, but that's too far for you to drive, so maybe just drop me off at my buddy's in Dexter."

"Don't be silly. I can drive you home. Brighton's not that far." I pulled back onto the expressway and started the ten-mile drive to Brighton. Out of the corner of my eye, I could see him looking at me. "So what happened with your car?"

"Fuel pump, I think. I was heading back from a scout meeting in Leonard when it went out."

"Bummer. Where's it at now?"

"Towed to a repair shop in Brighton. Tow-truck driver only wanted to take my truck and not me, so I was stranded."

"I see." The silence that followed was awkward, so I turned up the radio.

"Take the next exit and then turn right." Sam continued giving directions, taking us through multiple turns and curvy roads until we were driving down a gravel road. At the end of it, a large log cabin with mammoth windows sat in front of us.

"Wow. This is yours?"

"Yep."

I smiled. "It's really nice."

"I have ten acres, and there's a pond in the back. I've been fixing it up for a while. Pet project of mine, I guess."

"Impressive."

"You have time for a quick tour?"

I shifted my gaze to him, taking a long look. His baseball cap was backward, and a black scruffy beard covered his jawline. His demeanor seemed different, more mature.

"A quick tour is fine."

"Good." He smiled at me, the half-moons making my heart flutter.

A large wraparound porch with a swing greeted us as we walked to the door. Inside the house, I felt an instant sense of home. I followed him upstairs, letting him guide me through four bedrooms and two bathrooms. We ended in his bedroom, where doors opened to a balcony. The view from the balcony was breathtaking. The night sky, though brisk, was magnificent.

"This is amazing, Sam." I leaned over the balcony rail, taking it all in.

"Look." He nudged me, pointing to the night sky. "There she is." One star twinkled and nearly glowed.

I took my eyes off the sky and looked at him. "I can't believe you remember."

"There is very little about you I don't remember." As we stood there, my knees started to shake, and my body trembled.

"You cold?" He put his arm around me.

I avoided looking him in the eyes, knowing something might happen if I did. "You've made quite a life for yourself," I said, pulling away from him.

"It's not too bad."

"You look great." I was starting to stumble over my words. "I mean, your life suits you well."

"It's okay, G. I know what you mean." We listened to the night as it engulfed us. "You look exactly the same."

"Yeah, once a pale Irish girl, always a pale Irish girl."

"No, I mean from kids to now, you are still the same beautiful girl."

I wasn't sure what to say, so I just kept focusing on the trees moving softly in the wind. I could feel his eyes burning into me, leaving a lasting mark at every place on my body they traveled.

"Okay," he said, "I need to say something." He pulled at my sleeve. "Can you look at me, please?"

I shifted my eyes from the trees to Sam. "What's up?"

"I've wanted to call you for what seems like forever. I just couldn't do it. Too ashamed, I guess."

"There's no need for you to say anything. Really, I—"

He interrupted me. "Don't say another word, okay? I need to get this out."

A minute earlier, I had been cold, but now the heat inside my body was creating a near-inferno sensation.

"I'm sorry for what I did to you. I was going through a really rough time in high school—a lot of things really, but mostly I felt like I didn't deserve to be happy."

"It's really okay, Sam. Don't worry about it."

"G, just let me finish. This might be my one chance to say what I need to say."

"Okay."

He inched closer, placing his side against the rail, facing me. "I'm embarrassed by what I did. I tried to kill myself."

I bit my lip, wondering whether I should tell him I knew already. Instead, I remained quiet.

"That's why I vanished on you."

"I'm sorry. Are you better now?"

"Of course."

"That's good."

"But there's something else."

"What?" I couldn't look at him. I knew my resistance was weak to anything he might say or do.

"Okay. I'm just going to say it."

"What is it?"

He reached over and took my hand in his. As his hand enveloped mine, warmth darted through every inch of my skin. "I love you. I have loved you since we were kids. And I know it's not ideal because you're with Jack, but I had to tell you while I could. Every good thing in my life has been done with you in mind."

I stood there stunned, saying nothing. He raised his hand and placed it on the side of my face. I was confused, off-balance, uncertain about anything at the moment.

"Don't say anything right now. Just know I'm here and I'm not going anywhere."

"Thank you?"

"I get that I have horrible timing, but every time I try to get you out of my mind, the more I think about only you." He leaned in to kiss me.

I felt myself leaning in as well, not really in control of my body right then. Our lips were nearly touching when the sound of my phone broke through the night air. I stopped, stepped back, and took control of myself.

Jack B
Miss you. You done yet?

I looked at my phone and then at Sam, who stood there with the moon lighting up his face. I looked at my phone again, knowing that what I did next would take my life in a distinct direction.

Me
Just heading back now

Jack B
Where are you???

Me
Brighton

"Sam, I need to go."
"Jack?"
I nodded, stepping farther away from him.

"Like I said, bad timing."

"Thanks for the tour," I said, my words trailing off.

He walked up to me slowly, and my heart pulsed harder with every step he took. He wrapped his arms around me, holding me tight. He placed his hand on the back of my head; I could hear his heart racing through his shirt. We stood there for a moment before I pulled away.

I sat in my car outside Sam's house, staring at my phone.

Jack B
Why are you in Brighton?

Jack B
Are you with Sam?

Jack B
Call me.

As I made my way back to the expressway, I thought about what I should tell Jack. In the end, I decided to call and tell him the truth.

"Hey, Jack."

"Where are you?"

"Heading back from Brighton."

"What were you doing in Brighton?"

"I had to pick someone up and drop them off at their house."

"Sam?"

I hesitated for a moment. "Yes."

"I thought you had to run an errand for your grandma?" Jack's voice sparked with anger.

"It was for my grandma."

"Since when are your grandma and Sam besties?"

"They aren't, Jack. His mom is at work, so he called my dad for a ride, and my dad is out of town, so my dad called Teddy, who is also out of town, so that left my grandma or me to do it."

"And you graciously volunteered to drive all the way to Brighton to pick him up?"

"My grandma doesn't like to drive long distances at night."

"Doesn't he have any friends who could pick him up?"

"Apparently not tonight."

"I don't like it."

"Okay."

"Did you just drop him off?"

"Pretty much."

"What's *pretty much* mean?" This was a side of Jack I'd never experienced before.

"I picked him up in Deloitte and dropped him off at his house in Brighton. That's pretty much it."

There was silence on the phone.

"Hello?"

"You didn't go in his house, right? You just dropped him off?"

I bit the inside of my lip. "He gave me a quick tour, and then I left."

"A tour of what?"

"His house, Jack. What's this all about anyway?" I felt myself getting more defensive with every question he asked.

"You're either in this with me, or you're not."

"Funny, I could say the same thing about you."

"What?"

"Don't think I haven't noticed the disappearing act you pull."

"What disappearing act?"

"Not responding to texts, leaving in the middle of the night. It just seems strange to me."

"I have to work, Gracie. I have a demanding job."

"Okay."

"What, you think I'm up to something?"

"Maybe."

"That's crap. That's your own insecurities."

"And what's this? Why the third degree about me giving Sam a ride home?"

He was quiet on the other end the call. I watched the bright white dashes of lines on the road, waiting for him to respond.

"I just don't like it."

"Well, our parents are marrying each other, so he's going to be around, whether you like it or not."

"You're going to have to make some decisions."

"What do you mean by that?" I could feel my anger nearly overflowing.

"Me and Sam coexisting with you? I don't think so."

"Coexisting?"

"Yeah."

"His mother is marrying my father. That's as far as the coexisting goes."

"Really? Are you sure about that?"

"You're being ridiculous."

"All I'm saying is that I'm not going to stand around watching Sam stake claim on my territory."

"Territory? Are you calling me your territory?"

"You know what I mean."

"No, I really don't. 'Cause just now you made it seem like I was some property of yours."

"You're my girlfriend. Act like it."

Any other time, I would have loved hearing Jack call me his girlfriend, but right then it sounded like he was putting me in my place, like another trophy in his girlfriend display case.

"Bottom line is that Sam is going to be around for what I believe will be a long time, so either you deal with it or not."

"I don't want him around you."

"Well, too late, because it's already happening."

"You need to stay away from him."

"And if I don't?"

Jack was silent. Suddenly, I was a couple of miles away from the Highmore exit, not even remembering how I'd gotten from Brighton to Highmore.

"And if I don't?" I repeated.

"Then we're done."

I felt his words then. "Our parents are getting married. I can't stop Sam from being in my life. It's not fair of you to ask."

"Then we're done."

I glanced at my phone screen and saw his name disappear. He had hung up on me. I felt a blow to my heart. It was crushing and instant. Three times in a row, I called him, and each time the call went straight to his voice mail. My hands were trembling at the wheel, my leg shaking so bad I could barely keep the speed of my car constant.

I pulled in my garage, feeling the impact of his words hit me. They were all I could smell, all I could taste. I lay in the bathtub wondering how things had gone so sideways so fast. I had been his girlfriend one minute and then someone so insignificant the next that he was ignoring my calls. I picked up the phone and called him three more times, only to hear "You've reached Jack Bradshaw ..."

The tears came on like an avalanche I could not stop. An hour into my sob fest, I heard my phone chirp.

Sam
Thanks again for the ride.

Me
No prob.

I lay there with tears dropping on the screen.

Sam

Hope Jack was ok with it.

I looked at the words, my heart aching.

Me

All good.

I picked up the phone and called Chloe, who I knew would make me feel better.

"You busy?" I asked as I wiped my nose with my thermal shirt sleeve.

"You okay?"

Her simple question made my tears come quickly.

"What happened?"

I took a deep breath, trying to regain my composure. "Jack broke up with me." I was nearly sobbing.

"Why?"

"He thinks I'm cheating on him with Sam."

"Why would he think that?" I heard the tone of her voice change slightly.

"No reason, really."

"There has to be some reason he thinks that."

"Jack and I were supposed to do something tonight, but I had to pick Sam up and take him home first, and Jack got mad."

"Wait. Why did you have to pick Sam up?"

"His car broke down."

"In Highmore?"

"No, Deloitte."

"Doesn't he have any friends who could have picked him up?"

"Jack asked me the same thing."

"Yeah, 'cause it's a good question."

239

"My grandma called and asked me to pick him up."

"How did she get in the mix?"

"Sam called my dad, who called Teddy, and it ended up being me."

"Why didn't you take Jack with you to pick him up?"

I pondered her question. "I never really thought about asking him."

"And why might that be?"

"I don't know. Why does it matter?"

"Because it seems you are trying to hide something by not telling your new man you were going to pick up your old man."

"I told him."

"And you told him this information without him asking you first?"

I remained silent.

"That's what I thought."

"Anyway, I told Jack I didn't like his disappearing act."

"What disappearing act?"

"How he sometimes doesn't respond to my texts right away and how he leaves in the middle of the night. His excuse is that he has to work, but it seems strange to me."

"Gracie, he's an attorney who has to crank out like a gazillion billable hours each week. Not everyone has a job like yours where they can dictate when they want to work."

"You think my job's not demanding?"

"Not as demanding as his."

"Thanks a lot."

"I didn't say it isn't important, just that it's not as demanding. He's a partner in a major law firm, and he still finds time to date you. Pretty impressive if you ask me."

I was starting to feel bad about what I had said to Jack, questioning his whereabouts.

"And knowing Sam," Chloe continued, "I'm sure there's something else to this story."

I bit the inside of my mouth. "He told me he loved me."

"Of course he did. Typical Sam."

"It was nothing really."

"And what was your response when Sam professed his undying love for you?"

"Thank you?"

Chloe laughed. "Well, I guess that's better than telling him you loved him too."

"Jack doesn't want me seeing Sam, but how can I avoid it? Our parents are getting married."

"Well, you have a point there. Why do you think Jack is so sensitive about Sam?"

"I don't know."

"Think about it, Gracie. He's been burned before—cheated on and lied to. Clearly, he's ready to go all in, and then you show signs of bluffing, so he calls your bluff."

Chloe was right, as always. I had given Jack reason to doubt me. What was wrong with me? I had self-sabotaged my happiness again. "Now what?"

"Did you try to talk to him?"

"I've called him like ten times, but he's not answering my calls."

"You need to give him some time. When he's ready to talk, he will. Until then, find something else to do with your time—something else, that is, besides Sam. Got it?"

"Yeah." I felt sadness seeping through my pores.

"Just give it some time. I'm sure he'll come around."

"What if he does? He said I'll have to make some decisions about Sam. How can I not see Sam when he's going to be at basically every holiday and family function in my life?"

"Well ... maybe by then Jack will be in a better place, knowing you have no intentions of being with Sam. You don't, right?"

"I don't." I was glad Chloe wasn't sitting in front of me right then. I wanted to be with Jack, but the connection I felt with Sam was undeniable.

"Good. Keep it that way. Trust me, it would never end up the way you want it to anyway with Sam."

All I could think of was Jack. I needed to make it right with him. I had a chance at happiness with Jack, a real chance at a complete life. Jack wasn't a runner like Sam. I needed to get him back no matter the cost.

The next day I waited for Jack to call, but he didn't. I suffered through my day, feeling the effects that never hearing from him again might have on me. I tried three more times to call him, with no luck, before I went to bed.

By Friday morning, I could barely function, numb to my existence. I knew it would have been only a matter of time anyway before our relationship eroded. In the end, I knew my insecurities stood between us.

At least my classes kept my mind occupied for a while. As the clock ticked slowly, I tried to come to terms with my life. I had survived worse: death and loneliness and feeling lost in my own life. I wasn't sure why losing Jack was hitting me so hard. We had been together for only a short time, but I had felt different with him. Even though I knew he was out of my league, I had felt confident around him, a bolder, brighter version of myself. As my students dissected Emily Dickinson's "Because I Could Not Stop for Death," I felt like I was dying inside myself. Because I could not stop for death, as she said, it had stopped for me.

On my way home, a cold rain beat against my windshield, sending chills up my spine. The rain grew heavier; the chill, greater. I pulled into my garage and sat there for a minute, listening to the rain come down.

I walked from the garage to my mailbox and as I tugged at the soggy envelopes smashed inside it, I caught a glimpse of something on my front porch. I looked closer and saw him; he sat quietly on the swing, using his legs to move it slowly back and forth. His hair was wet, his head down.

I walked over and stood in front of him, feeling the rain wash over me. "Hi."

He raised his head, causing my heart to explode. He stopped the swing. "Hi, back."

"How was your day?" I asked.

He laughed. "I've had better." He reached out and pulled me to him. I inched closer to him, letting the rain run down my back. He guided me to the swing. His fingers intertwined with mine. "I just can't go through what I went through before—you know, with Angie."

"It's not like that at all. And I've thought a lot about it, and I'll do my best to stay away from Sam."

He looked at me, his eyes red—from lack of sleep, I suspected. "No. Your parents are marrying each other. You were right. It's not fair for me to ask."

"I understand why you did," I replied.

"You do?"

"Being cheated on has to be a horrible thing. I'm sure it brings with it a lot of residual doubt."

He nodded. "If I want to be with you, I have to trust you'll make the right decisions when it comes to Sam."

"Do you want to be with me?"

He looked down at his feet, beginning to slowly move the swing again. "Yes, I do."

I hesitated. "I'm not going to lie. Sam and I have a history. But it's history because it's in the past."

"And you swear there's nothing between you two?"

My mind flew back to Sam's profession of love and our near kiss. I wiped it out of my mind with my response. "Pinky swear." I held out my pinky.

He smiled, leaned down, and kissed it softly. "But we have to come to an understanding about some things," he said.

"Okay." I was nervous, wondering what he was going to say next.

"I work a lot. It's my job. I wish I didn't work so much, but I don't punch a nine-to-five clock. You have to understand that."

"Understood."

"And I can't always respond to your texts right away. If I'm working, I can't just stop what I'm doing to send you something back."

"I got it."

"That being said, I'll do a better job of staying in touch so you don't worry."

"That would be nice."

"I want you in my life, Gracie, but it might not always be easy."

Since Jack was laying his cards out on the table, I figured I might as well do the same. "And there's nothing between you and Angie?" I expected that his instant response would be no. It wasn't.

"It's complicated."

"How so?"

"I was going to spend my life with her, so I gave her everything— everything I thought I had to give, that is."

"I see." I felt my stomach churn. He wasn't over her yet. I shifted away from him.

"I'm the one who broke it off with her, so don't get the wrong idea. She brought out the worst in me. But she's like a tornado whenever I'm around her. I have to work really hard not to get caught up in it."

I looked away at the rain falling in front of my feet, just inches away from soaking my shoes. I remained quiet.

"Ah, now I've made you doubt me. I'm here for the long haul, Gracie. It's just that I need you to be patient with me. I feel like … no, I *know* you make me a better person. I'm just still trying to recover from Angie."

"I know."

"I never thought there would be anyone better than Angie, until now."

I looked into his eyes and leaned in to kiss him. Our mouths absorbed each other, fire emanating between us.

Jack's mouth moved to my ear. "God, I missed you." He wrapped his lips around my earlobe, slightly sucking on my skin.

"I have an hour before session. Want to go inside and make up?"

Later, lying on the living room floor, barely inside the door, I held onto Jack, his body sweaty and heavy on top of mine.

"Not that I want to fight, but the making-up part is pretty awesome," he said, kissing my shoulder blade.

"It does have its benefits." I looked over at the wall clock, barely visible in the near darkness of the room. "Crap, I have to go. My session starts in less than fifteen minutes."

We walked into the community center together, hand in hand. It was a feeling I hadn't experienced in a really long time—completeness. With a kiss good-bye, Jack headed to the gym, and I headed to the session.

Ginger looked up at me as I entered. "You look fabulous. What have you been doing with yourself?" She smiled. "Oh, wait, I think I just figured it out."

I smiled and took my seat next to her. "Sorry I'm late."

"Okay, now that we're all here, who would like to start?" asked Dr. Gretchen, sitting next to Sarah.

"I've had a pretty interesting week," I announced.

Dr. Gretchen motioned for me to start speaking.

"Well, it started off pretty rough but got much better."

"What happened?" Sarah inquired.

I knew it was a safe circle but I still hesitated for a minute, knowing Ellie was in the room. "I had to give my ex a ride home when his car broke down, and he professed his love to me."

"What did you say in return?" Ellie asked immediately. I knew that her question was more for Jack's benefit than for mine.

"Thank you?"

Sarah giggled. "Even I know that's a shut-down."

"Hard to explain that to others."

"I take it the new guy wasn't as convinced?" Ginger was dressed for work tonight, complete with black thigh-high leather boots.

"Not at first. Like I said, the week didn't start out great, but I finally convinced him."

"I usually do that with a good whipping." Ginger leaned back proudly.

"I picked out some of my mom's pieces, and they are going to be auctioned off at the benefit," Ellie said, changing the subject.

"Have you thought about putting them online as well for silent bidders?" Sarah asked innocently.

"Online? Well, no. I never thought ..."

"You could get so many more bids if they go online first," Sarah explained.

"How do I do that?" Ellie asked.

Sarah smiled. "It's easy. I catalog items at the library for archives and auction. I can help."

"That would be wonderful. I can't wait for you to see the paintings at the benefit."

"Well," Sarah said hesitantly, "I'm not sure I have anything proper to wear."

"Oh, I've got lots of stuff," said Ginger. "You can borrow something from me."

We all looked at Ginger, wondering whether she was really serious.

"I don't mean *this* stuff," she said, jiggling one of the chains around her neck that was doubling as a necklace. "My mom sold stuff online, like women's clothes. I have a lot of stuff that would work."

Sarah's face lit up. "Really? That would be really nice."

"There's a lot to do, I'm afraid, and not much time," Ellie said anxiously.

"We could all help," I offered, as did others in the room.

"Dr. Gretchen, for Tuesday's session, can we spend some time helping Ellie?" Mandie asked.

"Well, next week I wanted you to bring a special someone to session, but maybe we can push it back."

"This benefit means so much, especially now ..." Ellie's voice broke, tears flowing down her face. As she wiped away the tears, I noticed it: her engagement ring was gone from her finger. All that remained was the mark where the heavy diamond band had once rested.

"Ellie, what is it?" I reached over and touched her arm.

"It's Bruce. I found him ..."

"Dead? You found him dead?" Ginger's eyes widened.

"No, I found him with another woman ... in our bed," she said, her voice hiccupping.

"Oh, Ellie. What did you do?" Dr. Gretchen asked.

"I told him I was through with the lying and cheating." She wiped her nose with her lace shirt cuff.

Sarah dug into her purse and handed Ellie a packet of fresh tissues.

"Now I'm second-guessing my decision."

"Why?" Sarah asked.

"Maybe some people can't help but cheat," Ellie replied.

"What do you mean, they can't help it? I've been with lots of people, and trust me, they can always help it," Ginger boldly responded.

"Maybe there are circumstances when it's too tempting for someone to stay faithful," Ellie said, trying to reason with Ginger.

Ginger looked intently at Ellie. "I know you don't believe that, right?"

"All I'm saying is maybe he couldn't help it."

"Is that what he told you?" Ginger leaned in Ellie's direction. "Because if it is, it's total crap. I know you love him, but you deserve better, way better."

Ellie was blotting her cheeks where the tears had fallen. "Thank you for saying that. Can we just talk about something else, please?"

For the next hour, we talked about how we were going to organize the artwork for the benefit. Sarah seemed to have the best organizational skills out of all of us. She had Ginger take notes, and as each task was written down, one of us was assigned to it.

As the session drew to a close, Dr. Gretchen asked us to sit back down in different seats than the ones we had sat in when the session started.

"Now that you are all sitting in different seats, tell me how that feels."

"What do you mean?" Mindy asked.

"Does it feel strange to be sitting in different seats?"

"No," Sarah said, and we all shook our heads, agreeing with her response. "Why should it?"

"Exactly," Dr. Gretchen replied. "When we started, each of you had a specific seat you took that brought you a level of comfort. Now, each of you is seated in a different place, and being here still brings you the same level of comfort. What does that tell you?"

"We like all the seats the same?" Mandie responded.

"It means," Ellie explained, "that no matter where we sit in the room, we find the same level of comfort—with each other."

"Yes," Dr. Gretchen said. "Why do you think you are all so quick to help one another out?"

"We're good people," Ginger answered.

"I don't think so," I said, surprising the group.

"What, you don't think we're good people?" There was an edge to Mindy's voice.

"No, it's not that at all," I clarified. "The answer, I think, is that we're one another's safety nets. We want to catch each other before we fall because we know how it feels to hit the ground."

Dr. Gretchen smiled at me. "Yes," she said. "Now tell me another time you've felt like this."

"With my mother," Mandie said, tears filling her eyes.

"I'm not sure if I will always be able to give you a safety net, but I promise I'll help break your fall," I said, feeling emotional for an unknown reason.

Ginger looked at me. "You know ..." She hesitated before continuing. "I don't have a lot of friends—not a lot of people I trust. But you, I trust you with my life."

Then it happened. Ginger's leather pants, chain-link necklace, and glitter eyelashes faded away, and I just saw a sister. I knew she meant more to me than almost anyone, like the other women sitting around this bound circle with me.

Sarah said, "I feel like I can do anything as long as—"

"We have one another," Ellie said, finishing her sentence.

"What happened with you between the first day and now?" Dr. Gretchen looked at each of us.

I finally spoke on behalf of the circle. "We've changed."

Dr. Gretchen said nothing else but walked over to Ellie and took her hand. Ellie then took mine. One by one, we took hands until our circle was complete, unbreakable. We said nothing because we didn't need to speak.

As the session ended, Jack stood waiting for me outside the door.

"You know," I said, "I was thinking, maybe if Ellie's not busy, we can grab some takeout and start tackling your mom's pictures for the auction."

The art studio sat on top of the garage. Artwork leaned against the wall, lined up like dominoes. Finished canvases rested in egg crate slots, and pictures hung on the walls from floor to ceiling.

One painting caught my eye. It was a large canvas, painted completely black. In the bottom corner, there was a smudge. It moved up the canvas, and the larger the smudge became, the more color splashed onto the canvas, until near the middle of the painting, where a thousand brightly colored butterflies seemingly appeared. They took over the print, transforming what once had been blackness into a foray of color. Then, as quickly as they had taken over, they disappeared again, falling back into the blackness of the painting. It was breathtaking.

"You like that one?" Ellie stood next to me, eating sesame noodles one at a time as they dangled from a white box.

"Yes. I've never seen anything like it before."

"It was one of her favorites as well."

Jack glanced over at it, wiping the side of his mouth with a napkin. "That one's not for sale."

I continued standing there, captured by the butterflies. Was that how she had felt, coming out of the darkness into a world of color, then fading back into darkness again? The sound of my phone broke my thoughts.

"Hello?"

"Gracelynn? This is your grandma."

"What's up?"

There was silence on the other end of the phone.

"I mean, what can I do for you, Grandma?"

"We will not be meeting for breakfast tomorrow. There is still work to be done for tomorrow night."

"Tomorrow night?"

"Yes, Gracelynn. Did you forget?"

"Yeah, I know, the family dinner, but what's there to do? It's just us."

"I have a dress coming from the boutique for you. It will arrive tomorrow morning. It has been altered based on your current measurements."

"Wait, what? Why do I need a dress? I was just going to wear jeans."

"Not proper attire for a party."

"What party?"

"The one tomorrow night," she said, sounding annoyed.

"I thought we were just having a family dinner. Has something changed?"

"I decided to invite a few more people."

"How many more people, Grandma?" I knew where this was going, and I didn't like it.

"No more than fifty should be in attendance."

"Fifty? Is this a White House dinner?"

"It is a club dinner. Have you not heard a word? Are you wearing those earplug devices again?"

"Earbuds? No, Grandma. I'm just not sure how we went from a small family dinner to a party at the club."

"I thought it would be nice to formally celebrate."

"Isn't that called a wedding?"

"Please arrive at the club no later than half past five."

"Is this a plus-one event?"

She was quiet for a moment. "You may ask Mr. Bradshaw to attend."

I hung up and walked over to Jack, who was cataloging paintings. "So my grandma is throwing my dad and Lacey an engagement party tomorrow night at the club. Would you like to be my plus-one?"

"Tomorrow night? I need to be in court on Monday for this acquisition, and I'm not even close to prepared, so it's all about work for me tomorrow night."

I felt a wave of disappointment hit me. "It's okay. It'll be boring anyway, I'm sure."

"Want to get out of here and have some fun? Ellie's out like a light anyway."

I looked over at Ellie, who was beautiful even as she slept, unlike me. I drooled on my pillow and sometimes slept with my mouth open, letting high-pitched gasps of air escape, which sounded like a hyena being tickled.

The next day, the sound of my doorbell pulled me into the morning light. Jack lay next to me, the light of the day bouncing off his naked body. I shuffled to the door, feeling the coolness of the morning air. A large white box lay at my door. I knew I needed to call my grandma within five minutes of receiving the package, or I would never hear the end of it.

"Hello, Blake Desiree Honoree Smith speaking."

"Hey, Grandma."

"Gracelynn?"

"Yes, Grandma. It's me. And if you ever looked at your caller ID, you'd know it was me."

She was silent.

"Anyway, I got the dress. Thanks."

"Is it just you attending this evening?" She asked like she already knew the answer.

"Yes. Jack has to work. No plus-one tonight."

"I see. Try to do something with your hair. You are too pretty a girl to not show off your best attributes."

"My brains are my best attribute, Grandma."

"Unless you are going to wear your brains pinned to your chest, you need to work with what is on the outside. Storefront window, remember?"

"I have a boyfriend."

"You are not a thrift shop, Gracelynn. Remember that."

By three, Chloe and I were getting manicures and catching up on the week.

"So ... things with Jack back on track?" she asked, sipping a glass of wine.

"Yep. Hey, any chance you want to be my plus-one tonight at my dad's engagement party?"

"Can't. I declined when I got the invite from your grandma anyway. Why aren't you taking Jack?"

"You got an invite? I didn't even know it was a party." I sat there annoyed at my grandma for a minute. "He has to work on a big case."

"Oh, okay." She leaned her head back in her massage chair as it rippled along her shoulders. "Well, I'm sure it will be a night to remember."

We both looked at each other and laughed.

That evening I stood inside the entrance of the club, where I'd stood a million times before with and without my mother. Now I stood there with the realization that she was forever gone. I liked Lacey and knew her to be a kind, loving, and compassionate person. But she would never be my mother. I felt my knees grow weak. I was reaching over to touch the wall when his hand took mine for support.

"Sam …" I stumbled a bit. "Thanks."

"Wow, G."

I had forgotten what I was wearing—a deep plum dress with a plunging V neckline in the front and the back, the fabric gathering in a twist at my waist—and how I had ironed my hair in loose waves, tucked to one side with a diamond barrette. I had forgotten too the red lipstick and thick black mascara I had painstakingly placed on my lips and eyes and the tinted moisturizer with light flecks of glitter that I had gently rubbed on my face and neck. It was only after I saw my reflection in Sam's eyes that I remembered I had gotten ready at all.

"I've never seen anything as beautiful as you in my entire life."

I smiled, saying nothing.

"Gracelynn, Samuel, glad you could join us." My grandma approached wearing a beaded pantsuit with a gold sheer tank under the form-fitting jacket. Teddy walked slightly behind her, sporting black pants and a black T-shirt with the outline of a tuxedo on the front. I grinned when I saw Teddy, knowing he had refused to conform to my grandma's formal attire rule, unlike like the rest of us.

"Have you looked at yourself today? You should be in a magazine," Teddy said admiringly.

"I know, right?" Sam said, the half-moons nearly breaking his cheeks in half. "Teddy, would you mind taking a picture of us?" He asked, handing Teddy his smartphone.

Sam put his arm around my waist, pulling me to him. He wore a black fitted suit with light pinstripes, his tie was varying shades of purple, and his shirt was crisp and white. He smelled like how I imagined hiking in the woods would smell—clean, fresh, and with a hint of evergreen.

"How lovely," Lacey said as she walked up and stood next to Teddy. "Jeff and I should get in the picture as well."

My dad walked over and gently kissed Lacey. I was taken aback for a minute, not used to seeing him shower affection on anyone besides my mom. Quickly, about ten other people, mostly unknown to me, began taking pictures of us, commenting on how great the "new family" looked and how happy we must be. We stood there in the paparazzi moment until I was tired of smiling and tried to ease out of the frame.

Sam leaned down to me. "Race you to the bar?"

I couldn't get away from the moment fast enough. We stood at the bar, and not until I was on the last sip of my second vodka lemonade did I notice Sam staring at me.

"I know. I look hot. You can't take your eyes off me," I said, motioning for another round from the bartender.

Sam laughed. "Actually, I can't take my eyes off your drinking. Since when do you have a wooden leg?"

"Since about two hours ago."

He laughed, motioning for another drink as well. "You okay with this? You seemed a little shaky on your feet earlier."

"I really like your mom—I really do. It just makes me realize that my mom is forever out of the picture. I'm sure that doesn't make much sense to you."

"No, I get it." Sam took a long sip of beer. "I really liked your mom, G. She was super nice." He paused. "I don't think this is about replacing your mom, though. It's more like someone for your dad to spend part two of his life with."

"I guess." I looked over at him. "You cool with it?"

"Yeah, your dad treats my mom like she should be treated."

I looked over and watched my dad with Lacey, his hand on her lower back, supporting her. I was envious of Lacey for a minute, wishing my dad had been like that with me.

"Children, time for toasts," my grandma announced as she clapped her hands twice in our direction.

"I haven't been called a child in a really long time," Sam said as we walked toward the head table.

"Get used to it. We'll be in our eighties, and my grandma will still call us children."

"Your grandma is still going to be around when we're in our eighties?"

"Didn't you know? My grandma intends to live forever."

"Now that one I believe."

The six of us took our seats at the head table, with nine full tables of mostly strangers laid out in front of us. Grandma took a long drink of her vodka tonic and motioned for me to stand and give a toast. I sat there with my glass on the edge of my lips, not prepared to speak. Blood rushed to my cheeks as I remained motionless.

Sam, noticing my face, stood instead. "Here's to two amazing people getting to enjoy part two of their lives together!" He raised his glass to our parents. "G, anything you want to add?" He looked at me.

I slowly rose, feeling the effects of the vodka. I looked over at my dad and Lacey, smiles adorning their faces. My father and I would never be more than paper hearts to each other—fragile, imperfect, one-dimensional. But for the two of them, their love could be full of layers. To say anything less in that moment would not be appropriate and to some would even seem unforgivable.

"Being someone's first love may be great, but being their last love is nothing short of wondrous. Here's to lasting love." I raised my glass to them and sat down quickly. I finished my drink as the band began playing.

"Gracelynn," my grandma said, tapping me on the shoulder.

"Yes?" I looked up at her, expecting a lecture.

She kissed my cheek, saying nothing.

Teddy stood next to her. "She couldn't have said it better herself."

Just after the dinner plates were removed, my dad and Lacey stood. After thanking everyone for coming, they formally asked Sam and me to serve as best man and maid of honor.

We both nodded yes, as if we would like nothing more from life.

By the time dessert arrived, I was on my fifth vodka lemonade. Surprisingly, although I was tipsy, all my motor functions were still working.

I was dancing with Teddy when Sam tapped him on the shoulder. "May I cut in?" As Sam pulled me close to him, he whispered "I love you" in my ear.

I stepped back suddenly, realizing what he had said. I walked out of the room, out the door, and into the night air. Sam was right behind me.

"G, it's freezing out here. Come back inside."

"I need some air."

"Why did you leave me standing on the dance floor?"

"I told you, I needed air."

"That's not the reason. I love you, and you love me too."

"What are you talking about, Sam?"

"I wasn't sure until tonight, but now I'm sure. You love me." He reached for me, and I pulled away.

"You're out of your mind."

"I'm not. Give me a chance to make you happy."

"I can't."

He reached for my hand, and this time, I let him take it momentarily.

"Why not?" he asked.

"Because." I felt myself getting cold.

"That's not a reason. Give me a reason because all I know is the thought of spending my life without you is unimaginable."

"I can't count on you. Even you said you still run. We're not kids anymore. I need someone who is willing to stay put, stick it out. And that's not you."

"And you think that's Jack? Do you even know anything about him? If it seems too good to be true, that probably means it isn't true."

I kept my eyes focused on a busboy who was tucked away by the side of the building, taking quick drags off a cigarette.

"There are a lot of things I don't know, like how the future will play out, but I love you, G, and that's all I need to know."

"What do you want me to say?"

"I want you to say you love me."

"I don't."

"Look at me and tell me to my face you don't love me."

I knew that if I told him I didn't love him, it would be a lie. I did, even if I wasn't sure in what way. "I'm not going to do this with you, Sam."

"I know you've loved me since we were kids. Maybe I wasn't ready then, but I'm ready for you now."

"You had your chance, and you threw it away." I felt completely sober now and was trying to hold my emotions at bay.

"The biggest mistake of my life was letting you go."

"You left me like trash on the side of the road. You ran as far away from me as possible."

"And I've told you how sorry I am for that. I was messed up."

"And you don't think I was messed up? My mom died when I was practically still a kid. I was left to fend for myself, my dad barely acknowledging my existence, my grandma pointing out my every little flaw. And not once did it change the way I felt about you. I would have crawled on my hands and knees to the ends of the earth for you. That's how much I loved you." I stopped talking, tears flooding my eyes, anger filling my voice.

"It must have been hard for you." He looked out into the parking lot.

"Hard would be an understatement." We stood there in silence. "It's getting late. Party's over. I'm heading home."

"Can I at least give you a ride?"

"I drove myself." I walked back into the building, leaving Sam standing out in the cold.

Later, I lay in bed, phone in hand, still fully dressed. I wanted to see Jack; I needed to see him. I watched the clear night sky, a bright star holding my attention. At ten thirty, I felt the pangs of sleep pulling at me, the last ounces of vodka sending mini volts of pain to my head. I hadn't heard from Jack.

Me
I miss you. Come over.

Time fell away from me. I woke to the shrill overhead light of my room. The clock glared at me. It was after one. As I drifted off to sleep, I thought about the night, about Sam, about his words. Jack would be by my side soon after I found sleep again.

The world in my dream was bold, vibrant. I was running through a field of flowers. With every step I took, the colors became more intense. Thousands of butterflies surrounded me, dancing at my feet, their unified motion lifting me in the air. I felt myself being carried away by the butterflies, their wings giving me flight. Then the sky became dark and ominous, sending the butterflies into a frenzied state. They lost their grip on me, and I began descending into darkness, the blackness beneath me ready to swallow me up. His hands reached out and gently took hold of me. He kept me from falling, saved me from infinite darkness.

"Thank you," I whispered, feeling a sense of peace.

He said nothing. He just smiled, the half-moons staring back at me as he carried me safely home.

12

The dream stuck with me all morning. I couldn't shake it, even when Jack lay on top of me, whispering in my ear how good I felt, how amazing I was, how he wanted to stay inside of me forever.

As we sat drinking coffee, Jack reached over and squeezed my hand. "Hey, you okay?"

"Sure," I said, smiling at him.

"You seem distracted."

"I'm just tired. You woke me up early."

He laughed. "I can't help it. You bring it out in me."

"Did you get a lot of work done last night?" As I looked over at him, his eyes moved to his coffee.

"I didn't get it all done, but I made a good dent in it."

"You working today?"

"I should, but I'd rather spend the day with you."

"There's an Alfred Hitchcock film festival showing at the Palace. It's a fundraiser to save the theater. Interested?"

"Definitely."

As we sat in the dark theater watching *Rear Window*, I felt doubt creeping into my mind. Maybe it was the sense of paranoia all Alfred Hitchcock movies seemed to create, but something about Jack was bothering me. I took my eyes off the old large screen and focused on him. His eyes were closed, his breathing slow. His hand rested over mine as he slumped slightly in his seat. Two seats over, I saw a woman staring at him. When her eyes caught mine, she quickly went back to watching the movie.

At intermission between movies, as I stood in line at the bathroom, the same woman waited behind me.

"Excuse me," she said, tapping me on the shoulder. "Is that Jack Bradshaw with you?"

I looked at her. "Uh-huh."

"I thought so."

"Do you know Jack?" I asked.

"Not really. I met him through Angie."

I felt my limbs tense up as I turned back around.

After a moment, she asked, "Are you friends with Jack?"

"He's my boyfriend," I stated, without turning around.

"Really?" She seemed surprised by my statement.

I finally turned around again and looked at her.

"It's just that, well, I didn't realize they weren't together anymore."

"They haven't been together for a while," I said with confidence.

"I thought I just saw them together."

My confidence crumbled instantly, the paranoia taking over again.

"So," she said, trying to change the subject, "are you enjoying the films?"

I nodded, unable to speak. As a stall opened up, I nearly dove into it.

Back in the theater, Jack handed me a drink. I half-smiled. I couldn't say anything as anger and doubt ran through my veins.

"You okay?"

From the corner of my eye, I saw the woman take her seat again. Instinctively, I motioned to her and said, "Jack, I believe you know each other." I watched his facial expression, waiting for it to change.

He smiled. "Hello, June."

"Hey, Jack, I thought that was you." They stared at each other for a beat, saying nothing else. The lights flickered on and off, signaling the start of *North by Northwest*.

I tried to focus on the movie but knew it was useless. Jack seemed unfazed by his encounter with June. Instead, he ran his hand up and down my leg throughout the movie. By the time *The Birds* started, I was ready to go, as was Jack, as evidenced by where he placed my hand.

As soon as we got into the car, Jack pulled me to him. "Come here, you." His hand dug into my shirt as his tongue pressed against my lips, trying to force them open.

"Jack." I tried to pull away, but his strength outmatched mine easily.

"Let's do it in the car," he breathed in my ear.

"I don't think so." I shoved him back as forcefully as I could.

"Gracie, what's wrong?"

"Nothing. I just don't like being mauled," I said, trying to adjust my shirt, which he had nearly ripped.

"Whatever," he huffed.

We drove back to my house in silence. I hadn't seen that side of him before, and I didn't like it. As we pulled up, he turned off the engine and got out of the car. He opened my door for me. I tried to step around him, but he wrapped his arms around me.

"I'm sorry. I'm not sure what got into me back there." He kissed the top of my head. "Can I make it up to you?"

"How?"

"I promise to keep Mr. Happy in check tonight."

I laughed.

I fell asleep with Jack's arms around me, feeling warm and safe. I was the one who reached for him in the middle of the night. He willingly let me take control, and the power I had sent us both to new levels of enjoyment.

Afterward, we lay there naked, tangled in each other. "No words to describe being with you," he panted.

I smiled, moving my hand up and down his stomach slowly.

I awoke and rolled over at six and watched Jack sleeping next to me. I inched over and kissed his cheek. "Hey, you," I whispered. "It's six. You need to get going?"

He groggily opened his eyes. "Six? Already? But it's still dark outside." He pushed his head under a pillow.

"I'll make coffee."

"Come here first." He kissed me. "Okay, now go make coffee."

I was pouring my second cup of coffee when he spoke. "So about June ..."

I stopped and sat back down at the kitchen table next to him. "Yeah, so what about her?"

He reached over and took my hand. "I know her through Angie."

"She mentioned that in the bathroom."

He leaned back in his chair. "I don't know her too well, but I do know her."

"Did you know that was her sitting next to us before I said something?"

He nodded.

"Then why didn't you say anything?"

"What did you want me to say? There's my ex-fiancée's friend?"

"I guess that does sound weird."

"I knew it bothered you, so I wanted to come clean about it."

"Thanks." I hesitated for a minute. "Is that why you went all caveman on me in the car?"

"I'm not sure why I did that. I guess I was trying to reassure you."

"Well, next time, just tell me as opposed to mounting me in a car outside a run-down movie theater."

"Got it."

"She did say ..." I stopped, trying to decide whether I should bring it up or not.

"What did she say?"

"That she just saw you and Angie together."

I thought he would instantly deny it, but instead he just stared at me. I waited for him to say something.

"Were you just with her?"

"I was."

I felt my heart drop.

"But it's not what you think."

"I'm listening."

"Ellie had a few friends over, and Angie was there."

"And so were you?"

"Yeah."

"And did anything happen between you two?"

He was silent.

"Should I take your silence to mean something happened?"

"I think I'm in love with you," he blurted out.

I thought about what Sam had said: *if it seems too good to be true, then it probably isn't true.* "Jack, we don't even know each other that well."

"I know, but I swear, I've never felt like this before. Every minute I'm away from you is one minute too long."

"Maybe I'm just a rebound for you." My words surprised even me.

"How can you say that?"

"You still have feelings for Angie."

"Not like this."

I wasn't sure how to respond. "You're going to be late."

He stood up and started to walk out of the kitchen but turned back to look at me. "You're the farthest thing from a rebound, Gracie."

As I sat in my afternoon class, I thought about both Sam and Jack, trying to sort out how I felt about them. I decided to take matters into my own hands.

I pulled into the Egg in the Hole parking lot, skillfully prepared to talk to Sam. He had been more than willing to meet me, not even caring why. I was locked and loaded with a barrage of questions for him. As I walked in, he stood and smiled, the half-moons poking through his dark beard.

"Hey," he said, reaching out to give me a hug.

"Thanks for meeting me on such short notice."

"It was good to hear from you."

The waitress came over and poured us coffee.

"So ... I'm sorry I left like I did the other night." I smiled, feeling slightly nervous. *Stick to the questions*, I kept telling myself, *and all will be fine.*

"My fault. I caught you off guard." He smiled at me, and the half-moons seemed to light the world on fire. "It was just ... you looked so amazingly beautiful, I couldn't help it."

"I did?" I was already not sticking to the questions. *Get back to the questions*, I told myself.

"I forgot to even breathe when I saw you."

"You did?" *Not a question on the list.*

"How was the rest of your weekend?" he asked, stirring creamer in his coffee.

"I went to see an Alfred Hitchcock film festival at the Palace."

"I love that old theater. We went there, remember?"

I looked at him, clueless.

"We went to see *Amadeus* there for Music Appreciation class. You sat next to Chloe, and I sat in the row behind you."

"I sorta remember."

"Before I forget, our parents have decided they want to get married at my house."

"Bet my grandma will love that one. She's probably in a state of mourning right now, sitting in the club parking lot wearing a black veil over her face."

"Your grandma is handling the catering, the decorations, and the cake, so basically all I have to do is clean my house and keep the wild animals from eating people's faces off."

"Then all I have to do is show up and not have my face eaten off?"

"That sounds about right."

"So … can I ask you something?" I asked, my voice cracking.

"You can ask me anything." He smiled, displaying the half-moons.

"Have you been with a lot of women?"

He choked slightly on a piece of bacon. "Wow. Okay, well, I guess that depends on what you consider a lot."

"I don't know. I guess maybe more than ten."

"Ten? No, not ten."

"Nine?"

The half-moons played peekaboo with me. "Less than six."

"Oh, okay." I thought he would have been with more women.

"How about you?"

"Girls? Zero."

He laughed. "You know what I mean."

"About a dozen."

"Really?"

"Kidding. About the same as you."

"Lucky guys."

"What are you talking about? You were the first one on the list."

"Better if I would have been the only one on the list."

The waitress cleared our plates.

I took a small sip of coffee, readying my next question. "And how many of those women did you say 'I love you' to?"

"One."

I had thought I was ready for his answer, but I was not ready for that answer.

"How about you?"

"My point is that I'm not really sure you know what love is."

"How many, G?"

I bit my bottom lip. My questions were not going as planned. I looked down at my coffee. "One."

"It seems like we have something in common, then."

"Sam, you know I'm with Jack. And I'm very happy with Jack, by the way."

"You haven't even been with him long enough for it to be serious," he said.

"It gets serious quick when he tells you he loves you." Instantly, I wanted to shove the words back in my mouth.

"He already told you he loves you?" He rubbed his forehead. "Wow, fast mover."

"Not if you're sure."

"Are you sure?"

I hesitated, uncertain of what to say. "I'm not sure. Love is a big deal, you know?"

"I know."

"Why didn't you ever come looking for me if you love me so much?"

"Honestly?"

"No, lie to me. Of course I want you to be honest."

He shifted his eyes to the empty creamer cup. "I needed to prove I was good enough for you."

"What?"

"It took me a really long time to get my life together. I made a lot of mistakes, wasted some years. I would have ended up destroying us both. I had to wait until I was sure I wouldn't screw it up."

"But you never reached out before."

"I didn't trust myself. I have no resistance when it comes to you."

"I was with someone for a really long time—you know, before Jack."

"Yeah, I heard that guy was a tool. And knowing Chloe, she never would have let you marry a guy like that. So I knew I still had time."

"I'm not sure if Chloe would be happy about you."

"You're probably right."

"I'm with Jack now anyway."

"Him, I never saw coming. When I realized how much he was in the picture, I knew I had to go for it. Even if it means it will never happen with us, I couldn't waste my chance." Sam's honesty was refreshing, his timing horrible.

"I really like Jack. He's a good guy."

Sam nodded his head. "Just answer this for me, G. Do you ever think about me?"

I paused before answering quietly. "Yes, but this thing between us is not going to happen."

"So you acknowledge there's a *thing?*"

"I've gotta run." I stood to leave, ignoring his question.

Sam reached for me, and I shifted away. "Don't be a stranger, okay?" he said.

I smiled as I turned for the door, refusing to look back.

The next day, as I sat listening to oral presentations on gender bias in nineteenth-century literature, I thought about Sam. I hadn't responded to his text as I lay in bed the night before, although I had read it over and over.

Sam

I love you, G. It's my turn to crawl on my hands and knees to the ends of the earth for you.

Did I really stand a better chance at happiness with Jack? I felt uneasiness in my stomach as I thought about the benefit. I really wanted to go, but Jack seemed like he wanted me anywhere else but there. Why?

As I entered that evening's session with Rogelio's takeout in my hands, I was surrounded by artwork that Sarah was already busy arranging in groupings.

"Wow, Sarah, you're really good at this," I marveled, putting the large brown box of food on the nearby table.

"I know, isn't she?" Ellie stepped out from behind a large canvas of a sunrise on the beach.

"How did you get all these here?" I pondered.

Sarah smiled. "Jerry picked them up in his truck. I hope it's okay the way I've arranged them."

"It's amazing what you've done with these pieces," Ellie said. "Their groupings make them look so different ... so unique."

I nodded.

"These are amazeballs," Ginger said, standing next to Ellie. As they began talking, the sight of them together struck me. Ellie, dressed in designer clothes and with sculptured features, stood side by side with Ginger, dressed in tight satin pants, spiked boots, and a fishnet shirt. And as they leaned into each other, laughing with shoulders slightly touching, their connection made sense to me, here in our fractured world. Anywhere else, it would have seemed peculiar, awkward, and out of place. But in the world which we lived, it seemed perfectly normal.

It was our mothers who had brought us together, tragic, broken, some of us barely able to crawl into the room, hoping to make ourselves whole again. Thinking about my mom and all of life's moments I missed getting to share with her, I felt a pang of sadness, but I also felt a sense of gratitude to her for leading me to this place.

"Funny, isn't it?" Mindy broke my train of thought.

I looked at her.

"Ellie and Ginger go together like acid and ice cream anywhere else. The world hates when people like us do something like this."

"Do what?"

"We shouldn't make sense, but we do. Our puzzle pieces shouldn't fit, but we're only complete when we're together."

I nodded my head.

Ginger walked over to us and stood beside me. "I never thought I'd have a friend like you," she said to me.

"Why not?"

"Because you're so put together."

"Hardly."

"You got it all ... brains, looks, boyfriend. All I got is a great pair of legs and a good aim."

"I don't think you give yourself enough credit, Ginger. What would you really like to do? I mean, what's on your bucket list?"

"Bucket list? Well ..." She hesitated, seemingly trying to sort out what I meant by a bucket list.

"You know, the things to check off the list before you die."

"I really want to go to college." She looked down, like she was about to be punished for her thoughts.

"That's awesome! Then go for it."

"I can't."

"Why not? If it's about the money, I'm sure you can get financial aid."

"It's not that."

"What is it then?"

"I'm too dumb for school."

"You're not too dumb for school. I've taught thousands of students. Trust me, you're smarter than half of them."

She said nothing in response.

As we took our seats among the artwork, Dr. Gretchen began. "Who wants to start?"

"I want to go to college," Ginger announced to the larger group.

"And what's stopping you?" Dr. Gretchen probed.

"I don't know anything about college."

"You and most of my English lit students," I responded.

"What if I'm bad at it?"

"Thank you, Ginger. Hold that thought. For the rest of you, what would you do if you weren't afraid?"

"I would ..." Sarah's voice trailed off.

"Find your voice, Sarah," Mindy encouraged.

"I would become a party planner—you know, like special events, weddings, things like that."

"I would move back home and leave New York behind," Ellie said, almost sadly.

"I bet New York is exciting," Sarah said, her voice lifting.

"It's not the place that makes it great; it's the people," Ellie answered quietly.

Then it was my turn. I sat there for a minute. "I would celebrate my birthday."

All quizzical eyes were on me. "Who doesn't celebrate their birthday?" Mindy whispered to Ginger.

"I guess Gracie," Ginger answered.

"So for each of these," Dr. Gretchen said, "it is not for us to ask but for you to ask yourself, 'What would I do if I wasn't afraid?' It's time to do one thing that makes you truly afraid. And do it with a sense of purpose."

"How do we do that?" Ginger asked.

"That's a good question. Maybe for each of you it is a different answer," Dr. Gretchen replied.

"What are we going to do when this is over?" Sarah asked, a sense of melancholy in her voice.

"What do you mean?" Mandie questioned.

"I mean, what happens at the end of the six weeks?"

"I don't want this to end," Ginger stated matter-of-factly.

"Why does it have to?" Ellie wondered aloud.

"Well, technically, the session is over after six weeks, but perhaps I can see about starting another session in the next program series." Dr. Gretchen smiled as she spoke.

"When's that?" Ginger asked.

"January, I believe."

"What? We have to wait that long before we see each other again like this?" Sarah's voice sounded slightly frantic. "It's like losing my mother all over again." And with that, Sarah reached for her purse, recoiling inside herself again.

"I don't think so." Ginger stood up and grabbed the purse, holding it beyond Sarah's reach. "We're not going backward. It took us all this time to move forward. Backward ain't happening." Ginger was trying to keep Sarah from sliding back down the rabbit hole.

"Excuse me." Ellie stood, walking out of room.

We sat looking at each other until Ellie rejoined us.

"It's all settled," she said.

"What is?" Mandie asked.

"This room is officially rented every Tuesday and Friday from the end of this program series until the next program series starts," Ellie said, placing her designer bag down on the floor. "Now, where were we?"

"I can't believe you just did that," Ginger said.

"I did it for us," Ellie replied.

I looked around the room and saw each face lift with a renewed sense of purpose, a sense of hope; I suspected my own face must look the same.

"Okay, now how have your last few days been?" Dr. Gretchen lobbed the question out to any of us.

I was about to speak when I noticed multiple missed calls on my phone from my grandma. "Excuse me," I said, standing up and stepping out into the hallway. Five missed calls from my grandma brought a sense of panic.

"Hello, Blake Desiree Honoree Smith speaking." Hearing her voice made me feel even worse.

"Grandma, what's wrong?"

"Wrong?"

"You called me five times."

"Why did you not answer the phone?"

"Because I'm in a meeting," I retorted.

"Well, I will wait until the tone in your voice changes." She went silent, and I stood there, stewing.

"Very well, Grandma. What can I do for you?"

"I wanted to make sure you were prepared for Saturday."

It was my turn to be silent on the phone.

"For breakfast?"

"No, Gracelynn, not for breakfast. For Lacey's shower."

"That's Saturday?"

"Have you not paid any attention?" The more confused I sounded, the more irritated she sounded.

"What time on Saturday?"

"Five. Did you not read the invitation?"

"I don't think I got the invitation."

"Of course you received the invitation."

"I don't think so, and besides, I have a benefit to go to Saturday night in the city."

"No benefit."

"Excuse me?"

"It would be disrespectful to not attend your stepmother's shower. Rude, Gracelynn, just rude."

"Well, Grandma, I have other plans."

"That you will cancel in order to show support for your father's marriage."

"By buying his future wife some edible undies and a lace bra? Not going to happen."

"I have already purchased a silk nightgown and robe for you

to give her. You just need to be at my house by five. I will take care of everything else."

"Grandma, I am not going to the shower. I have other plans." I was adamant, and no one and nothing was going to change that.

"Then you can call Lacey and tell her you have prioritized something that happens every year over the once-in-a-lifetime shower in her honor. You know, she never had a real shower or wedding. She was married at the courthouse by a judge. Terribly sad."

I stared down at a crack in a floor tile, trying to sort out my next thought. I knew if I didn't go to the shower, it would send a loud and clear message that I didn't want to send. "Okay, I'll see you then." I hung up, feeling defeated once more by my grandma's words.

"Hey, babe."

Looking up, I saw Jack standing at the drinking fountain.

"What's wrong?" he asked. He walked over and kissed me lightly on the lips. Sweat dripped from his upper lip and fell near the corner of my lips. He wiped it away with his finger.

"Oh, nothing. Just that my grandma dropped this shower thing on me for Saturday night, which means I can't go to the benefit."

"Good," he declared.

"Why is that good?" I felt angered by his response. "Do you not want me there for some reason?"

"No, it's not that." He took a step back. "I told you I will be in Indy, and I don't want you there without me."

"I don't get that. It's a benefit for your mom. Why wouldn't you want me there to support your family?"

"I want everyone to see you there for the first time as my girlfriend, not just some girl who bought a ticket."

"Well, I can't go now anyway. I have to be at a shower for Lacey at five, so that blows the whole night out of the water. And I had a really kick-ass dress to wear."

"How 'bout when I get back, I take you someplace where you can wear that kick-ass dress?"

"Okay." Disappointment still rushed through my veins.

The room was full of conversation as I walked back in. "Gracie, we're all talking about the benefit on Saturday. You're coming, right?" Sarah asked cheerfully. "Ellie got us all tickets!"

"I even have a date," Ginger said, pushing her glasses back up from the tip of her nose.

"Really? That's wonderful." I smiled at her.

"His name is Bryan. He's an accountant."

"Is he one of your ... clients?" I was afraid of her answer.

"No. He did my taxes this year, and I guess he liked my itemized deductions."

"It's gonna be a blast with all of us there," Mandie exclaimed.

I half-smiled, not saying anything in return. I sat in silence as the other women laughed and talked about Saturday. I felt a weight in the pit of my stomach, knowing I would miss the chance to be with them.

Dr. Gretchen stood. "Everyone, before you leave tonight, please remember, do one thing that scares you this week, makes you smile, makes you feel alive. Have one really, super amazing moment, and we'll talk about it the next time we regroup."

Later that night, the light of the TV flickered across Jack's sleeping face. He was snoring lightly, his chest moving up and down in a hypnotic pattern. I looked at the clock. It was after midnight. Sleep somehow was evading me again. I rose quietly. I sat near the end of my couch, watching the stars in the sky from the window. I reached for my phone and read his words again.

Sam
I love you, G. It's my turn to crawl on my hands and knees
to the ends of the earth for you.

At another time in my life, I would have killed for those words. Now they just brought me confusion and sadness in a way I couldn't even describe.

By Thursday afternoon, my emotions were upside down. I still hadn't told Ellie I wouldn't be at the benefit because I was still trying to figure out some magical way to be at both places at the same time. Jack departed for Indy from my house in the morning rain. He left me with a long kiss and a promise that he would be just a phone call away.

I sat at my table flipping through my mom's recipes. I brought the handwritten recipe up to my chest, resting it near my heart. I wanted to pick up the phone and call her, ask her whether I was reading the recipe right, whether I should use real butter or if margarine was okay. I lowered my head slightly, knowing that would never happen. I traced my lips with the edge of the card, lost in the moment forever gone from me. A single day had changed my whole existence, and that day would greet me on Saturday, like it did every year.

I had just finished getting dressed after my bath when I heard a knock at the door. I peeked out the window to see Sam.

"Hey, G. Hope I'm not interrupting anything."

"Uh, come in." My skin was still damp and my hair wet from the bath. "What's up?"

"I was just in the neighborhood. Thought I'd stop by and say hello."

I looked at him, feeling awkward about both my appearance and the moment. I heard my phone chirp in the other room. "Would you excuse me?" I walked quickly into my bedroom in search of my phone.

"So this is where you get all your beauty sleep?"

I jumped a little when I heard Sam's voice. I turned and found him standing in my bedroom doorway. "Ha. Not sure about beauty or sleep, but yes, this is the place."

He walked over and sat next to me on the bed, our thighs touching. "I feel bad barging in on you. I'm gonna get going."

I looked at him. The half-moons looked back at me. I felt my heart jolt up and down, like it was being shocked. Our eyes locked.

"You don't make it easy, Sam."

He leaned into me, rubbing his shoulder against mine. "That's the point, G."

I thought about the session earlier in the week. "I don't want to go backward—you know, slide down the rabbit hole again."

"I promise that's not what this is about. I don't want to go backward either. I want to go forward, with you."

"Let's just focus on our parents. Okay?"

We stood, and as I walked him to the door, he said, "It will never change that you are the only person I'll ever love."

We hugged good-bye, and he left. I looked around my living room, Sam's smell still lingering in the air. It was then I noticed it: a white envelope sitting on my coffee table. On the front of the envelope, a neatly written "G" stood in stark contrast to the glaring white paper. I opened the envelope and read its contents:

RA: 6h 39m 15.70s DEC: 2 16' 22.7"
Star Name: Cassandra Marie Anderson
Owner: Gracie Anderson

G, I know you don't do the birthday thing but hope you're okay with this. I love you.
~ Sam
PS. Glad you were born. Life would have sucked without you.

I held the paper in my hand, reading it over and over. I felt tears rush to my eyes. Although I knew it was just one of a trillion stars in the sky, it brought me comfort to know she had a resting place. Sam had given her that—for me. I was reaching for my phone to text him when its ringing stopped me.

"Hello?"

"Hey, babe. Whatcha doing?"

"Hey, Jack. Not much." I stood looking at the paper, my fingers holding it so tight that I was leaving indentions.

"I miss you."

I couldn't take my eyes off Sam's words.

"Gracie?"

"Yeah?"

"Well?"

"I miss you too, of course." I set the paper back on the table and eased down on the couch.

"So I was thinking about Sunday."

"Sunday?"

"I'd like to take you somewhere special—you know, give you a chance to wear that dress."

"That's okay. Don't worry about it."

"Gracie, I love you."

I was silent for a few lingering seconds. "Jack ..."

"You don't have to say it back if you don't want to." I could hear his voice drop.

"No, it's not that. Those words mean everything to me. I just want to be a hundred percent sure before I say them because when I do, I'll feel that way forever."

He was initially quiet. "Sometimes love is a leap of faith."

"I'm scared."

"About what?"

I wondered whether I should tell him how I was feeling, about the doubt creeping inside of me, lurking in the corners of my mind. "I don't want to get hurt."

"Do you think I'd hurt you?"

"Not intentionally."

"Is that what's holding you back?"

"Holding me back?"

"I can tell something is holding you back from me. At first I thought maybe it was Sam, but now I think it's something else."

I hesitated, afraid that if I said what I was thinking, it would pull us apart. "Promise me this won't end badly."

"I don't want this to end at all."

I smiled at his words. "Me neither."

"It's settled then. We're stuck with each other."

After my call with Jack, I delicately picked up the paper and sat looking at the star's coordinates.

Me

I can't believe you gave me a star.

Sam

I would have given you a thousand of them if it would make you happy.

Me

I only need this one. And it's really mine?

Sam

Forever.

Me

It is the sweetest thing anyone has ever done for me.

Sam

You deserve it.

Me

Still doesn't change anything between us.

Sam

If you say so.

Me

Why didn't you stick around and give it to me yourself so I could thank you in person?

Sam

Now I'm regretting not sticking around.

Me

Probably better this way. I had an ugly cry going when I saw it.

Sam

Nothing about you could ever be ugly, inside or out.

⋆ ⋆ ⋆

I watched Sarah glide around the room, placing fall decorations all over our meeting space, transforming the bland cream-colored walls and bare tile.

"Sarah, I'm not kidding you. This is your thing. You should be doing this for a living."

Ginger's face appeared in the doorway. "Wow. This is super cool, but what are we celebrating?"

"Sarah wanted to breathe new life into our room," I said to Ginger. I tilted my head, trying to figure out what was different about her. Then it hit me. "Ginger, you have new glasses!" The cat glasses had been replaced with round, small, pink frames with little flowers etched on the earpieces.

"Yep." Her hair was pulled back in a side braid that cascaded over her shoulder. She wore a pair of jeans, ankle boots, and a blue sweater.

Dr. Gretchen entered and said admiringly, "Sarah, once again, you have really outdone yourself. You have a talent, that's for sure."

For the next two hours, we talked about life, about our week, and about making moments count. As Dr. Gretchen stood on the outskirts of the room, the six of us never let a moment become awkward, never let one thought fall.

I looked at each of my circle sisters—Ellie, with her one tiny strand of hair falling out of place; Sarah, with her big brown eyes that flickered slightly when happiness found its way to her; Ginger, whose mole near her upper lip curved into a heart when she smiled; Mandie, whose sole dimple on her left cheek appeared out of nowhere; and Mindy, whose small space between her front teeth made her look girlish even though she was every bit of forty. If I needed to, I could describe every detail, down to the littlest freckle, of each of these women. And that ordinary moment became my extraordinary one.

"Can I ask you something?" Ellie whispered.

"Sure." I inched in closer to hear her.

"Do you ever feel sad?"

I thought about the question. "I sometimes feel insecure."

"Life makes me sad sometimes."

"I wish I had a better body," I confessed.

"I wish I had your eyes," she answered back.

"I wish I had your legs," I retorted.

"I wish I had your strength."

My mouth opened, but words didn't come right away. "My strength?"

"From the first time I met you, I knew you had the strength of a hundred of us. Everything you've been through, and yet your strength is amazing."

"I'm just really, really good at pretending," I said, surprised by my own confession.

Our words fell away until the session ended. "How is everything?" I asked. "Have you talked to Bruce?"

"Yes. It's hard. He keeps telling me how sorry he is and how it will never happen again. He wants to get back together."

"I'm not an expert, but I know relationships are really tough even when you trust each other completely. Lots of things can happen to pull and push and cause strain. I'm not sure distrust makes it any easier."

"I don't trust him at all. For now, all I want to do is focus on the benefit. I'm excited you all will be there."

I hesitated, knowing I needed to come clean. "About the benefit, I don't think I'll be able to make it."

"Why not?"

"It kills me to think about not going, but I have this shower for my dad's fiancée. It's a once-in-a-lifetime thing, so I need to be there. Plus, I'm the maid of honor, so I guess it's my thing."

She nodded. "What time does the shower end? We usually go out afterward, so perhaps you can meet us out?"

"I'd love to! The shower should be over by nine. Just text me and let me know where you'll be, and I'll meet you guys there."

"It's going to be an amazing weekend."

At home I let the swing carry me back and forth in the night air. The temperature was dropping. I pulled at my coat, watching my breath blow cold in the wind. It was officially Saturday, and I knew the day to come would be full of haunting emotions. But maybe it would also be the day when I could finally release the weight of the past and let go of the chains that still bound me all these years later.

I smiled, hopeful that the day would take me to unimaginable new highs even as I tried to shake off the feeling that it would drag me to abysmal lows.

13

Chloe sat across from me, buttering her toast. "So you excited about tonight?"

"Yeah, thrilled beyond words," I said. My grandma had canceled breakfast in order to focus on last-minute to-dos for the shower, so Chloe and I were on our own this morning at the country club.

"It may be better than you think."

"Doubtful. And I'm missing the benefit for it, so that's a bummer."

"How is Jack? You hear from him today?"

"He sent me a text. Said to have a good day and that he loved me."

"Wow. Love, huh?"

"I know. I'm not sure how I feel about that."

"Pretty early on for the L word, don't you think?"

"I told him that."

"That's big for someone to say first. He really put it out there. What did you say in return?"

"Not much."

She took a sip of coffee. "It's only been, what, a month, right?"

"He said his grandparents knew each other for two weeks before they got married."

"Yeah, but back then, life expectancy was like forty, so if you didn't hit the ground running, you were an old maid by fifteen."

"True."

"What's keeping you from saying it back? And if you say Sam, I'm going to slit my wrists with this butter knife."

"Not Sam. That's a different story. No, with Jack, I'm just really scared of getting hurt."

"C'mon, you don't think everyone feels that? You don't think Jack had to swallow a million gallons of fear to tell you how he feels?"

"I'm not really sure he loves me. I think it might be more of a lust thing."

"Because he wants your jelly all the time?"

"It's great, but then I get worried that when it dies down, we won't have anything else in common."

"Maybe being intimate is his way of showing you how much he cares."

"I guess."

"Isn't it good?"

"It's amazing. It's just nonstop sometimes. I'm not sure how long we can keep it up."

"I wouldn't complain too much. Jack's just a physical guy, and I'll tell you this, girlfriend—he's an amazing specimen. I mean, he's damn lucky to have you, but just once, I'd love to run my fingers over a six-pack. The closest I come is when Rick hands me the beer to put away."

"I just wish we knew each other better. You know, it seems like we don't know what makes each other tick."

"Like you and Sam?"

"Maybe."

"Puke."

"I know, Chloe. I know."

"I'm not sure you do, Gracie."

"What do you mean?"

"Just because he's been in your life forever doesn't mean he deserves to have a permanent parking spot in it."

"It feels so comfortable when I'm with him, though."

"Comfort is different from happiness."

"I'm not saying I would consider it, but being with someone who knows me inside and out is nice."

"Hello? That's me."

"You know what I mean."

"This isn't one of those movies where Mr. Right has been in front of you all along. Wake up, Gracie. That's not who he is."

"And who is he?"

"He's a guy who thinks he can swoop in whenever he likes and you'll be there waiting for his personal entertainment."

"You don't think he can make me happy?"

"He doesn't know what happiness is."

"How do I get him out of my head?"

"Well, there are medications for those kinds of things, but in your case, I'd say avoidance."

"Avoidance?"

"Like do not initiate or respond to his texts. Do not answer his calls. Do not offer to give him a ride or help him move a couch or any other BS reason he comes up with to see you."

"You think that'll do it?"

"Either that, or he'll become more relentless because he'll see it as you playing hard to get."

"But I don't want to hurt his feelings."

"Sorry, kiddo. You're gonna have to smash that teeny heart of his to smithereens in order for him to get the message."

"There's no other way around it?"

"Like what? Write him a long, flowing letter and send it by carrier? This isn't nineteenth-century literature. It's gotta be quick, and it's gotta be dirty. You're gonna have to cut him off at the knees."

"That sounds unpleasant, for both of us."

"Well, you could always break up with Jack and run into Sam's arms and see what happens."

"Really?"

"Absolutely not."

When I got home, the bouquet of flowers I found on my porch was so large that I could barely get them in my front door. I pulled out the tiny card.

Until tomorrow,

Love,

Jack

A few hours later, I stood in my grandma's house, welcoming guests. As usual, she had gone overboard, but she was masterful at parties, so the compliments were overflowing. As the evening dragged on, I kept looking at my phone, knowing the benefit was in full swing and I was missing it. At nine, I was anxious to leave. The gifts were opened, the food was nearly gone, and the empty wine bottles were stacking up.

"I'd like to cut out, Grandma," I whispered.

"Hosts do not leave before their guests, Gracelynn. Remember your manners," she said, slurring slightly.

An hour later, I sat in the silence of my bedroom. I had texted Ellie twice but had heard nothing back. I had also texted Jack but hadn't heard from him either. I wondered when my life had become watching my phone, waiting for a reply back.

By eleven thirty, I had given up on going out. I lay in bed, watching the murky clouds cover the sky. In the distance, I heard my phone ringing. My heart was racing by the time I found it.

"Hello?"

"Gracie?" It sounded like Ellie, but there was something off in her voice.

"Ellie? How are you?"

"Not great. There was an accident. I hate to ask, but can you come to the hospital?"

"Are you okay?"

"Yes. A car hit our cab. I'm sorry. I know it's late. I wasn't sure who else to call."

"Which hospital?"

Halfway to Chicago, I dialed Jack's number. I needed to hear his voice, but instead I got his voice mail. It was nearly one when I pulled into the hospital parking garage. I walked into the emergency room, the labyrinth of hallways taking me through a maze until I finally found the waiting room.

It was quiet except for the muffled sound of a baby crying in the distance. An elderly woman in pale blue scrubs sat behind a large desk.

"May I help you?" she asked, barely making eye contact with me.

"I'm here for Ellie Bradshaw."

"Bradshaw?" She looked at her computer screen. "Room 14," she replied without looking up.

As I passed room 13, I stopped. Ellie and Angie stood in front of me, both in evening gowns. Their hair was in loose curls, and high heels were tossed on the floor near their feet. Even in her bare feet, Angie was statuesque. Her silver sequined dress featured a deep plunging neckline. I took a deep breath, reminding myself that I was there for Ellie and it was only a ride home.

Ellie walked over to me, a white bandage covering a small area by her collarbone. She reached for me and hugged me. "Thank you so much for coming."

"Of course."

"We just have to wait for the doctor," she said, stepping back slightly. "I hope I didn't wake you."

In my rush, I had thrown on sweats and a hoodie. My hair was pulled back in a barrette, and my glasses were slightly smudgy. "I'm just glad you're okay," I said.

"Hallo," said Ellie's friend, walking over to us. "I am Angie. You are Gracie?"

I looked up at her, towering over me. She was beautiful, and she knew it. "Yes, I'm Gracie. Hello."

"I say call cab, but she say no."

I was trying to figure out her accent; it was an American and European mix. She had likely migrated to the States at some early point in her career.

"If you'll excuse me for a moment," Ellie whispered, moving past us down the hall.

I stood there with Angie, neither of us saying anything. "Pardon me. I need to make a call," I said, moving a few steps closer to the entrance of room 14.

"Yes, I go inside and wait," she said, slipping beyond the curtain into the room.

I pulled out my cell phone, my hands trembling slightly as I dialed Jack's number. As it began to ring, I thought I heard an echo of the ring in the hallway. His voice message started, and I hung up. I held the phone to my chin, trying to decide whether I should call him again, knowing Indy was an hour ahead and he was probably sleeping. I could hear Angie's voice beyond the curtain, and the sound of it made me dial Jack's number again.

This time the ring I heard in my ear resonated just beyond the curtain. I listened to the sound of the ringing inside the room and then the silence when his voice message began. I felt my heart start to beat brutally, my legs shaking violently.

I slowly pulled the curtain back and stepped inside the room. Her hand rested on his stomach. "Oh, my baby, my baby," she said, kissing his earlobe. He wore a black tuxedo, his shirt partially unbuttoned, with monitors placed on varying parts of his chest. A smear of blood covered his shirt collar. A bandage with blood soaked through it was positioned just above his left eyebrow.

"I so worry about my baby. Dis one"—she motioned to Jack with her head—"and dis one," she said, motioning toward her abdomen.

I saw my reflection in his black shiny shoes, the anguish painted across my face. It couldn't be true. It couldn't be him, and it couldn't be real. I was standing there motionless, trying to wake myself up, when Ellie slipped back into the room.

"Good news. The doctor said they are going to release us. He thinks Jack can go home too. His vitals are good. We just need to keep an eye on him."

I inched back, watching Angie place her head next to Jack's. "We home go now, baby," she said in his ear. He began to stir.

"I'm going ... outside ... wait." I couldn't find any other words; the shock of the moment was sending me into a state of disorientation.

Ellie looked at me. "We'll come get you when it's time."

I shook my head and stumbled onto a chair in the cold, empty hallway. Two hours crept by, and I grew numb.

"Gracie?" Ellie stood in front of me. "Would you mind getting the car?"

I began to scramble for the keys in my coat.

"I'm sorry. I really am," she whispered.

As I sat in front of the emergency room, watching the hazards on my car blink on and off, I wondered why life played cruel tricks on me. I tried to be a good person, tried to be all things to all people, and now I found myself navigating another tragedy, another unhappy ending.

I heard the passenger doors open and watched from my rearview mirror as Angie got in the backseat first and Jack was helped in and placed next to her. She pulled his head to her shoulder; his eyes were groggy. Ellie took the front seat.

"Where?" I asked, barely able to speak.

"Jack's house, please."

"I'm not sure how to get there from here," I said, turning off the hazards.

"Okay, I'll direct you."

As we drove in silence, I refused to look in the rearview mirror, even when we caught every red light from the hospital to Jack's building. My eyes remained focused on the road in front of me, my mind in a state of utter shock.

I pulled up in front of his building and kept the motor running. Out of the corner of my eye, I saw Ellie turn to me.

"Gracie ..."

I shook my head. "Just please get out of my car, okay?"

She hesitated for a moment before opening the door. Angie began to speak, but Ellie cut her off. "Let's go."

I kept my head facing forward, but my eyes shifted to them. They pulled Jack out of the car and supported his weight between them as they walked. I watched them stagger toward the door, Ellie looking back at me as she struggled to balance Jack.

Later I didn't remember leaving the city. I was barely able to register when I crossed the state line. It wasn't until I was sitting in the park parking lot that I even remembered driving at all.

I walked toward the tree. The wind was cold, biting at my face. Leaves crunched under my feet. A light mist of icy rain splattered in my eyes. I tripped over a large root, hidden by the darkness of the night, and fell to the ground. I crawled to the tree base.

I found myself floating outside my body, moving back to a time and place I had wiped from my memories. I had wished that day away for twenty years, only to find it standing in front of me again, forcing me to take its hand. I lay back against the tree and closed my eyes, allowing the shackles to strangle me once and for all.

"Happy birthday, Gracie," my mom said as I staggered into the kitchen. "How's my girl today?" She took hold of the table, rising slowly to kiss me.

"I'm good," I replied, trying to push my bed-head hair back into place.

"What do you want to do today, love?"

"We don't have to do anything, Mom. It's fine to just hang out at home."

She leaned over and grabbed my hand. "Nonsense. It's your birthday—and my most favorite day of the year, by the way. We need to make it a day to remember."

"Mom, I'm not sure you're up for it," I said, wiping the sleep from my eyes.

"I have all this energy today for some reason. It must be because my baby is a year older."

"You look really good."

"Even have my favorite cap on," she boasted, pulling her Bears hat down slightly.

"What are we talking about?" my dad asked, entering the kitchen and stopping to give my mom a kiss.

"I was telling Gracie how I really want to make this day one she'll never forget. It's not every day she turns fourteen."

"True. Not sure it's a good idea to do too much, though." He was rubbing my mom's shoulders. "You don't want to overdo it."

"I want to do something as a family," she said.

"Well, what should we do?" My dad looked back and forth between us.

"Why don't we have a picnic in the park?" my mom suggested.

"Mom, it's too cold for a picnic."

"A matinee at the movies?" she offered.

"I have school, remember?"

"A quality education is overrated," she said, disappointed.

"How about this?" I took a drink of her orange juice. "Let's order takeout and have movie night with Grandma, Grandpa, and Teddy."

"That sounds great. I'll call your grandma," she said, motioning my dad to hand her the wall phone.

"Tell Grandma it's my pick since it's my birthday. No horror movies."

She smiled. "Oh, I just remembered Grandpa is out of town, but I'm sure Grandma and Teddy will want to come over."

That night, we sat on the couch, cuddled up next to each other, empty containers of Chinese food sitting on the coffee table. "Gracie's pick for the movie," my mom said, adjusting me slightly near her lap. I could feel her bones poking through her skin as her thin fingers ran through my hair.

"Cassandra, you should get some rest," Grandma ordered.

"Oh, let her enjoy herself," Teddy said, wiping the sweet-and-sour sauce off his "I See Scary People" T-shirt.

"It's like I'm cured today," Mom said, smiling.

"Gracie, what movie is it gonna be?" my dad asked, opening up the video cabinet.

"How about *Seven Summers of Horror?*" my grandma suggested.

"Negative, Grandma. How about *It's a Wonderful Life?*"

"I love it!" my mom declared, shifting on the couch.

"Of course you do—that is the only movie you two ever want to watch," Grandma grumbled.

"My birthday, my choice," I shot back.

"Why don't we do cake and gifts before the movie?" my mom proposed.

As the candles were lit and the birthday song was sung, I knew what I wanted. I closed my eyes and wished my mom a life with no more pain.

I opened the gift from my grandparents which was clothes. "Thanks, Grandma. Tell Grandpa I said thanks too."

"He is not happy about missing your special day. Those meetings can drag on forever," she gruffly responded.

After Teddy gave me cash and my dad gave me Bears tickets, I assumed the gifts were done.

"One more," my mom said, handing me a small wrapped box. "This one is just from me."

I peeled back the paper and opened the box. Inside was a star necklace. "I love it, Mom," I said, hugging her tightly.

Halfway through the movie, we took a time-out from the TV. Everyone went their separate directions except my mom and me.

"I'll never forget this birthday," I said, nuzzled up against her.

"Do you feel like sitting outside for a few minutes? I could use some fresh air," she said.

"It's kind of cold outside."

"Grab the blanket and let's sneak out before anyone sees us," she whispered.

Outside, we sat on the swing, moving back and forth slowly. She held my hand tightly.

"See that star up there?" She pointed at a bright twinkling star in the dark night.

"Yeah."

"That's where I'll be long after I'm gone from here." She rested her head on my shoulder.

"You're not going to leave us, Mom," I said, trying to shake off the dread I felt.

"Gracie, we both know my life here is fleeting, but up there"— she pointed to the sky—"I'll live forever."

"Are you scared?" A wave of sadness rushed over me.

"No, death is a part of life."

"You're okay with leaving me?"

"I'll never be okay with leaving you," she said, sniffling. "But one day you'll have a family of your own to fill the empty spaces."

"I feel like you're saying good-bye."

"Gracie, I couldn't say good-bye to you if I tried." She brushed the top of my head with her hand. "Maybe you should go back in before your grandma changes the movie on us. I'm not sure about you, but I'm not really feeling guts and gore tonight."

I laughed and went to pull her up.

"I think I'm going to sit out here a few more minutes. The night is so clear, the stars so bright. Go on in. I'll be right behind you."

I let my hand fall away from hers and went inside. I closed the door and started the movie. A moment later, my grandma and Teddy came back in the room.

"Where's your mom?" Teddy asked.

"She wanted to sit outside for a few minutes to look at the stars," I said, my eyes on the movie.

"It is cold out there," Grandma noted, looking out the window at the swing. "Maybe I should check on her?"

"Who?" my dad asked, walking back in the room with a bowl of popcorn.

"Cass. She's outside getting some fresh air," Teddy answered.

"She should really come in now," my dad said, tossing popcorn in his mouth.

My grandma opened the door. "Cassandra, you are going to freeze to death." She stepped onto the porch. "Cassandra?" I heard the door shut and the rustling of the swing. The screams of my grandma pulled us all to our feet.

I was the last one to the swing. I stopped when I saw her. My grandma held her, rocking her back and forth in her arms. My mom's head fell backward, her Bears cap lying at my grandma's feet. Her body was lifeless, her feet turned inward, as my grandma's hold on her tightened. Her arms fell outside the blanket, her hand dragging against the side of the swing.

I stood motionless as Teddy fell to my mom's feet, his face in his hands. My dad sat on the swing next to my grandma and Mom, his hand resting on her lap. "Oh, Cass ..." Tears spilled from his eyes, his voice cracking with despair and grief.

"Should I call the ambulance?" I frantically offered, thinking maybe they could make her better.

My dad looked up at me, tears overflowing from his eyes.

"We have to do something for her," I implored.

"Yes," Teddy said, lifting his head. "We have to let her go."

14

I felt a foot tapping against my leg and an arm shaking my side. I tried to brush them off, so lost in my memory-filled dream that I thought I still stood in front of the swing, watching her lifeless body, death shadows darkening the October night.

"Gracie?"

I felt the ground pushing against my side. A leaf beat at my nose. Hands reached under me and pulled me up, lifting me off the ground. My head seemed weighted down, my eyes unable to open; anguish filled my veins with cement. I heard the voice of someone speaking on a phone.

"I found her ... Not sure yet."

I tried to speak but could not.

"Don't know ... Most of the night, I think. Yes, I know it's cold ... I don't know ... Don't cry. It's going to be okay. There's no need to come here ... I know you're not that far away but just go home. She's okay."

I opened one of my eyes and felt the sting of the light. I couldn't see his face, but I knew he was there to bring me home. "Teddy?" My voice was gruff and scratchy, and speaking sent shots of pain down my throat.

"It's me, sugar." He wrapped his arms around me, hugging me tightly. "Thank God we found you." He kissed the top of my head.

"I didn't know I was lost," I whispered, my voice barely audible.

"Your grandma got a call from one of the girls in your group. Said she was worried about you. Said somethin' bad happened. Grandma sent me to your house, and from there, I started looking."

"Looking? How long could you have been looking?"

"Six, seven hours ..." His voice trailed off. "Your grandma wanted to call the police. I kept telling her they wouldn't do nothin' right away."

"No. I don't think it's been that long ..." I lay my head back against Teddy's chest, trying to get my eyes to focus. A few minutes later, I saw her boots, mud flying off each heel as she quickly approached. "Hey, Grandma."

She dropped to her knees, wrapping her arms around me.

"Doll baby, I told you she was okay," Teddy said, trying to pull my grandma off me.

"I needed to see her."

I looked up and did a double take. Mascara was smeared under her eyes, and her face was blotchy, her lipstick stain faded. Her always-perfect hair was strewn about. Her jacket was buttoned the wrong way, leaving a gap just above her belly button.

"What happened to you, Grandma?" I whispered, thinking she had been mauled by a wildebeest.

"Oh, Gracelynn." She pulled me closer to her.

"Can't breathe," I gasped, trying to pull air into my lungs; my supply was quickly being depleted by my grandma.

"We need to get her out of here. She'll freeze to death," Teddy said, trying to lift me to my feet. But my grandma would not loosen her grip on me. "Doll, you have to let her go."

"No, not again." Her hands were trembling as her heart beat rapidly against me.

"I'm okay, Grandma," I said, trying to reassure her.

"Teddy, we have to call Jeffrey. He left Columbus a couple of hours ago to get here. Oh, and Chloe. She and Rick were making calls to people."

Teddy was still trying to pull my grandma away from me. "Why don't you girls sit on the bench while I make some calls?"

I slowly rose, feeling the stiffness in my legs. I was cold now that Teddy's heat had been taken away from me. Grandma and I walked slowly together. I felt her body trembling next to mine.

We sat on the bench, saying nothing at first. I took a long look at her and then reached up and tried to wipe the mascara from under her eyes. She gently took my hand in hers and placed it in her lap. "Tell me what happened, Gracelynn."

I felt the rush of tears. "Ellie called you?"

"Eleanor Bradshaw? Yes, she is the one who called me."

"What did she say?" I closed my eyes, waiting for the hurtful words.

"She told me something happened after the benefit and said she was very worried about you and we should check on you right away to make sure you were okay."

I thought the tears would fall, but instead my eyes just hurt. "I didn't mean to worry anyone."

"Is it something with the Bradshaw boy?"

I looked at her, my eyes stinging. I rubbed my hand across the cold bench. "Yes." I looked over at the tree swaying ever so slightly in the brisk air.

"Is it as bad as I think it might be?"

"Depends on if you think 'bad' is that Jack told me he was in Indy on business when really he ..."

"Was at the benefit with that model girl?"

I nodded my head yes.

She said nothing for a moment. "Then it is as bad as I thought it was going to be."

"Fitting for the day, I guess."

"Not the best way to spend your birthday," she responded, her gaze turned to the tree as well.

"Maybe it's what I deserve," I said matter-of-factly.

"And why would you think that?" She reached over and lifted my head by my chin.

"Because, Grandma, nothing ever works out for me. That's all."

"Gracelynn, bad things happen to really good people all the time. I cannot explain why, but what you do now defines who you are."

"What do you mean?"

"I am constantly in awe of how strong you are … and maybe even a little jealous."

"You're kidding, right? You are tough as nails. Most days I feel like I'm just hanging on by my fingertips."

"You know what makes a person really strong?"

I shook my head.

"It is finding a way to persevere when most others would just give up. You dig in and you fight, and that is what sets you apart from everyone else."

"I'm not sure about any of that. I just keep going through the motions, praying the other shoe won't fall."

"How many people do you think, Gracelynn, could have survived—no, thrived—despite what has happened?"

"Not sure."

"Not many."

"Why can't things be different, Grandma?" I leaned against her, feeling my eyes sting again.

"I wish I knew. I have prayed so much for you to find real happiness."

"Well, it's not going to be with Jack, that's for sure."

"No, I am not talking about happiness with a man, Gracelynn. That is not what I mean by happiness. I mean completeness, fulfillment."

"But your life is fulfilled with Teddy," I replied.

"Yes, Teddy has made my life complete, but that is me. I need someone in my life to help define me. But you are different. You do not need that."

"But I do." I felt my heart crashing against the walls of my chest.

"You do not. You just think you do."

"Then what do I need to complete me?"

She replied with sadness in her eyes, "You need to know that what happened is not your fault."

"With Jack?"

She shook her head. "No one could have saved your mother. As much as we tried, it was just not meant to be."

"I know."

"And as much as I love your father, he has not been able to find room in his life for both you and his grief. That is his problem, not yours."

"It feels like my problem."

She nodded. "I am sure it does. Your father has never been able to manage his grief, and unfortunately, what is done is done when it comes to you and him."

"How have you been able to manage your grief, Grandma?"

"Everyone deals with grief differently. Your father let it swallow him up. I was lucky. I had—"

"Teddy," I said, finishing her sentence for her.

"No. I had you."

"Me?"

"Yes. You gave me a purpose, a reason to get out of bed each day. I had no other choice because I made a promise to your mother."

"You did?"

She nodded.

"What was it?"

"I promised her I would help you get on with your life."

"And you did."

"The truth is you never really needed me. It was then I realized how strong you were and that you would be okay no matter what."

"But you helped me, Grandma, in so many ways."

She laughed. "Well, if nothing else, it made me feel better to think I was helping, for you, for Cassandra, for myself."

"I'm so glad I've had you and Teddy. He's helped both of us so much."

"Without you, Teddy would not have been able to help me. I was lost when Cassandra and then your grandfather left us. It was you who helped me find a way."

I looked at her perfect hands, and for the first time, I saw the frailty in them. "I'm not really sure what to do now."

"About Jack?"

"Yes." I hesitated before continuing. "I'm sure he will be at the session on Tuesday."

"Why is that?"

"It's 'special person' night, so to speak. I'm sure Ellie will bring him."

"You have no plans to talk to him before then?"

"Definitely not. I'm humiliated by it all." I lowered my head, feeling the weight of my circumstances pulling me toward the ground.

"Then it is settled." She changed her posture, straightening her already-straight back up from the bench.

"What is?"

"I am going to the session with you on Tuesday."

"Uh, I don't think so, Grandma."

"And why is that?" I could hear the shift in her voice.

"Because it's not your thing."

"But it is yours," she quietly responded.

"No offense, Grandma, but you need to have an open mind about it. If you don't, then it's not really worth your time."

She was quiet. Leaves crackled in the distance. "Has it has helped you find perspective?"

"Yes." I knew for certain that it had changed me for the better in just a short period of time.

"Then I will go there with an open mind."

"Grandma ..."

Teddy's heavy footsteps drew us both away from the conversation. "Calls are made. Now we need to get you out of this cold," he said, helping me to my feet. All I wanted was to crawl into bed, cover my head, and wish away the world.

At home, nestled under the covers, I tried to lock out the memories of the night before. I drifted off for a while until the ringing of my cell phone brought me back to the light of the day. I lay in bed and listened until the ringing stopped. I closed my eyes again, only to hear the ringing resume.

It was nearly five when I heard knocking at the door. I peeked out from under my covers to see the shadows of the day outside. The knocking started again; I did not move. At seven, I climbed out of bed and called my grandma.

"Just wanted to thank you for earlier, Grandma."

"I will be there on Tuesday," she replied, her tone matter-of-fact.

"We'll talk about it tomorrow, okay?"

"Tuesday," she said firmly in reply.

I lay back down, not bothering to check the multiple text messages and voice mails on my phone. By ten, sleep had taken me away. It was midnight when my doorbell began ringing. I jolted out of bed, heart racing, and made my way into the living room, where I stood motionless.

"Gracie!" Jack was beating on the door. "I'll pound on your door all night until you talk to me."

I took a deep breath with each of the two locks I moved to the left and then opened the door. "What?" I tried to conjure up the acid running through my veins.

"Can I come in?"

I stood there looking at his shadow on the other side of my screen door. "It's late."

"Yeah, I know. You're not answering your phone, so I had no other choice."

"There's a reason I'm not answering my phone," I curtly responded.

"I can explain."

"I doubt it." We stood on opposite sides of the door, opposite sides of the world.

"Please?"

I opened the door, and he took a seat on the couch. I sat across from him. His face was bruised, his left eye slightly black. Scratches and cuts traveled from above his left eyebrow all the way down the side of his face. His left cheek was swollen, and a cut extended from just under his nose to his upper lip. In other circumstances, I would be offering sympathy and care; now all I wanted was to make him feel worse.

"You have three minutes to talk. After that, I'm done," I said, looking at him without blinking.

He coughed lightly, wincing as he held his side. "Sorry. Bruised rib."

"Is that what you woke me up to tell me?" I was incapable of any emotion other than bitterness.

"No." He looked at me. "Can I sit by you?"

I shook my head. "You have two minutes left."

"Okay ... well, first of all, I want to say I'm sorry for what happened."

I looked at him, anger rising. "I don't believe you."

"The last thing I ever wanted to do was hurt you."

"Too late."

He cleared his throat. "Will you let me explain what happened?"

"It's your two minutes. Do what you want with them."

"I never intended to go to the benefit, and I *was* in Indy."

I shook my head in disbelief.

"I swear, Gracie. It's the truth."

"Well, if it's the truth, how did you manage to be in a cab in Chicago, dressed in a tux, the night of the benefit?"

He winced, shifting his weight. "I finished up on Saturday afternoon and decided to come back and surprise you for your birthday."

"Yeah, you surprised me."

He continued. "Ellie called to guilt-trip me about the benefit, so I decided to go there for a little bit. Since you had that thing for Lacey, I figured it was no harm, no foul that I was there without you."

"You didn't think I'd find out about you being there? All the other girls were there, and you knew I really wanted to go."

"I know."

"And yet you thought it wasn't a big deal to go there without even telling me."

"I thought you would be so happy to see me that it wouldn't matter about the benefit."

"What about Angie? Were you there with her?"

"No. She was there, and I was there. End of story."

"Hardly."

"What do you mean?"

"At the hospital, she was all over you—'baby' this and 'baby' that. It was disgusting."

"I don't remember that. I was pretty out of it."

"Funny how Ellie calls *me* to pick you guys up from the hospital. It's almost like she wanted me to find out about you and Angie."

"There is no me and Angie."

"So you have no feelings for her?"

"I didn't say that. I told you before, it's complicated."

I looked at him, remembering what she had said. "And the baby? Does that make it more or less complicated?"

"What baby?" He looked stunned.

"The one she's carrying. Is it yours?"

"Baby? I'm not even close to wanting a baby. Being a father is the last thing I need right now. How far along she is?"

"So I guess the answer to that question matters?" I knew things between us were crashing and burning with each word spoken.

"Knowing her, it might not even be the truth."

"Could it be yours?" I didn't want to know the answer but had to ask the question.

"I swear to you, Gracie, I haven't been with anyone else since the first night we met."

"But before me, you were with her, and so it could be yours?"

"I'm sure I would know by now if it were mine."

We were both quiet for a moment.

"How did you end up in the same cab?"

"Ellie was going to crash at my place, and I was going to your place."

"And Angie?"

"She was going to stay with Ellie," he responded softly.

"At your place?"

He nodded.

"Well, that about does it." I stood up and went to the door.

"C'mon, Gracie."

"C'mon what?"

"I know it seems bad right now, but in the big picture it's not that big of a deal."

"I think it's time for you to leave."

"Why?" He looked at me, head tilted to one side.

"Time's up."

"How many more times can I say I'm sorry?" He remained seated on the couch, looking at me.

"None." I pulled open the door. "Bye, Jack."

"What do you want from me?" He did not move.

"I want you to be honest, no lies. I want you to give me the respect I deserve. I want you to love me like I should be loved." I felt my face flush with emotion as my voice rose.

"I do love you."

"If you loved me, Jack, you wouldn't have done this to me."

"News flash, Gracie—I'm not perfect."

"I never asked you to be perfect."

"Bull. You wanted me to be this perfect guy, so that's what I tried to be. But that's not who I am."

"Who are you?"

"I'm a guy who makes mistakes, and now I'm trying really hard to fix one of them."

"It's not that easy, Jack."

"You have this image of me where screwing up is not an option."

"You lied to me, and you were with your ex-girlfriend. Big screwup! Huge!" I yelled.

"And what about you?"

"What about me?"

"You and Sam?"

"There's no me and Sam."

"Sure there's not. He's just waiting to pounce, and you're giving him every opportunity."

"You're giving him this opportunity, not me."

"Tell me to my face he means nothing to you."

"Tell me to my face she means nothing to you."

We both stared at each other, waiting for the other to respond.

"I made a mistake, Gracie, one I wish I could take back."

I nodded, saying nothing.

"No more pretending, no more lies. This is who I am."

"Maybe I don't know the real you, Jack."

"You do know the real me. You just don't like the real me as much as you like the made-up version of me."

"That's crazy. You're saying I can't handle the real you?"

"It's easier to love the lie."

I closed the door and sat back down on the chair. "I don't trust you."

"No, it's more about me not being who you want me to be."

"I could say that same thing about you."

"How so?"

"I'm not one of your trophy girlfriends. I'm not arm candy, and that's what you want at the end of the day."

"That's your grandma talking."

"Supermodel Angie being by your side for photographers at the benefit was just by chance?"

He hesitated before answering. "I never asked you to be anything other than who you are. And I love every one of your perfect imperfections."

"You just said it."

"Said what?"

"I'm imperfect."

He grunted in frustration. "Are you the first person I've been with who wasn't a model or beauty queen? Yes. Are you the first person who has challenged me to be a better person? Yes. Are we a couple that may not seem obvious to everyone around us? Yes. Who cares?"

"Why do you think we aren't an *obvious* couple?"

He shifted again and eased back on the couch. "We come from different worlds, that's all."

"Meaning you're doing charity work by being with me?"

"No," he said, rolling his eyes. "You're so frustrating."

"I'm not a teenager anymore. I can't waste time with someone who thinks he's better than me or that he's doing me a favor by being with me. I'm past all that."

"Better than you? You really believe I think that?"

"Don't you?"

"There is no one better than you. Not for me."

I looked at him, feeling my heart pulse.

"I want you so much it kills me."

"That's just it, Jack. There's so much more to connecting than just sex."

"It's a big part of it."

"I know, but it's not all of it. I need to know we can connect in other ways too."

"Like what?"

"Like trust, like commitment, like compassion, like communication, like respect."

"Those are easy things."

"No, they're not. And that's the problem between us. You think those things come naturally, and I think you need to work to get them and work to keep them."

"So what are you saying?"

"I'm saying you confuse love with sex. They're not the same thing."

"Sex is a huge part of a relationship."

"Part of it, but there are so many other things besides sex. You think if we're physical with each other, that makes up for everything else. It doesn't."

"I'm a physical guy."

"I know, and I really like that. But how many times have you asked me about my work? How many times have you asked about Chloe?"

"Meaning ..."

"Meaning that connecting on a personal level like that isn't important to you. But sex only brings us together physically. It doesn't bring us together emotionally."

"See, that's what I mean. I've never been with anyone else who has challenged me to get my head out of my ass when it comes to relationships. That's why I need you."

"You need me?"

"Of course I do."

I went to him, and he took my hand.

"I'm so sorry, Gracie. I never want you to doubt me again."

"We need to establish ground rules when it comes to Angie and Sam."

"Agreed."

"After the wedding, I won't really see Sam too much."

"Good." He leaned in and kissed my neck.

"What about Angie?"

"I missed you," he said as he kissed my lips lightly.

I pulled away. "What about Angie?"

He looked at me. "Ah, c'mon."

"Are you going to cut her out of your life?"

"It's not that easy."

"Not that easy? Our parents are getting married to each other, and I'm ready to blow off Sam. How is it harder than that when it comes to Angie?"

"She's Ellie's best friend."

"Then Ellie needs to find other friends," I responded quickly. "Why does that matter?"

"Because my sister and I do a lot of stuff together, and I don't want to put Ellie in an awkward position by making her uninvite Angie to everything."

"But I can put my parents in an awkward position when it comes to Sam?" I pulled away from him.

"It's different with Angie."

"How so?" My anger was returning.

"She's been in my life a long time. My parents really liked her."

"Yeah, and the same goes for Sam."

"I told you no more lies, so I'm not going to lie about her."

I stared at him in disbelief. "Listen, I'm not one for ultimatums, but either do something about Angie or forget about me. There's not enough room in our relationship for her." As I was talking, his phone buzzed. "Kinda late for a text, isn't it?"

He stared at me, not taking his phone out of his pocket. "Probably Ellie. I told her I was coming over again to talk to you."

"And what did Ellie say about last night?"

"She told me you knew about the benefit, and I needed to figure out what I wanted and to stop jerking you around."

I nodded. His phone buzzed again.

"No more lies, right?" I said.

He nodded.

"Then take your phone out and let me read the text messages that just came through."

He inched his hand into his jacket pocket, pulled out his phone, and handed it to me.

El
Is everything ok? How is Gracie?

I breathed a sigh of relief until I saw the other messages.

Angie
U coming home 2 me?

Angie
Miss u baby, u gone 2 long from me.

I handed the phone back to him, stood up, walked to the door, and opened it. "Ellie's right. Please leave."

He sat there, not moving. "I'm not even sure what the messages say, but I know if they're from Angie, they don't mean anything."

"Read them after you permanently get out of my life." I held the door open. "Bye, Jack." I felt the rush of emotions consume my throat. Tears were clouding my eyes. I looked away, hoping he wouldn't see them.

"Gracie, just give me one more shot at forgiveness."

"Leave." I was barely able to keep my shaking hand on the door. I refused to look at him as he stood and walked out. I locked the door behind him.

My phone kept buzzing after he left. It drifted into background noise through the early morning hours.

By Monday, I knew I needed to get Jack out of my head. Thankfully, work kept me focused; my students were filled with more questions than usual, and I was grateful for it. My heart was heavy, but my mind was clear. If Jack wasn't ready to completely pull away from Angie, I needed to pull away from him. I could barely stomach my own insecurities, let alone the ones created because of her.

I purposely stayed late grading papers, not leaving work until after eleven. The drive home was quiet and peaceful. The stars were vibrant in the night sky. I was only a few blocks from home when I got caught at a railroad crossing. Sitting there watching the cars creak slowly down the tracks, I found the courage to read all my text messages from the last couple of days. The train was stalled; time belonged only to me.

Chloe
Got great news! Call me tomorrow.

Teddy
Message from your grandma—she will see you tomorrow night. Love u, doll.

Finally, I read Jack's texts from start to finish.

Jack B
Hey. Call me, okay?

Jack B
Just tried to call you. Call me.

Jack B
Just stopped by your house. You there?

Jack B
Not leaving until I see you.

Then came the messages from after we'd talked.

Jack B
I'm not really sure what just happened. Call me so we can talk.

Jack B
I can't control Angie. What do you want me to do about it?

Jack B
I'm lying in bed missing you.

Jack B
What the hell, Gracie? Be an adult and at least reply.

Jack B
Today sucks. I miss you so much it hurts more than my jacked-up face.

I deleted his voice messages without listening to them. As the last train car hiccupped over the tracks, my thoughts turned to Chloe. I was wondering what her news might be when something occurred to me. I dug through my purse, finally finding my calendar planner. I flipped back the pages, searching for it. I found the date and then flipped forward.

The railroad crossing bars lifted. I pulled into the gas station, pumped gas, and then headed into the attached convenience store.

A young clerk wearing earbuds rang me up and handed me my bag without making eye contact.

At home I sat on my bathroom floor, my back against the bathtub, waiting for the minutes to tick by. I knew it couldn't be. I knew I was just stressed. We had been very careful.

I looked at the timer on my phone.

In thirty-five seconds, I could put my mind to rest, put it behind me, get on with my life.

In twenty-one seconds, I could get a good night's sleep and wake up tomorrow with a renewed sense of purpose, a new direction.

In thirteen seconds, I could be free from the worry—discard it in the trash like I wanted to do with my weekend.

In four seconds, I could take out my dry contacts, wash my face, and maybe floss my teeth for the first time in weeks.

The timer went off on my phone. I reached up and grabbed it off the sink. I picked up the test, already knowing.

In zero seconds, my life as I had known it was gone forever.

15

As I drove by, I watched the newspaper boy delivering the morning news. He made his way from house to house, throwing each paper precariously toward front doors. Even in the age of social media, many people in my neighborhood still relied on the printed news, already slightly old by the time the words reached morning eyes. For those morning eyes, it was probably another ordinary day. For me, it was anything but.

I had been up all night and had been out of the house before five. I pulled into the parking lot, now able to make this trip on autopilot. Ever since discovering the meaning of the old oak tree, I had found it comforting to be near it. Chloe and I met here regularly for coffee. She appreciated the importance of the tree because she felt the love and loss of what it represented. I wrestled to pull the coffee carrier and bag of doughnuts out of my car.

I walked to the tree, stepping aside for early-morning joggers. Just like outside my window, here it was a normal day in the life of most people. For me, it was the start of something I had no idea how to manage, how to control. I felt like I was spiraling downward at full force, and I needed Chloe to bring me back to center, like she always did.

"Hey!" She stood by the tree, dressed in scrubs.

"Morning, sweetie."

We walked to the bench and sat down. I handed Chloe her coffee and the bag of doughnuts.

"What's my poison this morning?"

"Same as always, cinnamon and jelly-filled."

"Yummy," she said, taking a bite out of a cinnamon sugar doughnut. "Why are you up so early?" she asked as flecks of crystallized sugar fell from the corners of her mouth.

"I haven't really slept the last couple of nights."

"Really? Why?" She wiped her face with a napkin and took a small sip of coffee.

"Lots of reasons, I guess. Tell me your news." I tried to refocus my thoughts on her.

"I have bad news and good news. What do you want first?"

"Oh, well, the good news. I could use some good news."

"I got the promotion to director of surgery!" she exclaimed.

"That's fantastic!" I reached over and hugged her. "Do I want to know the bad news? I don't want anything to overshadow the good news."

"And that, my dear, is why I always get the bad news first—makes the good news better."

"Then you shouldn't have given me a choice," I replied, taking a sip of decaffeinated coffee.

"No baby again this month. I swear, some chicks bump uglies once with a random dude and get knocked up. Rick and I have been trying so hard and still are coming up empty. The next time I hear some ho-bag tell me she's got a bun in the oven, I'm going to lose it." She took another bite of doughnut. "So what's been going on with you?"

I sat there as her words sent me spiraling. "Jack and I broke up."

"What happened?"

I told her the story of Saturday night.

"Jesus. I'm sorry. Why didn't you call me?"

I shrugged my shoulders.

"So you've talked to him then?"

Nodding, I recounted our conversation from Sunday night.

"Frig. So that's it with him?"

"I guess."

"Well, you did the right thing. Until he can get it together and get that skank out of his life for good, forget about him. I mean, there's really no reason for you to ever see him again."

I bit my lip. "So that's reason a million and one I don't celebrate my birthday."

She laughed. "I certainly hope Sam doesn't see this as an opening, assuming at some point he finds out," she said. "I got the wedding invite in the mail, by the way. That must be your grandma's doing. It had Blake written all over it."

"Well, I think Lacey gave the final approval, but you know when it comes to my grandma, your approval is just a formality."

"Gotta love her, though. She's got balls of steel."

"She wants to come to my session tonight."

"Your grandma wants to go to your therapy session with you? I need to leave and do everything on my bucket list because the world must be ending."

I smiled. "It's 'special person' night, and she wants to go with me."

"I can go with you. Might be nice to see what I got you into anyway."

"Thanks, but she is determined to go with me."

"Well, better take a flask. She'll need it, and you might too."

I chuckled. We sat there awhile and watched the fall morning come to life.

She glanced over at me. "Okay, what gives?"

"What do you mean?"

"Something else is going on with you. I know it, so quit trying to avoid it. I walked you through your first tampon use, so everything is fair game with us."

"I'm scared to tell you." I looked at her for a second and then darted my eyes away.

"Scared to tell me? Now I'm scared."

We sat there, saying nothing. I could feel my heart in my throat; it was pounding so hard that I could barely breathe.

"Gracie, I can handle anything except losing you."

I reached into my pocket, pulled out the pregnancy test, and handed it to her.

Her eyes widened. "Jack?"

I nodded.

"It's just one test. Sometimes they can give false positives."

I reached back in my pocket and pulled out five more. "That makes six. I don't think all six can give false positives, right?"

She stared at all of them. "Six pretty much cements it, I'd say."

"I'm not even sure how this happened."

"Honey, if you're not sure how this happened, we have a much bigger problem."

"You have been trying so hard to have a baby, and I'm the one who ends up pregnant."

"Are you kidding me? Being a godmother is the next best thing to being a mother. It's great practice for me. I can make all the mistakes on this one, then raise mine to be perfect."

"What am I going to do?"

"Have you told Jack yet?"

I shook my head.

"When are you going to tell him?"

"He said he didn't want a baby."

"When did he say that?"

"When we talked about Angie being pregnant."

"Angie is pregnant? Is it his?"

"He said he would know by now if it was."

"Well, you certainly are, as evidenced by all the pee sticks we have lying around here."

"Not sure telling him is the right thing to do." I sniffled.

"You have to tell him. Your circles are too connected for him not to find out anyway."

"What do you mean?"

"Your therapy group? Your grandma's socialite gossipers? There's no way he won't find out. And anyway, he deserves to know."

"And what if he can't handle it?"

"Then at least you've given him the chance to decide what to do." She leaned into me. "And let me give it to you straight—you found fault in him for not being totally honest with you. Hello, kettle, this is the pot ..."

"You're right. I need to tell him."

"And speaking as your health care adviser, we need to get the blood test done to confirm it and get you on some prenatal vitamins. It goes without saying, no more booze or caffeine."

"Okay."

"I'll get you in today to see Dr. Simpson—best ob-gyn out there. We've known each other a long time."

"But I use Dr. Greenwich."

"Gracie, he's like a hundred. We need a doctor who might actually be alive by the time you deliver."

"He hasn't retired yet."

"Yeah, because he forgot he was supposed to about ten years ago."

"I need to tell my grandma."

"Good luck with that. I'll drink for both of us before that conversation."

"Maybe I should tell Jack tonight?"

"Good idea."

"What if I'm not a good mother?" I said, giving voice to the fear looming in my mind. "What if Jack doesn't want anything to do with the baby? Will I actually be able to raise it alone?"

"You will be an awesome mom, just like your mom was to you. If he doesn't want to be involved, it will be his major loss. And darlin', you wouldn't be alone in this if you tried."

I smiled, knowing Chloe was right about everything, once again.

By the afternoon, we sat in Dr. Simpson's waiting room with all the pregnancy magazines and six other pregnant Chicago women. Dr. Simpson was in high demand, and without Chloe's connections, I wouldn't have gotten my first appointment until the week I was due to give birth.

"Gracelynn?" When the nurse called my name, I found myself glued to the chair, unable to move.

"C'mon, Mama. Time to dance," Chloe said. She pulled me up by the hand, and we were led to an exam room.

"I'm Julie. I'm one of Dr. Simpson's nurses, and I'll be assisting today. Dr. Simpson will be in shortly, but first let's get some more information." As she began asking me questions, I felt like a teenager again, embarrassed by my poor judgment.

"Age of your first period?" she asked, typing at warp speed on a laptop suspended from the ceiling on a movable base.

"Thirteen."

"Age when you first had intercourse?"

"Sixteen."

"Date of last period?"

"September 28."

"Will she be having an ultrasound today?" Chloe asked.

"Yes. The urinalysis is positive, and her blood test will confirm the HCG levels, but Dr. Simpson will definitely want to take a look."

"So I'll know today?"

"You are definitely pregnant. We just need to do a thorough exam to make sure everything is as it should be."

"And she'll get her prenatal vitamins today?"

I was so thankful for Chloe. I sat on the thin paper sheet on the exam table, barely able to function. I kept shifting on the table, the paper underneath me crunching with every small move I tried to make.

"Yes," said the nurse. "Any previous contraception?"

I stared at her like a zombie.

"Have you been using contraception—the pill, condom?"

"Condom," I muttered. "And we always used them, so I'm not sure how this could have happened," I blurted out, trying to defend myself.

"It's been known to happen," she answered, clicking away at the keys.

"Well, you definitely don't need to worry about using them now," Chloe added.

"Number of previous pregnancies?"

"Zero."

"Do you want to list the father as someone we can provide information to?"

"My father? I don't see a reason why ..."

"The baby's father," she said.

"Oh." I looked at Chloe, who shrugged her shoulders. "Jack Bradshaw."

The nurse stopped typing. "Jack Bradshaw, the Chicago attorney?"

"Yes. Do you know him?" I panicked. Chloe was right. I was barely out of the pregnancy gate, and people were already making the connection.

"Uh, no. I thought he was engaged to Angelique, the supermodel. You know her?"

I couldn't form a response.

"I read a lot of celebrity magazines."

I stared at her blankly.

"My apologies."

"Gracie," Chloe interjected, "do you have his number so we can give it to Julie for the records?"

I looked at both of them, now in an utter state of shock. I pointed to my phone. Chloe nodded and read Jack's number off to Julie.

"Okay, Dr. Simpson will be in shortly. Please make sure everything waist down is removed. A sheet is next to you on the table." She started to leave the room and then stopped. "My apologies again for earlier," she said sincerely.

Jack had been right too. We were not an obvious couple, and now we were going to be not-obvious parents.

After undressing, I sat on the table, feeling cold and sweaty at the same time. Chloe sat across from me on a small chair. "Don't worry about it, Gracie. It's going to be fine," she said, trying to reassure me.

"It doesn't feel that way." I swung my feet back and forth, looking at my partially painted toenails. I was out of my league. I wished for my mom so much in that moment, and the loss of her hung heavily all around me.

Two quick knocks on the door, and the doctor entered. I hadn't thought to ask Chloe about Dr. Simpson. For some reason, I had expected a man, but Dr. Simpson was anything but, so I was more than surprised to see her. She stood before me, long blond hair pulled back slightly in a butterfly barrette. Her stark white lab coat covered most of her floral-print skirt. As she shook my hand, I noticed her multiple rings and the small tattoo peeking out from under her cuff.

"Gracelynn?"

I nodded yes.

"I'm Dr. Simpson."

"Hey, Dr. Simpson," Chloe said as she stood to give her a hug.

The doctor hugged Chloe back and then focused her attention on me. "So do you go by Gracelynn?"

"Gracie."

"So tell me a little bit about yourself, Gracie. Do you work?"

"Yes. I'm a college professor."

"Excellent. And what brings you in today?"

"I believe I'm pregnant." I wasn't sure why she asked me that. That I was pregnant seemed like the only obvious thing in the whole situation.

"Yes. I see that by the initial results. Is this your first pregnancy?"

"Yes."

"And I see there is a family history of cancer?"

"My mom."

"What type?"

"Ovarian."

She furrowed her brow slightly, nodding. "Any issues for you?"

"No."

"Your mother is deceased, correct?"

"Yes."

She nodded again. "Very sorry." She sat down on the stool. "Let's take a look, shall we?"

I placed my legs in the stirrups, like I'd done so many times before. This time, however, it felt different, almost awkward.

"Okay, ready?" Dr. Simpson asked before placing the ultrasound wand inside of me.

I nodded, not feeling anything, numb to it all. She began talking as I struggled to keep up. "Lining looks good, nice and thick. I think, yes ..." She began pressing buttons on the machine to focus. "Any history of multiples in your family?"

"Multiples?" I was confused.

"You know, more than one baby," Chloe explained.

"No."

"On the father's side?" She asked as she repositioned the wand inside of me.

"Uh ..." My mind began to race. "Jack is a twin."

"And Jack is the father?"

"Yes," Chloe said, answering for me. "Do you see more than one?"

"More than one what?" I asked.

"If you notice here," she said, pointing to a little black blob on the screen, "this is the first baby, and"—she shifted the wand slightly—"here is baby number two."

The blood pulsed so fast through my veins that I thought they would explode.

"Twins?" Chloe excitedly asked.

"Yes. It is more common if you, your mother, or your mother's mother was a twin, but the rate of multiples in general has increased over the years. Let's get the labs back to confirm the HCG levels, but that's what the ultrasound shows. I'll call you later to confirm everything." She squeezed my hand. "If you need anything, Gracie, you call me, okay? I'll make sure Julie gives you my contact information."

"When's her due date?"

"With twins you never know, but as of today, we're looking at the beginning of July. Oh, almost forgot." Dr. Simpson tore two black-and-white photos from the machine. "Your first baby pictures," she said, handing me the photos.

She walked out of the room as I inched myself up on the table, pulling my knees to my chest. Chloe sat on the stool and rolled over to me. I turned, dropped my legs, and let them dangle over the side of the exam table again.

"I just can't believe it," I mumbled. "Horrible."

Chloe took my hands in hers. "You're blessed, Gracie. These babies are a blessing. It may not seem like it now, but I know this is going to be the best thing that will ever happen to you."

"I never planned any of this," I replied.

"Life is sometimes about plan B."

As we headed to the parking lot, I looked at my phone. "It's almost four. I should go talk to my grandma."

"Want me to come with you?"

"Thanks, but it'll be a good warm-up for my conversation with Jack."

"I think telling your grandma will be easier than telling Jack. I have a hunch that he won't see this one coming, especially since you guys never played Russian roulette."

"Neither one will be easy, but my grandma can smell a potential scandal a mile away, so I better get her over with."

Chloe gave me a big hug. "Remember, it's a blessing. And boy, girl, animal, vegetable, or mineral, 'Chloe' better be in one of those names."

"Was there ever any doubt?"

★ ★ ★

Grandma and I sat in her kitchen, me with lemonade and her with a vodka tonic.

"It is nearly five, Gracelynn. We should be going soon. I do not want to be late for the session."

"We have plenty of time. We never start before six, and it's less than fifteen minutes away." I looked outside her stained-glass window and saw drops of rain beginning to fall.

"How was your day?" she asked, shaking her glass to move the ice around.

"Interesting," I replied, trying to find the courage and the words. "How about yours?"

"Frustrating. Do you know that Alyssa Stockard had the nerve to suggest she should cochair the Christmas benefit with me? The absurdity of it all," she declared.

"Wow. Unbelievable." I bit the inside of my cheek. "Where's Teddy?"

"He is contemplating buying a small waste-management company in Iowa, so he's going there to survey the area."

I nodded my head. "Grandma, can I ask you something?"

"I may choose not to answer, but you can always ask the question."

"Were you scared when you found out you were pregnant with Mom?"

She looked at me and set down the drink that had been nearly to her lips. "Yes, I was," she responded without blinking.

"Why?"

"I did not want to be a disappointment to my family. And of course, the timing could not have been worse."

"Because you weren't with Teddy?" I probed.

"Because I knew the disorder it would cause."

"Did you ever think about other ... options?"

"Options as in abortion or adoption?"

I nodded.

"Only a hundred times a day."

"Then why didn't you do either?"

"Back then, abortions were a risky move, unsafe and imprecise. I knew women who were promised a quick and safe procedure, only to be faced with dirty instruments and unlicensed medical personnel. Adoption was intriguing, but I could not imagine anyone raising my child except for me."

"How did your parents take it when you told them?"

"Fine at first, until they found out the truth about to whom Cassandra really belonged."

"Who told them?"

"I did, of course. I made the choice, so it was my responsibility to own it."

"Did you ever regret your decision?"

"It was not without pain along the way, but I always knew my choice was the right one."

"That's good."

"And the point of this conversation, Gracelynn, is what exactly?"

I tried to speak, but nothing came out of my mouth. The words felt like lead balloons in my throat, sinking further away from me.

She looked at me, taking a long sigh. "How far along are you?" And there it was.

"Almost five weeks."

"Who is the father?"

I looked at her, somewhat disgusted. "Jack is the father, Grandma. Of course, it's Jack."

"You have been spending time with Samuel, so I had to ask the question."

"No. I haven't been with anyone else like that except Jack."

"And how does Mr. Bradshaw feel about impending fatherhood?"

"I haven't told him yet. I just found out myself."

"Let me rephrase the question then. How do you think Mr. Bradshaw will receive the news that he is going to be a father?"

"Probably not well," I said, feeling dread over his reaction.

"Were you not safe? You know there are methods to prevent these types of things."

"Yes, Grandma, and I know about those methods. I thought we were always safe. I guess not," I said, defeated.

"And you know for sure there is a baby?"

I slowly placed two fingers in the air.

"Two babies?" She fell back slightly in her chair.

"Yes, twins."

"You have always been an overachiever. That is not limited to education and career, apparently."

"I'm sorry, Grandma."

"Regarding?"

"Embarrassing you, I guess. Yeah, being an embarrassment."

She touched my hand. "Had I not lived your life, I would not have a healthy dose of empathy regarding this matter. I was hoping for a nice courtship, marriage, and sprawling home for you first, but what I want does not matter. It is what you want that is most important."

"I'm not sure how to tell Jack," I sadly replied.

"You will not explore other options then?"

"I never considered any option other than keeping them."

"He may not take it well when first told, but if he is a good man, he will find his own way to be supportive."

"I think he's going to be there tonight."

She tapped her fingernails one at a time on the table. "Yes. I imagine he will be."

"I know you don't like him, Grandma."

"True, but if I am being honest with both of us, I have not really given him a chance to prove his measure of worth one way or another."

"That's nice to hear."

"Teddy is the one who told me I was not being fair, so you can thank him for my new sense of self-awareness."

"I need to tell Jack tonight," I said matter-of-factly.

"Then it makes sense for me to be there, for a number of reasons," she said, raising the tumbler to her lips.

"Do you need more vodka to stomach the night? We've got time."

She frowned at me at first, as if her response should be no, but then her face lightened. "Well, maybe one more," she said, reaching for the prepared crystal pitcher filled with vodka tonic. "When are you going to tell your father?"

"When is he back in town?"

"End of the week. You need to think through the timing since your news will likely be a shock to Samuel, who has his hopes for a future family life firmly set on you."

"I need to add him to the list."

"May I offer you a piece of advice, Gracelynn?"

"Sure, Grandma."

"If people choose to pass judgment on you, screw them," she declared, taking a long sip of her drink.

I laughed in half shock.

"Ready?"

I nodded, now knowing something my mom had figured out years before. Blake Desiree Honoree Smith had my back, and no one and nothing was going to mess with me as long as she was around. And that went for my children now as well.

On our way to session, Dr. Simpson called and confirmed that I was indeed pregnant and that based on my levels and the ultrasound, there were two babies growing inside of me. I expected my body to feel different now that I knew, but all I felt at that moment was nausea, knowing I would be seeing Jack soon.

As we stepped into the community center, Grandma instantly covered her nose. "What is that smell?" she asked in disdain.

"Chlorine ... and sweat," I said, taking her hand in mine. I needed to feel her strength since mine was quickly diminishing.

"A spritz or two of lavender vanilla would greatly improve this atmosphere."

"It's a gym, Grandma, not a boudoir."

"I think you could find a better establishment for this type of thing." She motioned to the cracked floor tiles as we walked toward the room.

I felt my feet freezing up on me, stopping me in my tracks. "I'm scared."

She squeezed my hand firmly.

"Hey, my girls," a familiar voice called out from behind us.

I turned to see Teddy. "Teddy, what are you doing here?"

He walked up to me, hugging me tightly. "Your grandma texted me and told me the news. I thought you could use some reinforcements."

I laid my head on his chest, thankful once again for Teddy and all that he represented in my life. "I thought you were leaving for Iowa."

"Iowa can wait. My girl can't."

"I can only have one person come in with me tonight, though." I looked at both of them, wondering what to do.

"I'm just gonna wait on that bench over there." He pointed to an old wooden bench just inside the center's main doors.

"But Teddy, the session is two hours long. That's a long time to wait."

He shook his head. "Two hours is nothing. I waited for your grandma almost my whole life."

My confidence as we walked in the room quickly evaporated when I saw them.

"Hello," Ellie said, approaching me. "How are you?"

I nodded, saying nothing.

"I am Mrs. Smith, Gracelynn's grandmother. And you are?"

"Mrs. Smith, we spoke on the phone. My name is Ellie. Nice to meet you." She extended her hand, and my grandma took it, shaking it firmly without taking her eyes off of her.

"Yes, Eleanor. We appreciated your call."

Ellie nodded, saying nothing.

"And who is this with you?"

"Sorry, this is Angie," Ellie said, motioning for Angie to come stand with us.

"Hallo, I am Angelique. I will like you call me Angie." She wore a tight white cashmere sweater that stopped above her belly button. Her breasts were pushed up and outward from her sweater. I noticed a hoop ring in her belly button; a gold chain threaded through it and wrapped around her waist. I was certain that Grandma noticed it as well. Angie's black satin pants clung tightly to her, showing the indentations of her hip bones. Her boots added four inches to her height.

Any other time, I dreaded Grandma's barbed responses, since

I normally found myself on the receiving end of them. This time, however, I looked forward to her drawing blood.

"Angelique, is it?"

"What they call you?" She stood a few inches taller than my grandma, but she was no match. My grandma was going to bring her to her knees.

"They call me Mrs. Smith."

"Yes, but no. What … you know … I am Angie, and you are who? Like they say, you first name? I like to be with you in a first-name way."

"I am going to allow you the benefit of being ignorant to proper etiquette, so take this as an opportunity to receive proper education, which clearly you are missing." My grandma leaned into her. "We do not know each other. I am fairly confident that even if we did know each other, I would not like you, so you may call me Mrs. Smith."

"You old, so I call you by last name?"

I almost felt bad for Angie then, for she had no idea she was dealing with a professional.

My grandma's back went slightly erect, like a python getting ready to go for the kill. "How old are you, Angelique?"

"Nine past twenty."

"I see. And did you attend school?"

"School?" Angie looked confused by the question.

"Yes, a place similar to this with books and a requirement to receive education on subject matters other than bikini waxes, unsightly tattoos, and artificial breasts."

"Some school, yes."

Grandma's eyes focused on Angie for a very long, uncomfortable moment. It was such a deliberate move that I could see Angie's face begin to change and her posture wither. She tugged at her sweater, trying to pull it down over her belly button ring.

"And your need to dress like this comes from where?"

"You no like my look?" She was clearly trying to recover from the shot of insecurity my grandma had inflicted on her.

"If your look is a form of self-expression, then I believe you need to reevaluate how you convey yourself to others—because right now, the only thing you are expressing to everyone is your need to be the center of attention. And no one here really wants or needs that, especially Eleanor. This is her night, not yours. If you are truly her friend, have respect for what this means to her."

Angie stared at my grandma blankly.

"Do you understand, Angelique?"

Angie nodded.

Grandma paused and then continued. "And for goodness sake, remove that piercing from your navel. That is a belly button, not a jewelry rack."

Angie looked down at her hoop ring, pulling at her sweater even more. She turned to Ellie. "We sit down now?" she asked, clearly feeling the need for flight.

"Oh, and Angelique?" my grandma added.

Angie looked at my grandma.

"Remember your place when it comes to my granddaughter, or I will gladly remind you."

Angie nodded in response, taking an open seat across the room.

Grandma looked to Ellie. "Angelique is the special someone you brought tonight?" she asked, innocently but with an ulterior motive.

"Well, I asked Jack, but he … wasn't up for it." Ellie glanced at me and then turned her eyes elsewhere.

"That is a shame. I was hoping to see him this evening," Grandma said, looking at me.

"Gracie!"

I jumped slightly upon hearing my name and turned to see who it was. "Ginger!" I said.

She approached me excitedly, holding hands with a short

man. Tonight, Ginger wore charcoal pants, flats, a black ribbed turtleneck, and a small chain with a ring on it around her neck. Her hair was pulled back in a loose bun, her makeup nearly nonexistent. Her skin looked fresh and clean. Her look tonight matched the person I had come to know, minus the facade of who she pretended to be. Ginger was beautiful.

"This is Bryan Bates ... my friend."

"Nice to meet you, Bryan."

"You as well, Gracie. Gin told me about you and the other ladies in the group."

"I could hardly wait for tonight. So exciting!" Ginger squealed.

I half-smiled, remembering the sense of dread I had felt the whole day while thinking about tonight. "Bryan, you're an accountant? Did I remember that correctly?"

He nodded. "I am. Own a firm in Highmore and one in Brighton."

"Brighton, really? I have friend who lives in Brighton."

"You do? Maybe I know them?" he asked.

"Oh, I'm not sure. Brighton's a pretty wide open space, right?"

"Who is it?"

"Sam Patterson."

Bryan clapped his hands, smiling. "Of course, I know Sam Patterson. Everyone knows him." He paused. "How do you know Sam?"

"We grew up together. Our parents are getting married to each other."

"Wait, is that you?"

"Sorry?" I was confused by his question.

"Sam's been telling everybody about you. He's head over heels for you, for sure."

"Of course he is," Ginger responded. "I can't believe you know the same person. It's like that so-many-degrees-of-separation thing."

I watched my grandma move toward us. "Ginger, Bryan, I'd like for you to meet my grandma."

"Hi, ma'am," Ginger said.

As my grandma shook Ginger's hand, I worried she would sniff out Ginger's occupation, the scent of bondage all over her. If she did, my grandma gave no outward inclination.

"Gracelynn is quite taken with you and the other ladies in the group."

Ginger's smile lit up the room. "I love Gracie. She's so awesome!" she exclaimed.

"Bryan, what is your occupation?" For my grandma, this translated to how much money someone had in the bank.

"I'm an accountant."

"Lovely. Do you own your own practice?"

"I do." He handed her his business card.

She stared at it like she was reading it, but I knew that unless it was written in seventy-two-point font, she couldn't make out one letter on the card without her glasses, which she had refused to bring with her.

I waited for her to say something caustic, but she surprised me. "My dear friend Teddy owns his own business and is thinking about changing accountants. Where are you located?"

"Highmore and Brighton."

"Brighton? Really?" She looked at me, one eyebrow raised. "Gracelynn has a longtime friend in Brighton."

"Sam Patterson. Yeah, just found that out. He's a great guy."

"You are acquainted with him?"

"Everyone knows Sam. He's a local celebrity in Brighton."

"Is that so?" Grandma raised both her eyebrows this time, making a clear point to me.

"Oh yeah." Bryan leaned in, excited to tell my grandma his big secret, which wasn't that big and wasn't a secret, at least not compared to the bombshell I was waiting to drop. "Said Gracie here is the love of his life. You might have an addition to your family soon, depending on how things play out."

My grandma smirked. "Your single-addition calculation may be off slightly."

I nudged her to be quiet, and she brushed me off with her hand, like an annoying mosquito.

"Grandma, I'm sure you're anxious to meet the other members of my group, so if you guys will excuse us," I said politely, pulling at my grandma's sleeve. I turned her in the opposite direction of the room.

"Gracelynn, that was extremely rude. I was having such a nice conversation with them. Ginger seems charming. What does she do?"

"Sales," I quickly responded.

Sarah stood nearby, holding hands with a man I assumed was Jerry. She smiled when she saw us. "Gracie. Hey, there."

I reached out, and she hugged me.

Pulling away, she quietly said, "This is my Jerry."

"Jerry, so nice to meet you."

He shook my hand, not making eye contact. "You as well."

"Sarah, Jerry, I'd like for you guys to meet my grandma."

Jerry nodded, and Sarah bowed slightly. "The pleasure is mine," Sarah said softly.

"You may call me Blake," Grandma responded.

"You no let me call first name for you," Angie said in the background, clearly listening to our conversation.

Grandma raised her index finger in the air toward Angie as if to shush her. Angie dropped her head in disgust.

"Thank you, ma'am, but with all due respect, may I call you by your formal name?" Sarah asked.

Grandma smiled.

I felt proud to be intertwined with this group. They had lives, plans, big deals, and small moments, and I was privileged to be part of it all.

Dr. Gretchen motioned for us to take our seats. "Welcome. It's with great respect that I thank you for coming tonight. Without a doubt, these ladies have inspired me to be a better person and to deal with the loss of my own mother in new and profound ways. I thought tonight we would begin with simple introductions. Who would like to start?"

Grandma raised her hand. "I would like to begin."

I felt nausea come over me again, the acid in my stomach starting to churn.

"Thank you," Dr. Gretchen replied.

"My name is Blake Desiree Honoree Smith. I am Gracelynn's grandmother."

Dr. Gretchen signaled for her to continue.

"I am from Westminster. I had a daughter, Gracelynn's mother. I also have a son-in-law and a very special friend, Teddy."

"Thank you, Mrs. Smith. Would you like to share anything else?"

"What else would I share?" Grandma's voice tightened. I was sorry I hadn't brought a flask to help her take the edge off.

"Anything that is on your mind."

Grandma straightened her already perfect posture. "I was not in support of Gracelynn coming here."

"Why is that?"

"Because I do not believe in this sort of thing."

"Which is?"

"Sharing personal details with those outside the immediate family, of course; I find it disrespectful."

"I appreciate your honesty. Some people do feel that way. Do you have someone you can talk to about your loss?"

"My loss?" Grandma flinched.

"The loss of your daughter. I'm sure it had to be extremely difficult dealing with the death of your daughter while being the matriarch of the family."

"Yes," Grandma said hesitantly. "I am grateful for Gracelynn. She helped me in many ways."

"I'm sure you already know, Mrs. Smith, how difficult it must have been for Gracie as well?"

"Yes."

"Do you feel like she could share her feelings with members of the family? Her father, for instance?"

"Jeffrey? No, that ability evades him."

"I see. And any other family member?"

Grandma looked at me.

"Not really," I quietly answered.

Grandma's voice cracked slightly as she remarked, "I am here because while I do not believe in therapy, I do believe in Gracelynn, and she believes in all of you."

"That speaks volumes about your support of Gracie, Mrs. Smith."

"I do not think therapy is the answer to problems," Grandma stated matter-of-factly.

"I don't see it as therapy," Sarah replied. "I see it as a place to be with people who know what it feels like on the inside. No one else understands what it feels like to deal with the hole."

"The hole?" Jerry asked.

"The hole that death carves out inside you, reminding you what's been taken from you," Sarah answered.

"The more you pretend it ain't there, the bigger it gets, until everything you feel falls into it," Ginger said.

"Then everything inside of you is gone, and there is nothing left to feel," Ellie gently responded.

"Do you really believe you have a hole inside of you?" Jerry asked.

"Yes," we all answered simultaneously.

"Not the way you see a hole, really," I said, "but the hole where you feel this emptiness that no one will ever be able to fill except your mother."

"I never thought of it that way," my grandma responded.

The room became eerily quiet. I imagined that all of us were feeling the holes grow larger as we thought about our losses.

"I'm Bryan Bates, and I'm glad Ginger asked me to come."

Dr. Gretchen turned to face him. "And how do you feel now that you're here?"

"Nervous."

"Why is that?" she probed.

He hesitated. "I was nervous meeting you all 'cause you're like her family, and I wanted to impress you. And what would happen if you didn't like me? She might not want to go out with me because your opinion means a lot to her."

"Your intention then," Grandma interjected, "is to be a lasting figure in Ginger's life?"

I rolled my eyes, hitting my grandma lightly on the elbow. "None of your business, Grandma," I mumbled under my breath.

"Heck yeah. I intend to be with her as long as she'll have me," he said, taking Ginger's hand. Ginger blushed, something I'd never seen her do before.

"She must be a hard one to tie down," my grandma said innocently. I nearly lost it.

"I am Angie," Ellie's guest suddenly declared, seemingly unaware that no one was paying any attention to her. "You call me Angie, okay? Yes, I here for El-lee." She said Ellie's name in two long syllables. "We together very long time."

"Thank you, Angie. Very nice to have you here," Dr. Gretchen replied.

"Hey, you're that supermodel, right?" Jerry perked up as he asked the question.

"I thought you looked familiar," Bryan added. "I've seen you on magazine covers. Nice-lookin' swimsuit on the one."

"Were you on *Trend* last month?" Jerry quietly asked. As we all looked at him, he shrugged his shoulders. "Lots of magazines on campus."

"Yes, yes." She rose slightly out of her chair, and her sweater crept higher up her midsection. I suspected that this was intentional. Vomit rose in my throat.

"A famous person right here," Jerry said, with Sarah shooting him a disapproving glance.

"I give her Bruce." The words slid out of Angie's mouth like a snake. "He still love you. You need be with him. Like me with my Jackie."

My body stiffened when she said his name.

"We no be without each other. He mama said so."

"What are you referencing?" my grandma asked.

"My mother really liked Angie," Ellie explained. "Said she and my brother Jack were destined to be together." Ellie tried not to look at me as she spoke about him.

"He mama say we make perfect babies. Say he to be with me like the bee to the flower. You know, the bee take to flower and need each other to make more of the flowers? We be married."

"That's nice. Perhaps we should move on with the introductions?" Dr. Gretchen offered, trying to steer the conversation back on track.

I stared at Angie as she spoke, my eyes glued to her for a completely different reason than the others in the room. I felt my grandma's hand graze mine. She was not ready to move past this conversation yet.

"You said you are getting married?" Grandma asked.

"Maybe yes?"

"Maybe or yes? I would think if you were set to be married, you would know it."

Angie looked at my grandma. "He just need to know I am good person."

"Why would he feel otherwise?"

"We had fight."

"A fight? I'm not sure what kind of fight would cause you to not be certain about getting married. Couples quarrel all the time. What did you argue about?"

If I were Angie, I would not have answered, but she was caught up in my grandma's web, so her answers came too quick and too honest.

"He no like my habits."

"Smoking?"

The rest of the group sat and listened to the conversation unfold; even Dr. Gretchen eased back in her chair knowing it was too late to stop the conversation.

"I no smoke. Bad for the lung."

"Drinking?"

"Bad for liver."

Grandma smiled, showing Angie her perfectly capped teeth. "Do you bite your nails?"

"No. My nails perfect like rest of me."

"Eat unhealthy food?"

"No, only pure go in body."

"I am somewhat confused then. It sounds like you are indeed perfect, which means this habit you speak of must be very minor. Perhaps it is not so bad after all?"

"I like be physical with other men."

"Physical with other men?" Grandma repeated.

"Yes. Yes. You know, I be with Jackie, then I be with other men. But my love only go to my baby, Jackie."

"I understand. You are unfaithful."

"Unfaithful?" Angie's eyebrows rose.

"You are ... what do they call it ... yes, yes, a whore." A small pin dropping in the corner of the room would have echoed like a violent thunderstorm. "Is that why Jack broke up with you?"

"We no broke up. He say no other men. I say okay, but Doug Dawes take me to dinner, and I no could say no afterward."

"Doug Dawes, the professional baseball player?" Bryan asked in awe.

"He play the ball with stick, yes, yes."

"You could not say no, or you did not want to say no when this gentleman asked you to go home with him?" Grandma asked.

"Go home with him? Ah, no, we no go home. We be physical in car."

"Very classy," Grandma retorted. She turned to Ellie. "And your mother was okay with this?"

"My mother just asked Jack to make the right decision when it came to Angie, knowing they made a great couple," Ellie responded.

"A great-looking couple, possibly, but I do not think a great couple in general," Grandma answered back.

"Regardless, there is now a sense of obligation when it comes to Angie and Jack," Ellie said sadly.

Grandma looked at Ellie. "May I inquire what happened with your fiancé?" she asked.

"He cheated on me …" Ellie's voice trailed off. "Quite often."

"And his infidelity is the reason you are no longer together?"

"I wasn't enough for him, I guess." Ellie dropped her head.

"I believe," Grandma said, "that people cheat for one of two reasons: one, because they need to feel the power, because they thrive on the rush of being with someone new, or two, something is lacking in their relationship that causes them to stray. And they seek that with someone else. The cause is not as important as the effect."

"Bruce loves power. He needs it to breathe." Ellie focused on the floor.

"You know," Dr. Gretchen said, "that his need for power has nothing to do with you, correct?"

"Maybe if I would have been different, he wouldn't have cheated."

"I am going to guess he was with someone else when he met you and cheated on that person with you. Would I be correct?" Grandma asked.

"Yes. He was with Greta Gerschaw."

"The actress?" Bryan asked. "Wow."

"I am not sure who this Greta is, but I do know once you cheat the first time, it makes cheating every time after that much easier."

"Greta Gerschaw was in *The House of a Hundred Horrors*, Grandma," I whispered to her.

"Really? One of my favorites," she replied.

"He told me he was a changed man."

"The fault in that is the belief it is true." Grandma's words sent waves of agreement throughout the room.

"I like the Bruce," Angie declared.

"You also like the backseats of cars. But let's leave it at that," Sarah countered. Quiet, introverted Sarah had just shouted from the rooftops.

Dr. Gretchen shifted in her chair. "Why don't we—" Her words were cut off by a knock on the door. "I believe we are all here. Excuse me for a moment." She opened the door and stepped outside the room.

As she reentered with the shadow of a person behind her, I felt the room spin.

"Everyone, please welcome an additional guest to the session." She motioned for him to step forward.

"Hi, I'm Jack Bradshaw."

16

As a little girl, I had been scared of the dark. I was not even really sure what I was afraid of, but I knew that when the outside lights began to dim, I wanted the inside lights to brighten. It was my mom who had helped me find peace with the long dark nights.

"Pretend you're sailing away in the night sky, using the stars to light your way. Don't let your fears define you. Use them to your advantage. If you do what makes you really afraid, the best adventures will find their way to you. You can either be crippled by your fears or be liberated by them."

Her exact words came back to me in that moment as I looked at him, feeling nearly paralyzed. The more I tried to calm myself down, the faster my heart raced. He took the only open seat; it was across from me, next to Angie. My psyche crumbled as I saw them blatantly exposed in front of me.

"Welcome, Jack. Our visitors have been introducing themselves. Would you like to go?" Dr. Gretchen smiled at him.

"Uh, I'm Jack. I think you all know that. I'm Ellie's brother and Gracie's ... uh ... her ..." He stopped short of defining his relationship with me.

"And is there anything you'd like to share with the group?"

I tilted my head, feeling my pulse begin to slow a bit, my heart calming itself.

"I lost my mom too. Guess that's kind of obvious." He wore a pair of jeans, laced-up shoes, and a hoodie. His facial bruises were beginning to dull slightly, but the cuts were still prominent.

I wanted to wave a wand and make our problems go away. Then I remembered that Angie was the least of our problems now. His eyes caught mine. I remained expressionless.

"Would you like to talk about it?" Dr. Gretchen asked.

"My mom was my foundation, my rock," Jack said. "Until recently, I felt like I had no center, nothing to hold me together, keep me sane, you know?" He rubbed his eyes.

"What changed?" Ginger asked.

"What changed recently, you mean?" He wiped his running nose with the cuff of his hoodie. "Someone very special."

My heart pounded as he spoke. I couldn't take my eyes off of him. I was thinking about going to him when Angie took his hand and kissed it.

"It okay, baby. Angie here now. Make it all better."

I was waiting for him to pull away from her. He did not.

"Is she your someone special?" Bryan asked, motioning toward Angie.

"My someone special?" He looked at Bryan.

"Yeah, the one you, like, love?" Jerry clarified, not looking at him.

"Uh, no, not this one," he said, pointing to Angie. "This one." He slowly moved his finger from Angie to me.

"Yeah, knew it!" Ginger exclaimed loudly.

"Ah, baby. You and me, like the bee to the flower."

He finally pulled away from her. "Angie, stop," he snapped.

"Angie, I believe my brother has made his decision," Ellie responded.

"No, no, he no make he mind up. He know we have baby," she insisted.

"Baby?" Sarah looked at her.

"I am with the baby. Yes, yes. Cannot you tell by my fat here?" She tried to squeeze her abdomen but was met with nothing but firm, tight skin.

"Really? And how far along are you?" Grandma asked.

"Onto the four months."

"Angie, you know it's not mine, even if it were true," Jack said, his voice rising.

"Yes, yes, you father to baby inside here," she said.

"I'm not going to talk about babies because I don't want any, okay?" he snapped back.

Grandma leaned into me. "I take it you never discussed children?"

I shook my head.

"You might want to have that conversation in advance next time."

"Yes, Grandma, good information to have now," I whispered back.

"We no make a good life without each other. You know, the three make the one," Angie said to Jack with confidence.

Jack looked at her and then over to me.

I let out a deep sigh.

Jack rebutted, "We're not a family, Angie. Not even close."

"Jackie, that no what you say last night." The words dribbled out of her mouth.

"Last night?" I questioned.

Jack glared at Angie. He shook his head at her.

"When we lay together in the bed, he and me."

"What?"

"Gracie, it's not—"

"No," I said, cutting him off. "Not from you." I pointed at Angie. "From you, tell me about last night."

"My Jackie so sad. I say we make the love, but he say no, no. He too sad to make he little boy stand up and be happy, you know?"

"You spent the night with her?"

"Not like that, Gracie. Can we step outside and talk about it?"

"No." I glared at him. "How much can you love me, Jack, if you already spent the night with another woman?"

"I do love you. I came here tonight to tell you I'm sorry. I want to make it right between us."

Everyone in the room fell away except the two of us.

"How do you know anything about love? You can't even stay away from Angie for a day. I mean, how are we ever going to have a life together? No bed is big enough for you, me, and her."

"I told you it's not that easy," he replied.

"That's the thing. It shouldn't be that hard to walk away from someone who is wrong for you and walk toward someone who is right for you. But there you sit, right next to her."

"I wouldn't even be here if it weren't for you. I came to see you." He ran his fingers through his hair.

"Doesn't seem like that at the moment."

"You're not being fair ... again."

"Okay, how about this? How about you look Angie in the eyes and tell her you choose me and that as much as it will change things, you can't have her in your life anymore."

He sat there saying nothing.

"That seems like a very reasonable request to me," Grandma interjected.

"Jack?" Ellie said, trying to prompt him to respond.

He remained quiet.

"Talk to her," Ellie said.

"It's complicated," he finally said. As the words left his mouth, my emotions exploded.

"Complicated?"

"Yes, complicated," he responded.

"Complicated? You have no idea what complicated is, Jack."

"Yes, I do. My life is complicated."

"Really?" I said angrily, rising to my feet. "You want to know complicated? Try being pregnant by a guy who doesn't want kids and who, oh yeah, by the way, is still hung up on his supermodel ex-girlfriend. How about that for complicated?" I was immersed in a pool of emotions I couldn't find my way out of. I was drowning in them. I was having an out-of-body experience, watching myself stand in front of him, nearly yelling.

"What?" He looked at me.

I stopped, realizing what I had just done.

"What did you just say?"

I took two steps back.

"Gracie, what did you just say?"

I opened my mouth to speak, but words suddenly eluded me.

"Did you just say you're *pregnant*?" He spit the word out of his mouth like it was rotten.

I stood silently by my seat.

"Did you?"

"I believe the answer to your question is yes, yes, she did," Grandma confirmed.

"Gracie, no way, right?" He looked closely at me.

I was dumbfounded in the moment, unable to find any emotion other than fear.

"Are you kidding me?"

I shook my head.

"Man, you got some swimmers!" Bryan yelped.

"Gracie, really?"

I nodded my head yes.

"How?"

I shrugged my shoulders.

All eyes were on me and Jack. Neither of us said anything. We just kept looking at each other, empty of words but full of emotions.

"I have to go," he finally said, getting to his feet. "I'm sorry, Gracie. I just can't." He was gone before I could even process his words.

I fell back in my seat and felt Grandma's hand grasp mine.

"Give him time, Gracelynn. He needs time."

I nodded, feeling the emptiness of the room without him in it.

★ ★ ★

As Jack walked quickly toward the exit doors, Teddy caught a glimpse of him.

"Hey, Jack," Teddy called out.

"Oh, hey, Teddy."

"Didn't know you were here," Teddy said, walking up to him, causing him to stop.

"Yeah, I came through the other door." Jack motioned to the hallway leading to the pool.

"Leavin' so soon?"

"I have to go," Jack said, pushing his hair back.

"You okay?"

"Not really."

"Want to sit and talk for a few?" Teddy asked, taking a seat back on the bench. "I was just waitin' for my girls, so I got time."

"Uh, I guess." Jack sat down on the bench, seeming somewhat uncomfortable.

"Hate to say it, but you look rough."

"Car accident last weekend."

Teddy nodded. "How ya feeling?"

"From the accident the other day, okay. From just a few minutes ago, not so good." Jack folded his hands together on his lap.

"You wanna talk about it?" Teddy placed his hand on Jack's shoulder.

Jack looked at him, his face pale and blotchy. "Do you know about Gracie?" Jack asked, eyes wide.

"I know she's the best girl around, next to her grandma."

Jack was quiet for a moment. "She is amazing, isn't she?"

"What's on your mind, son?"

After a long silence, he said, "Gracie's pregnant. And I'm the father."

"Lots to process, I bet."

He began rubbing his hands up and down his legs. "This has never happened to me before."

"Not sure that really matters. What matters now is what you do next. It's time to make some decisions."

"Decisions?"

"You need to decide if you're gonna be a boy or a man."

"What's the difference?"

"A boy runs; a man doesn't."

"I feel like running," he said with a loud exhale, like air being let out of a balloon.

"That's natural."

"It is?"

"Yep."

"How would you know?"

"Because I've been there."

Jack looked at Teddy. "And you stayed put."

"Oh, I ran, but I ran toward something. And when I got there, I stayed put, planted my feet in cement."

Jack turned quiet, looking at his hands resting in his lap. "I don't think I have it in me to plant my feet."

"I see," Teddy responded.

"We're barely into this thing, and now there's a baby in the mix—like an instant family."

"Not just any family, Jack, *your family*."

He looked at Teddy, mouth open but with no words. "I just can't," he finally said, standing.

Teddy watched Jack exit the heavy doors, feeling for the first time in a long time a sense of angst, wondering whether he should tell Gracie. He watched the clock tick by as he waited, feet planted in cement, like they always were.

"Gracie? Are you okay?" Dr. Gretchen asked.

I nodded, knowing full well I wasn't fooling anyone in the room. I was anything but okay.

"You have the baby with Jackie?" Angie pointed at me. "He my Jackie. No belong to you."

"Angie, please don't," Ellie replied. "Just leave it alone."

Angie sank back in her chair, pouting.

For the rest of the session, I said nothing. I could hear the voices of the other people in the circle, talking, laughing, questioning, sharing, but I remained silent. Even my grandma interacted with the group. The time dragged on for an eternity, something I had never experienced with the session before.

"Gracie?" I was lost in my thoughts of Jack and hadn't noticed Ellie approach me. "May I speak with you for a moment?"

I nodded, still trying to find my way back to reality. It seemed the session was over. "I'll catch up with you, Grandma, if that's okay?"

"Teddy and I will wait for you by the entrance."

"You wanted to talk?" I asked, looking beyond Ellie to Angie, who was texting on her phone.

Ellie glanced over to Angie. "Jack isn't the father of Angie's baby."

"That's good, I guess." I paused. "Is she really pregnant?"

"Yes." Awkward silence followed.

"Why would she say he is the father?"

"Because she wants it to be Jack so badly."

I nodded. "I feel horrible about telling Jack like I did. I just got caught up in the moment."

"He's just never been a kids kind of guy. That's not to say he won't eventually come around."

"I have to be okay with it if he doesn't." I felt a hiccup in my throat. "But I had to tell him."

"Of course you did."

"You know him better than anyone, right?"

Blinking, she said, "I believe I do."

"Do you think he'll ever come around?"

She said nothing.

"Never mind, I think you just answered my question."

"It's just that … he doesn't do chaos well. He needs to have order in his life. Any deviation throws him. That's why kids to him don't make sense. They are chaos in the best and worst way."

"I appreciate your honesty, Ellie."

"Can I ask you something, Gracie?"

"Sure."

"Even if my brother doesn't want anything to do with the baby …" She stopped briefly. "Would you let me be part of its life?"

I mouthed yes. She hugged me.

"Well, I better go. My grandma is waiting for me."

As we pulled away from each other, she said, "Gracie, don't give up on Jack yet. He might just surprise us both."

Down the hall, Teddy and my grandma sat on the bench waiting. I walked up to them and plopped down.

"How ya doing, doll?" Teddy smiled at me, his "I Eat Brains" T-shirt radiating slightly in the darkening corridor. An overhead light flickered on and off, causing the glow-in-the-dark lettering on his shirt to fade in and out.

"Oh, I've been better."

"I was just telling Teddy how charming I found the meeting participants," Grandma said. "They were very engaging in conversation. Much more educated than I expected."

"Grandma, losing their mothers didn't decrease their intelligence."

"Teddy spent a portion of his time tonight in discussion with Jack," Grandma revealed, looking at me for a reaction.

"You talked to Jack?"

Teddy nodded but said nothing.

"What did he say, Teddy?"

"He said he is going to be a father ... and he's scared." Teddy frowned slightly as he spoke.

"Did he say anything else?"

Teddy looked at my grandma. She nodded as if to say he needed to tell me.

"He said he's not sure he can stick around. Not sure the family thing is for him."

"I see." I felt my heart tumble into the pit of my stomach. "It's okay."

Grandma looked at me. "It is not okay, as a matter of fact. You deserve for him to stand up like a man and live up to his responsibilities."

"Give the boy some time, love. He's just been told he's going to be a father. Lots to sort out in his mind, you know?"

Grandma peered at Teddy and then relaxed her furrowed eyebrows. "How much time do you think he needs?" Grandma asked Teddy.

"I'm not sure. This is a big thing for him, especially when he never wanted a family in the first place."

"Perhaps, Teddy, you could speak with him ..."

"No," I said, stopping her. "We need to leave him alone. If this is what he wants, he knows where to find me." I felt the anguish about to drown me. "I am not going to beg him to be with me, to be part of this."

"I think that's best," Teddy solemnly replied.

"You do?" Grandma looked at him, surprised.

"Until you've been through it, you can't know what it's like."

He wrapped his arm around me. "You got us. Not the same thing, I know, sugar, but it's something."

I let his words sink in. "No. It's everything."

Intense and constant nausea began just after midnight. I wasn't sure whether it was the endless stream of bad dreams or something else, but the only comfort I found was when my head rested on the bathroom floor.

I watched the morning light begin to peek through the bathroom window and listened to the sound of a garbage truck moving from house to house in the distance. The nausea was relentless. Hearing my phone chirp, I pulled myself up and slowly walked to the bedroom.

Dad
Sorry I missed your call last night.

I forced a hard blink, trying to adjust my eyes to the letters on my phone.

Me
You in town?

Dad
Heading to Milwaukee this afternoon.

Me
Have time for me this morning?

Dad
Not sure. Busy morning.

Me
It's important.

Brushing my teeth resulted in dry heaves every time the toothbrush went beyond my front teeth. I sat on the toilet, head between my legs, wondering how I was ever going to survive. My dad knocked on the door as I still sat on the toilet.

Walking slowly to the front of the house, I opened the door and let him in.

"You okay?" he asked, taking a quick look at me before looking away.

"Not feeling well. That's all."

"Okay. So what's up?" He stood just inside the corridor.

"You want to sit down?" I asked, hoping he would so I could too.

"I can't stay long."

I nodded, knowing we were light-years away from each other. "I'm pregnant." I was too sick and too tired to ease into it, and my dad clearly wanted to be somewhere else.

"Really?" He sat down on the edge of the sofa.

"Really."

He was quiet for a minute. "Do I know the father?"

I looked at him. "Yes, Dad. It's Jack."

"Oh, Jack. Okay." He became quiet again.

"So ... I wanted to let you know."

"Does Dee Dee know?"

I nodded.

"I'm sure it was fun telling her."

I shrugged my shoulders.

My dad stood up, a sign he was ready to leave. "So what's next?" he asked, opening the door to leave.

"Uh, next? I guess I go to work."

"No, I mean with ..." He pointed to my belly.

"I have my next doctor's appointment in a couple of weeks. And then I just wait to get to the point I can't see my feet anymore."

He smiled but did not laugh. "Does Sam know?"

I shook my head.

My dad nodded. "Tough break for him."

"I'm not so sure how tough it will be for him."

He looked at me quickly, and then his eyes moved to the door. "Nice news, Gracie." His facial expression remained somewhat blank.

"Thanks, Dad."

I watched him drive away, wondering if anything would ever change between us. Maybe becoming a grandfather would change him, change the way he saw me, saw us. Somehow, I knew it wouldn't. I tried to shake off the nausea that clung to me like a leech and got ready to face the day.

As the day fell into night, I drove to the park. Teaching had been easier than expected, as long as I kept shoving crackers or a mint in my mouth whenever the nausea hit. I had thought the sickness would just last the morning, but it had stayed with me all day.

I buttoned the top button of my coat and walked to the oak tree. Sitting on the bench, I watched the leaves knock into each other violently as the wind took control of them.

"Well, Mom, guess what? I'm pregnant," I said into the wind. "I can hardly believe it myself." I watched the branches of the tree, some of them withered and brittle with the onset of November. "You would have been an amazing grandma," I whispered.

"G?"

Startled, I turned around. Sam stood behind me.

"Sam? What are you doing here?" I wiped my eyes.

"Your grandma said you'd be here. May I?"

I scooted over slightly. "What are you doing in town?"

"I came to see you."

I looked at him, barely able to see the outline of his face. "Why?"

"My mom told me your news."

I felt my heart beat hard.

"Are you happy about it?" he asked.

"Sure."

He leaned slightly into me. "You sure?"

"Sure I'm sure." We both laughed.

"And Jack? How does he feel about it?"

I shrugged my shoulders, feeling a chill slither up my spine. "He doesn't want kids, so this has thrown him … more than a little."

"And you don't want kids either?"

"I want kids."

"But he doesn't?"

I nodded.

"Then what are you doing with him? That's a pretty big deal breaker."

"The subject never came up."

"I bet it came up now."

"Uh, yeah." The moon, bright and full, threw a light over the bench. It was almost glowing in the night sky.

"Do you think he'll step up?"

"I'm not sure."

"You ready to go through this alone then?"

I took a deep, long breath. "Yes. What other choice do I have?"

We sat on the bench, neither saying anything for a few long minutes.

"Me," he said, breaking the silence.

"What?" As the wind whipped through the night, I was sure I had heard him wrong.

"Your choice can be me."

"Oh, Sam, that's really sweet, but I can't ask you …"

"G, I want to be with you no matter what." He kissed my forehead and laced his fingers into mine.

"Sam, I could never ask you to take this on. Your offer is beyond generous, but it's completely unfair," I said in a hush.

"Unfair? That's not how I look at it."

I shrugged my shoulders. "Then that makes one of us."

"I want this, and I want it with you."

I looked at his face in the moonlight, refined with age but still boyish in some respects. "You don't know what you're saying."

"I do. I want to have a family with you."

"Why?"

"Because life without you really isn't a life."

"You say this now, but it's only going to get harder from here."

"I know."

I looked him in the eyes; his gaze was full of compassion. "That's just so unbelievably kind of you." I felt a sense of relief, thinking about having Sam by my side. Then traces of grief overshadowed the relief as I thought about Jack. "You should run as far away from this as you can."

He kissed my cheek. "I have no reason to run and every reason to stay."

"Sam, it's not ..."

"Tell you what, why don't you think about it? I'm not going anywhere."

I smiled at him as the half-moons peered back at me. "Okay."

"Oh, there's one more thing, though. This seems like the perfect time and place to ask." He paused. "There hasn't been a day in my life when I haven't loved you. Even when things got bad and we were miles and years apart, you were always with me. I want you to marry me."

I placed my hands over my mouth, at a loss for any response.

"G, I love you. Say yes."

I lowered my hands to my lap. "I can't ..." Emotion filled my throat.

"You can." He placed his hand over mine. "I know you love me, G. You do, don't you?"

I nodded slightly.

"Then there's no reason to say anything but yes."

I looked at him, and my mind raced back decades to all those nights I'd spent wishing, praying, hoping that he would ask me to marry him one day. Now it was real, yet it felt different from what I had thought it would feel like.

"I can't."

"Why?"

"Even if Jack doesn't want anything to do with the babies now, he might change his mind later."

"He will have every right to his children. But they will be *our* children too, so we'll have to figure it out then."

"Sam, you deserve better than this," I said, touching my hand to his face.

"There is nothing better than this."

Saying yes would make life easier. I looked closely at him, knowing I would love him in varying ways for the rest of my life. But I knew my heart was connected to Jack, and I needed to give him a chance if he wanted one.

"I need time to think about it."

"So you're not saying no?" He smiled at me.

"I'm not saying yes, either."

"I'll take whatever I can get at this point." He leaned in and kissed me lightly on the lips. "I love you so much, G."

"That you would do this for me ..."

"There's no more you or me," he said, interrupting me. "There's us, and that's what I'm doing it for."

"Chloe is really going to love this."

He laughed. "Like a venereal disease."

17

"Ellie? It's Gracie."

"Hi, Gracie. How are you?"

"I'm okay. Hope it's not too late to call." I was sitting in my car in the park parking lot. Sam had left me a few minutes before.

"Is everything okay?"

"Yeah ... well, yeah." I paused. "Listen, I was wondering if you could tell me where Jack's at tonight."

"Have you tried to call him?"

"I did, just a few minutes ago. I got his voice mail."

"Maybe you should give him time to call you back."

"Do you really think he will call me back?"

I heard her take a deep breath. "Probably not," she said.

"I really just need to talk to him, face-to-face, you know?"

She said nothing.

"I'm sorry. I shouldn't have put you in this position. Forget about it."

"He's at my parents' house. He's staying there," she softly responded.

"Thank you so much, Ellie."

"You will need to get through the gates if you're going there now. I'll call Ernie. He's working tonight, so he'll let you in. But Gracie?"

"Yeah?"

"Just don't expect too much from him, okay? He's still having a hard time with it. He really doesn't handle chaos well."

As I brought the car to a stop at the gate, I felt so nervous; my hands were trembling at the wheel.

"Miss Anderson, I was expecting you," Ernie said. "I've opened the house gates for you as well. Have a good evening." Ernie disappeared back into the gatehouse.

I pulled into the driveway, wondering what I was going to say to him. Two lights shone deep inside the house.

I was standing silently at the front door, trying to gain my composure, when the front porch light turned on and the door opened. He stood before me in a long-sleeved baseball shirt and jeans. His feet were bare, his hair disheveled, his complexion ashy.

"Hi," I said, smiling briefly at him. "I hope it's not too late to stop by."

He just stared at me.

"Can I come in?"

"Uh, sure." He moved to the side so I could enter. We stood just inside the corridor.

I heard the faint sound of music in the distance. "Were you busy?"

"No. I was just thinking ... and drinking."

I nodded.

"You want a glass of wine?" He held a half-full wineglass in his hand.

"No, thanks."

"Oh, that's right," he said. He took two big gulps of the wine. "I need a refill."

I followed him into the kitchen, where a half-empty bottle of red wine sat on the counter next to an empty one.

He filled the wineglass and sat down. "Wanna sit?"

"Thanks." I took a seat across from him. The crackling of a fire and the soft sound of jazz took the place of any words at first.

"You really threw me, you know?" he said, looking at me.

"I know. I'm sorry. It was the worst way to tell you."

He stared at me as he took another long drink of wine. "No, I mean you. You came into my life out of nowhere."

"Oh."

"Like, at first, I thought it was going to be a pretty casual thing. But I learned pretty quick, you are anything but casual."

I watched him take another long drink. "Jack, maybe I shouldn't have come tonight."

"You called me, right?"

"Yes."

He kept looking at me, his eyes cloudy from alcohol and emotion. "Yeah, just wasn't sure what to say to you."

"I know."

"Pregnant? Jesus. Did I miss something? I can't remember a time we didn't use protection."

I shook my head. "You didn't miss anything. We were careful."

"Then how?"

I shrugged my shoulders. "I wish I knew." I felt the nausea return. "The nurse said sometimes these things happen."

"Nurse? So you've been to the doctor?" I hadn't seen him blink; his focus remained firmly on my words and his wineglass.

"I went to confirm I was pregnant."

"And I'm guessing you got the confirmation?"

"I got it."

"Angie's really pregnant, but it's not mine. You know that, right?" He refilled his wineglass as he spoke.

I nodded.

"You're really having my baby?" he asked, mouth open to accept the wine from his glass.

"Babies."

Wine spurted out of his mouth. "Babies? Shit, Gracie. What else?"

I said nothing in response.

He placed his head in his hands. "Babies, as in two? If you tell me there's more than two, I'm going to jump off a building."

"Two babies, yes. Twins."

"I didn't even want one, and now you're having two. That's freaking awesome." He raised his head, looking at me sideways.

"I'm just as shocked as you, Jack."

"Are you sure you're pregnant? They didn't make some mistake?"

I pulled out the ultrasound picture and handed it to him.

"These are them?"

I nodded as he squinted to look at the picture.

"For real?"

I nodded again.

He dropped the picture on the counter and pushed it away, saying nothing.

"Jack, I'm not here to ask you for anything."

"Well, that's good, I guess."

Anger began bubbling inside of me. "Even though I have every right to ask you because you are the father."

He shot a look at me before throwing back the last bit of wine from his glass. He clanked the empty glass on the counter. "What do you want from me? Money?" His eyes were murky, and there were traces of acid in his voice.

My voice became curt. "I just want to know if you're in this thing with me ... or not."

"If I say I am, then what?" He refilled his glass a final time, the last drops of wine from the bottle falling on the counter.

"I don't know ..." My voice trailed off.

"Marriage? A white picket fence? A family plucked out of one of your old movies?"

I was agitated now but trying to keep calm, knowing he was drunk. "I guess one day at a time, and we go from there."

"Huh." His eyes were planted on me. "And if I say I'm not in this thing with you?"

My insides trembled, and my voice shook as I said, "Then we go our separate ways, I guess."

"Is that what you want?" he asked, wiping the droplets of wine off the counter with his fingers.

"No." In that moment, I knew I wanted him—for me, for our children, for our future life. It would be hard, more challenging than easy, but my heart belonged to him. "Is that what you want?"

"No ... maybe. I don't know," he sputtered.

"You can walk away from this, but I wanted to give you a chance."

"A chance to do what?"

"Be part of my life—our life."

"Yeah, okay." He stood up to grab another bottle of wine.

"I don't think you need any more wine, Jack."

He looked over at me as he opened the third bottle. "I had a mother. I don't need another one, Gracie."

"Like I said, I shouldn't have come."

"Maybe your boy Sam can help you with this little situation of yours."

A volt of anger came to my throat. "As a matter of fact, it's not even his responsibility, and he does want to support me, be part of this thing with me."

"Bet you're happy about all this," he said, watching me from the inside of his wineglass.

"What are you talking about?"

"Thinking maybe you've trapped me. You've hit pay dirt with me."

Instinctively, I hit the wineglass out of his hand, sending it crashing. Red wine, like blood from my heart, splattered everywhere.

"I want nothing from you!" I screamed. "Understand? Nothing!"

He stood there dumbfounded, red stains all over his face and shirt. He mumbled something I couldn't understand, tears dropping from the corners of his eyes.

I walked out of the room. "Good-bye, Jack." I closed the door behind me.

★ ★ ★

"Why did you even go there?" Chloe asked me, handing me a glass of water. We sat in the darkness of her living room.

"I wanted to see him."

"But you knew he was drunk once you got there, right?"

"Yeah."

"Then why would you try to talk to him? That's the worst time to talk to anyone. If he had a rational thought, it was lost at the bottom of a bottle."

"I know, I know."

"You can't just run to him, expecting he's going to take you in his arms. It doesn't work that way. Wake up, Gracie. This is messy, and there is no way anyone is coming out of this unscathed."

"What do you mean?"

"Every decision you make has to be with those babies in mind. It's not just you anymore. Mommy lesson number one— they come first, no matter what. And if that means you carry a thousand pounds of emotional bricks on your back and sacrifice your happiness, you do it without question."

"He doesn't want me ... doesn't want these babies," I said, pushing down the nausea rising again in my throat.

"I'm pretty sure the only thing he wants tonight is an IV to get the alcohol in quicker."

"He might walk away from this."

"That's a definite possibility, one you have to accept."

I nodded. "I need to make a decision."

"What decision?"

"Sam asked me to marry him."

She sat up, turned to me, and pulled me up to look at her. "What?"

"He asked me to marry him tonight at the park. He said he wants to raise the babies as his own."

"Are you kidding me?"

"No."

"What did you say?"

"I told him I couldn't. I needed to try to figure things out with Jack."

"And ..."

"And he said he'd wait for me to decide."

"He's willing to raise someone else's kids as his own?" There was a tone of surprise in her voice.

"Yes."

"Sam freakin' Patterson. Out of left field, the guy proves he's got balls. Who knew?" She plopped her head back on the couch. "Of course, you're going to tell him no, right?"

"I'm not sure what I'm going to do."

"It's not fair to Sam to expect him to raise your kids. I can't believe I'm saying this, but Sam deserves better than that."

"I know he does."

"Do you love Jack?"

"Ironically, in the middle of the mess I created tonight, I realized I do."

"And Sam?"

"I'll always love Sam."

"You can't have them both."

I nodded. "I could walk away from both of them."

"You could, but you deserve better than that. You deserve happiness so massive you feel like you're being swallowed up by it."

"This is the last thing I expected in my life right now."

"Welcome to real life."

"I told my dad."

"How did that go?"

"Blah, blah, blank stare. You know, the usual."

"Sorry. He should have reacted better."

"I wish he would have reacted at all."

"Well, I know for a fact your mom would have been over the moon about it. She probably would be out buying baby clothes already."

I smiled and then dropped my head, feeling my fragile psyche crack. "I wouldn't say this to anyone else, but sometimes I wonder if ..."

"The wrong parent died? Yeah, I know."

We said nothing else for a very long time. We just sat there on the couch, watching the stars outside the window as they tried to fight their way through the murkiness of the night sky.

"Well, I better go," I said, knowing the night was slipping away.

"Listen, sister. Here's what I want you to remember, if you remember nothing else."

I looked at her.

"No more tears. No more pity parties. It's not those babies' fault how they came to be, and you need to do everything in your power to always make them feel like they were the best thing that ever happened to you—because they are."

I nodded.

"And you are never to use the word *mistake* when talking about them. Understand?"

"Understand."

"We have officially flushed plan A down the toilet. Plan B starts now."

I drove home thinking about plan B. I knew things were already changing; a new life was already in motion.

I spent the rest of that night and the entire next day with my head in the toilet, trying to live through the constant vomiting. Every time I ate something, it came back up. The vomiting became so intense that by Thursday night I had a hard time getting off my bathroom floor. I hadn't heard from Jack and had responded to only one of Sam's text messages. I was in survival mode and doing a bad job at even that.

As I lay on the floor, I heard my front door open. "Gracelynn?" my grandma called from the living room.

"In here," I responded coarsely, my throat raw.

She walked into the bathroom and knelt down beside me. "How long have you been like this?" she asked, pushing my hair out of my face.

"Like twenty-four hours straight." I laid my head on her lap, hoping the room would stop spinning.

"Have you phoned the doctor?"

I shook my head, trying hard to swallow the vomit rising in my throat.

"Chloe?"

"I don't want to bother her."

"Nonsense," Grandma replied, gently placing my head back down on the floor. She reached into her jacket pocket and pulled out her phone. "Hello, Chloe ... Yes, she is not doing well ... Twenty-four hours. Shall we call the doctor?" Grandma's brows dropped. "I see. That makes sense. Okay, thank you."

"Grandma, this just comes with the territory."

"Chloe said if you are still like this tomorrow, we need to call the doctor. In the meantime, we need to push fluids and try to get something to stay down."

"Good luck with that," I mumbled, already placing my head back into its new favorite hiding place.

★ ★ ★

The sun felt warm on my face as I struggled to pull my eyes open. I looked up and saw my grandma's face above me. I squinted, trying to focus. Looking around, I saw that I lay on my couch, a blanket covering my body, my head placed on a pillow that rested on my grandma's lap. She held a magazine slightly in the air, her red rhinestone reading glasses perched on the tip of her nose.

"Grandma?"

She lowered the magazine and smiled down at me. "Good morning, Gracelynn."

"Was I asleep?"

"Yes, for the better part of five hours."

"Really?"

She nodded.

"With my head on your lap the whole time?"

"Yes. I thought that would be the most comfortable place for you as well as the closest to the bathroom."

"Have you been up the whole time?"

"I have."

"I'm sorry, Grandma. I didn't mean to keep you up." I tried to sit up, but a rush of nausea sent my head back to the pillow.

"I would not have been able to sleep anyway, knowing you were sick, so it is better this way."

"What time is it?"

"Nearly eight."

"I have a class this morning. I need to get up." I started to lift myself off the couch and then inched back down. "I'm not sure I can stand up."

"I believe it is time to phone the doctor," Grandma sternly said, brushing the hair away from my forehead.

"This is normal pregnancy stuff, right?" I looked up at my grandma, knowing she would say yes.

Instead, she was quiet. "I think we should call the doctor."

The words weren't out of her mouth before I felt the vomit rising. I rushed to the bathroom. I had nothing left to give but stomach acid, which rushed past my tonsils violently. A slight tapping on the bathroom door brought my head out of the toilet.

"Hey," said a familiar voice.

I looked up to see Chloe standing there.

"How you doing?"

"Peachy." I slid down beside the toilet. "Just peachy."

"When's the last time you kept anything down?" She leaned against the bathroom sink.

"What day is it?" I asked, trying to wipe the dried spit from the corners of my mouth.

"When was the last time you had anything to drink?"

"The same day I kept food down, whatever day that was."

"Girl, why didn't you call me?"

I shrugged my shoulders.

"You might be getting dehydrated."

"Maybe I just have the flu?"

"Regardless, severe vomiting can cause dehydration."

"How soon before it passes?"

"You might need an IV to get your fluids replenished."

"Like hospital IV?" I shook my head. "I have to work."

"Gracie, you have to keep hydrated, or you could risk miscarriage."

Tears filled my eyes, a result of exhaustion, frustration, and worry. "I don't know what to do," I quietly said.

"Your grandma is going to call you off work, and I'm going to call the doctor. That's what *we're* going to do."

I nodded, trying to stand up. Chloe put her arm around my waist and pulled me off the floor. We walked slowly back to the couch. My grandma stood next to the couch with a cup of coffee in her hand, and the aroma of it sent me rushing back to the bathroom.

After a minute, both Chloe and my grandma appeared in the bathroom doorway, watching me with concern. "Not good," Grandma stated.

"Definitely not," Close responded. "I'll call Dr. Simpson."

I felt myself being lifted and helped out the door. A coat was thrown over my shoulders as I was gently placed in the car. I drifted off again. At some point during the ride, I was jolted awake. I opened my eyes, and my mother sat next to me.

"Mom, what are you doing here?"

She smiled at me. "We're going to the hospital to get you better." Her hand tenderly brushed across my cheek. "You are pretty sick. We have to get you well so we can keep those babies well."

"So you know about the babies?" I looked at her, trying to fight off the feeling she wasn't real.

"Of course, I know about them. It's my job to look after them."

"But you're not real."

She gave me a stern look. I blinked hard to see if the illusion of her would disappear. But she remained next to me in the backseat.

"I know you're sick, so I'm not going to respond to such silliness."

I touched her hand, and she in turn grabbed mine.

"I'm scared."

"About being sick?"

I shook my head. "About being a mom."

She laughed quietly. "Here's a little secret between you and me: I was scared out of my mind. I was so scared that your dad had to convince me to go to the hospital when I was in labor. I worried I would be a terrible mom."

"But you were an awesome mom."

"Correction, I will always be an awesome mom."

"Very true." I was quiet for a minute. "How did Dad convince you to go to the hospital?"

"He said I was starting with a blank canvas, and if I screwed up, no one would ever be the wiser. You would be my masterpiece, even if I messed up and painted outside the lines at times."

"You were perfect."

"Ah, I wasn't perfect. You only remember me that way. I made a ton of mistakes. Thankfully, I raised a very forgiving daughter."

"Am I really that sick?"

"You haven't been told yet, but you have hyperemesis gravidarum, which means severe morning sickness."

I looked at her, youthful, full of life. "Do you know what I'm having?"

"Twins," she stated proudly.

"Yes, twins, but boys, girls, one of each?"

"Ah, Gracie. There are so few good surprises in life. You should make this one of them."

"You're right."

"Of course, you will want to discuss it with your partner."

"Yeah, about that. Not really sure that's going to work out."

"Oh, it will be fine. Chloe is right; you definitely deserve a wonderful life."

"So will I end up with Jack or Sam?"

"Yes." She gave me a mischievous grin.

"Which one?"

"Ah, my beautiful, half the fun is experiencing it firsthand."

"But you know who it is?"

"I do."

"But you aren't going to tell me?" I wanted her to just tell me; I could hear the frustration in my own voice.

"One of the few things I forgot to give you was patience. You need more of your dad's, for sure."

"I guess."

"Regarding your dad, Gracie."

"What about him?" I asked, irritated that she had brought him up.

"Do not fault him for who he's not. Just appreciate him for who he is," she said without hesitation.

"He's definitely not you," I said, disgust in my voice.

"Nor should he be. One of the reasons I fell in love with him was that he wasn't like me. I didn't need someone just like me. I needed him to be him. Together, we were a perfect fit."

"He didn't seem too happy about being a grandfather."

"It was the same reaction he had when I told him he was going to be a father. His lack of emotion is from worry, not from indifference."

"Worry? About what?"

"About something bad happening. He has seen and heard it all and has sold a pill or read a case study about every single one of those things."

"I never thought of it that way," I said reflectively.

"Don't look to me as the better of the two parents. He kept me from falling off the edge of the cliff time and time again."

"I can't imagine that."

"You really don't know him. I'm not blaming you. He had a hard time managing it alone."

"He wasn't alone. He had Grandma and, for a time, Grandpa and of course Teddy."

"Yes, but I left him to figure it out on his own."

"It wasn't your fault you left. I never blamed you for leaving."

"But you wish he would have died and not me."

Hearing her say my thoughts out loud made them seem callous and abrasive, almost murderous. In my mind, I knew she wasn't really there, but my heart wanted to believe she was.

"You're going to leave me again, right?"

She smiled, saying nothing. She turned and looked out the window. "You're right, you know. It might get harder before it gets easier, but I promise it will get easier."

"What will get easier?" I asked.

"Life."

I nodded, now understanding.

I had forgotten how she smelled, what her voice sounded like, the rhythm of her heartbeat. It took only that moment to make her fresh in my mind again, alive like I was. "Will you stay with me?" I asked.

"Ah, Gracie, don't you know?" She leaned in to whisper in my ear. "I never really left you."

At first, the ambulance siren was soft, quiet, in the distance. Then it became louder and louder, until it sounded like it was barreling right through me. My body jumped, preparing for impact.

"Gracie?"

My eyes shifted over. He sat on the chair across the room, a newspaper on his lap.

"How are you?"

"Where's Mom?"

"Mom?" he asked with surprise in his voice. "Let me get the nurse."

It was then I realized I had been dreaming. She wasn't with me; she had never been with me. My heart sank.

"It's okay, Dad. I must have been dreaming." I looked around the room. I was tethered to an IV, with a monitor cuff placed around my other arm. I was in the hospital.

"Are you feeling better?"

"Well ..." I rolled my head slowly side to side. For the first time in days, I didn't feel like I was hanging on to the bow of a ship in a violent sea. "I do, actually."

He smiled. "That's good."

"What day is it?" I had no idea how long I had been out of it.

"Friday. It's just after ..." He looked down at his watch. "Two."

"After two? I missed my classes." I felt disappointed with myself.

"I'm sure your students probably didn't mind. Early Christmas present for them."

"You must know my students."

He chuckled. A doctor was paged overhead. We fell quiet.

"You were pretty dehydrated."

"I don't remember too much, except throwing up nonstop."

"You're on an IV for fluids, and they're giving you something for the nausea."

I closed my eyes and laid my head back on the pillow. "How long do I have to be in here?"

"Overnight, I think."

The room fell quiet again. "Dad, can I ask you something about Mom?"

He tensed up a bit. "Uh, okay."

"Was she scared to have me?"

"Your mom?" He laughed quietly. "Your mom was fearless. She was scared of nothing."

"I see." Now I was sure I had dreamed her, a response to my body's dehydration.

"Why do you ask?"

"No reason." Bringing it up would be useless. He would just think I was delusional. "Anyway, no chance I'm getting out of here today then?"

Before my dad could answer, a voice called out from the doorway. "Do you know what your fluids were like?" Chloe entered the room and plopped down on the side of my bed. "There's more water in a cactus than you had in your system."

My grandma and Teddy entered behind Chloe, and Teddy handed my dad a hot coffee.

"It's silly that you all are here. It's no big deal, really."

"Doll, it's a big deal. You're a big deal, and my great-grandbabies are a big deal." Teddy smiled, his hands folded over his T-shirt, which showed Frankenstein taking a selfie.

"And who do we have here?" Dr. Simpson asked, walking into the room.

"Hi, Dr. Simpson. This is my family."

The doctor smiled, nodding at each one of them. "Gracie, nice to see you again. Didn't expect to see you so soon, though."

"Yeah, this kind of came out of nowhere."

"How are you feeling now?"

"Better. I'd like to go home if I can."

"We need to monitor you overnight. You've gone through two bags of fluid already. You have severe morning sickness. Sometimes, the only way to manage its side effects is with an IV, like you're getting now."

"I don't feel nauseous anymore."

"We're giving you some medicine through your IV to help with the nausea."

"When will the morning sickness subside?"

Dr. Simpson leaned against the bedrail. "The good news is that in most cases, it gets much less severe as time goes on. Bad news is, if you have it with this pregnancy, you have a pretty good chance of getting it with every pregnancy."

"No worries about future pregnancies. I'm one and done."

"Well, you say that now, but your partner may feel differently."

I glanced over at Chloe, who shrugged. "You never know," she said.

"Okay, I'm off to a delivery, but I promise, as long as everything looks good, I'll try to spring you early tomorrow so you can salvage some of your weekend."

As soon as Dr. Simpson left the room, my grandma said, "I would like to review her credentials."

I rolled my eyes. "And why would that be, Grandma?"

"She seems very knowledgeable, but you are a high-risk patient, and I need to know she is capable of handling your case."

"Grandma, she's fine."

"Gracelynn, there are two types of professionals you never want to be just *fine*—your mechanic and your doctor. Both of them have the capability to keep you moving or not."

"Dee Dee, she's better than fine. She's one of the best around. I checked," my dad stated, his tone matter-of-fact.

I looked at my dad, surprised. "You checked?"

"Of course I checked."

All eyes were on my dad.

"We need the best," he said. "Anyone else is unacceptable."

"Dr. Simpson is the easy part; our patient here is going to be the tough part," Chloe responded.

I shrugged my shoulders, feeling tired all of a sudden. "What can I say? Never a dull moment with me," I declared, yawning.

"We're gonna get out of here so you can rest a bit," Teddy said. He stood, gently pulling my grandma up with him.

"We are?" Grandma did not want to budge.

"Yes, we are." Teddy took her hand.

"But what if she needs something?"

"She's in the hospital, sugar. If she needs something, I'm pretty sure she'll get it."

I watched them leave. Closing my eyes, I felt at peace for the first time all week. It was a strange feeling, almost numbing.

"Gracie?" His voice startled me.

I opened my eyes. "Did you forget something, Dad?"

"I was almost to the elevator when I remembered."

"Remembered what?"

"What you asked me before, about your mom. You know, about being scared?"

I nodded.

"I'd never seen her as rattled as she was the day you were born." He looked at me, hints of nostalgia in his eyes.

"Uh-huh?"

"Your mom was worried she would be a bad mother."

I felt the realness of his words then. "And what did you say?"

"I told her—"

"That she could create her own masterpiece? A blank canvas of sorts?"

His eyes widened. "Yes."

"I never knew her to be afraid of anything," I quietly said.

"Not even death."

"Do you think she's still with us?" I asked.

"I think she's wherever you want her to be." He squeezed my hand, holding it momentarily before letting go.

Just after he left, I thought I caught a glimpse of her outside my room. I waved, but she stood motionless. I blinked, and she was gone. I missed her so much; the ache inside of me was growing deeper, stronger. I dozed off, knowing that my body needed to heal but my heart never would.

"Can I get you anything?" a nurse asked as she finished checking my vitals.

I opened my eyes, shaking my head no.

"Oh, before I forget, your visitor said she didn't want to wake you but she'd be back to check on you later."

"My visitor?"

"Yes, she was here while you were sleeping. You're lucky to have such good genes. I'm amazed at how young she looks."

"Who?"

"Your visitor—why, your mother, of course."

18

The effects of being alone in the hospital hit me almost immediately after the nurse left. Dinner had come and gone, and the endless stream of TV channels didn't help. I looked at the clock, knowing the Friday session would be starting soon and I would miss it.

I felt a pang of sadness as I thought about the other women. The sessions had become part of my life, a bigger part than I had even realized until I thought about not being in one of them. I was lost in a mindless trance when a slight knocking on the door startled me.

"Gracie?"

Looking up, I saw an unexpected visitor standing just inside the door. "Ellie?"

She walked farther into the room, stopping a few feet from me. "How are you?" She reached out to touch my foot.

"Better. What are you doing here?"

"She came for the session," said Ginger, stepping into the room behind Ellie.

"Ginger?" I felt my heart leap. For some reason, seeing them made me want to cry. My emotions were running high.

"Hello, Gracie," Sarah said with a smile, pulling her coat off as she walked in.

"What are you guys doing here? You're a long way from our regular meeting spot," I said.

"It's not a session without you, Gracie." Sarah reached down and hugged me, as did each of the other members of our Highmore Circle.

Dr. Gretchen appeared with a man in scrubs, both of them carrying chairs. Once the chairs were positioned around my bed, the man in scrubs left, and each woman took a seat, completing the circle.

"I can't believe you guys came. It's so ..." My voice vanished, my throat filled with sentiment.

"Yeah, we're awesome. We know," Ginger declared. Everyone laughed.

"How did you know I was here?" I asked, confused.

"Your grandmother called me to tell me you wouldn't be in session," Ellie explained. "She told me what happened, and I let everyone else know."

"Girl, I hate to say it, but you're a mess," Mindy said, pulling snacks out of a large brown bag.

"Everything okay with the babies?" Ellie inquired, smoothing her one wayward hair back across her forehead.

"Yeah, they're fine."

She nodded, smiling as she lowered her head.

"It's okay we came to you, right?" Mandie inquired, scooting her chair closer to my bed.

"Are you kidding me?" I felt the emotion rising in my throat again. "It's one of the nicest things anyone's ever done for me."

"If this is the nicest thing anyone's ever done for you, we need to find you a better group of friends," Ginger declared, adjusting her push-up bra. Tonight, her false eyelashes and heavy eyeliner were present, but she wore a loose-fitting sweater and skinny jeans.

"You working tonight?" I asked her.

"Nah. I worked earlier today. Didn't have time to take it all the way back down to ground zero before we had to head out to come here."

"Well, I think you look great," I said, fully appreciative of her efforts to multitask on my account.

"My business never sleeps."

We all nodded, like she was talking about an office job. It seemed normal now, not taboo, to ask Ginger about her work. So many things had changed for us, I thought.

"I'd like to ask something," Ellie announced unexpectedly.

"The floor is all yours, Ellie." Dr. Gretchen motioned her hand to the inside of the circle.

"I just got into an argument with my brother, and I'd like some advice on how to deal with him. I mean, I'm not sure if it's all men or just the ones I know who act like immature teenagers."

"What did you fight about?" Sarah asked.

Ellie looked at me for a few seconds before answering. "It's not important what we argued about. It's just that he's so immature sometimes. It's very annoying."

"Conflict is one of the most challenging things to deal with," Dr. Gretchen explained. "Did you try to reason with him?"

"Impossible," she replied.

"I don't do conflict," Mandie said.

"Why don't you *do* conflict?" Dr. Gretchen asked her.

"It makes me feel bad to be mad at someone."

"Me too. Which is why it was so difficult to argue with him," Ellie noted.

"I argued with my mother once," Sarah quietly added. "I still think about it. I wish I hadn't."

"Why?" Dr. Gretchen pushed.

"Because the words I said were hurtful, and I feel guilty about saying them to her."

"But people say things they don't mean in the heat of the moment," Dr. Gretchen pointed out.

Sarah began to tremble. The reappearance of her fragile state worried me. "Today is my mother's birthday," she said through tears.

"Did you used to do anything special on her birthday?" Mindy asked.

"We would go for ice cream," she said with a smile.

"What kind?" Ellie inquired.

"We always got chocolate. It was her favorite."

"There's a coffee shop in the lobby that serves ice cream. How about chocolate in honor of your mother?" Mandie offered.

Sarah tried to catch a falling tear. "I actually hate chocolate. But I love vanilla."

We all laughed.

"My mom died on my birthday," I said suddenly. The words seemed to just fall out of my mouth.

"That sucks," Ginger exclaimed.

"She did?" Ellie looked at me, her eyes full and round.

I nodded. "That's why I don't celebrate my birthday."

"Maybe you should change your birthday," Mindy suggested.

"Kinda defeats the purpose of having a birthday, doesn't it?" I responded.

"Most people don't pick the day they're gonna die," Ginger said gently. "I'm pretty sure your mom would've picked any other day if she could."

"Maybe instead of focusing on her dying, you should focus on how she lived, right?" Sarah suggested.

"Sarah has a point. Is there something you used to do together that made you both happy?" Dr. Gretchen inquired.

"We loved to watch *It's a Wonderful Life* together but we were watching it the night she died, so it's hard to watch now."

"That's the one we watched together, right?" Mindy looked at me, puzzled.

"Part of my twelve-step program, I guess. It was really hard to watch it because, well, you know ..."

"Like I haven't eaten chocolate ice cream since my mom died," Sarah said.

"You don't even like chocolate, so why would you ever eat it again anyway?" Ginger asked.

"But if I don't, then I'll forget something about her."

I looked at Sarah as the gravity of her words leveled the room.

"I never thought of it that way," Ginger said, standing to grab a cup of water.

"But if you do something you don't like only because she liked it, Sarah, you run the risk of losing yourself in her," I said.

"Would that be so bad?" she asked in an imploring voice.

"Yes, because then it would be like you never existed," Ellie explained.

As I looked at Ellie, I knew I had to ask. "Did you and Jack fight about me?"

"Yes," she said, offering nothing else.

Sarah cleared her throat softly. "Is he going to take responsibility for ..." She pointed toward my stomach.

"I'm not sure," Ellie softly replied.

"They can't get enough of you when you got somethin' they want, but as soon as it's time to own up to it, they disappear," Ginger snapped.

"I'm not sure it's that simple with Jack," Ellie said, sounding defensive.

"Time to own up and be a daddy. Seems pretty simple," Ginger retorted.

We were deep in conversation when a nurse walked into the room. "Just checking to see if Gracie needs anything?"

"We should wrap it up for the evening," Dr. Gretchen announced.

We groaned collectively like a classroom of second graders.

"We will pick it up next week back at the usual place, assuming Gracie is out of the hospital by then."

"Thanks so much for coming," I said, hugging each one of them good-bye.

They all left, with the exception of Ellie. "You're really okay then?" she asked when the room was empty.

"I will be."

"I'm sorry about earlier—you know, bringing my argument with Jack up to everyone."

"Don't worry about it."

"I told Jack you were in the hospital."

I looked at her without speaking, waiting for her to continue.

"I asked him to come see you."

"He said no, right?"

"He said no."

I nodded, no longer surprised by his lack of interest in me or our situation.

"I'm so sorry, Gracie."

"It's not your fault, Ellie. It is what it is, I guess."

"I thought he would come around by now. He has a really hard time when things fall out of order."

"The night of the accident—you called me, but you could have called a cab. Did you want me to catch him in the lie?"

Her eyebrows lifted, making me think she would respond differently than she did. "Yes."

"I thought so."

"I love my brother, but you're right—he can't have it both ways. He has to decide what he wants."

"I'd take the supermodel if I were him."

"I wouldn't."

"It only gets infinitely more complicated from here. And it's already pretty complicated."

Ellie sat on the end of my bed, her weight barely registering an impression. "I heard someone wants to stick around."

"Turns out the runner isn't interested in running anymore."

"What are you going to do?"

I thought for a moment. "I'm going to take my time to figure it out. I have to make sure these babies bake like they should. I have to get them fat and healthy, so I'm going to focus on that for now."

"You're so brave, Gracie."

"Survival mode, mostly, I guess."

"Jack is a coward for doing what he's doing. He's throwing away his chance at an amazing life with you."

"Is that what you told him?"

"I did."

"I'm sure that didn't go over well."

"First real fight we've had in ... forever."

"It seems like things were fine until I entered the picture."

"My brother was barely living before you. It was a good show, but all smoke and mirrors. You breathed life into him, which is why I'm so angry with him. It's like he's choosing to not really live again."

"He has to do what he feels is right."

"I saw the picture."

"Picture?"

"Did you give him an ultrasound picture? There's one hanging on the refrigerator at my parents' house."

I was shocked. "I forgot it there. I'm surprised he still has it."

"For what it's worth, he does."

"Thanks for letting me know."

"My mom would have really liked you, Gracie. You're one of the good ones."

I smiled. She gave me a long hug before leaving.

Once I was alone, I slid off the bed and pulled my IV stand along with me into the bathroom. It felt good to be facing away from the toilet for the first time in a while. I washed my face and brushed my teeth. Physically, I was tired and looking forward to a good night's sleep. Emotionally, I felt suddenly renewed, ready to move on with my life.

I was halfway back to the bed when I saw him. He was standing on the opposite side of my bed, staring out the window. He turned when he saw my reflection in the glass.

"Hey," he said, facing me. He wore a pair of jeans and a form-fitting sweatshirt. His hair was slightly gelled back, a five-o'clock shadow outlining his chin.

"Hey." I eased down on the bed, placing my IV stand back in its place.

He stood there looking at me, his blue eyes vibrant and clear. The bruises on his face were fading, the cuts down his face healing shut. "How ya feeling?"

"Better."

"Okay if I sit?"

I nodded. He sat down, his hip touching the side of my leg. I felt a jolt of electricity run up my spine.

"Dehydrated?"

"Yeah, I'm on lockdown while they pump endless amounts of fluid into me."

"Ellie told me you were here."

"She mentioned that."

"I wasn't going to come," he confessed.

"Yeah, she mentioned that too."

His eyes met mine.

"So why did you?"

"How could I not?"

"I'm not sure what to say, Jack."

"I know." His hand moved halfway to mine. "It's been a really crappy week."

I laughed. "You're telling me. I've spent the better part of two days with my head in the toilet."

"I've spent the better part of two days with my head in a glass of booze. I think the end result for both of us has been pretty much the same."

"I want you to be part of this if you want to. You have that right." I knew it had to be said; I wanted nothing to be left unsaid if this was going to be the end of us.

"That's just it. I wouldn't want to do this halfway. I would need to go all in. And I'm just not sure I'm ready to go all in."

"Then I think we should each just do our own thing," I replied, more disappointed than hurt by the honesty in his words.

"When Ellie told me you were in the hospital, I freaked out. I thought I might lose you or the babies, and it really scared me, Gracie."

"I'm confused. Do you want me or not want me?"

"I want it to be like when we were first together; I want it to be easy again."

"It was never easy with us."

He looked out the window. "It's getting cold outside." He was trying to divert the conversation.

"That's what happens when winter is coming."

"I still can't believe this happened. I mean, this kind of thing doesn't happen to me."

"Apparently, it does." I was annoyed with him and growing tired of his poor-me attitude.

"I want to be with you, I really do. I'm just not sure I'm ready for the whole family thing," he said, still looking out the window.

"Well," said a voice near the doorway, "that works out perfectly for me then."

We both turned to see Sam step into the room.

"Sam? What are you doing here?" I asked, shifting up in bed.

Jack stood to look at him.

"How are you, G?" He grabbed my hand and squeezed it.

"Better, thanks." The room was so thick with tension that the air could have been cut with a surgical knife.

"Sorry, I wanted to be here earlier, but I got jammed up. Babies okay?"

I nodded, trying to determine what was going to happen next.

"Sam, we're kinda in the middle of something," Jack said curtly.

"Yeah, okay." Sam laughed at him.

"What's so funny?" Jack clearly found nothing funny.

"Unless I'm missing something, G tells you she's pregnant, and instead of manning up and taking care of her, you pout like a baby. You're kinda in the middle of something? Okay, right. You're an ass."

"Unless I'm missing something, she got pregnant by me, which means she wanted to be with me and not you."

"Good try, but she was probably already pregnant when I came back in the picture."

"And why were you out of the picture anyway? If you want to be with her so much, why'd you let her go in the first place?"

"Just go back to your trashy supermodel and leave us alone."

"What did you say?"

"Your money and celebrity mean nothing, but you think it means something. Money obviously can't buy you a set."

Their voices were escalating.

"Just stop," I said. But neither one of them was paying attention to me.

"Gracie doesn't want you. She wants me," Jack said, nearly yelling.

"Jack, keep your voice down," I implored.

"How do you know she doesn't want me? I asked her to marry me. Did she tell you that?"

Jack looked at me, stunned, before returning his eyes to Sam. "Bet she didn't say yes."

"She didn't say no, either."

They were inches apart from each other now, standing at the foot of my bed. Jack grabbed Sam's coat and shoved him back.

Sam tripped over the foot of the bed, nearly falling. He leapt up and flew headfirst into Jack's stomach. They both plummeted onto the windowsill and tumbled to the floor, Sam's hands reaching for Jack's throat.

I jumped out of bed and felt the IV yank out of my arm. "Stop it!" I yelled at both of them. I pulled at them, trying to release Sam's hold on Jack. "Enough!" I was struggling to tear them from each other, but they remained locked together.

A male nurse came running into the room. With one quick move, he pulled Sam and Jack off each other. "Leave!" he said, finger pointed at both of them.

I looked down at my arm. The IV was torn away, and medical tape dangled in the air as droplets of blood fell onto the bed.

"Gracie ..." Jack started to speak.

I shook my head. "Go. Both of you," I said, cupping my hand over my bleeding arm. "Walk out of this room and out of my life until I decide otherwise, or else I will keep walking and not look back."

I knew this was a defining moment for me and one I needed to own, the emotional chains and handcuffs bringing me a sense of gravity, a tether that finally belonged.

19

I stood just outside the gym doors, searching for him on the court through the window. It had been two months since that night in the hospital, the last time I had seen either Jack or Sam. I was finally ready to look Jack in the eyes and tell him how I felt. I had survived my first trimester and was actually starting to feel somewhat normal, even if this was a new normal.

I pushed the heavy door open and stepped onto the edge of the court. The squeaking of gym shoes against the floor was nearly deafening. Finally, I saw him, running down the court, motioning for the ball. His eyes darted over and caught mine, and his feet screeched to a halt.

With his eyes focused on me, he never saw the passed ball coming his way. It struck his head at full force, knocking him down. His body hit the hard surface with a thud. I ran to him, pushing my way through the other basketball players who loomed over him like giants.

"Jack!" I leaned down.

He opened his eyes and looked at me, his face contorted in confusion at first. "Gracie?"

I smiled at him.

"Is it really you?"

"Yes, it's me." I started to help him up, but he pulled me to him and hugged me. I could feel his heart thundering beneath his shirt.

"I never thought I'd see you again."

I pulled away from him slightly.

"I left you so many messages," he said, his voice hesitant.

"I know. I needed time. Listen, I—"

"No." He quickly sat up. "I need to say something."

"Jack, I—"

He interrupted me again. "Gracie, I know I said it over and over in my messages, but you gotta let me say this while I have you in front of me." His blue eyes, the color of waves, washed over me.

I nodded, sitting down on the court. "Okay. The floor is all yours."

He sat up on his knees, taking my hands in his. "Nothing makes sense without you." He paused. "You make my life mean something. You make my crazy feel normal. I want it all, Gracie, and I want it with you. And I want it today, tomorrow, and forever." He pulled my hands to his lips and kissed them softly. "Tell me I'm not too late." He placed the side of his face on top of my hands.

I felt the oxygen evaporating out of my lungs as he spoke. The court seemed to shrink as the other players surrounded us in a tight circle. "Jack, please look at me."

He lifted his head, his eyes meeting mine.

I gently touched the large knot forming on the side of his forehead where the ball had landed. I kissed it softly. I took his hand and placed it on my belly. "Anywhere you go, we go. I love you."

I was trying to pull him up when he rose to one knee. He took a deep breath. Not one shoe squeaked; the gym was silent.

"I'm not perfect," he said. "I'm gonna screw up sometimes, and there will be more imperfect days than I'd like to admit, but I'll take a million of those imperfect days with you over one perfect day with someone else. Marry me?"

I smiled, looking at him for a long moment. "I'm a fan of

imperfect days," I said, knowing my decision had been the right one all along.

★ ★ ★

Our children arrived exactly three weeks early on a warm summer night. My water broke as I lay in bed, and Jack literally fell out of the bed when I told him it was time to go. As we drove to the hospital, I noticed he had forgotten to put on shoes, his T-shirt was on backward, and the fly on his shorts was unzipped.

My labor became complicated, and the delivery took an unexpected turn with a surprising announcement from Dr. Simpson. "She needs a C-section," I heard her tell my family. "We need to get her prepped and ready."

Teddy leaned down and kissed my cheek. He wore his "World's Best Teddy Bear" T-shirt, given to him as an early present from the twins. Grandma stood next to him, wiping tears away.

"Grandma, why are you crying?"

"She would be so proud."

Ellie and Chloe stood next to each other in front of the window, their shoulders touching. "Oh, before we forget." Chloe handed me two boxes. "From their aunts."

In each box I found a small chain adorned with a gold star. I touched each star, feeling the impact of them. "Thank you," I said, my voice barely audible. "Best ... aunts ... ever."

"Yes, we know," Ellie declared.

"Hey, that sounds like something I would say," Chloe noted, rubbing her growing belly. She would become a mother herself by early winter, an event I would be with her to experience.

In the delivery room, Jack sat next to me, listening to Dr. Simpson walk us through the procedure. The first strong cry just before midnight brought tears to my eyes. The second cry arrived seven minutes later. Each baby weighed just over five pounds, and they would officially have different birthdays.

The Highmore Circle, as I had come to think of us, was full of activity. Babies, marriages, career changes, new relationships, incredible happiness, and unimaginable sadness were all part of our world. These women were so much a part of me that they had become my sisters. They were also the first ones outside our immediate family to receive the news about the arrival of the babies. We would continue to meet twice a week, without fail. How lucky it was that I had come to find them. They had given me perspective, laughter, hope, peace, and, most importantly, my mother again.

I hadn't seen her since my earlier stay in the hospital. I looked for her everywhere, trying to find her watching over us, but she evaded my eyes. I kept telling myself that she was with me, that she had never left me. Sometimes it made me feel better, but not always did the thought bring me comfort.

I thought about her as I lay in my hospital bed, with the babies by my side. One of the babies moved slightly and then became still again, deep in sleep. "I know you are with us, Mom," I whispered. "I'd like for you to officially meet your grandchildren, Elizabeth Chloe Faith and Cassandra Blake Eleanor."

As I watched the stars from my window, so bright they seemed to explode in the sky like fireworks, I felt her with us. I never turned my face away from the sky, but I knew she was there in the room. I caught her reflection in the window for a fleeting moment. She stood just beyond the darkness. I smiled, knowing there were just some things death could never truly steal away.

At that moment, I knew I would do everything in my power to raise my daughters like she had raised me. I would make sure they had a voice and an inner strength that no one could touch. I wanted so much for them. I wanted to protect them and keep them out of harm's way. I wanted to tend to every bruise, every heartbreak; kiss every boo-boo; and make sure they laughed a trillion times more than they cried, just like she had done for me.

Cassie stirred next to me, and Eliza was also starting to wake. I knew my greatest adventure was still to come, and I felt blessed to have my mom there with me for the ride.

"Time to take those blank canvases and create my own masterpieces," I whispered. "Thank you, Mom, for ..." I hesitated, trying to decide where to start. "For everything."

CPSIA information can be obtained
at www.ICGtesting.com
Printed in the USA
BVOW03s1635300617
488179BV00001B/3/P

9 781532 006760